MW01118557

Resonance

Book 2 of Recovery

RESONANCE

S. Alex Martin

CREATESPACE is a DBA of On-Demand Publishing, LLC

www.createspace.com

Library of Congress Cataloging-in-Publication Data

Martin, Scott Alexander.
Embassy / S. Alex Martin
p. cm. – (Recovery ; bk. 2)
SUMMARY: Arman Lance recruits archivists to catalogue the
island world of Daliona while the Dalish scientists develop the
Faustocine formula to combat Belvun's deteriorating ecosystems.
ISBN-13: 978-1517167646 (trade pbk.)
ISBN-10: 1517167647 (trade pbk.)
[1. Science-fiction. 2. Daliona. 3. Space travel.] 1. Title
[fic]

Printed in the United States of America

October 2015

Independent First Edition

To anyone who believes
they can become better than they are

"Remember to look up at the stars and not down at your feet. Try to make sense of what you see and wonder about what makes a universe exist. Be curious. And however difficult life may seem, there is always something you can do and succeed at. It matters that you don't just give up."

—Stephen Hawking

UNDIL

CORNELL

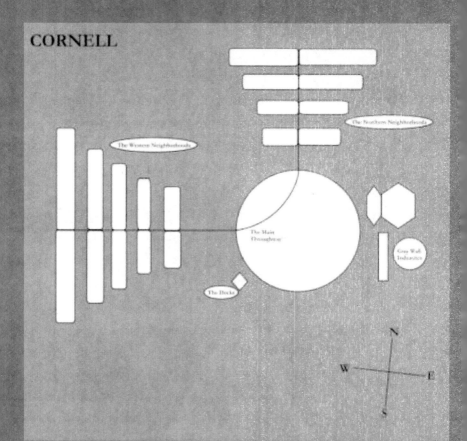

The Northern Neighborhoods

The Western Neighborhoods

The Main Thoroughfare

The Becks

Gray Wall Underwrites

N
W ——— E
S

THE UNDIL EMBASSY

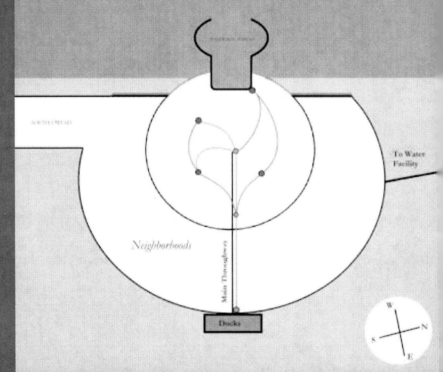

DALIONA

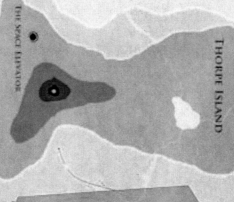

The Thorpe
Archipelago

LAKA ISLAND

LAKA GRAVITY RUN

RINGS ISLAND

RESNICK ISLAND

THE SPACE ELEVATOR

THORPE ISLAND

CORDELIA BIODOME

THORPE PLAZA

ARADIMA PIER

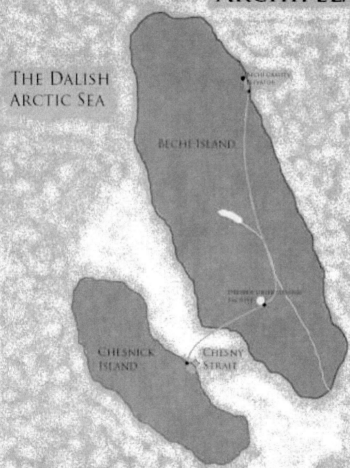

THE BECHI ARCHIPELAGO

THE DALISH ARCTIC SEA

BECHI ISLAND

CHESNICK ISLAND

CHESNY STRAIT

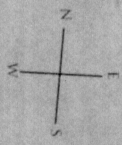

THE HOSSIARD
ARCHIPELAGO

HOSSIARD ISLAND

RONDALF ISLAND

THE CAVELLOR ARCHIPELAGO

VIZZONA ISLAND

THE MIZZONO-SUZU
PARTICLE COLLIDER

THE TAVIZZIO ACADEMY OF
RELATIVISTIC SCIENCES

CAVELLOR ISLAND

THE GÖMEN MUSEUM OF
THEANORETIC TECHNOLOGY

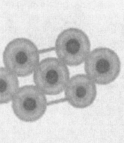

THE CYCLONIAL
GRAVITY WAVE APPLICATION FACILITY

N · E · S · W

THE WESTIN ISLES

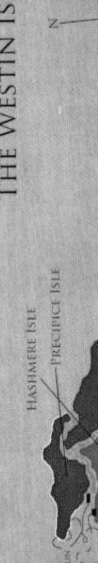

N
W — E
S

HASHMERE ISLE
PRECIPICE ISLE

HASHMERE
GRAVITY RUN

WESTIN ISLE

THE SALT MINES

THE SALT FIELDS

THE NOYA ARCHIPELAGO

N
W — E
S

NOYA ISLAND

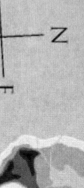

NOYA BAY

THE
ORCHARD
ISLANDS

GANO ISLAND

VOLCANIC SHELFS
COMPLEX

THE SELAYCHE ARCHIPELAGO

KILACHE ISLAND

LISHA ISLAND

ACHABAI ISLAND

TAHANI ISLAND

SELAYCHE ISLAND

REIICO ISLAND

N
W—E
S

RESONANCE

Part 1
The Archives

Chapter One

I STRAIN MY neck and pump my arms. My lungs burn, but I keep running. I *need* to run.

Wipe the sweat stinging my eyes.

Left right left right left right.

Break into a full-out sprint.

Pump my arms harder.

Crane my neck back.

Gasp for air.

"*Time.*"

The treadmill slows. I ease into a jog, then a walk. On the treadmill beside me, Glacia dabs her forehead with a small towel.

"So, how far?" she asks.

I check the distance on the treadmill's display. "Three-point-four—"

"*And the champ still reigns!*" she half-shouts, causing a few people to glance our way. "Four-point-one, mister. *Four. Point. One.*"

"You're insane."

"Thank you."

We reset the treadmills and leave the *Ember*'s fitness center. Most people are asleep by now, so the halls are quiet except for the dull hum reverberating in the walls. We ride an elevator up to Glacia's level and, like always, '*Floor 10: Vancouver Living Quarters*' glows on the wall opposite the elevator when we step off.

We head the opposite direction of the food court, and Glace opens an outer gate that shuts us into a private hall with two dorm doors on either side. She steps into her room and half-closes the door, then turns and lifts her chin expectantly. I lean in to kiss her...and linger longer and longer. When I pull back, Glace stands on her toes and pecks me one last time.

"Ready to get home?"

"'*Home*' is such a strong word," I say with every hint of sarcasm. "I prefer '*unfortunate birthplace.*'"

"Whatever." She smirks and shoves me out the doorway. "See you up there."

A half-hour later, we meet in the Observatory, the glass dome that spans a hundred yards down the center of the *Ember*. There are no walls, only the dome, so we can stand right at the edge and be level with the top of the station, as if we could walk right out into the void— which wouldn't be a good idea, considering we're both wearing our nightclothes.

Not to our surprise, several other people are already here, a few of them using the StarPad to figure out the exact moment the Kairos supernova will be visible. For now, the darkness is filled with stars and the other three stations in our space fleet. Above us is the *Drake*, and to our sides, the *Doppler* and *Blazar*. I can see people moving inside the *Blazar*'s Observatory, and know they're waiting for the supernova, too.

"Sometime in the next minute," the woman at the StarPad calls out, then she deactivates it to cut out the glare.

Excited whispers make their way around the Observatory, and everyone faces forward, toward the head of the *Ember*. Silence overtakes the room. We all watch the void, waiting...waiting...and then—

Flash.

An explosion of white, and the Kairos supernova graces our eyes. The white bubble churns in fast-motion, its wispy edges curling outward. The light deepens to a light yellow color, then a fresh shade of orange, then reddish. Within minutes, the supernova's light is days old, then weeks...

And then it vanishes.

❋　❋　❋　❋　❋

The sun glares through the window of the Bridge, pure white against the black backdrop. A brown crescent hangs far to our left, and we're aimed to intercept it. That's Undil, my home, the planet I spent my entire life wishing I could escape. Even now, I want to pass it by and venture on to some other planet full of beauty and life, not the dust and death that awaits me.

I drink the rest of my now-cold coffee that Orcher brewed before I arrived. He made sure the Bersivo Blend was a light shade of tan, but not *too* white—just the way I like it.

"Miranda hasn't said too much about Miss Haverns lately," Orcher says, looking down at Station Control, where Captain Fallsten is seated beside Glacia instead of standing behind her, criticizing her every move.

"She hasn't said that much about Captain Fallsten, either," I say. "What if they're actually becoming friends?"

Orcher chuckles. "No, I wouldn't go *that* far."

A string of data orbs zips across the Bridge, sent from an officer on the second tier to someone on the fourth tier. Between them, on the third tier, Victoria is conferencing with the lieutenants of the *Drake*, *Doppler*, and *Blazar* like she does every morning.

"When do you plan to discuss our idea with Lucas?" Orcher asks.

"After I write my expedition report."

Orcher promoted me to Head Archivist after we left Belvun, and the first project he wants me to work on is enhancing the archives database. The current program is—in Orcher's own words—*'grossly outdated,'* but he could never get Captain Blitner to develop a new program. And Lucas Starmile, the man who gave us the tour of the Embassy on our first day, is too busy in the education sector compiling Placement Reports and Secondary texts to manage the program all by himself. It sounds like a large task, but it'll give me something to do while

Michael moves forward with the Belvun Recovery Treatise. Come to think of it, I haven't seen Michael in days. Like on the expedition to Belvun, he stays in his living quarters working on the proposal he'll present to Daliona, where the newest Faustocine formula for Belvun's ecosystems is going to be manufactured.

"You'll get all the necessary support from Threshold," Orcher continues saying. "I'll see to that. And I expect Chancellor Green will have you hire your own team of archivists. As for the program itself, I suggest you take a look into Orvad's info systems sector. Remmit should be able to set you up with a techie there. Orvadians are always eager to grab contract work in the Embassy."

A grin flickers across my face. The notion of traveling to Orvad excites me. It's the city that sits beside the Undilaen Ocean, thousands of miles southwest of the Embassy, and it has a reputation for being one of the fastest-growing info-systems sectors in the galaxy. Not only that, but Victoria and Officer Remmit both grew up there.

"*All right, people,*" Captain Fallsten's voice suddenly echoes through the Bridge's intercoms. She's since climbed to her perch at the top of Station Control. "*We're closing in. Initiating approach sequence.*"

Undil grows larger with every passing minute. Its atmosphere shimmers along the curve of the horizon. Deserts, ridges, and canyons begin to define its surface. Soon enough, Captain Fallsten opens a comms link with Officer Remmit. They relay information to each other, speaking through gritted teeth and faking friendly demeanors for the sake of the approach.

"How about you engage those secondary reverse thrusters, Cap?" Officer Remmit's voice echoes when the fleet closes within five hundred-thousand miles of Undil.

"Engaging."

Captain Fallsten points at a station pilot, who swipes his finger up a panel. A hologram on the front display signals the activation.

"Is our docking clearance granted, Remmit?"

"Whoa, whoa. One step at a time."

"Just get it done."

A long silence, then, *"Clearance granted, Cap. Now take us in easy and have a nice—"*

Captain Fallsten cuts the link.

We move into orbit, approaching zero-speed with Undil's rotation. The other Embassy space fleets are spread in geostationary orbit. Lights blink on the stations secured to massive harbor bays, and transports and Molters zoom between them.

The *Ember* closes in... The thrusters flare... Slower, and slower...and we're docked. The *Ember* shudders, and a metallic groan reverberates through the walls.

"Systems stabilized," Glacia reports through the Bridge intercoms. *"Airlocks secure, transports cleared for departure."*

Orcher reaches down and taps an icon on his desk panel. "All non-mandatory personnel have clearance to depart."

With that, the commotion shifts. Officers on different levels of the Bridge shut down their workstations and file out the gate. Captain Fallsten is pacing behind the pilots now, pausing only to watch Glacia, who is reciting more data into her headset.

I meet Glacia once most of the crowds are gone, and we ride an elevator down to the docks on Floor 3. Several transports are lined-up for departure, zooming forward through the silvery light shielding us from the vacuum of space.

"Ten seconds to departure," a pilot announces after the transport we boarded is full and everyone secured.

The thrusters engage. The window panels haven't shut yet—they won't until we enter Undil's atmosphere—so the thrusters distort the air in the docks as we drift into the exit lane.

"Cleared to depart."

My body drags as the transport drifts toward the open gate. Silver light surrounds us...then darkness. Beyond the influence of the *Ember*'s gravity simulators, Glacia's hair ripples outward from her head, waving in slow motion with every slight movement. I can even feel a slight tug on my own scalp, the gentle wave of my own hair.

I *really* need a haircut.

We zoom through the space fleets. There's the *Aster*, which is hanging beside the *Jean*. Undil comes into full view when we pass the next harbor bay. The sun's glare burns along the horizon, but it isn't long before the window panels slide shut to protect the transport during reentry.

150 miles... 100... 75... 50... 40...

Turbulence. Flames and specks of other atmospheric particles blurs the video feed at the head of the chamber. Glacia's hair falls to her shoulders in an untidy mess and she tries to blow it out of her face while gripping the restraints. My body jostles around, and I fight to keep my neck steady until the shaking subsides. The transport levels out and decelerates. When the video feed clears again, Undil's barren desert dominates the view. Mesas jut up here and there, and a gorge—the remnants of the Mavine River—stretches toward a city caught in a thick haze:

The Undil Embassy.

"Preparing approach."

The altitude gauge refreshes: *40,000 feet.* The Embassy is still miles in the distance, but we're closing fast. I can see transports zooming toward the docking platforms ahead of us, and others circle the city as they await clearance to land.

The sun's evening glow casts shadows through the rocky desert, black pillars behind mesas and black spines under small ridges, while softer shadows fill the dry depths of the Mavine river gorge. And as we near it, the Embassy's form is also outlined. At its center, the Crown, the tallest tower on Undil. Standing around it are the three main branch towers, Shield, Horizon, and Threshold, each marking a corner of the inner city. Shield rises in the western corner, while Horizon and Threshold stand in the south and east.

A chill tickles my spine. The sight is more magnificent than when I first saw it almost three months ago. For a moment—a very *brief* moment—I'm almost okay with the idea of calling this place home. Still, I wonder how many people feel the way I do, especially people who have traveled to other planets. Who else secretly hates living on Undil and yearns to escape it forever, yet will always be forced to return?

Ha. Probably *everyone*.

"*Hurry up*," Glacia whispers to herself, her voice strained.

I look at her: she's breathing heavier, her face is turning pale, and her knuckles are turning white. She's staring intently at the disposal tube next to her seat. It's just out of her reach without releasing the restraints, and they won't unlock until the transport lands.

I shift my feet away, remembering the other girl who threw up when we flew Molters for the first time.

That was a mess.

"You better have good aim," I say, and I'm not joking.

Glacia is too preoccupied to respond. First her legs tremble a little—then a lot. She closes her eyes, controlling her breathing through her nose and flexing her fingers impatiently. A line of sweat forms in her hairline. Her breathing becomes erratic—

—and then she vomits. She hits the tube...*kind of.* Some mush splatters inside it, but for the most part, she threw up all over her restraint and chin. She spits, tears glistening in the corners of her eyes...

...and vomits again.

The stench reeks. I'm not surprised when the officer behind us vomits, except he's taller and manages to reach the tube.

I look away and breathe through my mouth. *Don't get sick.* And yet...somehow I don't even feel nauseous. Maybe my body is used to the trans-atmospheric flights. Orcher said some people get used to the transition from space to ground quicker than others.

"*Two minutes to dock,*" a pilot announces. "*Hang in there, people.*"

He must have seen Glacia on the cockpit display.

People grow restless as the transport nears the docking platforms. Chunks of Glacia's vomit start to crust over, and stomach acid drips down her seat. To breathe, I pull the collar of my uniform over my nose. Glacia herself has stuffed her hair behind her shoulder and is holding her head up—eyes open—apparently to keep her brain from spinning.

"Thirty seconds."

The Embassy slides out of the video feed as we curve to the left. The vast, darkening plain fills the view until the transport is low enough for us to see the docks. Another craft settles onto the platform, and then ours descends. The supports lock down, the restraints release, and the hatches open—much to everyone's relief.

Because it *reeks* in here.

"Get her some medicine," a man grumbles on his way out.

I hoist up my restraint and grab two packets from the medicine pouch next to the cockpit door.

"Weak," I whisper when I hand them to Glacia.

"Shut up."

She swishes the first liquid in her mouth, then spits it in the tube and drinks the second.

The cockpit opens and one of the pilots leans on the doorframe, thumbs jammed in his pockets.

"Cleaning station's through there."

He nods to a door at the rear of the chamber, beside a closet that contains racks of pressurized space suits, one for each seat. While Glacia's inside, I hear what sounds like a high-powered spray, and when she comes back out, her right pant leg is soaking wet.

We exit the transport and walk to the elevator that drops to the maglev station. Glace doesn't say one word to me the entire time, probably because I won't stop smirking whenever she looks at me.

I can handle something she can't.

HA.

Inside the bright white station, the monotonous voice relays departure times and destinations. We join a crowd of officers on a train bound for Crown Station. My body sways when the train propels forward, and soon we're rushing toward the center of the Embassy.

"Oy, Arman?"

I look sideways and see a blond-haired guy staring at me from down the aisle, hand held up in a half-wave.

"Lon Kelvin," he says when he walks up to us. "We kind of met at the opening banquet back in June. You remember?"

"Right. You're...Jeremy's friend?"

"That's me, *unfortunately*." He exaggerates a sigh. "Meathead went off and joined Shield Tower. He likes to make things go *boom*." Lon turns to Glacia. "And I remember you. Glacia Haverns, scourge of the Hologis arena."

She cracks a grin, breaking her steadfast attempt to look annoyed.

"Speaking of Meathead, he's meeting me up in the Crown. Just warning you."

The maglev train slows to a halt in Crown Station. Once back aboveground, we make our way to the Crown's most prominent room: the Hall of Treatises. In the center is the giant pillar where all treatises get signed, with the slogan *'Remember the Future'* engraved on its front.

"Seems like yesterday…"

Lon muses to himself for a few seconds, but the content look on his face is interrupted when we hear the shout.

"*OY! THERE HE IS!*"

Lon barely has time to turn around before a guy wearing a black and silver uniform clobbers right into him. Jeremy Pilkins, the guy Glacia and I sat next to at our opening banquet. His light ginger curls bounce on his head as he and Lon slap each other's backs, and then he steps back to look at me.

"Arman Lance, right?" I nod in response. "Score! First time, every time."

Then he turns to Glacia, who's already giving him an annoyed look.

"Hold on, I got this. Uh…"

He snaps his fingers, shaking his head as he mouths random names. Then his expression brightens and he shoves his finger in her face.

"Gloria! You were sit—"

"*Glacia,*" she interrupts. "My name. Is. *Glay. Shuh.*"

"Woah. All right. Chill."

Jeremy raises his hands defensively at the glare she gives him, but doesn't say another word to her.

"Let's go, Lonso. A bunch of us are throwing you a party at my place." He nudges Lon in the ribs. "Biz is gonna be there. About time you two got to know each other, right? Gonna get down to *Biz-ness*, right?"

Lon rolls his eyes and manages to say goodbye before Jeremy shoves him away.

Glacia slips her hand into mine as we walk toward

the Crown's southern gate. "Can we go back to Belvun?"

"Aw. Here I thought you were glad to be home."

"Yeah." She scrunches her face and looks behind us. "Except I forgot about *him*."

Chapter Two

THRESHOLD TOWER'S RECORDS Room is much larger than I remember, but that's probably because I'm so used to being cramped up in the *Ember*. But now the memories come flooding back to me: this is where Glacia showed off her Hologis skills on that tour we took our first day in the Embassy. I remember how annoying she was, how I just wanted to rush the day along and get away from her.

Now look at us.

Data orbs cling to the walls and fill the room with a blue aura. There are other officers sitting at workstations with their backs to me. It's going to feel weird working in the same room as all these people. I'm used to working alone, with Captain Blitner quiet by my side, the two of us surrounded by the dull hum of the *Ember's* engines. Not this. Not the tapping and muttering and people walking in and out every few minutes.

I sit at my assigned workstation and strap on a pair

of tendril gloves, then activate the expedition report and type in a code Lucas Starmile sent me last night. A screen with pre-filled information appears:

File Report: 061819
Expedition 1028
Belvun Recovery Treatise
Undil–Belvun, with return payload
Proposed by: Ambassador Conner A. Lance
Adopted by: Ambassador Michael T. Rafting

The entry fields below the heading ask standard questions: *Duration of Expedition, In-transit Emergencies, Delays.* Information that's easy to fill out. There's even a section where I have to type a summary of the entire expedition, start to finish. So, in my own words, what happened?

Um.

Yeah.

Okay, maybe this isn't as easy as I thought. Think...think...think. The longer I sit here staring at that blank screen, the more I realize how uninvolved I was until we reached Belvun. And it hits me two months too late: I need to be more than someone who just sits around sifting through information. Maybe that's the real reason Orcher suggested I develop a broader archives program. Being a station archivist—and now the *Head* Station Archivist—means understanding the little things that go on, the operations that make expeditions possible. I'm not just a member of the crew: I'm supposed to connect it.

'Don't build a crew. Build a family.' Those were Captain Blitner's first words of advice to Orcher, and they apply to me, too. That's my role, a role Captain Blitner

lost the ability to fill. Even though I work behind the scenes, I'm important to helping the crew function at its peak. A role that, two months ago, I never wanted to have.

So I type a personal report, whatever comes to mind based on the projects I saw and the people I talked to. That's another thing I should start doing: keep a day-to-day record. Why didn't anybody tell me all this before? Meh. It's common sense, I guess.

And I didn't have any back then.

Two thousand words is a lot more than it sounds. It takes over two hours to type everything I remember. Luckily I paid more attention to the things we did on Belvun, so it isn't difficult to recall *that* part of the expedition. I talk about the sites our excavation teams took samples from, locations on Belvun that have drastically affected by the droughts, fires, and super storms that have spawned more and more frequently through the past two years. There's even a watch list of cities and towns that are in *'elevated risk zones,'* anywhere the Belvish Embassy thinks will be the next to experience severe disasters.

Subari—Ladia's hometown—is second on the list. I remember how hot it was. How *dry* it was. The flaky grass, the wilting trees. The short fence that separated the neighborhoods from the desert on the other side. There was a forest of charred stumps stretching all the way to the mountains in the distance, and a haze hung in the air, so unnatural, so...*unclean*.

Belvun is dying.

I sit back and stretch my aching neck. My wrists twinge. I've *never* written such a long essay, not when I worked at Gray Wall, not even for the Embassy Placement Report.

I read through and change things here and there. It'll work, but it's not as detailed as it should probably be.

When I upload the report, a data orb forms in front of me. I take it to an empty slot on the wall that's designated for Orcher's fleet. Other orbs shimmer around it, expedition reports from years past.

I'm meeting Lucas Starmile at the Shady Barchan in twenty minutes, so I shut down my workstation and leave the Records Room. Soon I'm walking down Julian Street toward the Hologis Arena, which is directly across from the Shady Barchan. The Crown looms at the other end of Julian, rising higher than the rows of towers leading right up to it. A hot wind blows into my back and my uniform's cooling fibers get to work, sending a chill through my upper body.

I am *so* thankful for those.

✳ ✳ ✳ ✳ ✳

"So Orcher talked you into it, did he?" Lucas asks when we're settled in at the Shady Barchan. "Gonna try and get this program up and running?"

"Yeah. I need something to work on."

"Well, you'll be a load of help, bud. Truth be told, I'm terrible at multi-tasking."

He takes two gulps of seedberry juice, then cuts into one of his many killari sausage patties. What with his salad, five patties, five pancakes, and a bowl of fruit and kerns, I swear Lucas piled enough food on his plate to feed three people. And his hair... Geez. His spikey blond hair look more pointed than ever, as if he soaked extra gel into them this morning. Seriously. He could *stab* somebody with those.

"Let's get down to business," Lucas goes on. "We need more than a bunch of Records Rooms scattered all over the place, bud. That's just one heck of a disorganized mess and it's destined to fail. Sure, people can go in and grab any information they want, but that's too static for my tastes. Nah, we need more involvement. *Direct* involvement. Understand? I want to transform the archives into an active workplace. That way, we could analyze live updates, rather than sorting through a whole day's worth."

"So...*not* what Captain Blitner and I did."

"Exactly. His system was too slow, and I'm sure you'll agree when I say highlighting all that wasn't the most stimulating work. Staring at that stuff all day every day can make you go brain-dead," he adds with a short laugh.

"Tell me about it."

"My first assignment was the same as yours, bud. All archivists follow similar paths, so it's refreshing when we figure out ways to shake things up—or revamp the program altogether, just like *we* are trying to do. Believe me when I say you don't want to be stuck compiling placement reports the rest of your life. Nah. *Drives me nuts.*" He dumps a container of syrup on his stack of pancakes. "Let's play a new game. Data orbs make for good light reading, but when they're stuck on a wall for years, they're useless, right? So let's have live updates, on-the-spot analyses. We need to know what's happening *now*. A Molter loses pressure? I want our teams logging the malfunction in real-time. Artaans modifies its trade regulations? Our archivists should report it to the Embassy's council themselves, with side-by-side comparisons to other trade arrangements."

He sucks a smear of syrup off his knuckle and raises one finger to hold his thought.

"Some people think negotiations should be left to the politicians. I say it isn't so. We can't separate the problems from the people affected by them. Anyone can walk into a room and have an opinion, and a lot of times it's the wrong one. Nah, can't be like that. The people in the room should be the same people working in the field. Take Undil: we've been on top of space tech since Slater's Modern Embassy took root. But then some words were said, some hands were shook, and now Narviid owns half our industry and claims we need to expand our outlooks. And some say Narviid's not in it to build a better space fleet, because everything we've got is already top-of-the-line.

"Nah. I think the Narvidians are afraid of becoming too dependent on us. Chancellor Green won't even give them explicit mining rights in the Perihelids—not yet—and that's a big setback for anyone trying to make it good in the space tech industry. It works out for Undil, since owning the largest reserve of metal and fuel in the galaxy means we'll make one hell of a profit if anyone buys from us. But that's not gonna last, bud. Someone's going to cave. Long term, maybe this joint treaty will work out. Short term, not so much."

Lucas chops apart his killari patties and stuffs a forkfull into his mouth, chewing noisily. He washes them down, and then,

"Oh, and don't even get me started on Chancellor Green's reaction to the Joint Space Tech Treaty. You've probably seen how opposed he is, yeah? Well, ever since then, he's been pouring funds meant for the next stage of Undil's terraformation into our space tech sector. Talk about a giant step in the wrong direction, bud. If we ever want to gain our independence, Undil as a *planet* needs to become self-sustainable. We need to end our reliance on Artaans for food shipments...but that's a debate for another day."

"There is *one* positive thing I should mention: once this whole situation with Belvun settles, Daliona's eco-hacking days are over. Just watch. The Galactic Embassy Council will make all sorts of restrictions to shut those programs down, *if* they haven't already begun. Then they'll throw all kinds of support back into good old terraformation—and guess who gets to reap the benefits? *Undil.* All eyes will be on us, and that's exactly what we want. So, you get this program working, Ambassador Rafting will see that Daliona gets the Faustocine formula developed, and we'll be headed down the right path. You with me?"

"Yeah." I've been making mental notes, at least.

Lucas finishes his patties and gets to work eating his bowl of fruit. "Despite some flaws, Daliona, Yillos, and Artaans are the strongest planets out there. So there's another thing our new program will do: catalogue those planets. Figure out how those societies function. Outline their inner-workings. What they're doing right or wrong. *Anyway*"—he wipes his mouth—"we need to get you a conference with Chancellor Green and his council, and to do that, you need...?"

He looks at me expectantly, waiting for an answer.

"A proposal?"

"You got it, bud. The art of writing a treatise is knowing how to wrap things up in your words. It's called an agenda. Agendas drive politics, bud. The trick is figuring out which are worth pursuing. So slide this idea through Chancellor Green, and the rest will fall in place." He winks when my expression drops. "It'll be fun. Don't sweat it."

✳ ✳ ✳ ✳ ✳

Looking back, I should have chosen a different room in the apartment complex. The view from Room 811 isn't *bad*, per se, but it's boring. It faces north, looking right at the outer city, which consists mostly of low-lying residential buildings, some empty streets, and the desert beyond. If I look far enough to the left, I can see the docking platforms, but not Shield Tower or anything cool. Glacia, on the other hand, has a room up on Floor 12 that faces east, giving her a prime view of Threshold Tower and the sunset.

I adjust my elbow on the couch arm, then flip the page of *48 Light-Years*. I'm looking through this encyclopedia, trying to familiarize myself with Daliona before I get there so that I actually know what some of the plants and animals and ecosystems are—something I didn't do before going to Belvun.

Right now I'm looking at the picture of a large, fat lizard with a short snout. It's body is dark gray with crimson stripes, and spikes line its back. The description reads:

Ferron Marine Iguana
(Relocated to Daliona)

Native lizard to Earth's Galápagos Islands, and the only lizard species to forage in the ocean. To preserve this species, the creatures were transported on board the space vessel *Tether* from Earth to Daliona, where they were introduced into natural reserves similar to their original Earthly habitats.

Before I get any farther, I hear my apartment door slide open, and a few seconds later, Glacia drops onto the couch and cranes her neck to see what I'm reading.

"Oh, *those*," she says. "Ugly, huh?"

"Ha, yeah."

"Here—"

Glacia grabs the book from me, skims the pages until she finds what she wants, then hands it back.

"These are pretty."

The page is filled with pictures of tropical birds. Some have long necks and skinny legs, some are short and have giant beaks, and some have colorful feathers fanning around their necks. Almost every single bird is splashed with vibrant shades of blue, yellow, red, green, or pink. Under each picture is the caption, *'Relocated to Daliona.'*

"Why have I never looked through this?" I ask out loud, not taking my eyes off each page I flip to.

"Because you're *boring*, remember?" Glacia puts her head on my shoulder and hugs my arm.

"How was training?" I ask, still not looking up.

"Fine. Just practiced escorting transports. How about your meeting?"

"I need to write a proposal."

"Awesome. Your favorite thing ever."

"*Yup.*"

"Ask Michael. I'm sure he can help you. He's probably an expert by now." She sits up straight and looks out the window. "Nice...street corner. It really complements that mesa out there." She smirks and nudges my side. "Hungry?"

I drop the book on the couch. "*Starving.*"

We leave the apartment and catch a maglev train at Ceremony Station, which is across the street from the dome where our induction was held. We head across the city to the Shady Barchan, and after eating dinner, go to the Hologis arena because Glacia insists we see her display in the Hall of Fame.

Outside the stadium, soft colors sweep across the arena's glass panels: red fades to yellow, yellow fades to green, green fades to blue, and blue fades to red. The giant Hologis sphere above the entrance changes colors, too, bathing the intersection in its glow.

We go inside and follow a sign to the Hall of Fame, bypassing the spectator gates that lead to the inner stadium. The chamber at the bottom of the ramp we walk down has two halves: one side is devoted to groups of winners, and the other to people who ended up winning solo—which, so far, is *only* Glacia. Two holograms shimmer on the walls for each group. The first flickers with a picture of the victorious players, and the second replays the team's tournament highlights. The caption to this particular group of victors reads:

Brian Hems, Adria Baston, Lyn Everett
March 4311
37 KOs

"Look who it is," Glacia says, pointing at the fourth group of victors.

Harry Leopold, Lucas Starmile
June 4317
28 KOs

We watch the video feed. It shows Harry Leopold's highlights, then Lucas'. Glacia and I both say *"Ooooo"* when Lucas ambushes none other than Gort Buntem— our tour guide through Threshold Tower. Gort was dodging Harry when Lucas jumped out from behind a corner, kicked off the wall, and hurled his sphere from above. It smacked Gort's back before he could deflect it.

Victoria told us about this match, how Lucas beat Gort in the tournament's final seconds—a grudge Gort never let down. And now that Lucas has knocked him out cold-blooded *twice*, I'm sure their rivalry is even more furious.

Glacia walks to her lone plaque on the other wall, and a smug grin spreads across her face.

Embassy Arena Record
Glacia Haverns
June 4319
23 KOs

Her victory highlights play beside her picture. In one segment, she stalks three blue players, then attacks them, shoving two sideways and hurling a sphere at the third. Another segment shows her deflect two spheres at the same time—one near the floor and one near her shoulder—and then she charges toward a green player, who turns-tail and runs. But Glacia sends a Hologis sphere flying at his feet.

Out.

The video flashes to the final moments of the tournament. Glacia has her back to a wall. She sets one of her spheres on the ground—I *knew* she planted them to lure other players into traps—and then darts around the corner.

And there I am.

I don't even flinch until she slams me to the ground. She pauses—the moment when she snapped at me—then tags my head.

"That must've hurt."

I lift an eyebrow. "You think?"

Glacia tucks her arm under mine and smiles in admiration of her achievement. We stay a few more seconds, then walk up to the entry chamber and out into the warm night.

Chapter
Three

MY EYES FOLLOW Michael's stylus as he highlights a section of text, the opening line of his treatise proposal.

"It's easier than you'd think. What you want to do is create a strong case for *why* restructuring the archives program will benefit the Embassy," he explains. "So you'll need specific examples."

"Ha. *Great.*"

"It's really not that bad. Give it some thought. Better to have specifics than just, *'We need this because it will help.'* Two or three reasons will be good enough to start, but you'll want to expand on them."

Michael points at the first half of his treatise's premise, which reads: *Under the Recovery Treatise, Belvun shall give Undil permission to chemically test and alter biological compounds native to Belvun, including water and carbon-based matter.*

"Open with a general definition of your objective.

Keep it brief. One sentence—done. It'll be easier for councilors to work with on the spot while they're evaluating your presentation." He props one elbow on his desk and highlights the second sentence of the premise. "Break it into steps. What's your first goal?"

It takes me a moment to realize he's asking an actual question. "I guess...hiring people to work with me?"

"You sure about that?"

I stare at the premise to stall, then give up with a shrug.

Michael shakes his head. "How about asking for a location to house the archives?"

"Isn't that the Records Room?"

"Is it?"

He watches me carefully, making me even more unsure about the whole thing.

"I think so?"

"It either is or it isn't."

"Then...*yes.*"

Michael nods, still giving no hint of what I should include. "So what should the first step be?"

"Get permission to use the Records Room?"

"Write that down."

That's how Michael runs the session: he asks question after question so I can deduce the answers on my own, then goes through it a second time to refresh me. Afterward, he explains how I should organize the rest of the proposal. If this was a treatise, I'd have to write dozens of sections, but Michael says this type of proposal need only be two or three pages.

I'm not complaining.

"That's basic treatise anatomy. A lot to think about,

right?"

"Yeah."

"This is the sort of stuff you learn when you spend four years in post-Secondary Studies like I did." Michael sits back and crosses his legs. "I analyzed around two hundred treatises, Arman, and your father compiled a good number of those. Truth be told, I like how he did it. Appropriate trade-offs, good incentives, mutual benefits for all parties. You should see the treatises some other ambassadors wrote up. You'd think Undil was the center of the universe, all these one-sided arrangements screwing over other embassies. It's no wonder everyone liked dealing with your father. Hopefully I've learned a thing or two from him."

He laughs to himself, then sighs.

"You know, Arman, I've been wondering something: did you ever think you'd be chosen as the next ambassador?"

The question takes me by surprise, and I'm sure it shows on my face. "I mean...I thought that, like, there was a chance. I never wanted to though. No way."

"Guess that explains why you seemed so stressed. I suppose it's a good thing I took the Placement Report with you last year, huh? If I'd waited a year, you'd be in my seat. You would've had to go save Belvun single-handedly."

My nervous laugh makes Michael grin as he deactivates the display we were reading from, and then we stand together and walk to the door of his office—*Father's* old office.

"Your proposal conference is...?"

"The sixteenth," I answer.

"*So a little less than two weeks.*" He runs one hand through his loose black hair and lets it fall on either side of his face. "The premise should be easy enough. Can you get it to me Friday, and we'll go from there?"

"Sure."

He shakes my hand. "Good seeing you, Arman."

"Yeah. You, too."

I leave his office and board an elevator. During the ride down to the Threshold Entry Levels, I recite the steps in my head. *Get permission to use Threshold Tower's Records Room, reconfigure the room's basic systems, gain access to data feeds.* Those are the essentials. If they pass, it'll be up to me and Lucas to hire archivists, train them, and get the program moving we leave for Daliona in January, a little more than two months from now.

The elevator stops at the Pavilion—Threshold Tower's main level—and a group of people board, two of whom are carrying data orbs. A guy with short blonde hair gets on last: Lon Kelvin. When we exit the elevator, I walk up next to him.

"Hey."

He glances around, and his face lights up. "Oy, hey there. How're you?"

"Fine," I say with a shrug.

"Awesome." We climb the blue-lighted staircase to the surface level. "Oy, so, I got a question. Meathead's rounding up some people to go to Shield's proving grounds. You up for it?"

"Shooting?"

"Better: *the big guns.* And no ordinances to stop us." We both squint when we step into the sun's late morning glare. "You ever shot an ion cannon?"

"Nope."

"How about a tri-frag launcher?"

I shake my head, and Lon looks stunned.

"*Never?* That's gotta change. No better feeling than clicking that trigger and seeing stuff go *boom*." At the thought, his gaze tugs toward Shield Tower, which stands all the way at the end of the street to our right. Then he points in the direction of the Hologis arena. "Oy, I'm headed this way. Be at Shield by four, okay? And feel free to bring your girlfriend."

"Got it."

* * * * *

Glacia is meeting Ellin for a late lunch at three-thirty, or else she'd go with me to Shield's proving grounds. Or so she says. It probably has something to do with the fact that Jeremy will be there.

Shield Tower is a straight shot down the street from my apartment complex, so I leave ten minutes before four o'clock and arrive in the entry chamber a minute late. I pass some officers marching in a stiff line, and they don't even so much as glance my way before turning down a side corridor.

The entry chamber opens into Decker Hall, Shield's main hub. It's much more technical than Threshold's Pavilion and the Crown's Hall of Treatises. There are lots of screens, whole panels that display unit numbers and assignments. Some slots have *FREE* next to them, while others have locations like *Lower Central* or *Mili-*

tary Docks. Lines of soldiers and officers keep filing into the hall and stopping in front of the screens, then one person will step forward, recite the unit's next assignment, and they'll all march away again.

"Oy! He showed!"

Jeremy Pilkins is standing with Lon and two girls off to the side of Decker Hall. One of the girls is dressed in Shield's black-and-silver uniform, the other in Horizon's red-and-gold. Only Lon and I are wearing Threshold's dark blue, and personally I think ours are the best-looking.

"This is Arianna," Jeremy says, nodding at the girl from Shield. "That's Biz. Lon's got the hots for her."

Lon rolls his eyes and ends with a sideways glance at Biz, whose eyes are closed and mouth is pulled up in a smirk.

Jeremy jerks his head at a separate corridor labeled *Shield Station* and leads our group down it, walking two steps ahead of us. He pushes himself against the back of an elevator, sucking in his stomach as four officers in black and silver uniforms squeeze in with us. After they get off again, Jeremy exhales loudly and shoves me and Lon into the maglev station.

I feel so out of place. Like Decker Hall, all the officers stand motionless, arms crossed behind their backs. The loudest voice comes from the monotonous announcements of trains departing and arriving. Even Jeremy keeps his mouth shut until a new train glides in from a tunnel on the right.

"This one."

The five of us board the train labeled *Shield Outpost.* The station slips out of view and the windows plunge into darkness. A light rush of air whooshes around the train, but nobody talks. Someone to my left clears his throat, and that's it.

Then I see why no one's talking: a Shield Official is standing at the very end of the aisle. He's wearing a black uniform with three gold bars pinned to his chest, and a silver cap with a black brim sits atop his head, angled slightly to the left. His flat expression never changes, even as he sways in place with the motion of the train. We make eye contact, but I look away quickly, feeling like staring at him was the wrong thing to do.

The train slows to a stop. All the on-duty officers file into two lines and salute the Official as they leave, including Jeremy and Arianna. He returns the gesture and doesn't leave his post.

We walk through a security gate. A light flashes, followed by a beep, and on the other side, my face and information appear on a panel. A guard taps the image and a card similar to my ID slides out of the machine beside him.

"Cleared for two hours," he says when he hands the card to me. He repeats himself to Lon and Biz.

The moment we're past the security gates, Jeremy returns to his normal self.

"Place we're going is a couple streets over, right next to the gorge." He puts his arms around me and Lon. "Hope you little ladies don't mind the heat."

Lon pushes Jeremy's arm down and shoots a glance at another important-looking Official who's watching us leave.

The streets are wide enough for military-grade vehicles, and large compounds account for most of the buildings in the outpost. A squadron of tanks glides by. Each is twice my height, and they all have large turrets mounted on their tops.

Jeremy sees me and Lon staring. "Yep, those are the big boy toys. Fitted with sonic repulsors so strong they'd fry your ears right off and sizzle your brain. Those babies could shred Molters left and right all day." He straightens himself up and clears his throat. "*I have firsthand experience*. My instructor shot me down—"

Arianna spins around and walks backward. "Yo, it was a simulation. Get over it."

Jeremy's annoyed grunt is lost in a gust of hot wind that meets our faces when we cross the intersection. I glance at the industrial complex we're passing, and the words above its wide gates catch my eye:

Gray Wall Industries
Factory 3

This is one of the Embassy's space tech factories. In Cornell, I worked for Gray Wall's data management sector.

A guard at the entrance to a circular compound checks our clearance cards, and a second guard escorts us to the rear of the facility, a half-dome that faces the Mavine river gorge. Two Officials meet us inside a room that has shelves stocked with explosives and high energy weapons. A young-looking woman steps forward and paces in front of us. She has a small face and curly brown hair that's pinned up under the silver-and-black cap she's wearing, which is tilted to the left like every other important Official I've seen here. Her sharp green eyes study our faces—and then she speaks.

"*Goooood afternoon*, people. I'm Field Captain Sasha Verlan. Welcome to the Mavine Proving Grounds."

Her voice is, well, nowhere near as strong as I expected. It's high-pitched, chirpy, and...weirdly *playful*. She sounds ten years younger than she looks, honestly, and she already *looks* young. But I know she has to be at least twenty-seven years old. You can't hold any sort of official rank in Shield unless you've been in the program for seven years, and no one under twenty can join the Embassy at all.

"*Oookaaay*. This isn't your typical civilian range, folks. When you're here, you're under our direct supervision at all times." Her gaze lingers on me, Lon, and Biz, the obvious outsiders. "You don't pull any triggers, you don't press any buttons, you don't so much as touch any ordnance without my or Field Sergeant Kerdell's explicit permission, okay? You fire on *our* command and you cease fire on *our* command. Is that understood?"

"Yes, ma'am," Jeremy and Arianna respond together, both of them standing completely rigid.

Sasha frowns and narrows her eyes at me, Lon, and Biz. "I said, *is that understood?*"

"Yes ma'am," the three of us say in unison.

I'm trying to hold back from smirking. Her voice... No. I almost can't take her seriously. But the way her eyebrows pinch together, the way her mouth sharpens into a frown... I know she means business.

The man who has *F. S. Kerdell* embroidered on his chest taps the wall panel, and some of the weapon shelves go dark.

"Make your selections."

We're cleared to use five weapon types: ion, plasma,

tri-frag, incendiary, and concentrated particle turrets. I scan my clearance card over the ion cannon and CP turret, grab a set of tendril gloves, and then we all follow Sasha in single-file out of the weapons chamber, stopping in front of a larger gate. A long buzz, and the gate groans open. She leads us through a tunnel that ends in another gate, and when that one slides back, light pours inside and heat blasts my face.

Now we're on a long platform overlooking the Mavine gorge. It's several hundred feet deep and more than a mile across. A half-mile to the right, a gray pipe sticks out of the rock, crosses the gorge on a series of thick supports, and enters the other side. It's the Embassy's water pipeline, which supplies the city's underground reservoirs.

Sasha stops in front of a large platform enclosed by a low wall. Meanwhile, another gate down the compound opens up, and two officers tow out large hovercarts stocked with our weapons of choice.

"*Oookaaay.* Eyes forward, folks. You'll be shooting at drones. Everyone gets three cycles with their selected ordnance. If you are unfamiliar with how to operate these weapons, we'll show you. If you don't follow my instructions, I will escort you from this compound myself, your military clearance will be permanently terminated, and you will face a strict hearing in front of the Crown's Policy and Conduct Council. Is that understood?"

This time, all five of us give her an affirmative, "Yes, ma'am."

She jerks her thumb over her shoulder. "Elizabeth Pinna, IC-80."

Biz steps forward, jaw clenched nervously. She holds one of the ion cannons awkwardly at her side, pointed down. Sasha motions for her to step up on the platform, then guides her through correct posture and grasp. When Biz hoists the cannon onto her shoulder, she quivers under the weight, but doesn't let it slip.

A horde of target drones rises out of the gorge and scatters a hundred yards beyond the edge. Once they're in position, Sasha gives the all-clear.

Biz takes a deep breath. Adjusts the cannon on her shoulder. Places her finger on the trigger. A targeting array projects several inches from her face, and she takes aim.

The cannon whines—and a jet of blue erupts from the muzzle, blasting straight into...nothing. She completely missed. The jet of blue streaks forever forward and blends into the sky.

"*Oookaaay*. You have to hit them to destroy them, all right?" Sasha says.

Biz sets her finger on the trigger again and takes aim. The whining starts, she shifts her shoulder—and the blue beam explodes from the cannon. Flames. Smoke. Shards of debris. The explosion rips past our ears like high-pitched thunder.

She fires eight more times, missing two drones completely, clipping three, and destroying three.

"*Cease!*"

Biz lowers the cannon to her side and hands it over to Field Sergeant Kerdell, who places it back on the hovercart.

"Alonso Kelvin, TF-47."

Lon is quick about grabbing the gun from Kerdell.

Sasha refreshes him on how to use it: three explosive packs shoot out the barrel, and the explosion operates on a timer. Pulling the trigger in one click sets the timer, two clicks fires the packs.

A targeting system shimmers in front of Lon's eyes when he touches the trigger. It scans the distance between him and the drones, flashes green and beeps.

Click.

The packs whizz through the air, spreading farther, and farther, and—

"*B-B-BOOM.*"

Three explosions, dead on target. Five drones spin out of control, flames and smoke whipping around them. Two crash into each other and drop out of sight, and we hear the resulting explosion at the base of the gorge several seconds later. The crippled drones scatter, but it isn't long before their damaged engines burst apart. More debris drops into the gorge, and the air becomes silent.

When Lon finishes, it's my turn. Sasha helps me set up the CP turret, which stabilizes itself on a tripod, and I aim remotely to hone in on a single drone. Once I have a lock on it, Sasha gives me clearance to fire.

"*ZZZZZTTT.*"

A single, piercing zap. Until I look up, I don't think the turret fired properly. But I'm wrong: the drone I aimed at is falling...falling...falling out of sight.

"Total neutralization," Sasha says when she sees my stunned look. "The beam depolarizes the software grids and permanently deactivates all primary ops. Thrusters, comms, nav systems... The only shields that can sustain CP beams are industrial-grade Magnetic Resonance Repulsors, the ones that protect our space fleets from so-lar radiation and debris."

I shoot down four more drones. Each strike is the same as the one before: a powerful, piercing zap, and a quick flicker of green light around the drone before it drops out of the sky. The beam never misses. It even tracks the slight bobbing of the drones as they maintain a steady altitude.

Jeremy shoots an ion cannon, and Arianna tests an-other TF-47 tri-frag launcher. We continue this cycle, the explosions echoing inside the Mavine river gorge until we've used up our turns. Field Sergeant Kerdell taps a device, and the surviving drones retreat to the storage facility inside the gorge.

Chapter Four

I SPEND THURSDAY evening cooped up in Threshold's Records Room writing the premise for my proposal. Most of the other officers who work here have already left for the night, leaving me in silence to get this done. I've been staring at the display for twenty minutes now, reading and rereading it, wondering if there's anything else I need to include. I've covered the basics: ask for permission to use this room, integrate a new layout with new software, and hire a team. Yet I can't shake the feeling that I'm going to forget *something*.

Meh.

Oh well.

Michael will tell me.

When I take it to him the next morning, he spends a solid five minutes evaluating the premise line-by-line, slipping in notes or rearranging words.

"You don't need this bit..." He swipes his finger over

the panel, and a red line streaks through the words, erasing them. "Other than that, I think you're ready to write the main proposal. Good job. Now, moving on..."

Like he did before, Michael opens the Belvun Recovery Treatise as an example to follow. He scrolls past the premise to the body, and for the next hour we discuss what points to expand upon, how long each should be, and how to organize them into sections. He has me construct an outline so I don't forget anything when I compile the report.

"How about we meet same time next week?" Michael offers when we're finished with today's work. "I'll keep my schedule clear, that way I can look over it, fix what you need, and it'll be set for the conference."

"Sounds good," I say. "Thanks for this, by the way. I appreciate it."

"Any time." Michael reaches out to shake my hand. *"One more thing,"* he says quickly before I leave. "I talked to Ellin yesterday. She said John wants to—and I'm quoting here—*'get the gang back together'* and show us his office in Horizon Tower tomorrow after lunch. Does that work for you?"

John... Oh, right. Ellin's brother. Ugh. Of course *he* would want a reunion.

I force a half-hearted grin onto my face. "Sure."

✳ ✳ ✳ ✳ ✳

"I really don't want to," I grumble.

Glacia squeezes my hand. "It won't be *that* bad."

I slow my pace when we start walking up the long

ramp out of Horizon's maglev station. "This is going to be so awkward."

"How?"

"I don't know. What if he...hugs us or something?"

She snorts. "I'm sure you'll get over it."

At the top of the ramp, we enter Aperture Hall, the central hub of Horizon Tower. I can't help but notice how much it resembles the *Ember*'s bridge. Multi-tiered workstations line the perimeter, and officers pass data orbs across the room. It's almost relaxing to me now, because my time spent on the Bridge was always laid back, the commotion just a part of the background.

Glacia points to the left. "Over th—"

"Oh, you made it!"

Yup.

Here comes John, skipping toward us with a too-big smile on his face. He throws his arms open and wraps the two of us in a giant, uncomfortable hug.

"We were so worried you guys wouldn't find the place," he says when he lets go.

John looks different from the last time I saw him. His once-wavy hair has been neatly trimmed and rounded off by his ears and neck, but his wide eyes still shine with his...*unique* childish excitement. Michael and Ellin stand behind him, looking amused.

I groan quietly, and Glacia shoots me a glare.

"Do you like working here?" she asks him.

"Ha! Do. I. *Ever.* I've already had a promotion: apprentice to a fully-fledged interstellar cartographer." He clasps his hands in the air above his head, then relaxes and swings them at his sides. "One day I'll piece together the data you space explorers collect and make really intrepid maps from it."

"*Intricate*, John," Ellin corrects.

John throws one arm around her shoulders and squeezes her into him. "You know I gotta say, I missed you, sis. You were gone a long time, but you're still my favorite dictionary."

Ellin rolls her eyes, grinning at her brother.

His arm still over Ellin's shoulders, John turns and leads us down one of the corridors to an elevator that will take us up to his workplace.

"Got an office all to myself and it's the best view of the Embassy that Horizon has to offer, no doubt about it. My windows face the Crown and the entire city is just"—he throws his arms out, almost knocking Ellin's head into the closed elevator door—"*right there.* The whole wide wonderful world. Cartographers need those great views, you know? Better for all the visualization we have to do. I've mapped the Embassy so many times I've lost count." John pauses and holds a finger to his chin, tapping it repeatedly. "No, wait, I lied. Sixteen times."

The elevator slides to a stop and opens. As we exit, the words '*Floor 37: Cartography Arrays*' glow on the opposite wall, just like they do in the *Ember.* John skips to the right, still talking our ears off down the length of the hall.

"A cartographer needs all the practice he can get. We work with *very* concise instruments, mind you—"

"*Precise.*"

"—so we can't afford to misjudge a single thing. All the distances, shapes, and angles have to be spot on perfect, especially when it comes to interstellar travel like you guys just got done doing. People like *you* depend on people like *me*."

John abruptly stops walking, whips out his ID, and scans it on a panel. The door slides back to reveal a huge room nearly the size of Threshold's Records Room. An array of projectors hangs from the center, directly above a raised platform that has a ring of holography panels around its perimeter. A crescent-shaped desk sits off to one side, and a workstation stands on the other. And just like John said, afternoon sunlight pours through a massive window that gives him an impressive view of the city.

I can't help but be in awe of the place. Jealous, even. How did *John* of all people end up with such a professional room to work in?

Glacia gawks, clearly thinking the same thing. "This is your *office?*"

"You got it! Came with that promotion I told you about. Once I proved my excellent abilities to the Cartography Council, they told me straight upfront that I was destined for bigger and better things. I'll let you meet Leo! He's a good guy. And the Narvidians are contracting me for a few projects at the same time, so I'll be busy, busy, busy."

John hops onto the raised platform, straps on a pair of tendril gloves, and activates the projectors. Several data orbs materialize around him. He collects four in the center and sweeps away the rest so that they scatter and drift aimlessly around the room.

When he opens the first orb, more than a dozen maps spill out of it and arrange themselves in the air. Each map is a triangle: the Undil Embassy. The first map isn't all that great. It's fuzzy, with only a few notable towers drawn in. But each map improves upon the previous, and the sixteenth map is the most detailed of them all.

He expands it so we can see better: Julian Street, Delta Street, and Vernal Avenue all connect from the three branch towers to the Crown. Side streets are labeled in between blocks of other buildings, which, when he zooms in, have names shimmering above them. And when he flips the map upside down, the maglev stations and routes materialize below the city, and we can watch in real-time as trains wind their way beneath the Embassy.

"*You designed this?*" I ask, impressed.

"Yep! All by hand. I went to a few key locations, snapped a few pics, and mesmerized them."

"*Memorized,*" Ellin whispers, hiding it with a short cough.

"Then I rode the maglev trains for a week straight until I knew every turn by heart. Came back here and drew them." He points at Map 9. "That's when I started including the trains."

Now he's got my attention. I might be able to use this in the archives program one day. Michael catches my eye and nods. He's thinking the same thing.

"John, I have a question."

"*Yes-sir-ee,*" he responds, not looking up as he compresses the maps back to a data orb.

"I'm restructuring Undil's archives program, and I think your maps could come in handy. Would you be interested in making some for me? I can pay you."

John hangs his arms over the front of the panels and

smiles at me. "Don't worry about paying me any shims, Arman. We're all Cornellians here. I got your back for free."

He opens another data orb and more maps spill out. These aren't of the Embassy, but of Orvad, the city by Undil's ocean. This map isn't as detailed as the others were, but John explains he's still in the process of enhancing its features, like the water facility and the pipelines that distribute water to each of Undil's settlements. The last map he shows us is fuzzy, like static, and I can't help but feel like I've seen it before. Then it clicks: this is a section of the Perihelid asteroid field, just like Officer Remmit has in his lab on the *Ember*.

"I'll have this one done before you guys go back to Belvun," he tells us. "I'm on the team that gets to map what the asteroid field will look like when you go back through it next spring." He scrunches his face, suddenly sad. "I suppose that's about as close to the field as I'll ever—*Leo!* Come on, let's go meet Leo."

Without hesitation, his face lights back up, and he almost forgets to strip off his tendril gloves before leading us back out of his office. We go to Floor 42, which is labeled: *Cognitive Holography*. Everyone here seems to know John. Some techies look up and wave, and more than one person says hi as we skirt around the edge of the room. Even fresh recruits, whose faces I recognize from our induction, give him cheerful looks. This isn't the John I remember. He was awkward, flamboyant, shook hands with everyone—

Wait. That's still this John. How did he manage to become so popular? How did *he* make more friends than *I* did? *How?*

"Here we are!"

John lets us into a lab, where a bunch of techies are huddled around a circular podium, examining something in its center. They look up at our arrival.

"John!" one of them says, stepping away from the group. "Friends of yours, I presume?"

"And my family, Leo." He pulls Ellin into a sideways hug. "This is my sister."

"Yes, yes. Miss Ellin. He talks about you *all* the time."

She smiles. "I'm sure he does."

Leo laughs and takes us over to the other techies, who are standing around a pair of glasses that have tiny projectors right above each eye, and what look to be boxy data cartridges plugged into the sides behind the ears. It looks heavy and uncomfortable, and if they're trying to make it stylish, they're failing.

Horribly.

"These will be all the rage one day. I'm *sure* of it," one of the techies says to us, rubbing his palms together excitedly.

"One step at a time, Alec!" Leo chuckles, then runs one finger along the curve of the glasses. "About fifty years ago, Daliona pioneered an exceptionally complex project: neuro-optic holography. The goal? To transpose mental images into a holographic medium. Someone once jokingly speculated that because light is so easy to distort, and our thoughts are already so distorted, maybe we could learn to map our mental images for use in a visible medium."

He cracks a smile, waiting for us to laugh...but none of us are—except John, who hasn't dropped his beaming smile the entire time.

"Er, *anyhow*... Such a device would save time blueprinting cities and space fleets. Technological endeavors could be displayed as they're conceived, and memories could be laid out right before our eyes." Leo gives a smug smirk. "Daliona abandoned this project and developed opticons instead. Opticons are much cooler, mind you, but they can't do what *these* can. You could say we're at the forefront of this technology."

"What's it called?" Glacia asks.

"A Neuro-Optic Visor. NEO Visor, for short."

"John's been an enthusiastic tester," another techie says, interlocking his fingers near his chest. "He's managed to pull off some crazy stuff—more than the rest of us can brag about."

"I've just got *superior mental prowess*," John says, tapping a finger on the side of his head.

The techies laugh and Leo pats John on the back. "Once we get these working properly, we promised he could keep one. Could be months...years...or next week."

"My bet's on next week," John jokes. "These guys don't even stop to eat."

Another round of laughter, and then Leo hands the NEO Visor to John so he can demonstrate. He slips it around his ears and taps the side to activate the projectors. His expression hardens, eyes staring straight ahead at some point a few feet in front of him. Slowly, a blue glow appears. A dot focuses in the center of the glow and starts moving sideways, tracing a line. John's jaw tightens, and he grits his teeth. His breathing becomes heavier as he concentrates on moving the dot. He moves it upward, then sideways, then down, and then there's a square floating in front of him.

Nice.

He reaches out and turns it sideways, then repeats drawing the square again and again until a whole cube shimmers where there used to be nothing. It takes him all of a minute.

"Nearly perfect," one of the techies compliments. "Mine always look like a two-year-old drew them."

John beams at him. "No worries, Mr. Hanson. I know you'll get it...*one of these days.*"

"Draw the face," Leo says, shifting a glance at Ellin.

John taps an icon off to the side, and the cube vanishes. He squeezes his eyes and—after a few seconds—a new image begins to form: a face. As it becomes darker, I recognize Ellin. The eyes are a bit distorted, and the hair is shorter than hers actually is, but it's Ellin nonetheless.

One of the techies mutters his amazement. Glacia and Michael both look impressed, and a small smile flickers across the real Ellin's face.

"He likes drawing your face, Miss," Leo says after John hands the visor back. "You got a real man for a brother. Loves his sister, he does. He never—"

But Leo stops short as several heavy footsteps thud us, and we all turn around to see five men striding into the lab. I recognize two of them: General Corbard, the director of Horizon Tower, and Ambassador Ravad, a bald, tight-cheeked man with pale green eyes. He's the ambassador who shouted drunkenly at Orcher during our Induction Ceremony. The other men with them are Narvidians.

"I told you we'd find him here, Corbard," the ambassador announces. "He always is. Jonathan doesn't dilly-dally around, do you? Always on the go."

Ravad chuckles and gives John a sharp smile. John glances at General Corbard, who's staring right back at him.

The ambassador slips his hands into his pockets and takes a long look at the rest of us before actually recognizing who we are. "Oh, yes! The new ambassador. Rafting? Yes, my apologies. And of course, we have the *younger* Lance. How could I not have noticed?"

Behind Ambassador Ravad, General Corbard clears his throat. "John, report to me when you're finished here. The Narvidians would like to discuss your upcoming projects."

"I will, General."

"We tried to get ahold of you but you weren't answering," Ravad says, patting the holotab clipped to his leg.

"I'm sorry, Ambassador." John's fingers slide down to touch his own empty pocket, his hand quivering. "I left it in my office."

"No no *no*. It's all right. I'm sure you were excited to see your friends." Ravad bows his head and laughs. "Though I daresay if our tech people invested more time in developing *convenient* methods of communication, rather than, well"—he frowns and gestures at the NEO Visor—"whatever *that* is, we could have avoided this problem and never have needed to find you ourselves. But by all means, get around to it on your own time."

The techies glower behind Leo's back, who remains unmoved—on the outside, that is—and Ravad laughs at them, then points out the door.

"We'll see you shortly, Jonathan."

He turns and leads the Narvidians back to a waiting elevator, and General Corbard follows a few seconds after.

"He tried defunding us," Leo says when they're gone. He runs his fingers down the side of the NEO Visor. "Wasn't but a few years ago. Corbard won't budge, though. Ravad doesn't understand what developing this technology—and independently, at that—will do for Undil's future advancements. If we can sustain the processing power, imagine what we could create five, ten, *twenty* years down the road." He gestures out the window, where the Embassy is shining in the afternoon light. "We could construct whole cities from full-scale holographic projections and cut out all the guesswork. Map out prime locations for settlements on uninhabited planets without ever setting foot on them. Redesign our space stations on expeditions between planets. We need this technology"—he waves the visor at John—"and we need the very best minds using it."

Chapter Five

GLACIA RUNS HER hands down my sleeves to smooth out the wrinkles, gives the cuffs a quick tug.

"Repeat after me: you got this, mister."

"*You got this, mister.*"

She rolls her eyes, and I can't help but smirk.

"You're going to impress them."

"*I'm going to impress them.*"

"Run through the proposal, answer his questions, and get the approval." She steps behind me and flattens my collar. "Thirty minutes, in-and-out."

"*In-and-out.*"

Glacia comes back in front of me and grabs both of my hands. "This time next week, Undil will be on track to have a proper archives program"—she stands on her toes to give me a kiss—"and *you* get all the credit."

"And Lucas," I add.

"*And Lucas,*" she agrees, "but your name goes on top."

Glacia walks with me to Ceremony Station, where we stand and wait for a train to the Crown.

"Nervous?" she asks.

I rub my hands together. "How'd you guess?"

"Because I'm pretty sure this is how I looked before I had to fly in the Perihelids."

"Pretty much."

"But I have a hunch Chancellor Green won't smash you with an asteroid while you're presenting."

I half-laugh. "Don't tell Captain Fallsten. She'll change that *real* fast."

The intercom announces an arriving train seconds before one glides out of the tunnel to our left. The hatches slide up and people step off.

Glacia hugs me quickly. "Good luck!"

She steps back so I can get on, and when the doors slide back down, the train rushes out of the station. I pat my chest pocket to make sure my holotab is still there. Of course it is. I fold my hands in my lap, but that's uncomfortable, so I lean against the seat divider and cycle through everything Michael told me when he took one final look at the proposal: *Premise, Questions. Section One, Section Two, Questions. Section Three, Conclusion, Questions.* That's how the conference should go.

Should.

As the train rounds the tight left curve, someone down the aisle laughs. I glance over and see two Narvidian men dressed in their usual black and crimson uniforms. They're speaking Narvidian. I strain my ears to hear pieces of what they're saying, but don't recognize any words. The man who laughed catches my eye and throws a lazy salute my way. Not sure what else to do, I salute back.

I feel the sideways tug as the train decelerates. We glide into Crown Station, which isn't so crowded right now. I make my way up to the Hall of Treatises, then head up to Floor 35. An Official greets me when the doors open, and he escorts me to the conference room. There are no windows, and the lights are dim. I stand behind a podium and take a quick look at my small audience. Chancellor Green and his council are sitting on a raised tier in the very back, and the four tower directors are below that. There's General Corbard of Horizon, Commander Mannard of Shield, Henri Estilon of the Crown, and...*Orcher?*

All this time, and I never realized he was head of Threshold Tower. But of course he is. He owns a space fleet just like General Corbard and Commander Mannard, and he even told me he'd see to it that Threshold complies with my requests.

Once I'm settled, Chancellor Green speaks to the council and directors. "Today we welcome Arman Lance, Head Station Archivist of the *Ember* and primary founder of the proposed Live Archives Program." He gestures at Orcher. "I believe General David Orcher and Officer Lucas Starmile have wanted to enact this program for a number of years now, but were unable to set it in motion."

He pauses to glance at the display he's reading from,

then,

"Before you begin, Mr. Lance, we have one question: what inspired you to accept management over this program? Why do you feel you are best suited to organize it?"

I mull over an answer. I didn't expect to be getting questions right from the start. Then I remember everything Lucas said at brunch that one day, and decide to go with that.

"When I first talked to Officer Starmile about this, he told me Undil needed a way to monitor treatises, money transfers, and data anomalies in real time. Our current program is small. It started with three people, and now there are only two: me and Officer Starmile. I think it's important that we develop a larger archives program because Undil needs a team that will manually analyze information and catalogue expeditions in real time."

Chancellor Green scribbles something on his display. "Again, why do you think *you* should be in charge? Why not Officer Starmile, or some other officer who has spent a longer time in records-keeping?"

I look down at Orcher to stall. He crosses his arms and waits for me to continue.

"While I lived in Cornell, I worked at Gray Wall for three years. I wrote status reports and examined data. This will be similar, so..."

I can't think fast enough to find the words to finish my sentence, so I let it hang and hope they don't count it against me.

One of the council members leans over and whispers something to Chancellor Green. He nods, then sets his hands on either side of his display. "All right, Mr. Lance.

You may proceed with the proposal."

The display on the podium lights up. I access my proposal, take a deep breath, and read through the premise. Every time I glance up, some of the council members are taking notes, and others are watching me. Orcher nods after each paragraph. General Corbard circles something. Director Estilon looks up from his notes every now and then and gives me a reassuring smile—I think he is, at least. And Commander Mannard, who returned from Narviid two weeks before we got back from Belvun, stares at me the entire time, his mouth neither frowning nor smiling.

I pause after the premise, but nobody asks any questions so I move into the first section: permission to establish Threshold Tower's Records Room as the Live Archives Program's headquarters, and restructure it to suit our needs. I explain how we would need to install workstations, processors, and memory cores, as well as strip away some of the data orb panels and replace them with units linked to individual towers and space fleets.

I move straight into Section Two and explain how I will visit Orvad and see if any techies want contract work to code new software and redesign the archives chambers. I'll also work on assigning teams to each station of Orcher's fleet.

"What sort of compensation do you plan to give team members?" the councilman next to Chancellor Green asks. "How many shims per year do you propose?

This question takes me by surprise. I was so focused on what would go into the program that I didn't put much thought into that. Fortunately, Chancellor Green answers for me.

"We will discuss salaries when we move into evaluations."

Section Three covers future developments of the program and how it could be further integrated into the Embassy, though predicting future prospect was difficult without knowing *what* the system itself will be, and I probably won't know until after I visit Orvad.

I recite the conclusion, and then take more questions. Orcher asks if I've thought about sharing the program with other planets, and Director Estilon wonders how I plan to monitor the teams. When the room goes quiet again, Chancellor Green says a few final comments, thanks me for the presentation, and tells me he'll arrange a second conference after I return from Orvad.

The conference adjourns, and I'm free to go.

Chapter Six

JOHN HOLDS A glass of Sprice under Glacia's nose so that she's forced to sniff the overwhelmingly bitter scent. He bought us a round of drinks at the Shady Barchan to celebrate my first conference and has been pressuring Glacia into drinking a shot, insisting the Sprice makes it a *formal* toast.

It's nearly midnight, so the Shady Barchan isn't as packed as it is during lunch or dinner. A few people line the main bar, but the entire second level is empty. Out the windows, Julian Street is bathed in the yellow light pouring from the other restaurants. Cars glide past, a few people walk by, but for the most part, the Embassy has grown quiet.

"*Fine.*" Glacia grabs the glass from John, her nose scrunched. "Just one. That's it."

"And no faking!"

"*I promise.*"

John raises his glass. "To the success of Arman's

proposal!"

Our five glasses clank in the center of the table, then we gulp them down. Glacia squeezes her eyes and practically spits back into the glass.

"It's not *that* bad," I say.

"It really is."

"*Lightweight*," Ellin teases.

John spreads his hands over the table as if separating Ellin and Glacia. "Come on, sis. Leave her alone." He snaps his fingers to get the bartender's attention. "Hey, Neddy! Get us another round, but make one of them seedberry juice with a straw—*for the baby*."

Glacia's cheeks flush red. "*Make it five*," she grumbles, glowering at John.

Ned the bartender comes over with five glasses of Sprice, the red drink with gold flecks that reduced Victoria and Officer Remmit to fits of laughter on Belvun. Of course, they drank four glasses each, so it was to be expected. Even I'm cautious about drinking my second glass too fast. This stuff is strong.

"Thanks, Neddy!" John shouts as the bartender walks away.

"As always, Mr. John."

Ellin looks to John for an explanation.

"The Narvidians take me and the boys out every week," he explains with a smug grin, straightening his shoulders as if being treated out by foreigners is a huge privilege. "Let me tell you: those Narvidians can drain three pints of Arb Ale like it's nothing. Yeah. *Yeah*." He nods like it's the most incredible thing he's ever seen. "I tried it once, but...ugh. It's disguising."

"*Disgusting*," Ellin corrects, holding her hand out to

steady John on his seat.

He takes a giant swig from his new drink, then slaps the table and raises the half-empty glass in the air again. "To my...my *favorite* dictionary!"

And before Ellin can stop him, he chugs the rest.

By the time we leave, Glacia still hasn't touched her second glass. Michael and I split it so John doesn't, and then Ellin takes him outside, despite his insistence to take care of the tab.

"*Neck one's on me...on me,*" John promises when we're all outside again. He jabs his finger into his chest. "*Don't worry 'bout it... I'm heeah every week with the...the Narvs.*"

He smirks at his own nickname for the Narvidians, and Ellin does her best to keep him walking in a straight line. Fortunately, the sidewalks are clear this time of night and we don't have to worry about people staring.

"I'll walk with you," Michael tells Ellin. She nods and tightens her grip on John's wrist when he tries to pull away. Michael turns to Glacia and makes an obvious gesture at me. "You got him?"

"He's not going anywhere."

Glacia grabs my hand...which suddenly feels, like, *reeeaaally* far away. Ha.

Michael and Ellin walk John to the maglev station near the Hologis arena, and Glacia pulls me to the left, down a street that goes straight to our apartment complex. The farther we walk, the more I can feel it...my head swimming. Ha. That's the most Sprice I've ever drank at one time. I think. Yeah. Every car that whirs by us sounds like it's revving its engine...*vrrrmmm*...and all the lights dazzle my eyes, and whenever my grip starts to relax, Glacia squeezes my hand tighter and looks up at me.

Ha. She's so cute.

"You good?"

I nod and look at my feet: I'm scuffing the ground, dragging my heels on the sidewalk. Glacia notices and slows her pace. The apartments are only three blocks away now, so we aren't in any sort of hurry.

"I liked you better on Belvun," Glacia says.

"What you mean?"

"When you got all loopy from the air. But this, this is...sad." She bumps my shoulder. "You're boring when you're drunk, mister."

It takes me a few seconds to process what she said, and it really hits me hard.

"Sorry. I'll..." I swallow all the saliva pooling under my tongue. My head's getting fuzzy. *"Try...to be."*

She gives me a weird look, then sighs and keeps talking. But I'm barely paying attention. My stomach is starting to twist. I swallow again. Clench my jaw. Tighten my throat. One more block. Come on. I can make it. Come on.

"I hope Ellin talks to John," Glacia says from somewhere really far away. "He shouldn't be—"

Nope.

I keel sideways and vomit all over the sidewalk and against a building. Glacia mutters something, but I don't hear what. I stay bent over, spitting until the nausea wears off and I can close my eyes without getting dizzy. When I stand up again, she's watching me from a few feet away, waiting for me to finish puking. Then she moves closer and puts her hand on my shoulder to push me along. I barely remember walking into the apartment. Or going up to her room. Or slumping down on a couch.

"Here."

She grabs my wrist and curls my fingers around a glass of water, not letting go again until she's sure I'm going to drop it. After I drink it, I suck down a pouch of purple liquid she gives me, which rinses my raw throat and settles my stomach.

Neither helps my headache.

✳ ✳ ✳ ✳ ✳

I wake up and start to roll over—then catch myself before I fall off the couch. I drop one leg down the side and push myself upright. The room is mostly dark because Glacia's windows face away from the sunrise, but outside, Threshold Tower gleams in the yellow dawn.

I tilt my head back and close my eyes. The nausea has settled, but my head is hot and throbbing, so I gulp down the water that's still in the cup Glacia gave me last night—then go refill it. While I'm in the kitchen, Glacia comes out of her bedroom, dressed and ready for the day's flight exercises. A silver bar is pinned on each of her shoulders, right below the golden Undil Embassy crests that adorn them.

"Feeling better?" she asks, shaking out the cuffs of her sleeves and pulling her hair over her left shoulder like always.

I just shrug.

"Medicine's next to the fridge," she says, pointing. "I

have to run a simulation and meet Fallsten for escort exercises, so I'll be gone all day. Let's talk about going to Orvad and Cornell tonight, okay?"

"Mmhmm," I manage to grunt.

She steps up and kisses my cheek. Somehow, in my gross, disheveled state, I manage to smile.

After she leaves, I drink another cup of water and go up to my apartment, where I take a long shower and get ready for work, then catch a train to Threshold.

The Records Room is empty today. I'm thankful for the data orbs, whose pale blue glow I use as an excuse not to turn on the lights. There's not much I can do for the new archives program right now, not until I get approval from the council to move forward and hire a team. So I use the time to read up on Orvad's techies. The most prominent guy I can find in the city's info systems sector is Olivarr Cresson, the owner of Cresson Software Industries.

I make a note, then start working on what Lucas asked me to do today: read through historical accounts from 4230 to 4240 and pull out records to help him develop the Centennial Placement Report, which will be distributed to hopeful recruits next June.

Yes, my favorite kind of work.

Ha.

I'm interrupted only once, by a man searching for transport chamber layouts. Thankfully he doesn't turn on the lights. Other than that, the door stays shut and I'm left to read and highlight relevant sections of text. I admit, I don't mind the work. Not really. I'm used to working alone, or working with someone and not talking to them. That's how I operate. It's not, as Lucas put it, *'the most stimulating work ever,'* but it keeps me busy.

Still, hopefully something will come of this new program. Orcher wants it to be operational before we leave for Daliona, so that gives me...a month and a half.

Awesome.

Maybe our work on Daliona will be different. Maybe we won't just sit in a station or chamber all day reading semi-outdated historical records. That's pretty much all I've done in the Embassy so far. I know it's important for future generations to be knowledgeable about this stuff, but—again, like Lucas said—I don't want to be stuck in a room my entire life.

That's the reason I'm here, isn't it? To explore, to see whatever it is life has in store for me. Maybe I won't make a difference like Father did, but then again, I don't *need* to be just like him.

Hours later, I go eat lunch in Threshold's food court, two floors above the Pavilion. I get a bowl of spinach and poultry salad to prep my body to work out later. I've been slacking on exercise. Being trapped on the *Ember* with nothing to do half the day gave me all the motivation I needed...mostly because the fitness center is the brightest area of the station. Now I've strayed from my whole routine—

"Oy there."

I look up just as Lon sits down. He has a plate of seasoned killari beef piled on top of a heap of creamed pasta.

"Heard you're taking over the archives?"

"Yup."

He hurries to eat as much as he can, then says, "Had to hold a conference, right? How'd that go?"

I tip my head side-to-side. "Good enough."

"Taking applications?" he asks, to which I raise an eyebrow, so he says, "For the teams you're hiring."

"Not yet. I'm waiting for approval."

"Well tell me when you guys get around to it. You know I help monitor the Belvish matter samples on the *Drake*, so I've got inside info."

"Cool."

He scarfs down the rest of his beef, drops his tray at the cleaning dispensers, and then we leave the food court.

"I've gotta go meet Biz. I'll hit you up if Meathead takes us to the range again."

And just like that, he's gone as quickly as he came.

I go back to the Records Room. This time, two officers are inside, and the lights are on. It doesn't bother me now. My head is feeling *much* better than it was this morning.

I read reports from an expedition that returned from Yillos over the weekend. As far as I can tell, nobody's filled out the analytic data that needs to be done. Obviously I can't write up the report essay, since I didn't exactly travel to Yillos, but...gah, I hope I do one day. So I transfer stats into the report's blank fields, things like the duration of the expedition, which was thirteen weeks, two days, and fifty-six minutes—in Undilaen time, that is. Calculated in Yillosian time, the trip lasted only nine weeks, five hours, and forty-five minutes. So a day on Yillos is what? Almost forty-one hours?

Geez. I could *never* get used to that.

* * * * *

When Glacia walks into my apartment that evening, she sits on the other end of the couch.

"Not gonna get sick on me, are you?"

I fake a gag.

She rolls her eyes. "So. How about that talk."

Right, planning the trip to Orvad, and then Cornell for her brother's wedding.

Glacia projects a calendar from her holotab and expands the last week of September. "Jaston's wedding is on the twenty-seventh," she says, tapping the date's icon. "Have you thought about when you'll go to Orvad?"

"Like...whenever's good."

"And *when* will be good?"

"I haven't really thought about it."

Her cheeks tighten. "And when do you plan to start thinking about it?"

I hesitate. This is how she usually is after training with Captain Fallsten all day. I just need to stall and let her calm down.

It works. After a few seconds of me biting my lip, Glacia scrolls back a couple days on the calendar.

"Leave here on the twenty-fifth," she tells me. "Spend the day in Orvad, then meet me in Cornell."

"Got it."

"See how easy that was? Now send Orcher a message and tell him your plan."

I keep my eyes down as I get out my holotab and type out a message to Orcher. Once it's sent, Glacia taps *September 25* and puts *'Arman, Orvad'* under the date. Then she fills in her schedule for the next week: training with Captain Fallsten until September 21, followed by exercises with Shield Tower until September 25, and she'll fly to Cornell the next afternoon.

"I can pick you up from the dock," I say, careful not to agitate her more. "I live right by it...sort of."

She glances sideways. "Okay."

We don't say much after that. She leans back and closes her eyes, and I sit forward, press my knee against hers a bit. She doesn't react, so I resort to looking out the window at the city's outer limits.

I hate this view.

I glance at Glacia, and then, after some hesitation, push myself against the slant of the couch and gently massage one of her shoulders. It takes a few seconds, but she slowly tips her head back...pulls her hair over her left shoulder...and turns her whole back to lean into my chest. I massage her lower shoulders, the base of her neck, her upper back. Slow circles, taking care not to stray too long in any one spot. Her muscles flex and loosen under my fingers.

I don't remember stopping, but eventually my arms are wrapped around her, hugging her close. Glacia's chest rises and falls, her head propped in the crook between the couch and my shoulder.

"*Thanks.*"

She whispered it so quietly I thought it was just her breathing until she turns her head and settles her cheek on my chest. I kiss the top of her head.

Until I leave for Orvad, that's how we end our days. When I get back from Threshold and Glacia gets back from training, we relax together. Sometimes we look through *48 Light-Years* to learn more about what we'll see on Daliona, other times we go for late-night walks around the Embassy, when the streets are quiet and the air isn't so hot. On those nights, we walk to the edge of the city, stand in the loose dirt, and gaze out into the darkness. On those nights, we trace the constellations, or stare at the Andromeda galaxy, the smudged oval low on the northern horizon.

We look forward to the evenings, because the days are long and the nights are quiet.

Chapter Seven

SEPTEMBER 25
UNDILAEN TIME
STANDARD YEAR 4319

BY THE TIME I leave for Orvad, I still haven't heard from Chancellor Green's council. He said they likely wouldn't make a decision until after I get back from my trip, but I had hoped it would be sooner. Oh well. I'll just have to let it go for now...which shouldn't be difficult to do, considering the fact that I'm currently in a hover-craft with Victoria on a three-hour flight to Orvad.

We left the Embassy before the sun came up. I'm half-asleep, slumped sideways on the couch, staring at the newscast projected on the wall: a dust storm is blowing through Petrarch, Undil's smallest settlement. Then there's an update about a string of new regula-tions in Holistead after some guy's turret misfired and blew a crater near the city's Main Throughway.

At one point, I get up and stand by the window to watch the world rush by. This is the farthest west I've ever traveled on Undil. We follow the Mavine gorge to its end, where it seals up like a healed scar. The landscape shifts. Mesas dwindle away, ridges, canyons, and plateaus flatten out, and even the planet's surface changes color. The reddish-brown dirt turns dark tan, then takes on a rich, golden-brown sheen. The cracked ground smooths to dusty plains, and when I turn my gaze from the ground to the sky, I almost can't believe my eyes.

There are clouds.

At first they're thin, pale wisps that vanish in seconds, but soon they take on a whole new form. They aren't puffy, or billowing like the clouds on Belvun. No, these become...*dense.* Another half-hour, and the clouds look like a gray blanket being pulled across the sky. The sun peeks out here-and-there, casting pale, golden rays through the light haze.

"It'll clear up by midday," Victoria says, coming over to stand next to me. "Always does. At night, the temperature drops and the clouds move in. Sometimes it rains. But then morning comes, everything heats back up, and the clouds go away. Just watch."

She's right: the clouds gradually disperse, and in the bold sunlight, the features on the ground continue to change. There are ripples now, shifting in the golden dust or swirling in gusts of wind. Others loom like small mountains, cresting several thousand feet off the over the desert.

"Sand dunes," Victoria tells me. "Those big ones are

called barchans."

Barchans.

The Shady Barchan.

"You mean like the restaurant?"

She nods, and I hear her laugh once. "*Exactly* like the restaurant."

The barchans grow larger and larger, and sand sweeps from their tops in the gusty winds. Then, without warning, the barchans shrink, getting flatter...and flatter...until they're nothing more than ripples again. Except now there are strange lines etched into the sand, and another gust of wind uncovers a large gray pipe.

A *water* pipe.

And that means we're getting close. Miles ahead, against the southwest horizon, a silhouette quivers in the heat: a city on the sand. Soon I can see a curved wall protecting shorter buildings—neighborhoods, I assume—but in the very center, a cluster of towers stands against the Undilaen Ocean.

This is Orvad.

"*It's as big as the Embassy,*" I breathe, amazed by what I'm seeing.

Victoria looks down at me, only half-smiling. "Not quite. But it *was* almost chosen to be the Embassy, back in Undil's early years."

Orvad's main city is so tightly packed that there are almost no gaps between the towers. The city extends south, running behind the tall wall that has dunes blown along it. When I look north, I spot a separate complex several miles up the beach: the water facility. Massive pipes plunge into the ocean from the rear of the building, and dozens of smaller ones extend into the desert.

Some curve north, some stay straight, and the rest turn south.

"You grew up here?" I ask Victoria as the hovercraft makes its final approach.

"Twenty-one years. *Yep.*"

"Why'd you leave?"

"Do I look like a techie?" She half-laughs. "The city is smaller than it looks, too. Drove me *crazy.*"

"When's the last time you were here?"

Victoria doesn't answer. She looks out over the home she left without so much of a flicker of a smile. We just got here, and she already looks like she wants to leave. I can't help but think that this is how I feel about Cornell. I haven't seen my home in nearly four months, and to be honest, I'm not sure I'm ready to go back.

The hovercraft lands, we're given clearance to exit, and I step into my third Undilaen city. Well, kind of. The main city is still a mile or so away, but I'm at the edge of the neighborhoods and that's close enough.

Heat swamps my face—I was prepared for it, but this is so different from anywhere else I've been. The air is hot, but it's also...*heavy*. When I take my first breath, I can feel how thick it is, just like Victoria warned. It smells different, too. There's no dusty musk or stale odor of dirt. But it's also nowhere near the fruity-sour aroma like Belvun's air. No, this smells heavily of salt. It's also windy. *Very* windy. So windy that my uniform ripples and snaps. Even the hovercrafts have to physically clamp onto the platform instead of hovering above it like usual.

A maglev train is waiting for us out front of the dock. I welcome the stillness of the inside, savoring the air conditioning as we glide alongside Orvad's Main Throughway. We move closer to the main city until it's directly overtop us, the towers pointing straight into the sky—

—and the train dips underground.

My body drags forward as the train slows, and moments later we stop on a bright platform. The doors slide open and more people get on, but Victoria shakes her head to stop me from getting off.

The doors slide shut. The train accelerates back into darkness and speeds around a curve. I look around at the people who just got on and notice how much they resemble Victoria: shiny black hair, sleek eyebrows, narrow faces, golden-tan skin. Even Officer Remmit shares some similarities, though he has a rounder face. I can't help but think that if Glacia came with us, she would totally stick out with her blonde hair. I, on the other hand, blend in pretty well.

A minute later, my body drags again as we come to another stop. This time we exit the train and make our way aboveground, where towers rise around us and the sun is already past its peak. I'm surprised by how late in the day it is—until I remember that Orvad is four hours ahead. We left the Embassy at eight, and the flight was three hours long. I check the time on my holotab, and yep, it's almost one o'clock.

The tower closest to us is bronze, capped with a peak and antenna. There's a silver tower, a glass tower, another bronze tower, and more and more *and more*. Each stands well over sixty stories tall, but most are thinner than those in the Embassy. I count no fewer than six packed together per block.

Then we enter a small plaza—and my eyes get wide: there's *grass*. Real, green grass. It's contained to the circular plaza, but still. It's there. And sitting in the middle of it are three glass domes, each about two stories tall, and all three have several vents protruding at angles from their tops.

A plaque at the head of the plaza reads:

SANCTUARY PLAZA BIODOMES
Exoplanet Allen-17b
Renamed *Undil* upon Ryginese settlement in
Standard Year 3605
To Commemorate
Mission Commander Leeward Tyson Undil

"What do they do?" I ask, turning to stare up at them. It's hard to see inside because the windows are opaque.

"This is how most terraformation begins," Victoria explains. "Lucky for us, the Ryginese stuck to the standard model, unlike Daliona. First stage lasted three hundred years, recycling gases into Undil's atmosphere to make it breathable without masks. To live here during that... It's a crazy commitment, and probably the most selfless thing a person can do, to pave the way for humanity's future knowing you're going to die without seeing the result of your work." She laughs through her nose. "Something *I* could never do."

I point at the grass. "Are all the plazas like this?"

"Not all. But this isn't an unusual sight for Orvad, no. They're in the first stages of biological introduction, a crucial step of terraformation. And what grows here won't necessarily grow elsewhere. The Orvadians fine-tuned this grass to Orvad's climate. Some people even call it the Oasis of Undil."

We go back to the main sidewalk and see more of the city, and here and there I see patches of grass growing along walkways, in plazas, and even being watered by sprinklers. And as Victoria points out important towers, it becomes clear how small Orvad actually is. The city *looked* big from the air, but in reality, it's a mere seven blocks from end-to-end. That's shorter than the distance from the Crown to the Hologis Arena in the Embassy, if you don't count the neighborhoods or the stretch of buildings to the south.

The naval marina has the most expansive stretches of grass, and since it opens out toward the ocean, people are laying in the stuff, sunning themselves. I can't help but bend down and brush my hand through it, and *wow* is it soft. The Embassy needs grass. The color would brighten up the city in the best way, particularly the outer city, which isn't impressive at all.

I would know. I get to look at it from my apartment every day.

We check in at the Tidefront Hotel, which has tall windows overlooking a beach. Dozens of people are tanning on the sand, while others are skimming the waves or bobbing out in the deeper water.

Once our trunks have been moved to our rooms, we leave to go to our meeting with Olivarr Cresson, the techie I was looking into last week. He agreed to meet me and demonstrate the program his company developed.

Two blocks up past the marina, we walk into a rounded tower. *Cresson Software Industries* is projected at the back of the narrow lobby, and beside them, the picture of a man's chubby face. That must be Olivarr

Cresson: yellowish-brown skin, tightly curled black hair, a squared goatee, and thick white glasses propped on his large nose and ears...which I can't help but notice resemble the NEO Visors that the Embassy techies are creating.

"Head Archivist Arman Lance, escorted by Lieutenant Victoria Hofhen," Victoria announces to a thin-faced woman sitting at a desk in the lobby. "We're meeting Olivarr Cresson to discuss an Embassy contract."

The woman stands and motions at a narrow hallway. "Right this way."

The hallway has several elevators, and we ride one up to Floor 19. When we step out, she scans her ID on a wall panel.

"Olivarr is just in here."

A hidden gate slides back to reveal a wider, shorter room than the lobbies we walked through. Work panels line one of the back walls, and data orbs cling to the side of another. In the center is a round platform on which seven people are sitting behind panels, scanning data and watching video feeds from around Orvad.

"Olivarr, Head Archivist Arman Lance and Lieutenant Hofhen are here."

"Excellent!"

A short man jumps to his feet and skips down the platform to meet us. It's definitely the same man we saw in the projection downstairs, but he's about Glacia's height, and his large front teeth dominate his cheeky grin.

"Olivarr Cresson, CEO of CSI." He jabs two fingers on his chest. "That'd be me, if you haven't already guessed. *You* must be Mr. Arman. I knew I heard the rumors right, that the Embassy has a young guy running the show nowadays. Hope you came here looking for some ideas, Mr. Arman, because it's ideas you're going to get. Ideas are every Orvadian's specialty."

He spins on the spot and retreats to the work panels lining the back of the room.

"*Oh, to be a techie,*" Victoria mutters to herself as we follow him.

Olivarr slaps one hand on the back of a chair and nods at the panel. "Tell me what you see. What do we have here? And try not to overthink it. No wrong answers."

I stare at the panel. It doesn't look like anything I haven't used before. "Um...a workstation?"

"*Yesss*...and it's so *dull*, don't you think? We only keep these fossils to remind ourselves of where we, as a company, began. Now"—he waves up at the interface he was working at when we walked in—"tell me what *that* is."

I shrug. "A control center?"

He throws his hands in the air, exasperated. "*Use your imagination!* Somebody's been stuck in the void too long, I'd say." He winks at Victoria. "Mr. Arman, you're looking at the Real-time Archival Surveillance Program. RASP, for short. I always love a good acronym. Acronyms are fun. Though I probably could have gone easy on the Random Information and Network Surveillance Extrapolation Recorder. *RINSER.* You can imagine that didn't really catch on with the others..." He clears his throat and scratches his goatee. "We all have a bad idea or two in our lives."

That draws a laugh from Victoria. Olivarr grins, then

straightens up as tall as he can get—which isn't saying much—and sets his hands on his hips.

"Can you tell me what RASP does, Mr. Arman? Let's see if you did *all* your homework."

I grit my teeth and look away, at the interface. No, I didn't actually look further into what RASP is. I just know it's used for archival analyses and catalogues.

"I'm not...*too* sure about it."

Olivarr's face drops, disappointed, but then his mouth pulls into a dark smirk. "From the moment you landed in Orvad, RASP has been watching you. I know where you've been, how long you stayed there, if you ran or walked." He lowers his voice. "I could tell you how fast your heart is beating, if you're holding your breath, and even how tense every muscle in your body is, all with the tap of one...little...*button*."

He wags one finger in the air, and for several long seconds, he doesn't take his eyes off me. I stare back and try not to blink, try not to seem fazed by his warning. Even my throat clenches as I try not to visibly swallow.

Then Olivarr's face cracks, and he starts laughing.

"You look paranoid as all hell. You know that?"

I hear stifled laughter and see the other techies chuckling to themselves. A few glance my way and wave in amusement.

"Don't sweat it, Mr. Arman. RASP doesn't do *half* that stuff—and if it did, I wouldn't tell you. Besides, we'd be crazy to develop such an intrusive system. Ha! No, no. Like I said, RASP is the...the *core* of Orvad. It evaluates power usage around the city, monitors the water facility, runs checks on malfunctioning equipment, tracks inbound vehicles, notifies us of issues with the maglev trains, et cetera, et cetera. And, of course, it's all in a live feed. None of this next-day-analysis stuff the Embassy likes to practice. Lazy, if you ask me. Where's the ethic?"

Olivarr lets us step up onto the platform and look at the interface. Four people are relaying information about various system malfunctions to other teams in the city, and two others are examining a sort of...*map?* It's not like any map I've ever seen, though. Overlaying the city are what look like tangles of blue string, red string, and green string, and entire towers are connected by these webs.

"Do you see it yet?" Olivarr asks, his face suddenly next to mine.

"No...?"

"Data flow through the city, Mr. Arman. Another function of RASP. We have relay devices installed all over the place. Orvad's network web cycles through a sort of Fibonacci spiral, with CSI Tower as the source point. Look here—"

He traces his finger along the map, following the flow of strings, and I begin to see what he means. It isn't immediately obvious, not without *knowing* what you're looking at, but there's a shape hidden in the data web. A spiral—something that looks like an off-center galaxy, in fact—just like he said.

"Relays up the security of the data we're flinging around. Every bit is uniquely coded to Orvad's data flow. If we want to transfer data to the Embassy, say, a new software update, we'd have to encode the data into a language the Embassy's software can process."

That raises a question in my head. "Will that affect the archives program if we decide to use RASP?"

Olivarr swings his arms while he thinks. "Well, to make it easy, you could just install it wherever you need it. I would suggest upgrading the entire Embassy, but that's just me pushing for the integration of my own software. The Embassy wants to catch up to Orvadian tech, but we're advancing too quickly. Never gonna happen. All of us have been led to believe there's a sort of rivalry building, a grudge of sorts, perhaps? We've surpassed the Embassy's tech and come into favor with the Dalish... And now *you're* here looking to contract *me* to bring the Embassy's archives program up-to-date." He scratches at his goatee, another cheeky grin filling his face. "A curious situation, don't you agree?"

"The last head archivist wasn't exactly one for change," Victoria says.

"I see."

"Could we get this installed in the Embassy?" I ask, looking between them. "If Chancellor Green approves?"

"There are a number of outstanding factors you need to consider," Olivarr says, tipping his head sideways. "It takes time to configure new software over an entire city, for one."

"How long?"

He puffs his cheeks. "For the Embassy? Given what I know—and I've never been there, mind you—I'd say somewhere between one or two years?" He gestures around the room. "This whole setup took two months, and it wasn't hard to sync the rest of Orvad due to the rather *contained* size of the city."

"What about a space cruiser?"

Olivarr nods thoughtfully. "Hmm... That's a reasonable request if you need it done fast. I'd reckon a few weeks to get the primary systems integrated with the station's mainframe, then a few more weeks to tweak things around. I assume you would want an entire fleet integrated, correct? Not just one station? Quite frankly, that'd be counter—"

"Yes, four stations."

"Thought so... Yes, well we're always looking for ways to integrate our software into the Embassy." He claps his hands together. "This seems a perfect fit."

I look at Victoria. "It's doable."

She nods. "Definitely doable. What'll it cost?"

Olivarr taps the tips of his fingers together, clearly excited that he's getting attention from the Embassy. "Rough guess? A quarter-million shims per station. I'll have the actual quote in a week or so. I can send over relevant documents for the Embassy councils to look at, if you need."

I shake his hand. "Thanks. This looks good."

"No, thank *you*, Mr. Arman. I'm so very happy you're interested."

Chapter Eight

VICTORIA AND I eat a late lunch in a rooftop restaurant in a tower at the northern edge of Orvad. We grab a small booth in a shaded area to keep out of the heat, and outside the window, the tops of a dozen other towers rise up to challenge our height. Beyond them lie endless miles of windblown dunes.

The view is so different than what I've always seen in Cornell and the Embassy. Gone are the dusty plains broken by mesas and plateaus. The sand smooths the world, a constantly shifting landscape. I start to wonder how Victoria could ever hate living here, but then remind myself that she probably thought the mesas and gorges of the Embassy were more beautiful than her home, too. I wonder if what she said about Daliona was true, that I'll never want to leave. I felt that way about Belvun, standing with Glacia on the edge of the cliff where the stars dotted the twilight sky and the sun sank under the reddish horizon. If I try hard enough, I can still feel my skin tingling in the cool wind, hear the rush of the river and rustles of the trees.

Above all, I remember how I felt when Glacia and I locked eyes, how that powerful peace surged through me when I kissed her the first time. I knew, right then, that I was becoming someone better than I was before. It's a feeling I never want to forget, a memory I never want to lose.

"You're doing it again."

I snap out of my thoughts, *again*, and see Victoria watching me with an amused look on her face.

"I just...love it here."

She crumples a napkin and drops it on her empty plate. "I'm glad you think so highly of my home."

I watch her curiously. "You've traveled a lot, right?" She nods and grabs her glass of Armici tea. "What's your favorite place? Like, your favorite planet?"

Victoria sips the tea, her eyes narrowed in thought. "Yillos. It's cold—*very* cold—but I miss the tundra. Mountains, valleys, fields, rivers, herds of wild killari..." She sighs, and for the first time since coming to Orvad, she looks completely relaxed. "I miss the forests the most. Nothing like you've ever seen. They go on for thousands of miles, and when it snowed... Arman... It was so beautiful. And the smell of the pines stuck to you. We got a cabin overlooking the *Paysage des Montagnes Boissées.*"

She says the last part with a sort of funny, sophisticated accent, and the hint of a grin tugs at her mouth.

"That's where I'd live, if I could. Out there in the wood."

Once we're finished with lunch, we go down to our

hotel rooms for a short break. My room is a little higher than halfway up the tower and the window overlooks a grassy plaza that has the entrance to a maglev station at its center. Across the plaza are two identical towers covered in shiny blue panels. Three walkways connect them at even integrals, and both are topped with blue and silver pyramids. The colors remind me of Victoria's office in the Crown. It makes me laugh a bit.

She didn't leave *everything* behind.

I drop onto my bed and pull out my holotab. '*It's awesome here,*' I type to Glacia. '*The city's right on the ocean and there are sand dunes everywhere. We'll definitely come out when we get the chance one day. Let me know if you want to talk tonight.*'

After I send the message, I take a picture of the inner city and send that to her, too. Hopefully it'll cheer her up when she finishes training this evening.

A little while later, Victoria meets me in the hall so we can leave for our tour of the water facility, which begins at five o'clock.

"What's that?" I ask as we walk to the maglev station, pointing at the towers I saw from my room.

"Secondary."

"You went to school there?"

"For the first two years, but I enlisted in the Officiary Academy once I knew I wasn't cut out to be a techie like almost everyone else in this city. Lars graduated Secondary and joined the Embassy two years before I finished at the Academy." Her lips curl into a grin, and she glances down at me. "But see who's ranked higher?"

I raise my eyebrows, intrigued. "Do you know what his Report score was?"

"Nope. *He* claims the proctor congratulated him for his—and I quote—'*impressive display of abstract intellect.*' Whatever that means. Of course, then he went off and invented the MRRs, so I have to give him credit where it's due."

We board an express train to the water facility and speed into a tunnel that dips under Orvad's northern wall. When it resurfaces on the other side, the ocean is only a hundred yards away. Gray waves roll up the wide beach, then recede in a constant, mesmerizing ebb and flow.

The pipes of the water facility grow larger the closer we get. I thought they seemed big from a distance, and unlike my impression of Orvad, I'm actually right. They're *massive*. The pipes plunging into the ocean are at least fifteen yards wide, and the ones that run off into the desert are half that.

"Five o'clock tour?" the officer in the lobby asks when we walk inside.

"That's us," Victoria says.

"If you could just wait over there, and Director Hill will see you shortly."

No sooner do we sit down than a gate opens next to the desk, and a man in a blue and white lab coat walks out, his hands stuffed in the coat's pockets.

"Mr. Lance, Lieutenant," he says. "If you would..."

He takes us back through the gate and down a short corridor, where he unseals another gate that opens into the main part of the facility. The temperature drops thirty degrees and I start shivering after a few seconds. It's noisy, too. Generators whir, water churns in reservoirs, machines groan.

We climb a steep set of stairs to a walkway that runs around the entire perimeter, above all the equipment. The pipes enter the facility in the far wall, pass through a series of filters and processing units, then redistribute to the delivery pipes that exit the facility and transfer water around the planet. There are dozens of them, all with varying diameters, and each is labeled with a city. I don't see Cornell's anywhere, but the Embassy's pipe is unmistakable: it's the largest of them all, and the Undil Embassy crest is printed on the side.

"*Put these on*," Director Hill shouts above the noise, handing us each a pair of ear mufflers. Microphones are attached to them so we can talk to each other. "Are you here on assignment? Or just for a tour? Don't know any reason the Embassy would send you out here. Usually it's the inspectors."

I shake my head. "We were in Orvad on assignment."

"Got it. All right, this way."

Director Hill motions for us to follow him along the walkway until we're standing above one of the filtration units. He points at a series of large reservoirs connected to the exit pipes.

"We pump a quarter-billion gallons daily, process the water, and store it for distribution. It's transferred to the cities three times a week."

A branch of the walkway turns inward and crosses one of the reservoirs. These tanks are massive, at least fifty yards end-to-end and extending a hundred yards or more underground, according to the director. Below us, two officers move from tank to tank. Every now and then one of them taps the panels and reads off data while the other jots notes on his holotab.

It takes several minutes to reach the filtration units on the other side of the facility. The whirring noises are loudest here, and even with the ear mufflers and microphones, it's difficult to hear what Director Hill is saying. He talks about saline filters, heating and cooling units, and a machine he calls the Gurgler. Then we walk through a gate and out onto a platform that overlooks the larger pipes, which remain steady on their supports as gray waves surge against them.

Director Hill is talking to Victoria, but I'm hardly listening anymore because, miles to the left, Orvad stands tall against the ocean. The gray water forms a distinct line against the yellow, sandy coast. Tiny specks move on the beaches, people who get to go to the beach every day of their lives because they're fortunate enough to live on this side of the world, while all I had growing up was Cornell, a hot and hazy, unimpressive town built in the middle of absolutely nowhere. But even though I know Victoria has lost love for her home, I still can't help but feel a little jealous.

✳ ✳ ✳ ✳ ✳

"You should've come with me."

"I wish."

I stop walking and sit down. The sand crunches under my weight. I tried sitting closer to the waves, but underestimated how far they would reach and ended up soaking my shoes and pants. Glacia had the unfortunate pleasure of seeing me scramble out of the water.

Behind me, to the east, the sun has long since set below the dunes. Darkness covers the ocean, and thousands of stars twinkle in the sky. They've been disappearing, though. It took me a while to notice, but clouds are drifting in from the deeper ocean, where the air has already cooled enough for them to form. First it was just a patch here or there, and now a whole sheet edges toward Orvad, blacking out the stars as it moves inland.

In the hologram shimmering above my holotab, Glacia takes a bite of her dinner, then looks off-screen and says hi to somebody walking past her. She starts strumming her fingers on the table. Neither of us says anything for a while, which is awkward for her because she's sitting alone in one of the Embassy's restaurants, whereas I'm perfectly content on the dark beach, listening to the waves rush ahead of me.

"Hey, I'm gonna go to my room," she says when she's finished eating. "Let me call back in a few minutes."

"That'll feel like *forever*," I tease, but she's already gone.

The hologram disappears, leaving me mostly in darkness because the lights from Orvad don't reach this far down the beach. The wind isn't as hot as when the sun was out. I'd even say it's chilly—for Undil, that is. Being so far south, it shouldn't surprise me. Cornell and the Embassy are both situated near Undil's equator and have warm nights year-round.

At long last, my holotab buzzes again, and this time a hologram of Glacia sitting cross-legged on her bed shimmers in front of me. A faint orange glow warms her face: the sunset. She turns the view around to let me see it, also giving me a good look at Threshold Tower standing at the other end of the street.

"Miss this yet?"

"Ha." I turn my holotab so she can see Orvad glittering in the darkness. "I've got a *way* better view."

Glacia turns the holotab back on herself and pulls her hair over her left shoulder. "Nuh-uh. *Now* you have a good view."

"Eh, that's debatable."

She scoffs and narrows her eyes in a cute, annoyed kind of way. "*Watch it, mister.*"

I grin as she scoots backward on the bed to get more comfortable, then tell her about the dunes, the marina, and the original Rygin colony that used to be nothing more than three biodomes. I tell her how small Orvad is compared to the Embassy, and how Victoria showed me where she went to Secondary. Then I explain everything I can remember about RASP and how Olivarr Cresson will install it in Orcher's fleet—if the council approves the program, that is. And as I talk, I show her the pictures I took so she can see everywhere I went.

Afterward, I stare out at Orvad. Its green, blue, and white lights shine in the darkness. A memory suddenly pops into my head, and Glacia notices the grin that overtakes my face.

"What?"

I shake my head, still grinning.

"*Whaaaaat?*" she insists, sitting forward and tilting her head. She's so adorable. "What's so funny?"

"The night you dragged me out into the desert after our Induction Ceremony. It feels just like that...except you're not here."

I show her the view of the city again. Through the

back of the hologram, I see a smile settle on her face.

"Look up, mister."

And I do.

Except...there's one problem: the sheet of clouds covering the sky.

"Um, it's cloudy."

"Well, that ruins the whole mood."

We both laugh, and when we settle down again, I prop my arms up on my knees, holding the holotab above my eye level.

"Can you hear the ocean?"

She listens for a few seconds. "I think so. It's like...*whooooosh*, right? Unless that's just how you breathe."

I huff and puff loudly to amuse her. She cracks a smile, then asks, "Did you see the Hologis arena?"

"Nope."

"I don't think it's in the main city."

"Well, there's the problem."

Glacia lets out an exasperated sigh. "I haven't played in *months*, mister. I swear, if we don't play on Daliona, I'll die."

"Do you know if they have it?"

"They better. How else are we supposed to entertain ourselves?"

We stay up talking a little while longer, and then I begin the long walk back to the city because it's going to be an early start to a very long day tomorrow.

In the morning, Victoria and I eat breakfast before the sun comes up, and finish eating as the first rays spread over the horizon. It's still cloudy, so the sun is nothing more than a golden glow illuminating the clouds. And later when our hovercraft lifts off, Orvad becomes a dark silhouette, with miles of wind-blown dunes between us and the city.

From here, it's a one-way trip to Cornell.

I'm going home.

Chapter Nine

OVER THE COURSE of the flight to Cornell, the clouds clear away and the sun never rises any higher than we left it back in Orvad. The dunes harden into ridges, and the ridges flatten into plains. Now, as we approach Cornell from the southwest, I see the Gray Wall distribution center, the most distinct landmark in the settlement. It sits along the eastern edge of the settlement, a cluster of office buildings gathered beside the main factory, where much of Undil's low-class space tech is manufactured: software boards, thruster grids, energy panels, and more. When I worked there, I sat in a room, analyzing charts and writing reports for six hours a day, four days a week, for three straight years. No wonder I belong in the Embassy's archival sector. I'm good at handling the stuff everyone else finds boring.

My neighborhood connects to the western branch of the Main Throughway, about a mile outside Cornell. Cars glide in and out of the small city, all of them passing through the spot where Mr. Kirklan's car slammed into mine, the spot where Father was killed on impact. I was left with two broken ribs, a punctured lung, and a cut over my left eye. The surgeons mended me up, but kept my body numbed for two days until the scans said most of the pain had passed.

Now that the haze is clear, I can make out more of the inner city. Secondary, where I studied for four years, is a ring of buildings at the center of Cornell. Our Hologis arena sits several blocks directly south at the edge of the city. If I didn't grow up here, I wouldn't even know that place was anything special. Unlike the Embassy's arena, there's no colorful hologram shining over its entrance, no giant glass panels decorating its walls, no crowds flocking to watch a tournament. When people play in Cornell, they only do it to take a break from work, from the routine that keeps the settlement functioning properly. Life in Cornell isn't comfortable. We have no gardens to water or streams to swim in or grass to lie in. We have a decent fitness center and a pool that's always crowded with kids who have nothing to do. Living in Cornell is tedious at best, depressing at worst.

Yet that's the point. That's the life everyone born on Undil learns to live whether we like it or not. Father said it. Captain Blitner said it. Orcher said it. Even Victoria said it: our lives are just a step along the path toward a future that gets to live a life of comfort. It's true: people living on Undil right now may never see those days. But didn't Daliona start like this, too? Didn't Belvun? Didn't Yillos, and Rygin, and Narviid, and all the other planets humanity has settled? Nobody alive today has ever known war, to the point where the Galactic Council once met to decide if planets with military programs should be allowed to maintain them. The answer was *yes*, not to wage war, but to protect us from the one constant that would always seek to destroy us: nature. And on Belvun, nature struck back at the eco-hacking Daliona forced upon the planet. Five years ago, recovery efforts to reverse the damage failed.

They must not fail again.

The hovercraft lands and powers down. Victoria and I walk into the air conditioned terminal where I first met Ellin, John, and Michael. It's also the last place I saw Mother and my sisters, where Erinn asked if I was meeting Father in the Embassy, as if trying to convince herself that his funeral was just a bad dream.

And I had to tell her no.

"You need anything before I head out?" Victoria asks after I get my hovertrunk from the luggage line.

"I'm good."

I fake a smile. Now I know how she felt when we flew to Orvad. I don't want to be here. At all. For some reason, I feel like being here will suck me back into the life I used to live, the life I've tried so hard to escape.

She watches me carefully, as if she knows what's running through my head, then says, "I'll see you in a couple days."

Victoria returns to the hovercraft, and I go down to the lobby and out into the warm morning. An officer is waiting for me, a man Victoria called to give me a ride home. I don't say much aside from a quick hello, but the entire time he's driving to my house, he goes on about how he's always meant to visit Orvad but hasn't found the time. Really, though, does anyone in this town *have* the time? Unless you join the Embassy—or you're related to someone who's in it—you're stuck. Only people affiliated with the larger businesses get to travel. Glacia said that's how her brother met his fiancée. Their parents sent Jaston to Holistead to settle a textile contract, and two weeks later, he came back with Sophie. Apparently they like to joke that he took Sophie as payment for the deal.

Soon I find myself standing out front of my house. The officer has already driven away, but I haven't moved. I've never liked living here, and now that I've visited Belvun—even if it *is* burning up—I hate my home even more. The yards on Belvun had grassy lawns, leafy trees, and flowery shrubs. My yard has nothing but a metal platform that covers the cracked, lifeless dirt. Belvish houses had roofed porches, automatic garages, spacious windows, and large backyards for kids to play in. My house is long and rectangular, has only one-floor, and narrow windows keep out most of the daytime heat.

It's miserable.

I tap the buzzer. My breathing becomes erratic, my heart pounding so hard it hurts. I can't believe I'm nervous to see them again. It's only been three, almost four months, but it feels so much longer. I've never left home before. Never left Mother and the twins on their own like Father always had to leave me and Mother. And now...

Footsteps from inside. I hear Mother on the other side of the door telling the twins to stay in their seats. They must be eating breakfast. The door opens—and

Mother gasps. She stares for a second, then hugs me. When we pull apart, she holds me at arm's length, admiring my uniform and haircut and tracing her fingers over the golden Embassy crests embroidered on my shoulders.

"You're so handsome." She hugs me again, then lowers her voice and motions at the kitchen. "The girls are in there."

Almost on cue, we hear a fork clank against a plate, followed by two sets of giggles. Mother walks back in, pretending to check on them, and I follow a few seconds later. Erinn and Flavia are both facing the other way, so I sneak up behind them and stick my head between both of theirs. Erinn sees me first—and her scream practically pierces my eardrum.

I pull back as they stand in their chairs, arms outstretched. Erinn wraps hers around my neck, and Flavia hugs my chest. I heave into my arms and kiss their cheeks. Erinn clings to my neck, but Flavia lets go and runs into the front room. She returns with my hovertrunk in tow and pulls it down the hall to my bedroom. Only then does Erinn drop to the ground and chase after her. Mother and I both grimace when we hear a *thud*.

"They talk about you all the time," Mother says. A smile slips onto her face as she stares past me down the hall. "I caught Erinn pulling books off of your shelf a few weeks ago. She found his portfolios."

I laugh as I open my backpack and pull out the portfolio I made for them last week and finished this morning after adding a few pictures of Orvad. Mother unlatches the flat metal case and swipes through the pictures that project above it, smiling.

"How long were you on Belvun?"

"A little more than a week. Like, a week-and-a-half in *our* time, technically."

"How's Ladia?"

I shrug. "I, um... I didn't have time to see her. Met her father, though."

Mother closes the portfolio and hugs her arms to her chest. "I didn't know you were due back so soon."

"Thought it'd be a nice surprise." I lean my shoulder against the wall. "Um...do you remember Glacia Haverns?"

"Of course."

"I have to pick her up from the docks this evening. Her brother's getting married tomorrow, so...we're going to that."

Mother gives me a curious stare. "Are you—"

"*Yes.*"

Her mouth twitches. "I'm only wondering."

✳ ✳ ✳ ✳ ✳

I pick up Glacia at eight o'clock. She looks like she just woke up from sleeping on the hovercraft, what with her hair being tangled on one side and her eyes all red. She does her best to fix herself up on the ride to my house, but her hair refuses to smooth out.

"By the way, my sisters know you're coming," I say as we get out of the car. "I have to warn you: they're huggers."

Glacia runs her fingers through her hair one more time. "I'm ready."

We go inside. I half-expected Erinn and Flavia to be waiting on the other side of the door, but instead they're on the couch with Mother, bouncing eagerly. Their eyes widen when Glacia steps in behind me. Erinn smiles and Flavia grabs Mother's arm.

"It's nice to meet you," Mother says. She pats the twins' shoulders. "Say hello, you two."

Flavia waves shyly. "*Hi*," she squeaks. "I—I'm...my name ith Flavia."

Erinn bounces off the couch. "I'm *Erinn*."

Glacia smiles and crouches down to their level. "Your big brother has told me *all* about you. And you know what? I think he has a surprise."

The twins gasp and start jumping up and down, tugging on the bottom of my shirt.

"*Now, now, now!*"

"No... I'm saving it for bedtime." I give Glace a look to say, *why would you do that to me?*

"But I want it *now*," Erinn whines, pouting her lips.

"Tonight, okay? Right now Glacia and I have to do some stuff to get ready for tomorrow. Remember I told you her brother is getting married?"

Erinn lowers her head. "*Yeah.*"

"I'll be back tonight."

I ruffle the top of her head, making her giggle.

A gust of heat buffets our faces when I open the door. Thankfully the car is still cold. Erinn and Flavia wave from the front window as we pull away, and then we drive toward the Main Throughway and head into Cornell. The Throughway runs through the center of the city, curves north, and goes straight into the northern neighborhoods. Glacia points me to her house, which isn't all that different from mine. I park in the street and get out of the car.

"Jaston's here," Glacia says, looking at the cars locked in suspension above the driveway.

"They know I'm coming, right?"

"Um...well...*no*. I kinda forgot to mention that." She waves her hands in the air. "*Surprise!*"

She taps the buzzer and stands back, rocking on her heels anxiously. A few seconds later, Glacia's father opens the door. He looks just like her—or, she looks like *him*, I should say—except he's as tall as me, and his dark blond hair is short and wavy. They have the same hazel eyes, the same smile, even the same small ears.

Glacia throws her arms around him and presses her cheek into his shoulder. He clasps his own hands on her back, and a light smile settles on his face. Then he looks at me and lifts one hand in a short wave as if he knows exactly who I am—even though we've never met.

He extends a hand to me. "I'm Gavin. How are you, Arman?"

"I'm good, how about—"

"*Well*," Glacia interrupts, covering it with a fake cough.

Ugh.

Ellin is starting to rub off on her.

Mr. Haverns chuckles and puts his arm around her shoulder as we walk inside. "Staying for dinner?"

"I think so."

"Great. Jan and Jas are cooking it now. Killari beef wraps glazed in pricklefruit marinade."

"*Hello out there!*" Mrs. Haverns calls from the kitchen over the loud sizzling of the cooker.

"Hey!" Glacia calls back.

We walk into the kitchen. Mrs. Haverns is washing her hands and Jaston is shaking the pan with the beef cooking inside. Glacia hugs her mother, who has short blonde hair and dark blue eyes, and then Jaston spins around and bumps his hip into Glacia's, almost knocking her off-balance.

"Buy me something expensive for the big day, kiddo?"

"You'll have to find out."

Jaston glances at me, starts to turn around, and then does a double-take. "*Arman Lance?* She finally pulled you around, did she?" He wipes his hands clean, then gives me a firm shake. "I think you owe us a date at Emerson's Plaza. Doesn't he, kiddo?"

Glacia's eyes flash wide. "That's right! You totally turned us down after our Placement Reports, mister. *Nobody* gets away with that."

"What do you think?" Jaston says, perking one eyebrow. "Should he pay? I think he should pay."

He winks, then returns to tossing the sizzling beef in the pan.

"Glacia said you visited Orvad?" Mrs. Haverns asks. "How was it?"

"Awesome. It's so different from the Embassy."

"We've never been to either," Mr. Haverns admits. "Once Jas takes over the business, we want to visit Holistead, where Sophie's from. Maybe even travel around Undil a bit if we can."

"You two will have to tell us all about Belvun over dinner," Mrs. Haverns says. She smiles at Mr. Haverns. "If only we had the chances you two are getting. We're proud of you."

"I'm not," Jaston says over his shoulder. "They didn't bring me any souvenirs. Wasn't that the agreement? Buy your family stuff everywhere you go?"

"You're getting married tomorrow *and* inheriting the family business," Glacia snipes back, shoving him lightly.

Jaston waves his finger at her. "Watch it. I'm cooking *your* dinner."

✳ ✳ ✳ ✳ ✳

After we eat, Jaston drives me and Glacia to Emerson's Plaza, the large ice cream and dessert shop across the street from Secondary. Wallace Emerson, the owner, opened the plaza a year ago, and it quickly became one of the leading dessert distributors on Undil, even providing the Embassy with the ice cream and cakes at our opening banquet.

Jaston holds the door for us. I follow Glacia to the dispensers, and the three of us stand at separate panels to order. Jaston gets a seedberry sherbet swirl, Glacia gets a vanilla spike shake, and I get a bowl of mint chocolate cream. I'm about to scan my ID to pay, but Jaston stops me.

"It's on me, man."

We sit at a table next to the front windows. Glacia sits across from me, with Jaston.

"You two have your work cut out for you, joining the Embassy." Jaston points at me. "Especially *you*. The whole program's open to you and your sisters, once they're old enough. Why Threshold, though? Horizon's where all the cool stuff is. Exploring the galaxy, going where no man has ever gone before... You'd be gone a few years, but, *ha!*" Jaston laughs to himself. "It'd sure be one hell of a good time."

Glacia gives me a look. "You can tell who's never been on an expedition."

"Oh, it can't be *that* bad."

"Oh, *yes it can.*" Glacia sips some more of her shake, then says, "The trip back wasn't so bad, but *getting* to Belvun? That sucked."

"Didn't you guys have to take a mental evaluation?"

"Mmhmm."

"And?"

Glacia swallows another sip, then, "Cleared it, obviously. That doesn't mean the trip didn't still suck."

I grimace. It's something I never told anyone. The day before my interview with Chancellor Green, we took mental evaluations to make sure our minds were capable of handling interstellar expeditions. John didn't pass, but I'm pretty sure Glacia, Ellin, and Michael cleared with no problems. I, on the other hand, received a sixty-seven percent.

The cutoff score is sixty-five.

"I wonder where I'd be, you know? If I'd decided to go your route." Jaston raps his knuckles on the table and shakes his head slowly. "Wouldn't have to take over the business, for one, and at the worst possible time, too. Belvun's our biggest textile supplier. Shipments have been down these last few years, something like ten percent a year. You guys won't even get that chemical stuff to them until when...next spring?"

Glacia nods. "The Faustocine, yeah."

"We're looking at *at least* another two to four percent loss before then, not to mention however long it takes to actually fix Belvun and get shipments back on schedule. Wonderful inheritance, huh?" He shakes his head again and stares past me. "*Clothes manufacturing...* How'd our parents ever get in *that* business?"

Glacia answers him with a shrug.

"I'll tell you one thing: my kid is joining the Embassy, no questions asked. Maybe he'll be some sort of prodigy and they'll let him in early. Sophie and I could quit the gig and spend the rest of our lives traveling."

I grin. "That'd be the life."

Jaston perks up. "Wouldn't it? We were born to explore, you know? Born to travel farther than everyone before us. Consider yourselves lucky: some of us sit around all day waiting for a chance to hear the stories you people bring back. Sometimes I have to ask myself: *why Undil?* What were those people thinking, choosing *this* stinking planet to live on? Look at Belvun. Daliona. Yillos. Rygin. Mountains, trees, rivers, geysers... We don't even have a moon. Is it too much to ask? Did we miss out on some added benefits program?"

"I mean, Belvun doesn't have a moon," Glacia points out matter-of-factly.

"You're not helping."

"*Just saying.*"

"I'm just saying, we were born at the wrong time in history: too late to discover Undil on our own, and too early to see it terraformed like Daliona and Belvun."

"Maybe your standards are too high," I say, suddenly remembering something Captain Blitner told me.

Jaston frowns. "My standards?"

"Yeah. Someone once told me that Earth was both a blessing and a curse. It was a blessing because it was perfect for life as we know it, but a curse, too, because people wanted *every* planet to be like that. That's why we terraform, just like what we've been doing to Undil the last seven centuries. It's slow, but it's happening. The air wasn't always breathable. People had to wear masks and body suits for hundreds of years. All planets go through it, just...some take longer than others."

Jaston mulls it over in his head, then starts nodding slowly. "I've never thought about it like that," he says at last, his voice quieter than before.

"Belvun and Narviid are like...Daliona's experiments," I say. "They weren't terraformed, they were, um..."

"Eco-hacked," Glacia finishes for me. "Faster than terraformation—"

"—but clearly not as reliable," Jaston says quickly. "Belvun's burning up and Narviid's bound to follow."

I frown and shrug. "Maybe. But give it another one or two hundred years, and Undil might have its own trees and rivers and grass."

Jaston waves his hand over the table. "No, see, that's good and all, but there's one problem: I don't *have* two hundred more years to live."

"*Not with that attitude,*" Glacia mutters.

※　※　※　※　※

When I get home, Mother is helping the twins get ready for bed. My arrival interrupts that, though, because

Erinn runs into the front room and jumps on me just as I'm shutting the door. She's still wearing her mouth rinser, which is making her cheeks glow bluish-white.

I take her back into the bathroom, where Flavia is checking her own teeth in the mirror.

"Finish up," I tell Erinn. "I'll go get your surprise."

Her eyes light up at the mention of the surprise, and she starts washing her face without taking her rinser out.

I grab the portfolio, then go to the twins' room and sit between their beds. A minute later, the sinks turn off and Erinn and Flavia run in. Flavia slips under her covers and props herself up to see the portfolio better, but Erinn sits on her knees and clings to the edge of the bed, anxious to see the pictures.

"I have a story for you guys."

"Like Daddy's stories?" Erinn asks.

"Yeah, I went on an adventure just like him."

Erinn's eyes get bigger than I've ever seen them. "Did you see aliens?"

I laugh. "No, no aliens. But I did see another planet. It had mountains and rivers, trees and birds, and even *clouds*."

"What are cloudth?" Flavia asks, her forehead wrinkled in confusion.

"Clouds are big puffy white things that float really high in the sky."

Erinn's mouth drops open. "*Wow*."

"Why don't *we* have cloudth?" Flavia asks, still troubled.

"Because clouds are made of a lot of water," I say.

"And we don't have a lot of water?"

"Nope, not in Cornell. But I did see clouds a couple days ago by the ocean. There's a lot of water in the ocean."

"Where'th the ocean?"

"It's *really* far away."

"Oh. How far—"

"*I wanna hear the story!*" Erinn squeaks, shooting Flavia a glare.

Mother knocks on the doorframe. She steps in and kisses the twins on their foreheads. "Be good for your brother, girls."

"Goodnight, mommy!" the twins say in unison.

Mother leaves again, and I activate the portfolio. A block of pictures shimmers above the device. I expand the first one—a picture of the Undil Embassy from the sky—and start telling the story. I tell them about the maglev trains that zoom under the city, about the Crown and the other main towers. I show them pictures of the Molters and how I got to fly one by myself, leaving out the part where I almost got sick. Then I tell them about the huge Hologis arena and the tournament, and how Glacia won all by herself. I'm not sure the twins understand what Hologis actually is, but they both seem impressed.

Next I tell them about flying into space and all the other stations in orbit above Undil. I show them a picture from the *Ember*'s bridge, and even Erinn is at a complete loss for words. She takes the portfolio and stares at Undil and the space fleets as I tell them about the *Ember*.

As I show them the Perihelids, I look over at Flavia: her eyes are closed, head tilted sideways, mouth slightly open. Her blonde hair covers the left side of her face, and her breathing causes a few strands of hair to puff up and fall down every few seconds.

I look at Erinn: her eyes are still glued to the pictures.

"What's—" She stops talking suddenly when she sees Flavia is asleep. "*What's this?*" she whispers, pointing into a picture of the Perihelids.

"That's an asteroid," I explain. "Here, move over."

Erinn slides sideways, and I situate myself next to her. She leans into me, resting her head between my arm and chest to look at the pictures.

"What's an asteroid?"

"It's a really big rock. A lot of the asteroids in this asteroid field are bigger than our house."

"*Wow,*" she whispers again.

"Yeah. We had to fly spaceships through the asteroids for *two days.*"

"Was it scary?"

"A little."

"Did any rocks hit your spaceship?"

"A couple did."

"Did they hurt it?"

I laugh quietly. "No, the spaceship was fine. We had magnetic shields to protect us."

Erinn hugs my arm really tight. "Good."

"Remember Glacia?"

"Yeah."

"She had to fly *in* the asteroids. She was scared, but she's a really good pilot, so she didn't get hurt."

"Good, she's too pretty to get hurt."

My cheeks pull into a smile. "Yeah, she is pretty." I

kiss the top of Erinn's head. "Do you want to hear the rest of the story?"

She yawns, then wraps her arms around one of mine. "*Yeah.*"

I tell her about Belvun and show her pictures of the fields and trees and clouds. She loves the Dell Washers, the little gray-and-white birds Captain Blitner liked to watch, and insists that I need to bring one home as a pet for her. She gasps in awe at every picture of the Hania Reserve, sticking her finger through the holographic trees and mountains and rivers as if trying to touch them. But I don't show her pictures of Ellaciss City. She doesn't need to see...*that.*

Finally, I show the picture I was saving for last, the picture I took right before we flew back to the *Ember* and left Belvun: the Belvish Embassy. The glittering city sits atop its sloping hill, surrounded by the crimson forest and orange field. On one side of the picture, the maglev train glides toward the city.

Erinn pokes her finger through the center. "Can you take me there?"

"Only if you join the Embassy."

"I will!" She rolls over and kisses my cheek, then wraps her arms around my stomach in a big hug. "I'll go on adventures just like you and Daddy."

Chapter Ten

ROWS OF PEOPLE sit in silence as the notary gives a speech. Jaston and Sophie stand on either side of him, waiting for their turns to speak. Jaston is wearing a black suit, black pants, and a black tie, all of which contrast with his gelled-up blond hair.

Sophie is a whole other sight to see. She's wearing a double-layered, silky white dress that Mrs. Haverns personally tailored for the wedding. The top layer hangs down her shoulders and falls just below her waist, while the second layer folds around her feet. Green glitter is sprinkled on the dress and in her black hair, which is done up—as Mrs. Haverns called it—in a Loch Garden braided bun. Ringlets bounce down her shoulders, twin braids wrap together in a perfect circle on the back of her head, and a diamond crescent clasp is stuck in the top of the braids.

"And now, Jaston Bradley Haverns, you may present your final request."

Jaston takes Sophie's hand in his, and it's clear to see they're both trembling.

"Sophie Wates," he says after an extended pause. Then he laughs to himself and smiles. "Sophie *Meridia* Wates. You know, if it was up to me, we'd be getting married on Daliona, or Belvun. Somewhere we could be outside so your hair could fly in the wind, and the sun could shine on your face. If it was up to me, we wouldn't be stuck in this cramped auditorium." He pauses and looks down at Sophie's hand. "But it's not up to me. And you know what? *Everyone* on Undil dreams of having their wedding somewhere else, don't they? Who can blame them? But even though we aren't standing on a beach, even though there aren't any birds in the sky or trees to stand under, that's not why I'm holding your hand today.

"Sophie, if I let any of that take away from the fact that I'm marrying you, then I'm not good enough for you. We can't set our standards too high. We have to see the beauty no matter where we get married." Jaston laughs to himself again. "I know what you're thinking: *what's so beautiful about the inside of this auditorium?* I'll tell you what: you are, and all that you mean to me, and the fact that you've let me love you this long. And, of course, all the beautiful people who showed up to watch us make out in a few minutes."

A low rumble of laughter rolls through the crowd of about fifty people. Even Sophie holds a hand up to her mouth to suppress her giggles. As quiet returns to the room, she wipes a tear from her cheek.

"I'll ask you one last time. I promise, this is it." Jaston takes a deep breath. "Sophie Meridia Wates...will you marry me?"

Sophie's smile couldn't be any bigger.

"Yes."

They lean into each other and kiss, holding their hands between them. The crowd stands and applauds, and some people cheer when Jaston sweeps Sophie off her feet and spins her around. A man darts forward and snaps a picture right in front of them. Jaston steps down from the stage, carrying Sophie to the rear of the auditorium and through a set of doors. On the other side is an area prepared for the reception, complete with banquet tables and a dance floor. Knowing what the banquet hall in the Crown looks like, I can't help but think how this room is noticeably less impressive.

After everyone finds seats, chefs stream out of the kitchens with platters of food. They remove the tops, revealing trays of appetizers, steamy poultry dishes, and vegetables soaking in succulent sauces. Glacia and I end up sitting with two of Sophie's cousins, but make sure to leave three empty seats for Mother and the twins, who show up a few minutes later.

"It smells delicious," Mother says as we help the twins into their seats.

Erinn stares at Glacia, who's wearing the same blue dress and crimson shawl she wore at the Embassy's opening banquet.

"You're really pretty," she squeaks.

Glacia smiles. "Aw, thank you. I love your dresses."

Erinn giggles and plays with the bottom of her white dress, which has a red bow tied around her waist. Flavia is wearing the same outfit, except with a blue bow. Her eyes are transfixed by all the food on the table, and she tugs on Mother's arm, anxious.

"I don't think I'm *thith* hungry," she tells Mother.

Mother pats her shoulder, smiling. "You don't have to eat it all, sweetie."

"When do we get ice cream?" Erinn asks, looking around for it.

"After you eat dinner," Glacia tells her. "Want some help?"

"Yes, please."

Erinn sits back and lets Glacia scoop vegetables and cut a strip of poultry on her plate, then she grabs a fork and stabs a chunk of meat. Mother does the same for Flavia, and they eat without talking. Flavia must have been hungrier than she thought, because she asks Mother to cut up some more meat.

"What'th that?" she asks, pointing at a bottle of Sprice in the center of the table as Mother cuts the poultry for her.

"That's what grown-ups drink."

"Oh." She looks over to where Jaston and Sophie are sitting. "Why ith that girl'th hair sparkly?"

"That's Sophie," Glacia says. "She just got married."

"Oh."

Flavia keeps staring at Sophie, who eventually catches her eye and waves. Flavia blushes and looks down at her lap.

Across the hall, I see Mr. and Mrs. Haverns walking toward our table. When they reach us, Mrs. Haverns pats Mother's shoulder.

"Hello, you must be Mrs. Lance?"

"Yes," Mother says, hastily wiping crumbs from the corner of her mouth. "Mavella."

"I'm Jan, and this is Gavin."

"It's nice to meet you, Mavella," Glacia's father says.

Erinn waves at them. "I'm Erinn"—she points at Flavia—"and this is my twin sister, Flavia. When do we get ice cream?"

Mr. and Mrs. Haverns laugh. "Once everyone is done eating dinner," Mrs. Haverns says sweetly. "Is that okay?"

Erinn looks at Mother, who nods.

"*Yeah.*"

"*You can have all the ice cream you want,*" Glacia whispers in Erinn's ear.

They talk a little longer, and then Glacia's parents return to their table to sit with Sophie's parents. A few more minutes go by before a high-pitched chinking sound resonates from the front table. Jaston and Sophie are both standing, so the banquet hall goes quiet.

"We have an announcement we'd like to make," Jaston begins. "There's, uh, something we've been holding off telling everyone until now. Our big surprise. Sophie?"

Sophie tugs at a ringlet and glances over at her parents. "I'm pregnant. It's a boy."

As the crowd applauds, the photographer ducks to the front table and snaps Jaston kissing Sophie's hand. They both smile around at everyone, mouthing '*thank you.*'

Jaston stretches his arms outward. "All right! How about some dessert?"

The chefs return and replace the dinner platters with cake trays and bowls of ice cream. Erinn grabs a spoon and digs into the bowl of mint cream Glacia puts in front of her, while Flavia nibbles at a slice of cherry-glazed cake.

"No Lemon Swirl." Glacia sighs, dismayed. "I'll be right back. Need to make a quick trip to Belvun."

She ends up grabbing a few lemon fudge cubes, and I eat what's left of Flavia's cake. Erinn, on the other hand, finishes her ice cream, then tugs on Glacia's elbow and begs for a second bowl.

It isn't long before Jaston and Sophie stand again, and this time they walk to the center of the room. Light music starts playing. It has no words, just a slower, airy sort of rhythm. A relaxing rhythm...spritely pulses mixed with low, drawn-out swings. Jaston and Sophie move together, one hand on each other's shoulders, and the others clasped out to the side. Sophie's dress ripples over the floor, and Jaston sets each step to avoid catching it under his feet. The photographer crouches between two tables, snaps a picture, then shuffles across the floor for a different angle.

Foreheads touching, they slide to a stop as the music fades. Then more people stand and fill the dance floor. The tempo picks up. The energy flares. Little kids wiggle their bodies and swing their arms. Some girls toss their hair back and laugh, dancing together or dragging guys into the mix, some who seem particularly reluctant. I'd never be able to do that, be the center of attention. If it wasn't for Glacia—

I feel a poke on my shoulder and look to the right: Glacia is staring at me. Erinn pokes my shoulder, too, and giggles. Glacia pokes me again, and Erinn mimics her, giggling again. Then Glacia leans down and whispers in her ear.

Erinn hops off her chair and tugs my hand, trying to get me to stand up. My heart thuds so hard in my chest it hurts, and I give Glacia a wide-eyed stare, trying to say, *'why would you do this me?'*

"*Come on!*"

Erinn strains to pull me off the seat, and I finally give in. But I don't give Glacia the satisfaction of a second glance. Nope.

Instead of just taking an open spot at the edge of the dance like I would do, Erinn drags me all the way through the crowd and starts swinging our arms as high as she can. Heat swims into my face and I bite my cheeks, looking only at Erinn and the floor. I'm too busy panicking to care that anybody's watching me at this point. Just change the song. Please. Give me that.

This is awful.

Glacia and Flavia join us after a few seconds of this torture. I do my best to ignore Glacia's smirks, but it's hard to keep my eyes off of her, especially when she's wearing that dress. Even her hair is styled like it was at the Embassy's opening banquet: two curls hanging beside her eyes, and the rest pulled over her left shoulder. Her crimson shawl is back at the table, which is probably for the best because Erinn might have tried to grab it.

"*Gotcha*," Glacia whispers in my ear when the song fades out.

Erinn lets go of my hand and takes Flavia's instead. Glacia takes the chance to grab my hand and kiss my cheek.

"You *really* need some Sprice, mister."

"Do I?"

She pushes us apart, then twists back and forth to the beat of the new song. I clench my teeth harder, but stop resisting. Loosen my arms. Pivot my feet in sync with Glacia's twists.

People start laughing, and a circle forms around Erinn and Flavia. Flavia's eyes are wide with fear as Erinn twirls her as best she can, but Erinn is having the time of her life, and almost falls down from laughing so hard. Another little boy pushes his way through the legs of the watchers to join them, but Flavia runs away to Mother at the dinner tables, and Erinn chases after her. The little boy stares after them, waiting to see if they'll come back, then skips off to his parents when they don't.

The music changes to a slow song. Glacia and I have since moved to the outer edge of the floor so I don't feel so trapped. Here I can focus and think and not feel as embarrassed. I pull Glace against me, one hand on her waist. She lifts her arms over my shoulders, and we sway. I have no idea how to dance formally, so I just shift...shift...shift...and sway back and forth like other people are doing. I keep my eyes on Glacia's face. The soft light brightens her hazel eyes, the ringlets of hair bounce down her cheeks. In my hands, her silky dress folds and stretches as we move.

A burst of chimes plays in the music, and the corners of Glacia's mouth flicker upward. "*It reminds me of the stars,*" she whispers.

She shifts her arms. I don't say anything, but make a mental note to ask Jaston for a copy of this song. Glacia's birthday is February 21. We'll be on Daliona then, and it's the perfect song to give her there. It's the kind of song that's both happy and sad at the same time, the kind of song that latches onto your heart and makes you wish it would never end. A song that feels so distant. A song you yearn to rediscover forever.

Glacia's eyes flick up and down, so, instinctively, I lower my head to hers until our foreheads are touching—then our lips. A tingling flutters in my chest. My hand squeezes her waist ever so gently. Her arms pull around my neck, pressing down just enough to hold me there. The song fills us, and I absorb it, knowing that in these quiet moments, I will hear it play.

Chapter Eleven

"ALWAYS KNEW YOU'D come through, kiddo. Never doubted you for a second."

Jaston runs his hand down the quilt Glacia and I bought on Belvun, the one that has the blue river and reddish forest stitched across it.

"What do you think, Soph?"

"It's beautiful."

"*And*"—Jaston lowers his voice—"it's a hell of a lot more original than half these other gifts. If you ever need a toaster, give us a call. We got three. One even doubles as a coffee maker."

"I've been saying we need some color in the house," Sophie says while Jaston and I fold the quilt. "We'll be spending a lot of time in whatever room it goes in. And of course, you're always welcome to visit. Holistead's not bad! Not as hot, and a bit homier, too. The people are nice—"

"That is, once you can figure out what they're saying," Jaston interrupts. "Can you believe she used to talk so fast, I'd just nod at whatever she was saying and work it out later? I'm still not sure if she actually agreed to go on a date with me the first time I asked."

He winks at Sophie and slips his hand into hers.

"*Jeremy Pilkins*," I mutter to Glacia. She rolls her eyes.

"Who's that?" Jaston asks.

"A guy we know. He never shuts up."

"And he thinks my name's Gloria," Glacia adds.

"He sounds like a typical Holisteadian," Sophie says. "Did he join Shield Tower?" Glacia and I nod, impressed by her guess. "A lot of them choose that route. Really, the louder they are, the more they like playing with guns."

Jaston looks around the emptying banquet hall, his eyes fixing on one spot, then another, and another, as if he's trying to remember every detail of the night. The dance floor is long-quiet, the music lowered to a level where it's barely a part of the background. Then I remember I need to ask him to send me a copy of the song Glacia liked.

I catch his eye and nod subtly to the left, away from Glacia and Sophie. He gets the hint, and we walk away from the girls.

"Is there any chance I could have that first slow song you played?"

"Mine and Sophie's?"

"After that, like—"

He holds up one finger to stop me. "*Stelle Adiis*, by the Narvidian composer, Jahn Hakliin. Beautiful piece. Traditional orchestral style. You want it for...?"

"Glacia's birthday. She really liked it."

"Gotcha. Yeah, I'll send it to you in the morning. What time you guys leaving?"

"Eight."

He utters a low whistle. "It's almost midnight now. What are you guys still doing up?" he asks, laughing. "Yeah, I'll get it to you. And Arman?" His eyes flick at Glacia again. "Have fun out there."

✳ ✳ ✳ ✳ ✳

Erinn squeezes her arms around my neck, sniffling. When she lets go, she rubs her eyes and pouts her lips.

"W—why do you have to leave?"

"I'm working on a big project. A really *important* project."

"When will you come back?"

I lift her chin with one finger. "As soon as I can. I promise. I'm traveling to another planet soon, so I'll bring back more pictures, okay?"

"*Mmhmm.*"

"I love you." I squeeze her in another hug and kiss her cheek before turning to Flavia. "You guys be helpful to Mommy. Promise?"

"We promise."

Flavia's chin quivers, but she holds back her tears. I give her a hug and kiss her cheek, then stand up and face Mother—and now *I* fight to hold back tears. I hug her, say goodbye, and then turn my back and walk with Glacia up the ramp to the hovercraft.

It's just us in the hovercraft today. The lounge feels

empty without any extra company. We sit on the same couch, but for most of the flight, we don't talk. The world outside zooms by, canyons and mesas and ridges passing below. Newscasts from around Undil play on the projection on the wall, but there's nothing new from two days ago.

After nearly two hours, the Embassy crests over the reddish-brown horizon. Glints of sunlight reflect in the sky, other hovercrafts approaching from other cities. A haze hangs in the air, and the wind buffets us when we step onto the platform, so Glacia and I speed-walk to the elevators and descend to the maglev station. We board a train, stop at Interchange Station to let more people on, and a few minutes later we're standing across the street from Ceremony Dome, a block from our apartments.

I message Orcher to tell him I'm back in the Embassy. He notifies Chancellor Green, who ends up calling to schedule the final proposal hearing.

Chapter Twelve

AS IT WAS when I first presented to the council, the conference chamber is dark except for the lights surrounding me and the panel of directors. Orcher, Commander Mannard, General Corbard, and Director Estilon talk quietly amongst themselves as we wait for Chancellor Green and his council to arrive.

I lean against the podium and let my head hang. When he called the other day, Chancellor Green made it sound like his council approved the program, so I shouldn't have anything to worry about. Still, I'm anxious. This is my first official project. Its success depends on my decisions determination.

The council finally arrives. Chancellor Green gives me a reassuring nod as he sits, and pushes up his black-rimmed glasses before saying, "Lieutenant Hofhen told me your business in Orvad went well."

"Yes it did, sir."

"And General Orcher tells me you attended a wedding with Miss Haverns yesterday?"

"Her brother's."

"Good to hear. I've never been to one myself." He chuckles, then folds his hands in front of him. "You spoke with Olivarr Cresson about installing RASP aboard our fleets—"

"Just General Orcher's, for now," I correct quickly.

"A mobile arrangement to be expanded to other fleets should it prove successful. Excellent." Chancellor Green taps his panel and a screen shimmers to life in front of him. "You'll need to monitor how RASP affects a number of factors before we decide whether to expand it to the other fleets. I've settled the payment, and Olivarr Cresson has organized his teams to install simulation software that will train you before its application in the fleet...which brings me to my next question: have you begun preparing your teams?"

I stop to think but then realize the truth: I talked to Lon about *possibly* hiring him, and that was only in passing.

"I've talked to some people."

Some members of the council shift in their seats. A woman highlights a line from the proposal. "You say here you need a total of—*at minimum*—twenty members, five per station. So, Mr. Lance, how will you go about recruiting these members?"

I shift my feet and look at my holotab, my eyes searching my notes. "I think we were going to put out a notice—"

The councilwoman raises a hand to stop me. "General Orcher will get you in touch with the lieutenants in his fleet. You need to arrange individual interviews, preferably engineers, records personnel, and anyone associated with planetary sciences who understands what you'll be cataloguing on Daliona. Then evaluate them with someone qualified—by that I mean the lieutenants of the fleet—and from there, decide who you will hire."

I make a note of everything she says. When I look up again, I see Orcher nodding his approval.

"The rest of your proposal seems to be in order." Chancellor Green motions around the room. "We approve the Live Archives Program and its integration with RASP. I'll get in touch with Olivarr Cresson to finalize the contract. In the meantime, you may proceed."

Chapter Thirteen

OCTOBER 9
UNDILAEN TIME
STANDARD YEAR 4319

"JACLYN LANDER. TWO years aboard the *Drake*, four aboard the *Blazar*." Lucas slides the information display toward me, with her personal credentials listed below an image of her face. "She loosely worked under Captain Blitner. I say *loosely*, because whatever archives program Lawrence was supposed to be overseeing wasn't functioning as we would've liked...for obvious reasons."

He takes the display back and sits back in his seat.

"Right, then. Call her in."

I do, and she sits across from us in the same seat that so many others have over the last several days. We're in Lucas' office, on Floor 40 in Threshold Tower.

The hall outside is filled with people from Orcher's fleet, a number of officers, techies, analysts, engineers, and others who were selected by their lieutenants to interview for my teams.

"Your current supervisor is Lieutenant Marlick, correct?" Lucas asks her.

"Yes."

"Tell us about your old work."

"When I worked for Captain Blitner?"

"Correct."

Jaclyn pauses to think, then says, "I never saw him face-to-face, since we worked on different stations, but I had to write reports and transfer them to him."

"You say you collected data?"

She nods. "Every day. I'd scan and log major output systems, note any trends and inconsistencies, then compile a report and send it to him."

"And did Captain Blitner ever provide you with feedback?"

"Not that I'm aware of," she says. "Before every expedition, he'd send the same message about what data to collect and how to organize a report. But only Lieutenant Marlick checked on me if something about my report wasn't clear."

Lucas bobs his head. "That's consistent with most of Lawrence's evaluations. His last ten years as Head Station Archivist followed a rapidly declining trend"—Lucas holds a hand up to Jaclyn, who looked worried at the comment—"none of which reflects poorly on you."

He asks her a few more questions, we let her go, and then the next person comes in. That's how these past few days have gone: strings of interviews until lunch, followed by strings of interviews until dinner. Lucas does most of the talking, and I just listen, trying to decide who I could get along with...or who I wouldn't last a day with. Some people drone on and on, answering Lucas' questions with no enthusiasm at all. Some people are straight up annoying, spewing their own ideas on how we should be developing the program.

I'm just looking for a team, people.

"Who's next...?"

Lucas closes Hadley Briton's information and opens the next file: Randeroy Harmat.

"Holisteadian." He makes a face. "Spent two years in Shield, but was voluntarily discharged and transferred to Horizon's planetary sciences sector for three years before General Orcher recruited him in the wake of the Belvun crisis. Didn't work under Lawrence, so that's a relief. Bring him—"

But the door slides open before Lucas can finish, and a guy with flat-buzzed brown hair saunters inside and drops into the seat. Even sitting down, he's tall. Lucas stares at him, and he stares back, one finger tapping the armrest.

"You guys are supposed to interview me, right? That's how this whole thing works?"

"Right," Lucas says. He clears his throat and skims the list he just read me. "Randeroy—"

"*Rand.*"

"Okay, Rand. We couldn't help noticing you were voluntarily discharged from Shield six years ago."

"That's still on there? Damn. Thought it'd be off by now." He raises both hands. "I'm not a nut job, if that's what you're thinking. They'd have put me down. Nope.

Quit for a noble cause."

Lucas' jaw is slack. He's clearly thinking the same thing as me: this guy is something else. Maybe it's typical Holisteadian behavior, like Jeremy Pilkins. But it doesn't explain Lon...

"It says here you specialize in *localized* planetary sciences. Can you explain?"

"What's it sound like? I'm an environmentalist." Rand grins, flashing us a white smile that contrasts with his heavily tanned face. "I deal in joint contracts. Still got ties to Horizon even though I'm assigned to Threshold. These days, I monitor Undil's terraformation—if that's what we're still calling it—and Belvun's deterioration. All this eco-hacking shit's has been giving me work like you wouldn't believe. Even Narviid's calling in favors, asking us to analyze planetary data to see how soon until they get to ride the same path Belvun went down." He taps one finger on the side of his head. "Predictions say Narviid's first ecosystems should collapse in the next few years, followed by accelerating exponential decline, just like Belvun. Has the Narvidians on edge."

He fakes a smile and clasps his hands behind his head.

"*But have no fear!* Undil shan't follow that dreadful road. In fact, we needn't worry, not *one damn bit*. Sure, the Ryginese opted Undil for traditional terraformation, but our oh-so-environmentally-conscious chancellor has decided that Undil's greener days can wait a few years. It's not like we're already decades behind schedule. But I'm sure the techies are just *loving* all the funding he's pouring into them. We might be taking the long road, but at least it'll be a paved one."

This actually gets a chuckle out of me and Lucas, which prompts Rand to smile all big and sweet, one of the fakest smiles I've ever seen.

"So, getting back on track..." Lucas folds his hands on the desk. "You've been to Daliona?"

"Oh I've been there, and I'm more than ready to go back. What is it...thirty days till we leave?"

I nod in response. Rand eyes me up, a scowl on his face.

"Oy. Do you even talk, man? Awfully quiet over there. Don't I have to work under you?" He gestures at Lucas. "He knows how to talk. Comes in handy, *talking*."

I bite my lip to hold my expression steady. Lucas tenses up a bit, too, but that doesn't stop Rand.

"You *are* Lance, right? The guy running this whole program?"

"Yeah, I'm—"

"*He speaks!*" Rand claps his hands and leans forward over the desk. "I've got a few questions of my own for you. Number one: let's say I don't come into work one morning. Too tired. You know how those expeditions can get. What are you going to do?"

It takes a second for my throat to unclench. "Call you to—"

He stops me with another wave. "Say my holotab's off. I like my beauty sleep. Makes my skin glow. What do you do?"

I hold eye contact with him, however much I want to look away. For some reason, I feel like doing that won't help me here. But I'm taking too long for him, and he slaps both his hands on the desk, rattling *everything*.

"Let me make this simple, Lance. You better come

wake my sorry ass up and drag me down to work. Sound the alarms if you have to. Nobody's got time for people who shirk their duties. You heard what Orcher said at that captain's funeral. The crew's your family. We all have responsibilities, and we're not always gonna like them, but in the end, this isn't about you, or me, or this guy." He nods at Lucas. "It's about *all* of us, Lance. It's about the mission. Why we do what we do."

He offers out his hand. I'm hesitant, but I shake it.

"I'm not saying we can't have a little fun. Hell, when we get to Daliona, you can bet I'll be the first one to take you down a gravity run. But here, you're the head archivist. You're my boss—act like it."

He sits back and clasps his hands behind his head again.

"So, go on. Interview me."

✳ ✳ ✳ ✳ ✳

At dinner that night, I tell Glacia and Ellin about Rand. We're in the Shady Barchan—as usual—and a few Narvidians who are sitting at the bar keep roaring with laughter and drowning out our conversation. It gets to the point where I have to repeat myself several times so Ellin can hear me across the table.

"Well, he's not *wrong*," Glacia says, poking at her sautéed chicken parsley. "You aren't exactly the most assertive guy around. And it doesn't help that General Orcher threw this on you after Captain Blitner died."

I shrug, now only half-listening as I strain to catch some new words from the Narvidians. One of them sees me looking their way and turns to face our table.

"*All vadianni?*" he grunts. The other men at the bar snigger. He looks at Ellin, furrows his forehead, and jerks his thumb at me. "*All vadiaatni? Anaat vakii!*"

Ellin looks taken aback. The man gives her a hard stare, then turns around again when one of his colleagues hands him another shot of bronze liquid. He tips his head all the way back, swallows it, and slaps the glass on the table with a satisfied grunt.

Glacia rolls her eyes. "*Well then.*"

"*Yeah,*" Ellin agrees. She spins her fork in her salad and glances up at me. "So Arman, um…someone said some Orvadians are installing new equipment in the fleet?"

I nod. "RASP. For the new archives."

"What's that?"

I forgot I never talked to Ellin about the program. We haven't seen each other since that day with John, and I've only seen Michael in passing. It feels weird to have come in together as recruits, and now we're separated most of the time.

"The Real-time Archival Surveillance Program," I say. "We're going to use it to catalogue other planets, starting with Daliona."

"Sounds like you're really moving up." Ellin smiles, but it's short-lived. "I'm jealous. I can't go to Daliona with you guys."

"Why not?"

She looks at me like I should know. "Because of you, I think. They assigned me to a team that's reprogramming Threshold's Records Room after it gets redesigned…and now it turns out to be your archives."

I grimace. "Sorry about that."

Ellin fidgets with her fork in her empty salad bowl. Glacia absentmindedly thumps her foot against her chair in rhythm with the song playing in the background, and I stare straight ahead, once again trying to pick up what the Narvidians are saying. I keep hearing *'Chaklii! Chaklii! Chaklii!'* whenever one of them chugs down a whole pint of Arb Ale, but there are other words thrown in, too: *tapiams, geragrin, lediams, amar*... At one point, two of the Narvidians stand up, say, *'Maak, anta wass,'* and leave, so that must be some sort of goodbye.

Eventually all the Narvidians leave, several of them stumbling and nearly knocking into our seats. When they're gone, the Shady Barchan is unnaturally quiet.

I keep reciting the words over and over in my head, paying attention to how I heard the Narvidians pronounce them. The *a*-sounds and *i*-sounds seem to be the most prominent in all the words, whereas the *e*-sound is low and flat.

Glacia nudges me, and only then do I realize I'm mouthing the words to memorize them. I remember that day on the *Ember* when she made fun of me for trying to learn the language to impress Ladia. Except at the rate I'm going, I won't be impressing anyone anytime soon.

✳ ✳ ✳ ✳ ✳

Lucas and I continue interviewing people over the weekend. Jared Sprig is a technical systems engineer on the *Doppler*, someone like Ellin who works with engine and guidance software. He's flown on seven expeditions with Orcher over the last five years, and before that, spent eight years working for Horizon Tower developing data processors. Noah Belraus has been in the Embassy three years and played a part in the evacuation of Ellaciss City. I recognize Chloe Marshal. She was in my recruit class. Lucas recognizes her, too, and we come to find out she was the girl who stuck with me and him during the Hologis tournament.

The final round of interviews is with more people from the *Ember*. I recognize a lot of them from passing them in the halls every day, but I've never known their names: Emilie Pargo, Kile Arlington, and a number of others who happen to be from my recruit class.

"*And that's that,*" Lucas says when the last person leaves. He drums his fingers on his desk. "Now comes the hard part: evaluations."

"Awesome."

He catches my air of sarcasm. "I did my half, bud. You sat there and smiled for moral support. It might be *our* program, but these are *your* teams, people *you'll* be communicating with on a daily basis. Choose wisely."

Over the course of the next several days, I meet with each lieutenant of Orcher's fleet and review the applicants. I spend the first day with Lieutenant Marlick, from the *Blazar*. He tells me his personal observations of each candidate, and in the end gives special recommendation for Jaclyn Lander, Langston Clafford, and Hazel Bridger.

On the second day, I video conference with Lieutenant Rivets of the *Drake*. We review most of the applicants fairly quickly, but when we get to Lon, he goes off praising him left and right.

The third and fourth days blend together—in a bad way—because I've been stuck reading interviews and reports for so long. Fortunately, Victoria is enthusiastic about the whole process, which perks me up a bit. We spend the afternoon in her office on the Crown's thirtieth floor and evaluate everyone I interviewed from the *Ember*. Rand Harmat stuck out most to me, so I jot his name on the list.

✳   ✳   ✳   ✳   ✳

Lucas gives me a supportive smile before we walk into the conference chamber. "Last presentation. All set?"

I take a deep breath, let it out. "Yup."

It's gotten easier to talk in front of the council. I don't feel the same anxiety as when I made the initial proposal.

"And remember, you're doing all the talking." He slaps the door panel. "After you, bud."

Lucas and I walk into the conference chamber and stand behind the podium. As before, Orcher sits with the panel of directors, and the Chancellor and his council sit in the tier above them.

"Good morning, gentlemen," Chancellor Green starts. "You've made your selections?"

"Yes, sir," I say.

"How many team members did you choose?"

"Nineteen across the fleet, with me being the twentieth. Five people per station."

I project the list and recite the teams we've assigned. Each person's picture fills the projection when I read their name, and when I'm done, they're organized into four sets according to the station they'll be working on.

"Have you assigned team leaders?" a councilwoman asks when I finish.

"Yes. Elliot Writway will be the *Blazar*'s, Baxter Krebs as the *Drake*'s, Samuel Scott as the *Doppler*'s, and me as the *Ember*'s. And as I said in my proposal, I will be in contact with each team on a daily basis, and all reports will come to me."

"And you report to...?"

"General Orcher," I say, nodding in his direction.

The councilwoman's eyes flick to Lucas. "And Officer Starmile, where do you stand in all this?"

Lucas steps forward and folds his hands behind his back. "My part begins, more or less, when the expedition returns from Daliona. By then, the teams should be well-trained and using RASP to its full potential, and we should have enough data to determine if pursuing an embassy-wide installation of the program is in our best interests."

The councilwoman jots another note. "Thank you."

The chamber goes quiet as the council deliberates among itself. Chancellor Green converses with the man next to him, and General Corbard whispers something to Orcher, who shakes his head in response.

After some discussion, Chancellor Green looks back at me and Lucas. "Gentlemen, everything seems to be in order. Should I or my council have any further questions, we'll give you a call. Otherwise, you are authorized to proceed with training. Good luck."

* * *

* * * * *

Over the next few weeks, my workload increases tenfold. I knew managing the teams would be difficult, just like Rand and Lucas warned. It's like a shadow has been looming over me ever since that day three months ago, when Orcher promoted me to be his fleet's Head Archivist. But up until the last conference, all I had to do was write proposals and bring RASP into the Embassy. Now I have to do the actual work.

The actual work sucks.

Everywhere I look, I have responsibilities. Remember meetings, analyze reports, keep track of dates, record meaningful notes whenever I talk with someone in the program. As promised, Olivarr Cresson arrives with a team and installs a RASP training program in Threshold Tower's Records Room. Before heading into orbit to reconfigure the fleet, he spends two days training me and the other team leaders on it so we have a basic understanding of RASP, and then the four of us have to train the rest.

During the first week, we work with the *Blazar*'s and *Drake*'s crews. I learn—and quickly, at that—that some people have natural talent with tech systems, while others...not so much. Elliot Writway, the *Blazar*'s team leader, is able to run a software defragmentation in less than a day, whereas it takes Hazel Bridger three days. And on the *Drake*'s team, Lon spends more time asking questions than actually practicing—but by the end of the second day, he's able to run biometrics and telemetry scans.

The rest of the week, Lon ends up teaching his crew how to use RASP, so I have him help me train the *Doppler*'s and *Ember*'s teams the following week. And at the end of October, after we finish our final day of simulations and training, I can't help but think this is starting to feel like a real program. All that's left to do is set ourselves up in the space fleet and begin the expedition to Daliona.

Chapter Fourteen

NOVEMBER 1
UNDILAEN TIME
STANDARD YEAR 4319

I'VE ALWAYS LIKED November.

At nine days long, it's the shortest month of Undil's recognized year. Our calendar resets with the Standard calendar, which is measured in hours, not days. Some planets only have a handful of months, such as Belvun. Its Standard calendar resets on September 14th, whereas its solar calendar resets almost three months later. Undil's solar calendar spans fifteen months, but only the scientists pay attention to that.

Another thing about November is that ten days from now, on January 2nd, I'll be 21 years old.

But this year, there's one reason I'm glad November is finally here: the expedition to Daliona leaves on Janu-

* * *

ary 1st. When I joined the Embassy five months ago, I never imagined I'd travel there. Back then, I didn't care where I went, as long as I made it to Belvun—to Ladia.

Now, everything has changed. Now, at night, Glacia and I look through *48 Light-Years*. Of the nine planets humanity has settled, Daliona is the only one covered entirely by an ocean. Three hundred archipelagos, tens-of-thousands of individual islands, and one small continent, called Kiana. The life, the color, the nature, the technology... The longer we look at these pages, the more I crave to blast seven light-years across the galaxy, to breathe the air of that world and feel the light of that sun, to dive into those waters and see the creatures that exist only there.

Glacia closes *48 Light-Years* and turns over, slipping her feet over the end of my couch and yawning as she lays her head in my lap.

"What do you want for your birthday?" she asks, her eyes closed.

"We'll be flying to Daliona. What more could I really want?"

"I have a few ideas. You've never flown outside the stations, for one."

I scoff at the idea. "If I remember correctly, you didn't enjoy flying outside."

Glacia opens her eyes and points her finger up at me. "There's a *big* difference between flying in the *Perihelids* and flying in free space. The Perihelids aren't exactly a walk in the park." She pokes the bottom of my chin. "But flying in the void? *Totally* different experience. Even better than trans-atmospheric flight."

"Oooh, *pilot lingo*."

"Shut up."

I poke her nose back. "You're cute when you talk nerdy to me."

Glacia fakes a gag. "*Wooooow.*"

"Quiz me. I got this."

"It'll go right over your head, *Mr. Archivist.*"

"Try me."

"What's the Hohmann Transfer Orbit?"

"The Hohmann Trans—come on, start with something easy."

"It's basic spaceflight terminology! The orbit that shoots you from one planet's orbit to another's...*as long as they're in the same elliptical plane.* Otherwise we have to do all sorts of crazy math that I'm pretty sure only Officer Remmit enjoys." Glacia sticks her tongue out. "Okay, what's modulation?"

Easy. That popped up all the time when I worked at Gray Wall.

"Adjusting a radio frequency."

"Close enough. How about achondrite?"

"Sounds like a rock."

"What kind of rock?"

"Um...a meteor?"

"It can be. It's any meteor or asteroid with no magnetic properties. So like, every time we mine an asteroid in the Perihelids, it becomes an achondrite."

I shake my head. "Nope, never learned that."

"Pilots do because we have to run scans while we're flying through debris and asteroid fields. Just another way we're saving your life."

"Yeah, well, once my program kicks in—"

"Ha, *please.* What can your program do that can't already be done by a holotab?"

"Biometric scans."

"Holographic pictures."

"Fleet synchronization."

"A phone call."

"Radiometric Interference Scans."

Glacia narrows her eyes suspiciously. *"You made that up."*

"Fine. Temperature and humidity control."

"Okay, *stop*. You're embarrassing yourself." Glacia twists and props herself up on her elbows. "Admit it, mister: this *'archives program'* is just Orcher's excuse to give you a job."

"I'll pretend not to be offended."

Glacia sits up all the way and sets her chin on my shoulder. "You're lucky, though."

"You have quite a way of saying that."

She tucks her head against my shoulder, but I look out the window. The last of the evening's light fades from the boring intersection I got stuck with when I chose this room.

Then it hits me.

I finally remember *why* I chose this room: the Kairos supernova. It hung low in the sky the day we toured the apartment complex. The sight fascinated me: a second sun with dark orange ripples pulsing both night and day. I didn't need the city, only the sky. The sky was where I wanted to be, because Ladia was out there somewhere, way beyond where the blue changes to black and the safety of the atmosphere becomes the hostility of the void. Back then, my life was a string of unfulfilled wishes. The supernova made me think they

● ● ●

were finally coming true.

And now it's gone.

A wave of shame hits me. My gaze drops. I stare at the top of Glacia's head and let myself feel her hands in mine. One of her fingers twitches as I carefully slip my hand out from between hers and put my arm around her. She leans into my chest more, and the tightening knot eases. Because my wishes *are* coming true, except it wasn't the supernova that made them happen. It was Glacia, and what she taught me. How I can be happy with what I have—with *who* I have—and how I need to let myself experience the things I've been missing out on. She taught me that sometimes the greatest journeys don't happen around you.

They happen within you.

Chapter Fifteen

"SET FOR LAUNCH."

A few seconds of silence, then,

"Four, three, two, one—"

The transport shudders. In the predawn darkness, the bright blue glow of the thrusters illuminates the platform. It's just me and the *Ember*'s archives team in this transport, but three others are trailing us, one headed to each station in our fleet.

My body presses into the seat when the transport accelerates. One thousand yards...five thousand...ten thousand... Long video panels newly installed into the walls of the transport display the world outside. Only the Embassy shines beneath the stars. The Crown is a golden pillar at the heart of the city, crisscrossing streets shine white and yellow, and blocks of light are scattered on the sides of several towers. The rest of the landscape is shrouded in shadow, from the grayish silhouettes of plateaus and mesas, to the black depths of the Mavine river gorge. And just as we're able to see the curve of Undil's horizon, the sun peeks over the planet's western edge.

The transport trembles: turbulence in the upper atmosphere. When the tremors pass, my body loosens beneath the restraints and my uniform ripples with every tiny movement. At the other end of the row, Allison Vetch's hair floats around her in slow motion, forcing Rand Harmat, who's sitting next to her, to turn his head sideways and wave it out of his face.

"Oy, tie it up next time, Vetch."

The altitude gauge crosses the one hundred-mile mark and continues to climb. At two hundred miles, long specks of light appear in front of the transport: the space fleets, dozens of stations latched onto harbor bays locked in geostationary orbit above Undil.

"*Normal flight pattern achieved,*" a pilot announces. "*Smooth rendezvous with the Threshold Space Fleet expected.*"

We fly below the Horizon Space Fleet, what with its stations that are designed for long-term exploration. Each is equipped with habitable landing pods that deploy sustainable settlements. Horizon's stations are wider than Threshold's, and they don't have the same bulging observatories or bridges. Even their engines look different. Rows of vent thrusters line their sleek wings, rather than massive twin side-thrusters.

Then Threshold's fleet comes into view, and we glide past harbor bays that completely dwarf the transport. There it is: the *Ember*. Its name glows beside the Bridge, and a silvery light pours out of the docks, awaiting our arrival. The other transports break out of formation.

One arcs up toward the *Drake,* and the other two swoop around to the *Doppler* and *Blazar* on either side of the *Ember.*

We enter the dock, and weight immediately returns under the artificial gravity. I take a deep breath and pause to see how my body is reacting. I didn't throw up when we returned to Undil, but that doesn't mean I won't *now.* My stomach tingles and saliva leaks into my mouth. I clench my hands, waiting...waiting...

But nothing happens.

I breathe a sigh of relief and unlatch my clamps.

The same can't be said for Kile Arlington, another guy I hired from my recruit class. As soon as the transport lands, he fumbles with his restraints, drops to his knees, and vomits into the disposal tube.

"Good to see some friendly faces!" Officer Remmit calls as we make our way out of the transport and walk toward him. "Olivarr's good company, but I miss being the smartest guy in the room."

"And what, the rest of us are just blithering idiots, then?" Rand retorts.

Officer Remmit's jaw goes slack. He glances at me, then clears his throat and says, "We should get up there. Olivarr's expecting us."

Rand is the last one to walk through the gate.

We take an elevator up to Floor 11 and walk to the Records Room—except it's not called that anymore. The new label beside the door reads: *Live Archives Chamber.*

"I need to warn you, Arman," Officer Remmit says before we go inside. "Olivarr did a *little* remodeling."

We hear a thud, then a grunt. Olivarr Cresson appears a second later, holding one shoulder and wincing.

"Don't listen to him, Mr. Arman. It's not so bad. Only thing we need is a set of windows. I miss the sun. Never realized how crazy you people really were until I started waking up in the dark every morning." Olivarr steps back and lets us inside. "There's just nothing like a good old fashioned Orvadian sunrise...that is, once the clouds clear away. You would know, Mr. Arman. You saw it. But *some people* left Orvad and never came back...and forgot to take their nostalgia with them, it would seem."

He makes an obvious nod at Officer Remmit, who retorts, "I've seen the sun rise over half a dozen planets, Olivarr, and a few moons as well. Yillosian sunrises are particularly beautiful, especially if they break over a light snow."

"Yes, *well.*" Olivarr pinches his thick glasses and lifts his chubby chin. "While you've been off trotting around the galaxy, I've been at the drawing boards inventing RASP, the very program Mr. Arman here selected to operate his database"—he sets one hand on my shoulder and the other on his heart—"for which I am *ever so grateful.*"

Officer Remmit looks unimpressed, but doesn't push the debate, and lets Olivarr show us around the chamber's new layout.

The workstation pillars where Captain Blitner and I would sit are gone, replaced by five panels set into the wall opposite the door. There's more space to maneuver the room because all the equipment is set around the perimeter except for a machine in the back that looks like a smaller version of the Observatory's StarPad.

"Goodbye, holotabs. Please welcome RASP's state-of-the-art Augmented Conference Interface. It's about to become your new favorite toy, Mr. Arman. You didn't know it, but you saw my team using one in Orvad, and now I'm providing it to the Embassy. I like comparing it to the Dalish *lucidity interface*, an advanced neuro—"

Rand starts chuckling off to the side. "Are you kidding me? This is as rudimentary as it gets for the lucidity interface." He gestures at Officer Remmit. "Come on, genius. I know you've seen it. You can't stand there and let him compare the two. It's an insult to Dalish techies everywhere if he thinks *this* holds any merit against lucidity. The Interface isn't some fancy hologram projector, it's a budding frontier in—"

"—in neuro-transcendence technologies. I'm aware." Officer Remmit lowers his head toward Rand without actually facing him. "However, *Randeroy*, you of all people should know that Undil's current infrastructure can't support that level of processing power on such large a scale. Infrastructure *feeds* infrastructure. You should know all about how slow these processes are. Or should I be asking you, *Mr. Environmentalist*, why Undil is still a pile of rocks?"

"*And sand*," Olivarr mutters to the side.

"Where are the forests and fields we're all so anxious to see?" Officer Remmit continues, ignoring Olivarr's comment. "Our cities can't pump out clean air forever."

"I'd ask you the same thing," Rand says flatly. "An Embassy techie who's concerned with terraformation? At least Cresson here comes from a city that's making progress in terraformation."

"And I'm an avid supporter of Project Oasis, you should know," Olivarr adds, raising a finger.

Officer Remmit shoots him a look, which sets Rand off even more. "Oy! At least he's investing in Undil's future. So I'd ask you, Remmit: if you're so suddenly supportive with advancing the next stage of Undil's terraformation, why haven't you gone to Chancellor Green and assured him you techies don't need *more* funding? Put a word in for me, thanks. Tell him Randeroy Harmat thinks sitting in the shade would feel nice, will you?"

Rand and Officer Remmit glare at each other, both of their faces red. One of Rand's fists is clenched at his side. Olivarr sees that, too, and clears his throat.

"So where were we? Ah, yes, *the ACI!* How about a demonstration?"

He goes to the machine at the back of the room and grabs a black visor, which is nothing more than a metallic headband with a thin screen at the front. He slips it over his eyes, and the rest of us wait for something to happen.

"Nice and snug," he says, patting his ears. "Has to cover *all* your vision, or else you'll get a real headache. Augmented reality is tricky like that."

He must be able to see through the visor, because he sets himself up in the center of the machine just fine. The visor's edges glow blue, and he reaches out to tap an invisible icon. At the same time, a single word displays on one of the machine's panels: *Drake.*

"Hello, Turner!" Olivarr waves at someone we can't see. "Don't mind me. Just giving a demo." He laughs at something the other man says. "Of course! Send somebody over."

A few moments later, a new person appears in the projection array: Lon. His eyes grow wide when he sees us.

"This is *weird*."

His voice sounds off somehow, separated from the projection, and the only sign he's wearing a visor is the fact that his ears are pressed flat against his head. Then he crosses the room in a curved path, avoiding people the rest of us can't see.

"Now you understand why we had to clear the room out," Olivarr explains. Still wearing the visor, he walks between Allison and Kile. "Precautionary measures. Don't want you ramming your shins."

"What happens if I leave the room?" Lon asks. His voice still sounds separated, and the more I try to ignore it, the more it annoys me.

"The visor deactivates. These chambers are the only rooms in the fleet equipped with this tech...*for now.*" Olivarr faces Lon and points at him. "Alonso, is it? We need to get a move on. I'm sure we'll see you later."

"You definitely will."

Lon vanishes, and then Olivarr takes off his visor and returns it to the rack.

"That's always fun. My boys in Orvad love the ACI. The very first Hologis arenas relied on the technology, actually, until real-time spatial holograms refined the sport." Olivarr clasps his hands behind his back and looks up at us. "Let's get you settled in, shall we?"

※　※　※　※　※

"I take it back."

"Too late."

Glacia pouts up at me from my holotab's projection. "*Mister...*"

"Acting cute won't cut it," I say, trying to make my voice sound flat.

"What do you mean, *acting?* I'm friggin' adorable."

"Keep telling yourself that."

Glacia giggles and pulls her hair over her shoulder. I sigh...then she sighs...then I shoot her a look and sigh again. The corner of her mouth tugs upward.

"When do you get here?" I ask. "I miss you."

"Same morning we leave for Daliona."

"Gotcha." Silence, and then, "So, things good down there?"

Glacia shrugs one shoulder. "Worked with Shield again, so no Fallsten. We practiced diving maneuvers."

"Cool."

"Then we wanted see who could get closest to the ground without crashing."

"And?"

She bites her lip. "All you need to know is I didn't get hurt"—she raises one finger to stop me from speaking—"but this one guy clipped a ridge and smashed his windows to pieces. Like, there was glass *everywhere.* And this other girl tore off an engine."

"Geez."

"It's not like the captains would let us get killed, though. We know what we're doing. I think the worst injury they've ever reported was an amputation."

"Oh, good. *Just a scratch.*"

We get quiet again. I stare above Glacia's head, at the blank wall behind my desk. Before she called, documents and pictures shimmered all around me. I was organizing for the expedition. Now the room is dark except for her projection. It feels so empty in here. The only sound is the station's dull hum.

"I'm not reckless." Her voice is quieter than before. She shifts in her seat, and the projection grows until only her neck, shoulders, and the back of her bed are visible. "You know that, right?"

"I know."

"Hey." She perks up. "Don't forget I'm taking you flying once I get up there."

"Okay."

Glacia puts her hands to her lips and blows me a kiss. "Night, mister."

I smile for her. "Night, Glace."

The hologram shuts down, leaving me with only the glow of my holotab's screen.

I don't want to stay in here, cramped. So I wander the halls for a while. The *Ember* is empty. The station's hum fills every corridor. No one passes me, no voices drift out from behind any doors. Some halls are dark, unused since the day we returned to Undil. The fitness level feels eerily quiet. I'm used to seeing dozens of people lifting weights, jogging on treadmills, and swimming laps in the pool. Now the fitness rooms are dark, and the surface of the pool remains still. Floor 11 is the only level with any sign of activity: light spills out of the archives chamber, where Olivarr is making installations to RASP.

I head up to the Observatory. Undil is shrouded in night, though I can see a sliver of light where the sun is setting in the east. It disappears within minutes.

I lie on one of the loungers and stare up. Thousands

of stars fill the black gap above the planet. My eyes trace two constellations: Etymus the Scroll and Arcen the Bow. I don't recognize any others from here.

Silence.

The hum fades behind my thoughts. Up here, I'm isolated from every person I've ever known. Drifting. If I squint, I can see a tiny speck of light in Undil's night: the Embassy. It's several hundred miles to the east—from *my* perspective—and it's the only visible city on Undil. Glacia is there. Victoria is there. Ellin, and John, and Michael. Orcher, Lucas, Chancellor Green. Everyone but the few of us on the *Ember*.

As I lay here, I remember the song from Jaston's wedding. *Stelle Adiis*. I find it on my holotab and let it play in the quiet night. The music floats around me. A ring of chimes, a low roll of air, a pulse on a string. It's a song that plays within your chest. A song that brightens the stars. A song that makes you close your eyes just to let it take over your thoughts.

The music goes on longer than I remember, a melody that's just as painful as it is addicting. And when it finally does end, I keep my eyes closed and let the remnants of the notes float through my head.

It's a song of desire...

A song of anger...

A song of hope...

A song of solitude.

Chapter
Sixteen

WITH HELP FROM Olivarr, my team syncs RASP to the fleet's databases and explores the range of operations available to monitor. This system is so much simpler than the painstaking work I did on the trips to and from Belvun. We can access a two-dimensional display of any room on the *Ember*, log the readings we need, and move on. No more walking down to Captain Crowe's office, or Life Support, or Officer Remmit's labs.

One room, one system.

As the week progresses, transports ferry up supplies and crewmembers. The food reserves are restocked. Orcher and Captain Fallsten arrive on the fifth day and conduct a full systems check. Officer Remmit tests the MRRs, Captain Fallsten gauges the engines, and Captain Crowe initiates the long-term life support systems.

The halls get louder, the food courts fill with clanking utensils and conversations. But despite all the commotion and growing excitement surrounding our departure, I start to miss the silence. The first couple nights, I could walk the halls to unwind from the day, or go to the fitness center and not be surrounded by dozens of people. Most of all, I miss having the Observatory to myself, when I could just sit back and stare at Undil. On the second night, I even watched a space fleet arrive and dock on a harbor bay. Now when I go to the Observatory, people are always lounging on couches or using the StarPad or looking up at Undil and the stars. To be alone, I have to either wait until after midnight to use the Observatory, or stay cramped in my room—and I hate being stuck *there*.

On the final night before launch, the crew is busy as ever with the final checks and preparations. I decide to go to the archives chamber and try out RASP's augmented interface again. I slip the visor around my head and a display appears in my view. I select the *Drake*'s archives chamber, and in an instant, I'm there. To the onlooker, I'm just a guy wearing a black visor standing in the middle of the room, but to me, I'm on an entirely different station.

It turns out nobody from Lon's team is working right now. All five visors are hanging on the wall, all the panels are deactivated. One of the seats is pushed away from the others, but there's nothing I can do to move it. In the *Drake*, I'm just a projection.

The door is open. I walk to it, hoping maybe I can go into the *Drake*'s hall, but no. When I stick my hand outside, it disappears up to the wrist, replaced with a blue outline of my hand in the *Ember*.

Weird.

I pull my arm back inside when I realize how stupid

I must look. If someone walked by right now, they'd see a guy sticking his hand out the door for no reason. Hopefully Olivarr will have time to extend the ACI so we can use it around the entire station rather than being confined to the archives chambers. I laugh to myself when I think about it: we could really mess with the other crews.

✳ ✳ ✳ ✳ ✳

Transports glide through the silvery barrier and land in their designated slots. A minute later, Glacia staggers around the side of one, followed by her hall mate, Kerin Richter. Glacia keeps running her fingers through her hair, trying—to no avail—to flatten out the puffs that formed during the flight.

"Hold it down this time?" I ask.

"One of us did," Kerin says.

Glacia wipes the corner of her mouth and mumbles something.

We walk to their private hall on Floor 10. Kerin goes inside her own dorm, but Captain Fallsten assigned Glacia to the departure shift, so after we empty her trunks, we head to the Bridge and go our separate ways: me up the ramps, she down to Station Control. Officers are gathered on the platforms, relaying commands and priming the launch sequences. Data orbs zoom between platforms, status updates flash on displays. And keeping watch over the Bridge from the top platform is Orcher, who's dressed in his dark gray uniform with gold buttons and cuffs.

"Coffee?" he offers when I reach him, but I decline.

He sips at his steaming mug of Bersivo Blend, and sets it down gently before saying, "Larson told me you've synced the fleet?"

"Yup. We're all set."

"And the catalogue?"

I nod in response.

"Excellent. Good to see you've been busy."

I grip the railing and look over the Bridge, out at the harbor bay and Undil beyond, where dawn is creeping eastward. I pat the rail like Orcher always does, sigh, and look at the other stations: their engines glow blue, and the lights that outline them are blinking, one-two...one-two...one-two...

"Daliona's days are shorter by an hour," Orcher tells me, sitting with his arms crossed now. "Thought you'd be happy to know that."

"Ha. That's *way* better."

The roughest part of the trip from Undil to Belvun was the difference in the length of the days. The gravities were similar, but adjusting from twenty-eight hours to thirty-four hours wasn't fun.

At all.

"Daliona's gravity is another matter," Orcher goes on saying. "We'll adjust the simulators tonight, but come morning..." He makes a small shrug. "Well, you shouldn't have trouble sleeping."

I don't know if I should be worried or not. Falling asleep in-transit has been an issue for me. Hopefully he's right about my body being exhausted.

It isn't long before the fleet is cleared for launch. The docks are sealed, the MRRs are activated. A short groan reverberates in the walls when the clamps release the *Ember* from the harbor bay—and then we move. The motion is slow at first, but soon we've retreated into a new orbit beyond the ranks of the other fleets. When our trajectory is set and we've pushed beyond Undil's influence, Captain Fallsten contacts Orcher.

"Coordinates locked, engines engaged."

"On your command."

"Initiating."

The hum intensifies as the engines shove us out of Undil's orbit. We're aimed straight for our sun—or just to the side, at least.

The minutes drag on. The sun grows larger, and larger, *and larger*, and after a half-hour, a pilot activates the solar filters to dim the Bridge and Observatory. Even now, Glacia and her copilots are holding course against the sun's gravity as we arc around it, thrusters accelerating. At only a few million miles away, the sun is so massive that the top and bottom are impossible to see. Flares burst and plasma roils and sunspots patch its surface. It's crazy to think that this is the star I lived under for twenty years, the star whose heat I've hated but depended on to survive. It's always been large in the sky, especially compared to Belvun's smaller, cooler sun, but now...*now* I see it for what it is, and the sight blows me away.

How can anything be so *huge?*

Orcher leans over and sets his arms on the rail. "To put this in perspective... Our sun is ten-thousand-times the size of Daliona's, which is twice the size of Belvun's. And you see that sunspot?" he adds, pointing at an oblong black dot amid the plasma. "That's fifty-times the size of Undil."

"*Wow.*"

My holotab buzzes in my pocket: a notification from RASP. As I'm reading it, Officer Remmit's voice echoes through the Bridge, reciting exactly what the notification says.

"*Incoming radiation. MRRs powering to max.*"

I look at Orcher, but he waves off my concern. "Dense solar wind is typical for a flyby, but several times more powerful than when we enter the void."

I'm about to ask what he means, but then a sheet of green and pink engulfs the entire fleet: an aurora. It blankets *everything*, and all at once. Streaming, waving, cresting around us—but the MRRs are strong enough to hold the aurora several yards above the station's hull. And just like that, we're free of the radiation. The aurora vanishes, gone in an instant.

When the pilots deactivate the solar filters again, the sun is nothing but a shrinking speck of light, another dot among the dots, a star in someone else's constellation. Even Undil is out there somewhere, too distant to see at all. Now all that matters is a planet orbiting a star that lies ahead.

Daliona awaits.

Part 2
The Island World

Chapter
Seventeen

I DON'T NOTICE the ache in my body until I try to sit up. Every muscle burns. My arms, legs, neck, back... I feel like I just ran five miles on a treadmill at high resistance. But Orcher was right: I slept the entire night.

I hold my arms above my head and count: *one...two...three...four...five...six—*

And I have to let them drop. It felt like I was lifting my hovertrunk—except *without* the hover setting. This...this is going to take some getting used to.

By the time I force myself out of bed, shower, and put on my uniform, I'm on the verge of exhaustion again. At breakfast, I grab extra portions of kerns and fruit and killari patties. Then the struggle of actually eating: cut the patties, lift them to my mouth, move my heavy jaw.

Cut, lift, chew.

Cut, lift, chew.

When I'm done, my left shoulder and wrist are beginning to cramp, not to mention my jaw almost locking up.

Eating.

What. An. Ordeal.

Then it's time for work. Normally I'd take the elevator, but I know this won't get easier if I skimp out on exercise. So I take the ramp. Halfway up, I have to stop and stretch my back, and by the time I reach the archives chamber, my legs are sore.

The archives door is closed, which is unusual because Rand and Trey always arrive before me. I can't blame them for being late though. This gravity really took its toll on—

"Happy birthday!"

I reel back in shock—or sway, actually, since my feet seem rooted to the ground. A small crowd of people is standing inside, with Glacia at the front and my team all around her.

Glacia hoists her arms up to hug me, her arms quivering as she fights to hold steady. "Fallsten'll kill me if I don't get to the Bridge like *right now*, but I'll take you out flying this afternoon!"

She stands on her tiptoes, gives me a quick kiss, and then ducks out of the chamber with a quick goodbye to the others. Her heavy footsteps thump down the hall as she attempts to jog to the elevators, but it isn't long before she slows to a walk.

Rand crosses his arms and tips his head toward the door. "So, Lance. How'd you manage to land *that?*"

I ignore the question, because it was really Glacia who got me, not the other way around. But I'm not about to tell him that. Let him believe what he wants.

We set up on the work panels and access the feeds we need to report. It won't be a long day. RASP collects operational data overnight, so all we need to do is analyze it, write reports, and distribute them to Orcher, Captain Fallsten, and Officer Remmit.

It's livelier than the time I spent with Captain Blitner. Rand and Allison already know each other—at least a bit—because they've both been on the *Ember's* crew for the last few years. As I think back, I remember seeing them during the expedition to Belvun. Here and there in the halls, the food courts, the fitness centers, even on Belvun itself. But until the interviews, I'd never talked to them...or anyone who wasn't involved with my work, for that matter. But like Rand said, talking to people comes in handy.

✳ ✳ ✳ ✳ ✳

In the evening, I meet Glacia at the docks, where she's already registered us to fly outside the *Ember*. Because we'll be free-flying in the void, we're required to wear pressurized suits. They're sleek, fit right over our uniforms, and will protect us from space exposure, should anything go wrong.

"You're cleared for a half-hour," the pilot monitoring us says. "The Barrier has a three-mile radius out here, so you shouldn't have any problems keeping your distance. As per regulation, Mr. Lance is not allowed to pilot this craft." He nods sharply at Glacia. "Take it easy on him."

Oh, great.

I strap into the seat and seal the helmet to the suit. Glacia powers up the thrusters and activates the exit sequence, shifting her fingers this way and that to adjust the gauges. Floating toward the gate...through the silvery light...

And into the darkness.

Every last ounce of the simulated Dalish gravity releases my body, and I'm suddenly very aware of the fact that this will be *nothing* like when I flew the Molter in the Embassy.

Maybe she's stalling, or maybe she's taking it easy on me, but for the first few minutes, Glacia concentrates on navigating around the *Ember*. She's totally focused. Her fingers twitch, making the slightest movements to adjust the Molter. In a transport, the changes would be gradual, but in the Molter, I feel every little jolt. The smaller jerks, the larger drags. I have to clench the arms of my seat and steady my breathing.

"Hanging in there?" Glacia asks. I guess it looks like I'm going to puke.

"*Mmhmm.*" I don't trust myself to actually speak.

Light swamps my vision when we fly over the Bridge, and Glacia hangs in place above the half-dome. It's weird seeing the Bridge from the side, how layered it is. The platforms are terraced, and the ramps seem so much steeper than they feel. Station Control sits at the very bottom, from and center, where Captain Fallsten is in her usual seat, her frizzy red hair a colorful splotch against the light gray of the Bridge.

Glacia drifts backward along the length of the *Ember*. The Observatory slides past, its glass bubble rising from the top of the station. Then the engines slip by, glowing dark purple as they power the station in FTL. Only now do I realize how fast we're flying, so many times the speed of light, hurtling toward one indistinguishable dot set against thousands of identical dots, all of which are dwarfed by the brown bulge of the Milky Way's core in the backdrop.

I notice Glacia looking around, and then she deliberately turns the Molter to face a certain direction. We've rotated so much that the fleet is directly above us, *pointing up*, so that I'm looking straight into the rear of the engines. I nearly get a headache just trying to wrap my head around it. This is so disorienting, so...*mind-bending* to think that we're still moving with the fleet despite facing a completely different direction.

Space is weird.

"I think this is it," Glacia whispers, her eyes searching the stars. I look to her for an explanation, but she just shakes her head. "Just watch. One of Officer Rem—"

Flash.

It happens before she finishes. A black patch of the void suddenly explodes into a dark red ball that's getting brighter by the minute. The gases condense, turn orange, and churn in fast-motion before our very eyes. I know what that is, I just didn't think I'd see it *again*.

"*The Kairos supernova,*" I finally manage to say.

Glacia tilts her head toward me, but doesn't take her eyes off the spectacle. "Yeah, but in reverse. One of the astrophysics guys told me it'll be three hours before it looks like a star again." She reaches for my hand. "He also told me they ran some spectrum analyses and matched the supernova to a magnetar-forming variant, instead of a neutron star. Maybe that's why I'm *sooooo* attracted to you."

I roll my eyes, at which Glacia squeezes my hand tighter and hugs my arm, resting her head—her helmet, rather—on my shoulder.

"Happy birthday, mister."

I look down, and our eyes connect through the helmet visors.

"I wish I could kiss you right now."

"I would, but"—she knocks on the front of my helmet—"we'd get in so much trouble for taking these off."

"It'd be worth it."

"Probably."

The Molter is so quiet. The fleet is still above us, still powering its way through the void, and the stars shine, unwavering. I can almost see the distance, however far this section of forever stretches.

"This is the universe, Arman. All of...*that*. We might never see most of it, but it's there."

A chill runs down my spine as she speaks, because it's true. One day, we're going to die and pass the responsibility of furthering the human race to the next generation, and they'll pass it to the one after that. It's how we've survived for two thousand years since leaving Earth. The thought is both scary and beautiful, to think that we're one step along a path that, in the end...

Leads nowhere.

"Not many people know what it's like out here. To just, like, I don't know..."

"To just *be*," I finish for her.

She lifts the corner of her mouth. "Yeah."

Our fingers flex together, and for several moments, we sit in silence and take it all in. I think about how the fleet doesn't even look like it's moving, yet we've flown millions, maybe billions of miles in the fifteen minutes since we left the *Ember*. It's so surreal...and now I know why Glacia took me out here for my birthday. Because *this* is one of the feelings I've craved my entire life.

"What's the Barrier?" I ask, remembering how the pilot told us something called the Barrier had a three-mile radius.

Glacia hesitates. For the first time, she loses the wonder in her eyes. Her hand tenses, as if she wants to pull away. Finally, she says, "I can't really explain it. I'd have to show you...but we can't stay long."

"Why not?"

She pulls her hand away. "I'll make it quick."

Glacia fires the thrusters and spins the Molter around, swooping under the fleet until only the blinking lights on the bottoms of the stations are visible. Using one hand, she switches to a new proximity gauge, and to my surprise, the distance isn't getting larger: it's getting *smaller*.

But what are we getting closer to?

Just as the units transition from miles to yards, I hear Glacia mutter something about *'so much trouble,'* but she doesn't hold back now. She reverses the thrusters and levels out the Molter. One hundred yards...fifty yards...twenty yards...

And we lock in place.

I can hear a voice shouting in Glacia's helmet, but she grits her teeth and ignores the voice yelling at her.

"Hurry up and look."

I do. At first I see nothing, but then...*a ripple.* An ebb and flow, as if there's an invisible sheet distorting the stars and making the pricks of light quiver in the middle of the void.

Then it hits me.

"Is that—"

"Arman, I'm so, *so* sorry."

Without any more warning, Glacia fires the thrusters and swerves up toward the fleet. My body flattens against the seat, and the force is too much to handle. I eject my helmet, twist sideways—

And my stomach wrenches.

Chapter Eighteen

"DRINK THIS AND return to your room." The pilot hands me some medicine, then rounds on Glacia. "Miss Haverns—*come with me.*"

I take one last look at the mess I made. I managed to throw up on only my side of the cockpit, so it's not as bad as it could have been. My right foot is covered in slime, as is the passenger hatch and floor. Two pilots get to cleaning it up: one reels out a hose and sprays down the cockpit while the other calls me over and sprays off my leg. Over at the control area, the pilot escorts Glacia to a private office and seals the door behind them.

I go to my room to change my pants, then sit around and wait. Glacia shows up a half-hour later. She doesn't look upset, but she isn't herself, either. Her hands stay tucked under her arms, and she's biting her cheek.

"So...?"

"A week's suspension."

"He can suspend you?"

"He called Fallsten down."

"Oh."

"And General Orcher. And if I fly anywhere near the Barrier without orders ever again, I'll be discharged from the fleet." She exaggerates a smile. *"Fun stuff."*

"Could've been worse," I say, trying to lighten the mood. "We could've been tossed into the void, never to be heard from again."

She doesn't react. On second thought, it probably wasn't the best thing to say.

"Hey, it was still cool. Like, now I have to plan something really reckless for *your* birthday."

There's the laugh.

✳ ✳ ✳ ✳ ✳

At work the next morning, Rand shows me the data RASP generated while Glacia and I were flying outside the fleet. There are individual stats for both of us: our body temperatures, heart rates, and even anxiety levels. My graphs are off the charts. My heart rate started at 77 beats per minute, rose to 110 as Glacia flew us to the Barrier, and then soared to 159 right before I threw up. As for Glacia, her heart rate stuck around 65 until we flew to the Barrier, where it rose to 90, and then peaked at 100.

"You're as sensitive as they come, Lance. I'm starting to rethink taking you down those gravity runs." Rand props his elbow on the edge of his work panel and sizes me up. "You know, I've seen kids—hell, I've seen *toddlers* with a tighter stomach than you got."

Somebody coughs, and we turn just in time to see Kile look away from us.

"*Then again,*" Rand mutters so Kile can't hear, "you could be Arlington. I don't know how he manages to digest anything."

"Excuse me, Arman? Can I have a word?"

Officer Remmit is standing in the doorway. I jump up, relieved to get away from Rand for a bit. But instead of going down to his office, we head up to the Observatory. It's not too crowded, given that it's still early in the morning and most people are on duty, so we have room to talk in private.

"Vicky told me what happened last night, with you and Miss Haverns. Quite a stunt. Not one I'd ever condone you do again, and Miss Haverns was certainly aware of the consequences...but so be it. You've seen the Barrier, as anyone who travels should, in my opinion. The more informed you are about the realities of interstellar flight, the more careful you are to avoid—how should I put it?—*unfortunate situations.* Now you know one more of the many mysteries early-era physicists had to solve. Here..."

He jumps up into the center of the StarPad, the highest point of the Observatory.

"Tell me what you see. Go on, no wrong answers."

I glance around and shrug. "The Milky Way, the stations, the stars—"

"Off to a good start." He steps past me, facing the rear of the *Ember.* "Now, what's there?"

I scan the void for anything unusual, anything he might want me to notice. But everywhere is the same: stars and blackness.

"Just...the void?"

"*The void*," he mutters, leaning back on one of the panels and crossing his arms. "Years ago—*millennia*, I should say—even before the dawn of interstellar travel, we discovered something about the void: it's filled with dark matter and energy. We had no way to interact with either, no way to harvest it, not until nearly a century after the first settlers landed on Daliona—a journey that, back in those days, took twelve years in one direction."

"*Twelve years?*" I gawk at him. "Who would want to wait twelve years?"

Officer Remmit puffs his cheeks and throws his hands in his pockets. "A madman, that's who. And given what we know of that era, most people were out of their minds. Quite frankly, I'm glad we advanced beyond primitive space tech. *Ion thrust propulsion*... It was practically the stone age." He stands upright and stares straight up. "Developing the means to generate energy from the dark forms would open up the frontier of *commercially viable* interstellar travel—and then it happened: we discovered that dark matter is a substance, a physical medium, like water...or gel, more accurately.

"So we solved one question, but now people were asking, '*How do we interact with it?*' The answer came late in the twenty-fourth century. Dark matter behaves quite astonishingly when you propel a massive object through it at a critical velocity: we push it, we...we *drag it along*, rather than pass through it."

That concept seems familiar, how certain substances act differently than others when force is exerted. And then I remember my Basic Matter States and Properties course in Secondary.

"Non-Newtonian? Dark matter is a non-Newtonian substance?"

Officer Remmit's eyes widen, his face lighting up more excited than I've ever seen before, and the words fly out of his mouth. "*Yes, Arman, yes!* Boosting into FTL exerts enough force on dark matter to interact with it, *and thus...*"

His eyes shine with the hope that I'll be able to finish his sentence for him. But remembering the term 'non-Newtonian' was a feat in itself. I'm an archivist for a reason. Most techie-talk goes right over my head.

"*The Barrier*, Arman! It forms the Barrier. It's wrapped around us, moving with us, and more importantly, we can harness its energy *as we move through the void*. It's the ultimate fuel source."

I don't think he's showing off: he's genuinely trying to help me understand. The problem is I'm getting a headache just listening to him, forget trying to comprehend it all... This doesn't explain why Glacia got in trouble for flying too close to the Barrier, why the pilot warned of the radius we were confined to.

"What if we fly past the Barrier in a Molter?"

Officer Remmit leans on one of the StarPad panels. "What happens if you fill a balloon with too much air?" He makes a quick popping gesture with his hands. "It bursts. Like I said, we're moving with just the right force to stay within the Barrier. Apply less energy, and we slip out. But apply *more* energy, and it explodes." He pats the top of my shoulder when my face drops. "That's what my equations *say* would happen, at least, and physics loves sticking to equations."

"So if Glacia *had* hit the edge...?"

"I wouldn't say you and Miss Haverns were in any immediate danger, Arman. She kept you at a safe distance, and I'm sure the force required to disturb the Barrier in any catastrophic sort of way is much larger than what the bump of a Molter would produce—though I wouldn't attempt it. Some theories are better left untested."

✳ ✳ ✳ ✳ ✳

My brain still hurts at dinner.

Even trying to explain what Officer Remmit told me, I don't find myself understanding it any better than the first time I heard it, and I'm sure I'm butchering the actual details. Out of my archives team, Trey seems the most keen to hear what I have to say. The other day he was telling us about software codes and mathematical formulas he developed for various research collaborations within Horizon, so learning about dark matter and energy fascinates him. Allison shows no interest in it and goes on eating. Kile shoots quick glances my way from the end of the table, listening to snippets of the conversation, but never joining in. Rand, on the other hand, seems the least impressed, despite being the one who understands what I'm talking about.

"You're thinking way too hard, Lance. Don't hurt yourself."

Trey gives him a look. "You don't think this is cool?"

"You know what I think? I think whatever the hell

works, works. Nothing Lance just said changed my life. It's all old news. Let's focus on the real problems, like fixing Belvun, terraforming Undil, and getting some meat on your bones—because *damn*." He squeezes my arm. "Don't you exercise? You can't just sit around and expect your body to magically adjust to the gravity. It's all about the *push*." He taps the side of his head. "You wanna think like your techie friends, Lance? Eat up. The brain uses most of the body's energy." He shoves an un-cut slab of killari steak into his mouth and chews it noisily. "Notish how I'm alwaysh eating? It's becush I'm alwaysh thinking—*har har*."

✳ ✳ ✳ ✳ ✳

"So what's Fallsten making you do while you're suspended?" I ask Glacia after we get back from the fitness center that night.

"Observation." She drops backward onto my bed and heaves a long sigh. "Fifteen hours in Station Control and fifteen hours of void flight with Fallsten." She scoots to the back of the bed and pulls her knees up. "I deserve a plaque in the Belvish Embassy: *Quickest Suspension from Duty*."

I laugh, and she reaches for my hands and pulls me down beside her.

An hour later, my body is exhausted, but I can't fall asleep. My eyes keep opening. The time above the door reads *13:43*, only five minutes until today's midnight, because each day of the expedition is four minutes shorter than the last. Beside me, Glacia's arms are pulled to her chest, but I know she's awake. She keeps shifting. With my eyes adjusted to the darkness, and aided by the glow of the time over the door, I look down and see that her eyes are open, too. She blinks a few times, yawns, and continues staring straight ahead.

I turn so that I'm completely facing her. She looks at me. Her eyes reflect the blue glow, and a small smile flickers on her face.

"Everything okay?" I ask quietly.

"Mmhmm."

"Can't sleep?"

"Just thinking."

I move my arm under the pillow to lift her head a bit. "About what?"

She shrugs, but doesn't take her eyes off me. "I never said thank you."

"For what?"

"For coming back that night on Belvun, when you stopped me and—"

"*Glace.*"

Her eyes move up and down between mine, looking more and more anxious as she waits for me to say something.

"It's not about what I did for you. It's about what you did for me." I slip my fingers between hers and push our hands up between us. "Now it's about what we do for each other. So let's get to Daliona and have fun. Sound good?"

Glacia nestles her head closer to mine. "Mmhmm."

✳ ✳ ✳ ✳ ✳

"I'm visiting the *Drake* real quick," I tell Rand and Allison, who are each close to finishing their morning reports.

"You better make it quick, Lance. I'm starving."

I grab a visor off the back wall and strap it over my eyes. The out-of-place objects on the *Ember* glow light blue, like the outlines of Rand and Allison, but the *Drake* come through in solid color. There's Lon, sitting at an exact copy of the work panel I just left.

"Have a seat," he says as I walk toward him.

I pull my actual chair around and sit next to him, then slide my hand back across my visor to make the *Ember*'s background disappear. Lon shows me a feed of the *Drake*'s containment facility, where the Belvish samples for the Faustocine formula are stored. Large, pressurized containment units are evenly spaced throughout the room. RASP has access to the individual readings, allowing Lon to monitor them remotely.

"Each unit's sterile, has climate control, and is perfectly preserved," he explains, tapping icons over the units to view their individual data. "The Dalish need them kept uncontaminated. Take a look at these soil and root samples from Fleerard Forest: Belvish reports say the original formula from five years ago poisoned seventy percent of the forest's root network. Trees stopped getting water, seed germination ceased, and the soil went stale."

"You'd like this, Rand," I say, even though I can't see him.

"*I'd like what?*" His voice sounds a bit muffled from the visor around my head.

"These samples from Belvun."

A pause, then, *"Are you thick, Lance? Who the hell do you think collected some of those samples? Not the environmentalist. Oh no, never."*

He might as well have slapped me in the face.

"Oy. Done talking to the ghosts?" Lon asks, indifferent to the short exchange. I nod, and he continues. "Daliona's job is to synthesize a Faustocine formula that *won't* attack Belvun's ecosystems."

"They have to create a different strand for each ecosystem, right?"

"Each and every one. And chances are most won't work on the first try"—Lon goes back to the video feed of the containment facility—"so it's a good thing we packed lots and lots of samples, else we'd be flying back and forth for years."

"And you said the units are stable?"

"Yep, we keep regular checks so they don't degrade." He laughs nervously. *"That* would ruin someone's day."

Three of Lon's teammates walk into the chamber: Anna Barr, Baxter Krebs, and Heather Vale. Baxter's carrying a tray of sandwiches, a pack of seedberries and kerns, and four glasses of juice, one of which he hands to Lon. I notice, however, that he keeps the food all for himself.

He gives me a look when he sits down and waves his finger at me. "That's seriously weird. You're floating, in case you didn't notice."

None of them can see the chair I'm sitting on. But it's there, as real to me as theirs are to them.

"You know what's worse?" Anna asks, pointing at Lon. "When he goes on the *Doppler*, he doesn't shut up.

Yaps on and on about genetic mutations to some invisible girl while the rest of us are trying to be productive."

"I talk to *Chloe*, first of all, and we were discussing proper genetic coding. So many people pretend to know how that stuff works when they really don't. It was extremely enlight—"

But Anna's not listening anymore. She turns the other way and starts talking to Baxter as he eats.

"I'll shoot this over to you in a bit," Lon tells me, gesturing at the report he's compiling. "Need anything else?"

I think back to the list Rand helped me compile to keep track of items to include. As far as I remember, there's nothing else.

"Nope."

He scowls at the others, but they don't notice. "I'll try to get these three to work, then, since Bax is incapable of *managing the team*." He raises his voice and draws a look from the others. "See you tomorrow."

"See ya," I say, and with that, I deactivate my visor.

The *Drake*'s chamber vanishes, and when Rand sees I'm back, he stands up and points out the door.

"Oy, let's get food. *Now*."

✳   ✳   ✳   ✳   ✳

I pump my arms faster, push my legs harder. The distance on the treadmill flashes when I reach two miles. The last five days, I've stopped here because my legs couldn't handle the exertion under Daliona's simulated gravity. But today's different. I feel like I could go at least another quarter-mile, hopefully more.

Next to me, Glacia works her arms back and forth, sweat coating her forehead, strands of hair stuck to her eyes and cheeks. She always runs harder than me, but today she seems more determined than ever. I glance at her distance: *2.74 miles*. When she reaches three, she slows to a walk, practically choking on each heavy breath before guzzling down her water. I stop a minute later because my legs really *are* about to collapse.

2.21 miles, just short of my goal.

Glacia glances at my distance. "Not bad."

"I'm gonna puke."

"How do you think *I* feel?"

"Like you could go another mile."

She chokes under another gulp of water. "I want to run four miles in twenty minutes by the end of the expedition. If this was Undil's gravity, I'd have hit seven by now."

"You're insane."

"No, I'm *eccentric*." She offers me the last of her water as we leave the fitness center. "But you'll probably reach three by the end."

"Not a chance."

Glacia goes back to her room and I go to mine, where I take a shower and get ready for dinner. We meet my archives team in the food court for dinner and stack our plates full of meat, fruits, and kerns. Living and exercising in gravity that's just under twice as heavy as Undil's has gotten my body accustomed to eating a lot more, not to mention the fact that my metabolism is off the charts. When we flew to Belvun, eating was almost an inconvenience. On this expedition, we eat every couple hours. It's never a question of *when*, but *what* and *how much?* Poultry, beef, ham, fried vegetables, several varieties of kerns, salads, and more. I want to feel refreshed afterward, rather than craving a nap and then not being able to sleep at night.

That *never* ended well.

✳ ✳ ✳ ✳ ✳

"Expeditions to Daliona are some of the easiest," Orcher tells me when I meet him on the Bridge the next morning. This is the first time I've seen him since the second day. "It's the closest to Undil in travel time, and there are no asteroid fields. All the makings of a smooth trip."

"I thought Narviid was closer?"

"No, it's three days farther, but to the celestial southwest, rather than the north. And Belvun is to the celestial west." As he speaks, Orcher points his fingers in several different directions and chuckles. "We're scattered all over the place."

I nod and look out over the Bridge. Today Glacia is stuck shadowing one of the pilots. Orcher refrains from saying anything about what happened with her.

"Larson told me he spoke to you about the Barrier. He called it a learning experience."

"He did. Have you ever seen it?"

"Not with my own eyes, no. Only renderings in Larson's lab." Orcher looks down at Captain Fallsten. "Miranda once offered to take me out there, but I'm not keen on free-flight. I prefer being...*contained*. I take it you enjoyed it? The flying, I mean."

He doesn't *seem* angry. Not right now. If he is, he's hiding his disapproval.

"Yeah, it brought everything into perspective."

"Sometimes a bit *too much* perspective." Orcher shifts the elbow he's leaning on, and his eyes drift to the head of the Bridge, to the stars beyond. "We look out there and see how impossibly *big* the universe is. Not many people truly understand that we are such a small part of it. Nobody asks to come into existence, yet we're all here, and we're all just trying to see how far we can go. We aren't in a fair fight, so to speak. The universe doesn't care about us. It inherently destroys whatever it creates. We live in a universe governed by chaos, where true survival is impossible and we have however long it takes for our bodies to degrade to enjoy life." Orcher pauses and holds up a hand as he thinks. "I know it's not the most *eloquent* way of looking at it—"

"Not really," I agree quickly.

He strums his fingers on the desk. "Have you been checking in with the other teams?"

"Every morning."

"Good, good... Miranda hasn't complained about your reports, so you must be doing something right. Have you planned an itinerary for Daliona? You'll want a schedule for each team to follow, or else they could end up cataloguing some of the same locations."

He looks down at where Victoria is sitting by herself, reading through notes on a work panel.

"I'm sure Lieutenant Hofhen would be glad to help you get started, since she seems to be your go-to trip advisor."

We sip our coffees together, just like we always

used, *before* I got assigned to managing these teams. I don't come to the Bridge every morning like I used to. I miss starting my day like that, walking in here and watching the station come alive before I left to join Captain Blitner, where I'd be stuck in silence. Now it's the opposite... I have to come *here* to catch a break. At least Orcher hasn't forgotten how I like my coffee: it's not too dark, and not too white, but a nice shade of tan.

Just the way I like it.

Chapter Nineteen

AS THE EXPEDITION continues, life gets easier. The ache in my muscles eases, the days are nearly an hour shorter, and the archives teams are running smoothly. Olivarr installs new updates into RASP by night, so he's never around during the day unless we need him. And after finding ways to occupy herself during the lulls in her week-long suspension—mostly by reading *White Soils* several times over—Glacia is granted a modified work schedule.

Michael is hosting another conference today to discuss Daliona's role in the Belvun Recovery Treatise. I normally sit with Orcher during conferences, but Captain Fallsten took my seat, and Victoria is on his other side. Officer Remmit and Olivarr are sitting at the opposite end of the room, probably to be as far from Captain Fallsten as possible. I sit a quarter of the way around the table, and farther down, Glacia is with the other off-duty station pilots. Michael himself is standing in the center of the room, surrounded by projections of the documents he's composed during the expedition.

The conference runs much the same way it did on the trip to Belvun. Michael recites the premise, skips over the sections meant for the Belvish Officials, and delves into Daliona's objectives. People ask questions, Michael takes notes. Orcher repeats sections for clarification, Michael takes more notes, and the conference ends forty-five minutes later, much better than the two hours the first one lasted.

As people file out of the room, I see Officer Remmit waving for my attention and pointing at Olivarr.

"Just wanted to check in with you personally, Mr. Arman," Olivarr says. "What have we got? Three days left?"

"Two."

"Ah, yes. Two days. *Right.*" He twirls a finger in the air. "This space travel stuff is messing with my head."

"*That's not the space travel,*" Officer Remmit mutters to the side. Then his face perks up as Victoria walks by. "Vicky! I've been meaning to talk to you."

He hurries over to her and they disappear into the hall, leaving me alone with Olivarr.

"RASP is still functioning properly, I assume? No complications I should be aware of?"

"Nope, it's working fine."

"*Working fine...*" Olivarr chuckles. "Just wait until we really get it going, Mr. Arman. You'll have full access to the fleet's external video feeds soon, and after that we'll integrate the Life Support systems and upload the crew registry. I expect that will take another two weeks, three at the most"—he raises a finger—"*but no longer than that!* And no extra charge, either. Throw it in as a bonus for taking me along for the ride. This is my first time visiting another planet, Mr. Arman, and I fully intend to make the most of it. Dalish technology is *fascinating.* I've only had a taste of it in Orvad, but to finally *go* there..."

A boyish grin takes over his face, his eyes lighting up like Officer Remmit's did in the Observatory the other night. Is this what I looked like when I first stepped foot on Belvun? I don't remember much of those first few minutes except for Glacia slapping me after Belvun's air made me loopy.

"Belvun was...colorful," I tell him. "You had to dig to find anything brown."

"I believe that's what most people refer to as *dirt,* Mr. Arman." We laugh together, and then he says, "I hear Daliona has lots of green. Green leaves, green grass, green mountains, green moss... Perhaps even the rocks themselves are emeralds. Imagine that, Mr. Arman: emerald mountains behind emerald cities on emerald beaches."

"My girlfriend and I have this book called *48 Light-Years,* like an encyclopedia about all the planets. Have you heard about the animals?"

He claps his hands. "*Yes!* Sea creatures and birds and lizards and fish. Do you know how many times we've sent people to the bottom of the Undilaen Ocean? *Hundreds.* And they all come back empty handed. Not a speck of bacteria to speak of. But Daliona, Belvun, Yillos, Artaans..." Olivarr lets out a happy sigh. "The beauty of it. So much *life.* Isn't it amazing, to think that we can co-exist with other creatures? That there are whole other beings that eat and sleep and move as we do. Imagine if there was no life, that all these stars and rocks were floating through space, and nothing else was happening, anywhere. What point would there be in a universe that could not experience itself?"

He shakes his head, and when he speaks again, his voice is lower, barely a whisper, as if he's having trouble remembering the words. *"We aren't meant to sit and wait, but go where we are sent. Above all else, remember this: we cannot be content."*

I raise an eyebrow, intrigued. "What's that?"

"The last lines of the Gateway Manifesto. *'We Cannot Be Content'* was the so-called rally cry that drove our ancestors off Earth for good. The whole reason we're here, Mr. Arman, out among the stars."

✳ ✳ ✳ ✳ ✳

We drop out of FTL the next afternoon.

I'm in the Observatory, trying to catch a glimpse of the Barrier as the fleet decelerates into Daliona's solar system, but I can't even tell when we drop below light-speed. The only sign is that the star in front of us is suddenly a little bigger.

Daliona's sun.

As the evening progresses, the sun continues to grow. We're flying on an intercept course toward a pale blue dot that's separate from the starry background, and after dinner, Glacia and I use the StarPad to learn about the other planets in the solar system. The outermost planet is the massive blue, white, and purple gas giant, Vanoss. Dozens of moons orbit it, and, according to the description, the Dalish have built mining settlements on several of them. There are two more planets billions of miles across the solar system, Gheen and Loveila, but they're too distant to see with the naked eye.

By morning, we've made our flyby of Daliona's sun and are headed for the sharp blue crescent beyond. Two pricks of light hang near the planet: moons.

The activity in the Bridge swells as the crew prepares to enter orbit. Data orbs zip through the air, officers deactivate non-essential operations, and Captain Fallsten monitors the orbital trajectory.

Daliona fills our view now, its plainer features becoming more and more apparent. Clouds loom over the ocean, some twisting in massive swirls with holes in their centers. In other places, the teal-colored ocean is wide open, not a cloud in sight, nor any distinguishable islands. Sometimes I glimpse tiny blacks dot zooming across the face of the planet, and realize they're satellites.

It isn't long before Daliona's small continent slips over the horizon and shifts...shifts...shifts into view.

"That's Kiana, right?" I ask Orcher.

"It is," he says with a subtle nod. "Humans don't live there. Not a single person. After the Yillosian tundra and the Artish ranges, Kiana is the third-largest nature reserve in the galaxy. Think of it as an accelerated evolutionary breeding ground, of sorts. It hosts Daliona's most diverse range of species, many of which will be relocated as more planets become terraformed."

The southern regions of Kiana are greener, and in

some places, flatter than the darker, more mountainous ranges in the north. Misshapen lakes, twisted rivers, jagged fjords, and a light brown desert span the continent, which, according to Orcher, is only two thousand miles from one side to the other. Not even close to half of Daliona's diameter.

"Where are the islands?" I ask as Kiana slips below the western horizon and we drift into the shadow of night.

"Most are too small to see from high orbit." Orcher peers inside his empty coffee mug before saying, "You should be able to see some of the larger ones here in the dark, if the skies are clear."

Just then, Officer Remmit's voice comes over the Bridge's intercoms, stopping our conversation. He and Captain Fallsten relay information to each other as we descend into a lower orbit. Once stable, Captain Fallsten orders the pilots to cut the main thrusters. Now we're zipping around the dark side of the planet, where specks of white and blue light flicker among the clouds.

"Thunderstorms," Orcher says when I look to him for an answer. "Or...possibly a hurricane. Can't quite tell. You've never seen rain, have you?" I shake my head, curious. "It's not often a hurricane hits an island at full force. The Dalish have damping systems implemented around high-risk areas."

Daliona's eastern horizon shimmers with gold light as the sun reappears from behind it, and soon we're flying into the dawn. The two moons come into view again: the larger one is yellowish instead of white, while the smaller is light gray and closer to the planet.

"Lide and Docho. The Dalish are in the early stages

of settling Docho—the yellow one there. It won't be habitable within our lifetimes, that much is certain."

A new object sticks out high above Daliona. Captain Fallsten orders the pilots to engage the reverse thrusters—and I see why. A sort of cable hangs under the object, which, it turns out, is a conical spaceport that's several times larger than the *Ember*. The cable protruding from its base drops several hundred miles to the surface of Daliona, and I realize it's not a tether: it's a network of tubes. And as we lock into a synchronized orbit, I see large pods shooting up the tubes, which eventually disappear inside the spaceport.

Officer Remmit's voice echoes over the intercoms again. *"Good job, people. Now get your stomachs ready for the space elevator."*

"Looks like it's about that time."

Orcher stands and motions for me to follow. We make our way out of the Bridge and down to Floor 3. He goes inside the *Ember*'s docks, but I hang back to wait for Glacia, who shows up a few minutes later with Rand and Allison.

"Oy! Come *on*," Rand says the moment he sees me. "Failed us again, Lance. Thought you'd have saved our seats, but of course now we gotta fight the damn rush. Good going."

He walks past me without looking down and gets in line to board a transport, then looks back and waves us toward him, muttering something about *'no damn sense of urgency.'*

He was right about fighting for a seat. Usually Glacia and I sit in the front row of the passenger chamber, but now we're stuck in the middle, knocking into the knees of people who are just as eager to leave the *Ember*.

We drift through the silvery light and zoom into open space. Daliona's endless teal-blue ocean gleams below us—that is, somewhat to our left, though now the transport is rotating to line up with the docks opening in the side of the spaceport. The ocean shimmers, the water lighter near the planet's equator and darkening to the north and south. The blue is so much more vibrant than Undil's gray ocean. And where the space elevator descends into the atmosphere, there's a patch of four green islands: a large one with three smaller ones off its western shores.

Our transport enters the spaceport and lands in a designated slot. We exit and make our way to the central hub of the port, where a spiral ramp connects to the space elevator's pods. There are twenty in all, and each look like they can carry two hundred people.

Then I see my first Dalish man.

He opens a gate to let us board one of the pod. As we walk toward him, I can't help but stare—and grin: his face is rounder and flatter than any I've ever seen, and his skin is dark bronze, a bit lighter than Trey's. And...wow. He *has* to be two feet taller than me, and is more muscular than I could ever believe.

This guy is *huge*.

And it's not just him. It's *all* of the Dalish. They have the same relative build and features, and they're all dressed in blue, green, and white uniforms that have the Dalish flag embroidered on their shoulders. Some of the men are bald, others have slick, black hair. Many of the women have twisted braids, or hair that's cropped just under their ears. And I have to do a double-take when I skim over the officers working the control panels: no, I'm not seeing things. Their eyes are *glowing*. There's a blue ring around their pupils, and many of them are moving their hands through the air as if arranging things the rest of us can't see. One woman squeezes her earlobe, and the ring vanishes, leaving her eyes a normal color.

We board the pod and sit in the farthest empty seats, because the aisles are so narrow and there's no room to be picky.

"Attention, all passengers," a thick, slurred voice says over an intercom. *"Please properly fasten your restraints to ensure maximum safety."*

The announcement plays over again, and a projection shines on the window for us to watch: a Dalish officer demonstrating the proper way to secure our restraints. The harness slides down over my shoulders, pressing me firmly into the seat. Then there's a hiss, and the harness inflates, cushioning my chest and legs so I can't squirm around.

"Please place your arms on the armrests," the same slurred voice says, this time near my ear.

I do, and four cushioned clamps hold my arms down. Glacia and I look at each other with the same nervous expression. This is *not* what we expected. What did we just get ourselves into?

"I thought this would be relaxing."

We can move our heads, but that's it. Fortunately, I feel comfortable, or this would be a whole lot worse. My body doesn't care, though. Claustrophobia sets in, my body ignoring my every attempt not to panic. It's trapped. *I'm* trapped. Trapped, like I was when the car smashed into mine and killed Father. I couldn't speak. Couldn't call for help. I could see shadows moving in the light, but I could also smell—

"*Four,*" says the voice, "*three, two, one, descent.*"

The pod drops.

"*HOOOOOOOOLY—*"

The initial force of the drop shuts me up, fast. We plummet out from the bottom of the spaceport, straight toward Daliona's surface. I'm being shoved up into the cushioned restraints. My hands ball into fists. Someone in the pod is yelling with excitement, but it's definitely not Glacia. I dare to peek over at her and see that her face is as white as mine feels, her eyes wide and jaw clenched tight.

This is not going to end well.

For *either* of us.

Daliona grows larger by the second. All I can see from here are oceans and clouds, and what might be the hazy form of another island hundreds of miles to the west. The horizons are forever away, so much wider than Undil's and Belvun's, and seemingly without end because the ocean stretches in every direction. No mountains, no canyons, no forests or dunes. Just the teal aura of the planet and the star-filled darkness above.

Down...down...down. We're ten minutes into the drop, and it's impossible to see the curve of the planet anymore. My stomach feels weak, weaker than any of the trips to-and-from the *Ember*, and I'm already scared of throwing up.

"*Pressurizing.*"

Though the pod is still plummeting through the atmosphere, I can tell it's slowing down—if only slightly.

The force on my shoulders relieves, and I let my face relax again. A steady rush of air whips against the bottom of the pod, and only then do I notice how quiet it was until now.

We drop lower, toward the clouds—then we're level with them—then they're above us. A green mountain peaked by a black volcano rises two or three miles away. Lakes fill wide valleys and rivers flow to the island's shores. And just on the other side of the mountain, a city of glittering towers stretches for miles along the coast.

The Daliona Embassy.

Before I can see any more of it, the mountain ridge is too high to see over. We've slowed down a ton more, and we're almost level with a forest of odd-looking trees. Thick, stringy moss covers the twisted branches, and wide leaves sprouting from bright green stems sway heavily in the wind.

Darkness covers us again when the pod drops underground. Now we're inching downward, even slower than an elevator. A crease of light widens, revealing a docking chamber where more Dalish officers stand near the gates, waiting for the pod to lock down. At the control stations, I see video feeds of other pods dropping toward the island, and one by one, they all descend into the chamber.

There's a long hiss, and the restrains on my wrists and elbows unlatch. I push up the body harness and take shallow breaths as my head swims. I'm *freezing*. My chest is tight, my body is shaking. Even my hands and arms broke into a cold sweat. Allison hurries to retrieve medicine from a pouch outside the pod—but it's too late. I run after her—spot a giant arrow flashing at a line of tubes just outside the pod—and throw up in one.

I'm not alone. Glacia is right behind me, and several other Undilaen officers, too. For a long minute, all I hear are the strangled noises of people hunched over tubes, vomiting. Only when I take the medicine Allison hands me is my body is quick to normalize.

Still...*ugh*.

The four of us walk up the spiral ramp to the top of the chamber and follow the crowd of Undilaens to a station at the end of a long tunnel. The words *Outbound FAST Track* is etched above the gate, and when we walk inside, there are dozens of sleek white shuttles waiting to be boarded, with many of them bound for *Thorpe Plaza*. Every few seconds, one lifts onto a central track, people board, and then it zooms forward with almost no noise.

"Loooaaad up here!" a Dalish officer calls out. "There's plenty of room to fit all your scrawny arses!"

His voice booms over the commotion. And he has a point: the Dalish are so big compared to us that the seats were made for people their size. As a result, Glacia and I both fit into a single seat, and even though my feet barely touch the floor, Glacia's swing a full six inches off the ground.

"These people are *huge*," I say, looking out the window at the man waving people toward this shuttle. He towers above every Undilaen that passes him.

Rand slings one arm over his seat. "Didn't you do your homework, Lance? It's the oxygen. More oxygen in the atmosphere makes everything bigger. Bugs, lizards, fish, people. *Everything*. I've been here twice, I would know."

"That explains why everyone acted so high on Bel-vun," Glacia says, nudging me. "It was the air."

Rand nods. "Belvun like to boast that they have the happiest population anywhere. You notice how no one seems too bothered by the fact that their planet is burning up? They're so high, they don't freak out until the bodies start dropping."

I think about it for a second—and yes, that explains *a lot.*

The shuttle loads into the central tube, and then—gone. We zoom forward in a black tunnel underneath the mountain, but not even five seconds after we leave the station, the lights in the shuttle go dark and the tunnel opens into a massive cave, at which point the shuttle slows down to let us look around. Pointed columns of rock hang off the ceiling, and similar columns stick out of the water. The cave is glowing pale blue, though, and the light is coming from weird, bubbly strings made up of...goo?

I nudge Glacia's arm. "Reminds me of Glowbull."

Rand hears me and twists back around. "See, it's funny you should say that, Lance. Those bubble-looking things are Lumis Leeches. They feed off the bacteria in this lake, and their excrement is bioluminescent." He points up at the glowing strings. "In other words, *that's their poop.* How do you think Glowbull is made?"

My face drops. "Are you—"

"I have no reason to lie, Lance. Look it up." He shrugs matter-of-factly. "*The more you know.*"

"That's...disgusting."

Rand shrugs. "Hey, gotta come from somewhere."

The shuttle moves through the cave, revealing sloping walls, more of the massive rocky pillars, and other dark holes that might be more caves. At the other end, we accelerate up an incline and burst aboveground, speeding through a tube that's standing high above a wide expanse of pastures and vineyards.

"Thorpe Island, home of the Dalish Embassy." Rand counts off on his fingers. "You've got parties, fireworks, reef dives, sailing, stunning vistas, hover-cross courses, gravity runs, cyclo facilities—"

"Gravity runs?" Glacia asks, her eyes fixing on his with a flare of curiosity.

"You heard me, Haverns. Here I thought a Hologis junkie like you would've known about the runs. But no doubt in my mind you'll love them." Rand jerks his thumb sideways at me. "Lance on the other hand? *Not a chance.* He doesn't strike me as a guy who would like streaking through tunnels at breakneck speeds on nothing but a maglev sled. That's not gonna stop me from taking him out, though. We'll make a man out of you yet, Lance."

Now Glacia's eyes *really* flare with excitement. I can almost sense the adrenaline pumping through her. Rand's right, though: that's sounds downright terrifying.

He arches an eyebrow at Glace. "Got your attention? Most of the islands have a track or two, and a few hotels have family-friendly courses. They give you a medal for every track you conquer, proof that you've mastered one of the most extreme sports in the galaxy. I've got fourteen, all engraved with my motto. I'm gonna try to conquer Tahani this time around, then I'll test my luck at some hover-cross." He adjusts his arms so he's leaning toward Glacia more. "How about it, Haverns? Want a few medals of your own?"

Glacia's grin is as wild as it was when she won the Hologis tournament last year, and that's all the answer Rand needs.

"Thought so. Once of these days I'll let you meet the other members of the Undilaen Gravity Run Racing Club."

"What's your motto?" Glacia asks when her initial excitement subsides a bit.

"*No fear*. I say it at the top of every run, right before I shoot off. The key to facing your fears is figuring out how to forget them. Sure, it's scary as hell when you're about to shoot off, but once you're flying down the track, adrenaline takes over."

"Have you ever crashed?"

"Better question is *how many times?* More than I count, Haverns." He rubs the side of his left arm. "Broke this twice in two weeks my first time visiting Daliona. I got friendly with a couple walls. A bit *too* friendly."

Out the window, elongated glass domes take over the pastures, and beyond those, the southern sector of the Embassy. Within seconds, towers surround us. White and silver and glassy, some with large spheres hanging off their sides, some twisting, some arranged in odd shapes: arches and half-cubes and narrow terraces. And when we round a turn between two towers, something swoops around a tower and straight over the shuttle. More of them appear from the spot where the first came from—except now that I see them...

"Are those people *flying?*"

Glacia presses her face to the window, too. The people are one block away, heading the same direction as us, dipping and diving between towers and skywalks.

Allison snorts. "Firsties…gotta love them."

Rand smirks in agreement. "Cyclo suits, Lance. That Talbot guy built one from scratch last time we came here. Saw it myself. Relies on some complicated physics your know-it-all techie friend would be able to explain in excruciating detail. But I'm not so sure you could handle those, not with what I've seen so far."

I try to ignore his last comment and just watch the people fly. They look so *free*. Able to go anywhere and everywhere, masters of the sky. And whether or not I can handle it, I want to try it.

Our shuttle curves to the right and crosses a gap in the city. A clear river runs below us, bending gently back and forth through the city on its way to the ocean.

"Rainbow River," Rand says. "Might not look like much now, but just wait until nighttime. Lights up the whole city."

At long last, the shuttle slows and slides into a slot that another shuttle just shot away from, bound for a new destination. We get off and follow the crowd along a skywalk that overlooks a decorated courtyard set in the heart of the city. Two narrow towers stand at the other end of it, joined at the base and splitting apart higher up. They're the tallest peaks in the city, and the Dalish flag waves at the top of each: a blue background, a green circle, and a white web surrounded by nine white dots.

When we're back on solid ground, Rand heaves a breath of fresh air. "Take it all in."

Trees with bristly trunks and sharp-looking leaves

are spaced every twenty feet along the plaza's paths. The paths themselves are dark blue, contrasted by rows of white sand along their edges. Bright green grass fills the plaza's emptier areas. There's even a sunk-in amphitheater, at the center of which is a fountain where several jets of water spray fifty feet into the air. Further along the walkways, water gurgles down a series of steps into a hole and erupts as a geyser every thirty seconds or so. A garden is spread across a whole section of the plaza, with various flowers Glacia and I saw in *48 Light-Years*. Some have pink petals striped with green veins, and there are some bulbous, light blue flowers with dark spots on them, and even some white and red flowers with yellow stems. The aromas remind me of Belvun, these sweet alien scents that my brain scrambles to process.

I flex my fingers and swing my arms and take a deep breath. My head tingles, not in a dizzying way like on Belvun, but in an energized way, a surge of clarity. I see everything, hear everything, *feel* everything. I want to run. I want to run *a lot*. My mind races. My muscles are restless. I'm more awake, more alive than I've ever been in my entire life.

It's not just me. Glacia springs with every step, her fingers twitching. Even Rand and Allison seem jumpy, and they've both been to Daliona before.

Then I look at the upper heights of the towers surrounding the plaza. Each of them has to be at least as tall as the Crown back on Undil, which makes Thorpe Tower close to twice that height. People in cyclo suits fly overhead, and FAST tracks two wind through the towers, suspended fifty, one hundred, and even up to two hundred yards high. And now that I'm looking, I notice the city isn't divided into blocks. In fact, I don't see any roads at all, just walkways that branch into more walkways. Plazas and courtyards flush with life fill almost every other gap in the city.

As we pass them, Dalish officers look down and greet us with wide, white smiles. For being such large people, they're all friendly in a quiet way. And their eyes are strikingly vibrant: bright green, watery blue, yellow hazel, foggy gray... Most people on Undil have brown or blue, with hazel sprinkled in, like Glacia's family. I've never actually *seen* someone with green eyes until now.

A blue-and-white craft descends onto a landing pad near Thorpe Tower, and a handful of Dalish officials exit it. Orcher is at the head of our own procession, and he salutes a man who is well over a foot and a half taller than himself, and whose hand is so large that it would completely cover Orcher's.

"Good to see you again, Dillon," Orcher says. "Been too long."

"Ah, a good deal too long, David," the massive Dalish man greets, his voice deep and slightly slurry. "Things here have been wonderful as ever. Wonderful, as, *ever*. Though I daresay the weather could be a tad more cooperative. We've already warded off three hurricanes this season. *Thuh-ree!* We're growing weary of the rain." He extends his giant hands skyward. "You managed quite a day for your arrival. Hardly a cloud in the sky. Could not have planned it better myself." He fixes on someone's face, and his eyes light up. "Ah, Remmy! You faring well?"

"I can't say I'm not, Mr. President!"

"Elon's down in the Aelic Archipelago, else he'd have seen you in. He's developing the High Orbit Shuttle Track you two discussed all those years ago. Project is a go, of course. He sends his wishes, and he promises to get in touch during your stay. Pay him a visit, perhaps! See how your idea turned out."

Officer Remmit claps his hands. "Excellent news, Mr. President. And I'll bring along my new friend here, Olivarr Cresson from Orvad. Bit of a brainiac. He's installing some toys for our new archives."

President Okana salutes Olivarr then turns his large eyes on Orcher, puzzled. "How did you manage to convince Blitner to—"

"I'm afraid Lawrence passed away during our stay on Belvun, Dillon. Conner's son heads the program now. He's been developing it for a few months now."

"My condolences." The President rests his large hand over his heart and bows his head. Then he gives Orcher another curious look, and his large eyes scan the crowd. "But you say Conner's son is with us? Where?"

"Arman. Yes. I'm not sure where—ah, over there."

Orcher spots me from a few yards away and motions for me to come up front. Up close, the President is two feet taller than me, and his arms *have* to be twice as thick as my neck. It's absolutely intimidating, standing next to him.

"Dillon Okana," he introduces. "You should be very proud of yourself, for all you are doing, and for all your father did. Your name holds a rich legacy, Mr. Lance."

"Thank you, sir."

He puts a large hand on the side of my arm, keeping his grip gentle, because he's well aware that he could crush me in an instant. But his dark bronze skin is rubbery and warm, and a sweet, powdery fragrance surrounds him. Wow. Do *all* the Dalish smell this good?

He looks over to where I was standing and gives Glacia, Allison, and Rand all a warm smile. Then he turns the other way and looks down the line of Undilaens. Unsure of what to do, I stay standing next to Orcher, even though I'm itching to go back to Glacia and the others, away from the center of attention.

President Okana glances skyward again, this time at the FAST station, where another shuttle just pulled in and let off more Undilaen officers.

"This plaza will be filled to the brim if we linger any longer, and I see no reason to keep you. But join us tonight! Our host celebrations shall be held on the Abadima Pier at eight o'clock. There shall be plenty of food, so bring your good cheer and starving stomachs!"

Chapter Twenty

"IT'S ONE GIANT party, Lance," Rand says when I ask what tonight's celebrations will be like. "If you don't remember it tomorrow, you did something right."

We leave Thorpe Plaza and turn down a wider sidewalk. There are elevators to FAST stations on the corner of every block, and just by looking around, I can see how deeply the tracks are integrated into the city. Some are stacked on top of each other, branching off in different directions and connecting every plaza in sight. I watch one enter a station, unload, load, and zoom away again in a matter of seconds, only to have another slide in and repeat the process before shooting off to another part of the city. This is nothing like the Undil Embassy's maglev trains. These are sleek and short and quick, whereas ours are long and tubular and stay in stations for a minute or more. And when Rand tells us that FAST stands for *Frictionless Aerodynamic Shuttle Transportation*, I can't help but think of Olivarr: he's probably in love with that acronym.

More people in cyclo suits soar high above us, as well as several slim crafts that I've seen anchored to the sides of towers. As far as I can tell, there are no ground-based vehicles. The ground is for walking, for taking time to see the sights and smell the flowers—which Glacia does every time we pass a garden patch. She runs up and sticks her nose into a flower, and comes away with spots of pale yellow dust on her cheeks and nose.

A few blocks in, we reach the edge of the Rainbow River. The canal is one hundred yards across, with narrow footbridges spanning it here and there. People lying flat on single-rider water crafts skim the surface, and six people in cyclo suits are diving in and out of the water, swooping over bridges and around boats until they vanish around a bend.

Upstream, where the river breaks west toward the mountain range, the city opens up into a plaza so huge it might as well be a small jungle. Groves of trees surround grassy parks and vibrant gardens. At least two dozen towers make up this sector of the Embassy, several of them architectural works of art so elaborate that it boggles my mind how they stand on their own...until Rand tells us the Dalish use cyclo technology to build their cities. Apparently that's how the space elevator stands on its own, too, instead of being thousands of miles tall and fixed in geosynchronous orbit like the primitive elevators were.

One tower coils around itself in a double spiral. Another arches over the river and has balconies and glass pools sticking off its sides. One structure doesn't even *look* like it should be building: it's made up of two-dozen spheres scattered within a tangle of crisscrossing beams. The tower nearest us glitters blue and white and green, and it's rotating in place, ever shifting its shape.

"Reservation Plaza," Rand announces as we walk in the shadow of the rotating tower. "You've got your hotels, your shopping centers, your fancy restaurants. Oh, I should tell you: shims mean nothing on Daliona. Everything's free. The Dalish take pride in their hospitality. They have a sort of work-order system in place to keep it that way." He points at the hotel that's arching over the canal. "If you want the best view of the Rainbow River, check out the Kulean. My personal favorite is the Mauka, though, and the Malihini offers various vacation packages if you want to immerse yourself in the Dalish experience but don't have time to travel—which doesn't apply to us, *obviously*."

He tells us a little about each of the hotels in Reservation Plaza, but in the end, the Kulean wins me and Glacia over. The lobby itself is more elegant than any hotel Belvun had to offer—and to be honest, I've never been inside any hotels in the Undil Embassy, though I can't imagine they're all that special. Undil isn't exactly known for trying to impress foreigners.

In the Kulean's lobby, clear tubes filled with water run floor-to-ceiling in. Bubbles float up them, fading from green to yellow, blue to purple, red to pink. Twin chandeliers decorated with cut glass hang between two staircases, and a red and gold carpet covers the floor. Water slips down textured walls into rows of bright-colored flowers, the scents of which sweeten the air. Above it all, sunlight pours through slotted windows, bathing everything in a natural glow that blends with the light chimes and drumbeats in the lobby's ambient music.

The attendant smiles as we approach. Her dark eyes slant inward, and small yellow flowers adorn the black braids wrapped around her head. She's several inches taller than Rand, and he's the tallest of our group.

"Hello!" she says. "Have you reserved your rooms with us?"

"We're just in from Undil," Rand says, glancing farther down the counter at another Undilaen who's making reservations.

"We welcome you! Have you stayed with us before?"

"I have, but we've got two firsties to Daliona here." He grabs my shoulder and pulls me up to the counter. "This one here took my professional advice. I said you guys have the best view of the river."

The attendant smiles, her perfect teeth bright white against her dark face. "You didn't tell them wrong, sir."

Rand waves his ID between his fingers. "You got three rooms open?"

"I'm not staying," Allison says, taking a step back. "I'm going to the Pakalo."

"*The Pakalo?*" Rand raises an eyebrow and sizes her up, unimpressed. "Whatever. Suit yourself."

The Dalish girl checks the system as Allison turns to leave. "We have two Rainbow Suites available. Rainbow Suites have complimentary—"

"Yeah, yeah, those," Rand interrupts. "Get them quick, before that guy does." He jerks his thumb at the other Undilaen officer down the counter. "Don't need anybody taking my room, not after Lance here couldn't even save me a good seat on our transport."

The attendant smiles again, her eyes staying fixed on the panel as she registers our IDs.

"Enjoy your stay!" she says when she hands the back with our room information.

The ride to Floor 39 is quick. Glacia and I find our room and walk inside—then stop three steps in. The right wall curves up and over in a quarter-circle, and the window overlooking the river is trimmed in colorful stained glass. Two large orbs that turn out to be hollow seats with cushioned insides face the window, and float above disks set in the floor. Out the window, the river flows through the center of the Embassy four hundred feet below. If I look far enough to the right, I can just see the green humps of the mountain and the black-capped volcano at Thorpe Island's southernmost point. Behind those, the space elevator rises into the sky, a dark line that vanishes into the atmosphere.

A short hall leads to the bedroom, where there's a large bed decorated with a canopy of blue and green drapes.

Then we walk into the kitchen, which has complimentary fruit—and *geez* there's a lot of it. Fruit on the counter, fruit on the table, fruit on small stands or in baskets. Fruits I've never seen, like a wrinkled yellow melon three times the size of my fist, dozens of squishy orange berries with tiny black seeds, a crunchy green fruit with brown spots on its peel, and so many others.

Fruit for *days*.

✳ ✳ ✳ ✳ ✳

Dusk is falling when Glacia and I catch a northbound shuttle to Abadima Pier. The shuttle shoots through the city and descends into the pier's station, where we join the crowds of people making their way to the celebrations.

The city basks in the evening's waning glow, and clouds cover the sun before it sinks behind the mountain, giving way to a few stars gleaming in the darkening sky. The walkways light up with dazzling lights. White arrows slide under our feet, guiding us to the pier—not that it's hard to miss. The host celebration is exactly what Rand said it'd be: one big party. Music shudders the air, pillars of fire roar into the night. Lanterns float up...up...up into the sky, and I even see a man juggling five torches blazing with fire.

People are gathered around a stage in the center of the pier, cheering on a group of Dalish cycloists holding metal rods. As they swing the rods around, electricity arcs between them, flickering, zapping, exploding in sparks. They arrange themselves in patterns, and sometimes plumes of fog engulf them, flashing with every burst of electricity.

Restaurants line the edges of the pier, and Dalish waiters are carrying all sorts of entrées: trays of seasoned crustaceans, slabs of peppered fish, fat brown tentacles smeared in globs of glaze, seaweed salads, and even *more* fruit.

Glacia and I go with the flow of the crowds, because trying to push through would be useless. And despite being a foot shorter or two shorter than the Dalish, the Undilaens mingle without hesitation. I have to wonder what it's like for Glacia, though, being around all these people who are well over two feet taller than her.

We stop at the other end of the pier, where Rand said he and Allison would meet us. A fresh, cool breeze blows against our faces. Dark waves ripple toward the shore, and there, on the horizon, two bright crescents rise over the water: Daliona's moons. The pockmarked, pale yellow one is larger than the smooth gray one. And in their light, I notice black silhouettes jutting up out of the ocean several miles away. There are hundreds—no, *thousands* of the objects. But I don't see an island, nothing that—

"Arman."

Glacia taps my shoulder and points into the sky behind us, taking my attention off the objects. I look up and see a thick white line rising into the dark blue sky: the space elevator. Even though it's behind the mountain, the sheer size of it still dwarfs the Embassy. And at the top of the line, a few hundred miles above Daliona, the spaceport looks like an explosion of white light, brighter than any of the visible stars and planets. Only the moons outshine it...*barely*.

Glacia twitches, then tucks her hands under her arms. "I'm getting chills."

I put my arm around her waist and kiss the top of her head. We lean back on the rail and look at the space elevator, the city, the people on the pier. To the south, Thorpe Tower stands tall above the Embassy. The twin peaks glow bright blue and green, and spotlights illuminate the flags waving atop the spires.

"Oy! Ignoring my calls now, Lance? About time we found you."

We turn around and see Rand and Allison walking

toward us. Rand is wearing a shirt that fades from tan to black, with the black shaped like silhouettes of the palm trees. Allison, on the other hand, braided her hair and dyed several strips of it blonde. A lazy smile is slapped on her face, her eyes kind of just...staring around. And she smells smoky, almost, but with a sweet odor.

"I...am so...*starving.*" She speaks slowly, not looking at anyone in particular. She bends over the railing, keeping her neck arched to look at the moons. "Wow...it's so...*pretty.*"

"Kalupa," Rand tells me and Glacia, not bothering to keep his voice down. "It's this oil stuff they let you bathe in in the Pakalo's spas. Makes your brain go soft."

If Allison heard him, she doesn't seem to care. She sighs happily and looks over her shoulder at us...her eyes still distant. "You should've seen the way she was eyeing up the fondue a minute ago. Weirded me out."

Allison looks over her shoulder, her eyes freakishly wide, and whispers, "*Chooocolaaate.*"

He pulls Allison away from the rail. She doesn't put up a fight as he guides her back toward the crowds, looking for a place to eat. Most restaurants are serving buffets for the night, so we end up gorging ourselves in trays of Leeka Trout, Sea Sander, coral shellfish, barkal, Blue Merka, and all sorts of other fish and crustaceans I've never seen served on Undil. There's a wide selection of fruits: squishy red ones, lumpy blue ones, clumps small green berries with black pits, and even some that were grown in the ground. *The ground!* When I go to get a drink, I grimace in disgust at the Glowbull and instead pour a glass of palm leaf water, which is too bitter for my liking, so I try some kern milk instead. It's ice cold and sweet and goes well with the fish.

A half-hour later, I stare down at my stack of empty plates, wishing my stomach could hold more. Glacia's eyes wistfully flick back to the buffet. Not even Rand touches anything else, despite his gloating about needing to eat a lot to keep in peak mental shape. Allison seems unfazed by the fact that we keep slipping our leftovers onto her plate whenever her eyes wander to a laser show that started up in place of the electricity-shooting cycloists. She eats...and eats...and eats. Rand and I somehow manage to hold back from laughing, but Glacia *loses* it. When Allison stabs into the last crustacean we snuck onto her plate, Glacia snorts into her drink and sprays it all over her face.

As the night goes on, we walk around the pier some more. It isn't long before a drunken Dalish man lumbers up to us, a sloppy grin on his face. *"Tiny Undilites!"* he bellows, and then he proceeds to toss coils of woven flowers around our necks. Allison freaks out—then calms down when she realizes the flowers aren't strangling her to death. She gives the drunken Dalish man an embarrassed smile, but he just lumbers off in search of more Undilaens.

We spend the next hour watching the laser shows and cyclo aerobics and Dalish dancers dressed in nothing but skirts and headdresses of flowers and ferns. At one point, dozens of people in glowing cyclo suits race around the entire pier, swooping over people's heads, ducking under the pier, and landing on rooftops and railings. The Dalish cheer them on, and I hear people shouting their names and taking pictures of them as they fly in formations.

'Heyyy, Kayo!' I hear someone shout as a woman flies by upside down, giving high-fives to anyone tall enough to reach her.

'Marnakov, over here! Over here!' another says.

'Blessenka! Score a few for me against those Scars tomorrow!'

These people must be celebrities of some sort. Athletes, I'm guessing, now that I see how groups of them are wearing cyclos colored in the same designs.

They create shapes in midair, their suits flashing colors and even pulsing with the music. A few of them even plunge into the waves, and we watch their glowing suit lights zoom through the water, then burst above the surface again. That's when I remember the objects I saw sticking out of the water.

"I have a question," I ask, looking up at Rand.

"All ears, Lance," he says, still watching the athletes, clapping whenever they do something impressive.

"What are those things out there?" I point where I saw the silhouettes, though the moons are too far above the horizon to see the poles anymore. "Like, in the—"

"You mean the gyrobines? Thorpe Island's first and last line of defense against hurricanes. They absorb energy from the ocean and surface winds, and account for about eighty percent of the Embassy's power grid. By the time hurricanes reach Thorpe, they're just thunderstorms, otherwise the city would get flattened in minutes. Imagine two hundred foot waves slamming the city, and winds like you wouldn't believe. Not exactly an ideal vacation."

At long last, the music cuts out and the crowds settle down—but the night isn't over. A voice echoes around the pier: President Okana's.

"Let us welcome our Undilaen visitors. Everyone, everyone!"

On cue, the Dalish applaud us. A few even go around shaking hands.

"You may be aware that our sister planet, Belvun, is still in need of our assistance," President Okana keeps saying. "The Undilaens have worked tirelessly to bring Belvun closer to a full recovery, and we have a part to play. Let this mark the beginning of the end of their efforts. Daliona opens her arms to you, our guests. Welcome!"

The pier rumbles with applause again, and everyone turns around to watch tiny lights whizz high into the sky—then explode in sizzling flares of color, their booms reverberating against the city. Some fireworks twirl, some change colors, some snap, crackle, and pop. Smoke drifts over the pier, engulfing us in a sweet, charred scent.

The celebration lasts long past midnight, but Glacia and I don't stay to the end. We beat the crowds and return to the hotel, and back in our room, we look out over the Rainbow River. It's living up to its name, and *wow*: the bridges and walkways along the canal glow soft pink, green, blue, and yellow, and the water itself is lit so brilliantly that the river flows like a fluid aurora. Even the towers along its banks are bathed in the light, so that the whole riverfront is a myriad of color.

"If I could stay here forever," Glacia whispers. "Just right here...looking at this."

I nod in agreement, thinking of Mother and my sisters. If only they could be here. If they could leave the dust of Undil and see the things Father saw, the things I'm seeing now... I want them to know how big life can be. Not just our world, but the other worlds as well.

Has anyone ever visited Undil and *actually* fallen in love with it? Will Undil ever look like Belvun or Daliona? Will it ever *feel* like these planets?

Glacia hugs my chest and stares up at me. Our eyes close, our lips touch. We're still wearing the flowery coils the drunken Dalish man threw around our necks, and the fragrant scents engulf us. In a blur, I feel the bed against my arms. Glacia's hair fans under us, and her hands are on my shoulders. Up my neck. Down my chest. Glacia's head sinks into the pillow. My hands sink into the blankets.

And as we kiss, I can taste the flowers' nectar.

Chapter
Twenty-One

THE NEXT MORNING, we start cataloguing the Embassy. Right now I'm working with Lon and Rand, but Rand is going to leave later because he has to attend a planetary sciences convention. We have a list of facilities and towers we need to link to RASP's database that will let us map the city's network flow and archive data for future access.

The three of us catch a shuttle to the Embassy's southern sector, and even before we get off, I can see how this end of the city is much more clustered than the northern: the plazas are few and far between and less appealing. Gone are the sprawling gardens and fountains and walkways. Multiple towers line each block, packed so tightly together that they almost remind me of Orvad. Even the relaxed atmosphere has been replaced by restlessness. I don't see people flying in cyclo suits, and the FAST stations are loaded to the brim.

When we squeeze out of the station, Rand looks over

his shoulder, mumbles something I can't hear, and then cranes back his neck to orient himself.

"All right, should be this way."

We move fairly quickly, but it's a pain when people cut us off without looking twice. Down here, people just want to get to work. No time for talk. And it doesn't help that we're so much shorter than everyone. It's like they don't even see us.

The towers open into what must be the sector's largest open space, two blocks wide by two blocks long. But it's not empty, I was just looking too high above the crowd. A large glass dome sits the center of the would-be plaza. Hexagonal windows make up its exterior, and a steel gate encloses its front. Giant exhaust vents circle the top of the dome, all of them connected to tubes running along the inside of the glass.

"The Cordula Biodome," Rand says in admiration. "Beautiful, huh? It's the oldest remaining biodome in the galaxy."

Biodome. The word resonates in my head until I remember where I heard it before: when Victoria and I visited Orvad, she showed me Sanctuary Plaza, Undil's first Ryginese settlement—three biodomes. And after he was discharged from Shield, Rand became a planetary scientist for Horizon. *That's* why he's so in awe: it's the very foundation of his work.

"Cordula was constructed in the middle of the twenty-third century, more than a hundred years before humans left Earth for good." He points up at the vents as we walk closer to the gate. "Daliona's atmosphere was toxic to us back then, so we had both habitats and automated biodomes pumping gases round-the-clock to dilute the atmosphere. Took a few centuries, but that's terraformation at its finest...until eco-hacking became a thing and screwed Belvun over."

A long hiss follows us as the outer gate closes and then the inner gate opens. A wide path goes into a jungle of trees and ferns and flowers. These are nothing like Belvun's forests and fields, though. Vines wrap around tree trunks, and leaves larger than my entire body hang from stems as thick as my wrist. Rubbery fungi grow around knots in trees, and stuff that looks like twisted string hangs off the branches of others. Everything is soaked from the humidity. Even *I'm* already sweating.

The sound of running water mingles with the chirps and buzzes of insects and birds. Animals live here, *real* animals, just like on Belvun.

The path takes us to a group of long shelters surrounding a three-sided monument. This is where some of Daliona's first settlers lived. Where humanity broke free of Earth, of the early worlds in that solar system, and found a fresh home.

Standing next to the monument, I see words that are laser-etched into each face:

WE CANNOT BE CONTENT

Below this, two more lines are etched in smaller print:

From the Gateway Manifesto
of Benedict Drake, Wander Enterprises

"Olivarr told me about this," I say, remembering the

talk he and I had after Michael's conference.

Rand's mouth goes flat. "*Of course* he did. Techies worship this guy. Drake owned the space tech company that developed the first FTL drives. According to the books, Earth was dying and Drake came out a full-fledged hero...the *savior of humanity*." He rolls his eyes. "Yeah. Whatever. If you dig a little deeper, you figure out nobody *needed* saving. It was all staged." Rand chews his lip and shakes his head at the monument. "See, history remembers people for the good things they did, or the evil, but never both. It's skewed to support the people who made it out alive." He claps both me and Lon on the shoulders. "Why don't you two read that manifesto when you get a chance? *Really* take a look at it. I'm not convinced this Drake guy was out to protect everyone. Seemed to me was leaving some people behind. But that wouldn't sound so heroic, would it?"

"And yet, we're here," Lon says, shrugging his shoulders and giving Rand a sharp glance, clearly put-off.

"*And yet...we're here*," Rand repeats in a low voice, not glancing back.

But I feel the same way as Lon: here we are, walking in the footsteps of the first interstellar settlers, and Rand thinks it was all was rigged.

In his own words... Yeah. *Whatever.*

Rand waves us on toward one of the shelters. As Lon and I follow him, I think about all the books and notes and documents I've read over the years, especially those I saw when I worked with Captain Blitner. Zacharias Slater's name always popped up because he was the founder of the Modern Embassy program, but Benedict Drake isn't familiar to me at all. Of course, if he lived two thousand years ago, he wouldn't be relevant any-more, and *definitely* not to Undil.

The shelters are all one-story tall and divided into four rooms each. One is filled with work panels that monitor conditions both inside and outside the bio-dome. Instead of showing Daliona's current conditions, though, they're set up to show the environments as they were two thousand years ago. Oxygen dominated the atmosphere at levels so toxic it would kill a human in a matter of hours. Biodomes all around Daliona diluted the air, pumping gases like nitrogen and argon while the planet's ecosystems served as natural filters and adapted over time.

The next panel displays the current atmospheric composition, and the change from then to now is star-tling: even though there's about half as much oxygen as there was in the twenty-third century, there's still twice as much oxygen as nitrogen, with only trace amounts of other gases.

"What's Undil's atmosphere like?" I ask.

"Nitro—"

"*Mostly nitrogen*," Rand says loudly, cutting Lon off. "Take these numbers and flip them and that's pretty much what we've got." He wafts the air toward his face. "You can feel the difference, can't you? Like there's a gallon of coffee running through your veins? Oxygen is a miracle drug to us lesser life forms, Lance. Don't forget that."

"Tell that to the Dalish life spans," Lon says. "They live...what? Fifty, sixty years?"

"Somewhere around there. The Dalish have the best tech, but the shortest lives. Kind of a shitty trade-off, but they've made do."

Elsewhere in the living chambers are interfaces that were used to control drones and explore other islands, as well as blueprints for the construction of the space elevator, which apparently gets torn down and rebuilt every century.

One panel plays the video journal of a man who was part of the original landing crew, who came here before Benedict Drake was even born. He describes the bio-dome's ventilation system and lists several of the creatures that, to this day, reside within it.

It turns out most of the original crews recorded video journals, because when we walk into the other rooms, more faces talk to us about plans for future expeditions, or how they want to balance the biodome's ecosystems with the outside world.

As I watch another video log from a man who constantly traveled between Daliona's surface and an orbiting cruiser, I can't help but feel the eeriness of this place. Some of humanity's earliest interstellar explorers lived here. They slept in these bunks, ate in these kitchens, maintained the jungle ecosystem to preserve the life they brought with them. Generation after generation after generation worked to make this world possible for humans to inhabit, without ever reaping the rewards. All they knew—all they *hoped*—was that their efforts would pay off.

And they did.

"*I work so you may have a future,*" I whisper as I move away from the recording.

Rand looks down at me. "What's that from?"

"It's my father's motto."

"Nice. I like it. We all have our mottos, don't we?"

At first I nod in agreement. But then I think about it...and realize no, *I* don't have one, no motto to stamp my name to, no message I'm trying to spread.

That needs to change.

*　*　*　*　*

After we leave Cordula, Rand leaves for his conference, something about discussing potential adverse effects that another failed Faustocine formula would create on Belvun. He even compiled a log of environmental issues that could result if these efforts fail, some of which he claims are irreversible.

So Lon and I get to cataloging. We go to five of the Embassy's biotech facilities, meet with the directors, and link the networks to RASP. We're only cleared to collect basic data from projects in-development and future outlooks, but Lon says we'll be able to extrapolate more information when we analyze it for reports. We also generate interior maps of the main facilities for RASP to convert.

We eat lunch at a rooftop café along the southern waterfront, right beside the wall that separates the main Embassy from the military compounds and marina. The towers on either side of us rise about a hundred feet higher than ours, but we have an open view of the ocean: small boats cruise in the deeper waters, leaving white trails as they speed along the surface, and closer to shore, people glide on parachutes. Farther up the coast, I spot a few people gliding around in cyclo suits, diving into the waves and racing around what looks like a floating midair course that's designed specifically for cyclos. I watch them, wishing...

"Your lunches, sirs."

A waitress is standing beside our table, holding a platter of seafood. She's taller than both of us, but is more on the petite side—for a Dalish girl. She's wearing a dark blue skirt with yellow stripes, flowers are coiled around her wrists and forehead, and her dark bronze skin gleams in the overhead sun.

"Freshly caught and broiled today," she says and she sets the platter in the center of our table. "Should either of ya need anything, gimme a shout."

She walks away, and Lon starts drooling over his plate. "This...looks...*delicious.*"

A sauce that's speckled with green flakes drips over his slab of fish. My own plate is stacked with meaty crustaceans: barkals. The orange shells have black and gray spots, and a clump of seaweed is stuffed between each pincer.

"Oy—look." Lon spins my plate around so I'm face-to-face with the largest barkal. "He's smiling at ya."

"Glace would be *so* jealous."

"Don't worry. This'll be our secret."

I crack the shell: chunks of white meat spills out, which I dip in gooey red sauce. It stings my tongue at first, but the aftertaste is sweet, like spiced honey.

"They should've served *this* at our banquet," Lon says between bites of his fish.

I bob my head as I swallow the last of the meat and crack open a second shell. This food is so much better than anything Belvun or Undil serve, even at the fanciest restaurants. Fresh out of the ocean, not shipped across the galaxy. In my experience, fish meat usually tastes bland, but this...this has *all* the natural flavor.

"I heard we can go fishing on some of the islands," Lon continues. "They take you out over the water and you reel in your own catch. Can't get much fresher than that."

I chuckle as I swallow another bite. "Nope."

When we finish, Lon folds his hands behind his head and lets the afternoon sun warm his face. After a while, he opens his eyes and stares at something above me—I'm guessing the space elevator—and smiles.

"Been a while since I've been this happy, man."

"Tell me about it."

"Really, though. Before my dad transferred to Holistead, I grew up hearing about Daliona every day. Most Orvadian tech has Dalish influence." He spreads his arms. "Now I get to see it all for myself. *And*"—he holds his finger out in front of him—"I've got Chloe."

I give Lon an amused look. "Careful, you're starting to sound like Jeremy."

He laughs. "I don't even care, man. I'm in love with life. What more could I ask for?"

We both get quiet and stare past each other: me at the endless ocean, and Lon at the space elevator. The waitress comes by again to take our empty plates, but we sit there a while longer.

"What's Glacia up to?"

"Training. She has a weird schedule."

"Gotcha." Lon leans sideways in his seat. "You hear about those gravity runs?" I nod in response. "Think you're gonna have a go at one?"

I shrug. "Maybe. You?"

"Maybe. I heard all the courses are different. The one island, uh…" He snaps his fingers a few times. "Tahani, I think. People say Tahani's the one to conquer."

I remember Rand saying yesterday how he wanted to go down the Tahani track during this expedition. If Lon's heard about it already, it must be a pretty big deal.

Lon pushes back from the table. "Okay… How about we finish what we came here for?"

With one last glance at the ocean, we leave the rooftop restaurant and ride an elevator all the way back down. I take out my holotab and check the towers we still need to link today. After this week, we'll travel around Daliona in our station teams to catalogue other key locations.

"Where to now?" Lon asks.

I point to the left. "Koilun Tower. Looks about a block away."

We meet the director of Koilun and run a scan that gets relayed to orbit, where RASP logs the tower's internal systems and synchronizes a link. The same goes for the Breegan facility, the Karthal laboratories, and a number of other notable towers in this sector. The plan is that by the time we leave for Undil again, RASP will have the galaxy's most comprehensive planetary catalogue of Daliona—the first of many on our list.

✳   ✳   ✳   ✳   ✳

The sun is falling behind the mountain when we finish for the day. Lon and I catch a shuttle back to the northern sector, back to the plazas and gardens and towers of all different designs. I feel so free on this side of the city, because the south was so cluttered and busy. Whenever I look up, the evening glow sets the backdrop for the skyscrapers, splashes of orange and yellow between the tops of towers. The streets light up white and gold, and the Dalish moons rise earlier than they did yesterday. I still can't get over them, those two balls of light in the sky with visible pockmarks, craters, and ridges.

Lon and I go our separate ways: he to his hotel, me to Abadima Pier, where I'm meeting Glacia. I stand at the rail and listen to the rush of the waves against the shore. It clears my mind. I feel my surroundings, the cool metal railing under my wrists, the laughter behind me, the salty breeze. For a moment, I can pretend that I've lived here all my life. I've *always* listened to this ocean, *always* stared at those moons, *always* seen the space elevator trace its way through my sky.

A pair of arms wraps around my waist, and Glacia's cheek presses into my back. When I turn around, she stares up at me, her eyes reflecting the moonlight, and then she spins us around so that she's leaning backward against the railing and I'm in front of her, facing the ocean. My hands slide down to her waist, and hers cling to my arms as we kiss. She closes her eyes, and her fingers tighten around my arms, then relax. When I look at her again, her mouth is pulled up in a little smile. The wind flutters her hair around, but neither of us makes a move to settle it.

"Hey, Glace."

"Mmhmm?"

I curl a strand of hair behind her ear, but don't say

anything else.

Another smile flutters over her lips. "What?"

"I just like saying your name."

She breathes out a laugh and leans into my chest. Our fingers slip together. I kiss the top of her head and close my eyes. We sway together, the breeze gently pushing us to-and-fro.

"We should go out on the water sometime," Glacia says quietly.

"We will."

"Also I want to swim in the ocean and see the reefs. Oh, and remember those lizards we were looking at a while ago?"

I open my eyes and laugh. "You mean the ugly ones?"

"Yeah. I want to see them, too."

"We'll do it all."

I touch my forehead to hers. Neither of us speaks for a long time. My mind keeps flashing back to last night. I can't get it out of my head. I just want her. And I want to feel her weight on top of me again. Feel her hair fall around us. Feel the warmth we—

"You know what I saw today?"

"Hmm?"

She lifts her head to look at me. "A cyclo training arena. It's inside the flight center."

"Did you—?"

"Nope." She bumps her nose on mine. "But I *did* get us a training reservation for Thursday at nine."

"Seriously?"

"Hey, I had to make up for that mess we called your birthday *somehow*, didn't I?"

Glacia suddenly ducks under my arm and pulls me

away from the railing. We walk down the pier all the way to the edge of the city.

"The Molters have special flight courses around the islands." She points at several rows of lights lining the water at the other end of the Embassy. "We start at the Aulina Marina and fly north, then go around the mountain and the other islands in the archipelago. I flew over the Embassy's gravity run, too."

"Does it look cool?"

"Couldn't tell. It's a giant tube that just dives straight into the ocean. It was on...Laka Island, I think." She hugs my arm, her eyes full of excitement. "Arman, it's so pretty from up there. You can see straight to the bottom of the bay, and the clouds were sliding down the back of the mountain this morning, and there's a big lake that feeds into the Rainbow River."

She lowers her hand to mine as we turn toward Reservation Plaza, making our way back to the Kulean Hotel. People crowd the gardens and walkways. Lanterns hang in the trees and music blasts through the air from a party in one of the recreation areas.

Glacia gives me a look. "We should crash it."

I scoff—and she gives me a look. *She's serious.*

"Um, I..." But my voice fails.

Anxiety floods my brain.

Nope, nope, nope.

She nudges my arm. "Let's do it, mister. Come on."

My hand tightens around hers. It's so tempting. It's just a party. Nobody would know who we are.

But I don't want to.

Yes, I want to.

I *really* don't want to.

I really *want to.*

Breathe in.

Breathe out.

No fear, Rand would say.

So I take a step toward the music. Glacia suppresses a laugh, because she knows I'm freaking out. So she drags me harder. I resist even more. She grabs both my hands and eggs me on.

I'm squinting with embarrassment, grinding my teeth. We're almost there. The music is louder. I can hear glasses chinking, people laughing. Then we're in the middle of it all, and there's food, drinks, torches, flowers, floating lanterns, glowing hats, flashing glasses, and—wait.

Robots?

Robots are floating around cleaning up messes, serving drinks, blasting music, and even projecting holograms of sporting events from around the planet. A large crowd is gathered around one in particular, their cheers rising and falling with the action and excited voices of the commentators.

Glacia and I find a spot where we can watch, and see two team names on the sides of the display: *Scartones* and *Cove Runners*. Two teams of players in cyclo suits—half of them bright green, the other half blue and yellow—fly through a stadium, throwing a red ball to each other and trying to score in floating goal posts. One man gets clobbered from the side by a smaller black ball and loses the one he was carrying. A woman dives after it, then hurls it to her teammate in the other direction. Loud groans resound from the crowd gathered around the hologram. *"Nooooo!"* one man shouts, pulling at his hair. *"Blessenka! Poss eet to Blessenka!"*

On another projection, I see six racers riding thin hover bikes on tracks that climb several hundred feet in the air. The names *Makoza, Affoerijøn, Blijørckel, Chovan, Mirahami*, and *Tarskov* are lined up along the bottom, switching places as the racers pass or fall behind each other.

My nerves ease the longer we stay. It's like half the people staying in Reservation Plaza came out for this: Dalish, Undilaens, Yillosians... People from most of the planets are here, it seems, though I don't see any Narvidians. I listen to their accents, their words. Notice every difference in their heights, faces, skin, hair, and eyes. This is where I want to be. I'm free. The whole world is within my reach.

And the night is still young.

Chapter
Twenty-Two

BY THE TIME Thursday evening rolls around, we're on track to finish cataloguing the Embassy on Friday. Orcher's happy, I'm happy, and the entire archives team is eager to get out of the city and start cataloguing more of the planet.

Right now I'm riding a shuttle to the Embassy's military sector, which lies southeast of the Cordula Biodome. When the shuttle rounds the final curve, I see Aulina Marina, the Embassy's naval base and military support sector. It's several times larger than the marina in Orvad, and the ships and submersibles outnumber Orvad's twenty-to-one, at least.

Glacia is waiting for me in the shuttle station. She's been training at the flight center all day, and it's obvious how anxious she is to finally fly in a cyclo suit. We're both tense when we hold hands. I can't wait to do this, but I'm nervous: what if I can't fly?

The flight center and massive aircraft hangars take

up a huge section of the marina. Inside the complex, we walk down a corridor that has a long glass window, on the other side of which are dozens of Dalish aircrafts: sleek, triangular crafts with streamlined thrusters under their wings and low-ceilinged cockpits.

"Dynasty jets," Glacia says when she sees me looking at them. She puts one hand on the window and looks at one. "Fast as hell. I get to fly one in two weeks."

The corridor branches into two smaller hallways, one labeled *Pilot Center*, and the other *Cyclo Center*. We follow the second and enter a small chamber filled with Undilaen and Dalish officers, all of which seem to be military personnel. Next to them, I can't help but feel like I'm the least-qualified person in the room.

Me, the archivist.

How exciting.

A Dalish military Official salutes us when we enter the chamber. "Aye, you have ID?" he asks in a thick, slurry accent. We show him, and then, "Good. You know how to size up?"

"Yes," Glacia says before I can say the opposite.

He gestures at two free panels. "Aye. Go on."

Glacia shows me how to register by syncing my ID to the system and getting a biometric scan. The machine measures my body's dimensions, takes my weight, mass, and density, checks my vitals, and records my current brain activity. All the data displays on the panel for me to see, even though I'm not sure what it means.

When it's done determining how much space I take up in the universe, the panel beeps and *Cyclo Unit 18* flashes at the bottom of the screen.

The next room has storage units built into the walls,

each containing a cyclo suit. The empty units glow red, and the available ones glow green. I open Unit 18 and grab the cyclo suit that's inside. I watch other people put their suits on, then mimic them, shimmying my arms into the vest portion and latching the clasps. The suit compresses on my body, legs and all. Not *too* tight, but still firm. The retractable helmet attaches at the neck and seals shut, and the dozens of squishy nodes that line the inside tingle my skull. The cyclo's torso has an array of components, most notably an energy disk on the center of the back.

Someone taps the side of their head to retract the helmet, so I make the same motion: the front visor folds down, leaving only the nodes touching my scalp.

"Own-uh-ly activate your suits inside the arena," the Dalish Official announces, looking right at me. "I would advise you leave the amateurs some ex-tuh-ra space. Don't want any accidents."

He opens the gate to a short corridor, which leads right into the cyclo arena.

It's *massive.*

I saw the facility from the train, but only briefly. Now that I'm here, the sheer size of the place blows me away. Not even the Cordula Biodome can compare. Most of the arena is open space, but obstacles are scattered around, too: platforms that hover in midair, ropes that dangle from bars, clusters of tall columns, and, at the very top, a spiral ramp that connects to a glass dome in the ceiling. An observation deck, I'm guessing. But nothing can be reached from the ground. The lowest platforms are twenty yards up.

To use this arena, you *have* to fly.

"Activate your suits. You recreational users may go your own way. The combat sector is open. First timers are required to stay with me."

Again, he looks right at *me*.

The other officers jump into the air, and within seconds, they're dispersed all around the arena.

The Official steps in front of us. "I am Cap-ih-ten Aray," he says in his thick accent, tapping the name on his chest. "Your names?"

"Glacia Haverns and Arman Lance," Glacia says.

"And you are a pilot?"

She nods.

"And you?" he asks me.

"No."

"What do you do?"

I have to clear my throat because it tightened up. "I'm the Undil Embassy's Head Archivist."

I can't help but notice the way his mouth twitches.

"Aye, then. Let's see what you've got."

We tap our headsets in the same place he does. A light sensation overcomes my body, almost like I'm weightless, and the nodes touching my scalp tingle again. But when I try to shift balance onto my right foot...

I can't.

Because I'm not touching the floor.

I'm floating an inch off the ground, and so is Glacia. She kicks her feet, and her body wobbles in place, but stays upright. Then she really starts to kick and swing her arms, apparently trying to flip over, or move, but nothing works. I try it, too, and it feels like an elastic force is tugging against my torso.

Captain Aray waves a large finger at us. "Ah-ha. First mee-stake. The mind controls the cyclo. Aye, it will take getting used to, but once you have mastered control, you will have one hell of a good time." He rises higher into the air, does a slow flip, and then stabilizes in front of us again. "The best users exercise clarity, focus, and discipline. Daily meditation helps achieve this balance, for a calm mind is a strong mind. Try and *feel* your movements. Let them come to you. You will know the sensation when you feel it. Go, go."

Feel a sensation? Uh...*go up.*

Nothing.

I imagine myself rising, picture myself looking down from high in the air, but to no avail. I don't move an inch.

Feel. What does he mean, *feel*? How can I feel something in my brain? How do I calm my brain down to feel something in it? What am I trying to—

The nodes.

The tingling.

I stop my train of thought and focus on the sensation of the nodes. Feel where that light sensation tickles my skull. I focus on the front of my head—

And drift forward.

The movement shakes my focus and I wobble to a stop, which feels strangely like the resistance of a repelling magnet. Now I'm hovering six feet off the ground. Glacia looks up at me and frowns. She hasn't figured it out yet, and I can't help but grin. I've found another thing I'm better at than her.

Ha.

I test it again, this time feeling the sensation at the

back of my head. My body accelerates backward, and then up. Down. To the left. To the right. Down again, to the floor. When my feet touch the ground, all the weight returns to my body, and I can feel a subtle vibration on my back, a sort of constant whirring.

Glacia still hasn't figured out how to move without flailing her limbs. She's over there screwing her face up, mouth thin and forehead furrowed. She brushes hair out of the way, then looks at me and frowns even more, almost accusingly. I just smirk and drift around, practicing how to control the movement while keeping my body upright. It's difficult. At one point, I manage to flip heels-over-head, but because of the cyclo suit, I *feel* like I'm oriented upright and it's the room that's upside-down.

Geez, that's weird.

After several failed tries, Captain Aray has to tell Glacia exactly what to do, step-by-step, until she gets it. I've already dared myself to float twenty, thirty, forty feet in the air, and I'm learning how to stabilize myself. As long as I move my muscles right, my body works with me.

"Become aware of your body," Captain Aray tells us after Glacia's had a few minutes to practice. "Master the placement of your limbs. You may not feel their weight, but you can sense their position."

He recites his instructions without emotion. He's so calm, and his voice matches his movements. Steady, smooth, controlled.

"Aye, be aware of two things at all times: your body and your environment. You must understand that you are not flying. You are moving through space relative to other objects."

"*Falling with style*," I mutter to Glacia, who's struggling to stay upright a few feet away. She hears me, but is too focused to respond.

Captain Aray points at a platform fifty yards above us. "Land on that. Go, go."

I relax my body, feel the sensation in my brain, and rise higher than ever before in a perfectly straight line...so straight, in fact, that I have to use my fingertips to shuffle backward when I hit the underside of the platform. I grip the edge and effortlessly climb up, at which point all the weight returns to my body.

I walk to the edge and stare down at Glacia. She's slowly rising, wobbly though she is. She starts going faster—then abruptly stops, adjusts her path, and speeds up, over and over until she reaches the platform and climbs up. I have to look away before I laugh: she looks like she's going to be sick.

"Aye, good enough," the Captain says when he lands softly between us. He extends his hand over the edge. "Now jump off the side."

He says it so casually, it takes me a second to realize he's asking us to fall almost two hundred feet to the ground. When I look down, anxious adrenaline rushes through my body. I'm safe. I know I am because I have the cyclo suit. But my body doesn't care. It's a death sentence if I screw up. But I *want* to jump.

Do it.

Shake out my limbs.

Come on. You got this.

Then I remember what Rand always says.

"*No fear.*"

And then I jump.

Wind rushes in my ears.

Tears sting my eyes.

My stomach flips, chills run over my body.

Falling...falling—*now.*

I focus on the nodes at the top of my head. Squeeze my eyes shut, grit my teeth. Focus, focus. Open my eyes...and my fall slows until I'm hanging in midair like three feet above the ground.

Woah.

When I look up, I see another body drop off the platform—and thirty feet down, Glacia starts slowing down.

Really? Already?

Please.

It takes her a full ten seconds to reach the ground. Somehow, her hair is messed up, but she's fine otherwise.

"That was so scary."

"You? Scared?"

"Shut up."

Captain Aray dives toward us, clapping slowly. "Aye, I have seen more daring jumps from that height, but you aren't dead. Try it again. Maintain stability. Be *confident.* Confidence improves stability."

So we fly up to the platform and jump again, and again, and again, until we have some sort of basic control over our falls.

Before each jump, I whisper *'no fear.'* It works just like Rand said. My jumps are getting smoother, and I get so confident that I start diving headfirst off the edge. I have about three seconds to slow myself before hitting the ground, but I don't even notice the time passing. The pulse of exhilaration, the spike of adrenaline that floods me when I look down, the drag of air when I pull out of the fall... I'm not trapped. Not anymore. Never again. I can go anywhere, do anything. And by the end of our training session, I'm not afraid of the fall.

Not one bit.

Chapter Twenty-Three

ORCHER PUSHES A cup of coffee toward me. "How does this compare to Bersivo?"

I sip at it, and my eyes widen. It's strong—*very* strong—and has a rich, spicy cinnamon flavor. It's creamy, too, with a layer of tan froth floating on top.

"That's...wow." I take another sip, but I'm not sure if I like it. The taste would be fine if it wasn't so strong.

"Didn't add a drop of cream," Orcher admits. "Kloia Brew tends to blend best undiluted."

I take another cautious sip before setting the mug down to cool. "Hmm."

We're sitting in Orcher's temporary office in Thorpe Tower, which is decorated, unsurprisingly, with shimmering murals of Undil's landscapes. Mesas, red rocks, blustery dunes, and dried-up river gorges. Seeing these glimpses of home when I'm so far away... It almost looks like a decent place. And I'm sure anyone who hasn't lived on Undil their whole life would see these and think they're some of the most beautiful sights in the galaxy.

The room itself is designed for people our size, too, which is a relief after having to sit in the huge Dalish-sized chairs for most of the week. Orcher and I can see eye-to-eye, both feet on the ground, with no craned necks or sore backs.

"So, to business." Orcher opens a file on his desk panel and scrolls down. "According to your schedule, your teams should have finished cataloguing the Embassy...yesterday?"

"Yeah."

"And did you?"

"Yeah," I repeat. "It's all linked to RASP."

"Excellent." He rubs his chin as he reads more of the report. "What's your plan moving forward?"

"Dividing into teams."

"I take it each has its own itinerary?"

"Yeah. We leave in the morning."

"What's your first destination?"

I rack my brain, trying to remember the map I looked at. The islands weren't that big, and there were only two of them.

"The...Bechi Archipelago, I think."

He chuckles and flicks his eyes up at me. "Well I hope you've done your homework. Bechi lies to the far north. This isn't Undil, or Belvun, for that matter. Bechi lies in an arctic region."

"Arctic?"

He grins. "Did you pack a coat?"

I shake my head. Of course I don't have a coat.

"Well, I advise you get one there, then. The Dalish arctic isn't as brutal as the Yillosian tundra, but you can still expect to see some ice and snow. The weather can be fickle around those parts."

My eyes get wide, and Orcher laughs again. Then he goes back to looking through the report, nodding here and there.

"How are the other team leaders doing? Everybody keeping up with their work?"

I don't answer immediately. I haven't checked in with anyone but Lon since we finished cataloguing, and he's not even a team leader. I received the final reports, compiled them, and sent them to Orcher. But I keep forgetting to check in with the leaders.

"They're doing great."

I nod for emphasis despite clenching my jaw nervously. Hopefully he didn't notice the waver in my voice.

"Good to hear." He swipes the panel again. "Have you spoken with Olivarr recently? How close is he to completing RASP's next installation?"

I can't lie this time. "I haven't talked to him."

"You'll need to do that before you go to Bechi. Preferably, contact him after you leave this meeting, and write a report for me, to be delivered by this evening. No later." He gives the panel one last tap, then leans back and folds his arms. "Can you do that for me?"

"Yes, sir."

"Excellent. Thank you, Arman. You're doing a great job." He smiles, his gray-blue eyes creasing at the edges. "I have nothing further to discuss. Enjoy your trip."

✳ ✳ ✳ ✳ ✳

Olivarr messages me back at lunch, and we arrange to speak in the evening. So after dinner, Glacia leaves to hang out with Kerin—her hall mate on the *Ember*—and I go back to the hotel room to wait for the call.

"That's a right fancy place you got there, Mr. Arman," the hologram of Olivarr says when I show around him the rooms. "Could you get me closer to the window? I've heard so many stories about this river..."

It's not dark enough for the Rainbow River to shine, but he's impressed all the same.

"I'll tell you what, Mr. Arman, I can't wait to do a bit of exploring myself. The moment we finish this installation, I'll be out there, I promise you." He pushes his glasses up his small nose. "It's maddening, really. I lost a whole night's sleep thinking about what I *did* see while I was down there that first day. Ended up sleeping on a couch in the Observatory. I couldn't get enough of the view."

Olivarr's hands move out of sight when he returns to working on a panel in the *Ember*'s archives chamber.

"You say Orcher wants to see a status report? All right. I'll send over—up?—down?—a list of upgrades my boys installed this week with details of each. You'll be pleased to know we are *finally* developing a station-wide network for the Augmented Conference Interface. It's not my priority, it's Dany's, but you can expect she'll have it finished by the time we're waving goodbye to Daliona. Need to reroute the projector arrays and code the network to the ACI, and we should be up and running." He sits back and clasps his hands behind his head. "Two...one...*now*."

Right as he says '*now*,' my holotab buzzes and a notification appears in the bottom corner of the projection: Olivarr's status report.

"Got it," I say.

"Great."

"Who're you talking to?"

Olivarr glances over his shoulder. "None of your business."

A second later, Officer Remmit's disembodied head floats into the projection. The rest of his body appears when he crouches beside Olivarr.

"I don't know what lies he's been telling you, but don't listen to a word he says. He's been slacking all week, Arman. Likes to go off and play with the StarPad."

"You would too, if you'd never seen the stars your whole life."

"Excuses."

Olivarr rubs his forehead. "I'll have the installation completed this week, Mr. Arman. Good luck with your cataloguing."

"If you see Vicky, tell her hi for me," Officer Remmit requests, squeezing in closer beside Olivarr. "She has no idea how dull it is babysitt—"

The link cuts out before Officer Remmit can finish.

Laughing to myself, I go sit in the green spherical chair floating by the window and read through Olivarr's report, then start typing my official one for Orcher. It takes longer than usual—mostly because as night settles, the Rainbow River begins to glow and I catch myself staring at it multiple times. Fireworks explode along the oceanfront, and a small boat drifts down the river. The people on it jump into the water and swim around the boat, and then they're too far down river to see anymore.

I wish... I wish...

A while later, Glacia gets back from hanging out with Kerin and walks straight to the window...except I don't think she realizes I'm here, sitting inside the orb right behind her.

So I test my theory.

"*Boo.*"

Glacia twitches and twists around, then lets out a half-laugh, half-sigh. "*Whyyyyy?*" She pouts her lips. "I hate you, mister."

"No you don't."

"Yes I do."

"Mmmmm...*nope.*"

She squeezes in next to me and waits until I send the report to Orcher, then wriggles her hand into mine.

"Excited for tomorrow?" I ask. She's joining us for the first week of cataloguing, and after that, will meet us as her schedule allows.

"*Mmhmm.*" She kisses my cheek, then shimmies her way out of the lounger and walks around to the bed to put on her night clothes. "You?"

I watch her reflection in the window as she moves behind me. "Orcher says it's cold. We need coats or something."

"Yup, I know it is."

I stick my head out of the lounger and give her a sideways look. "Were you planning to tell me?"

Glacia sits crossed-legged on the bed and strokes a brush through her hair as she waits for me to join her. "You didn't think to look it up?"

"I mean, I looked at a map. I kind of just assumed it

would be warm."

"Why, because it's an island?"

"Well..." I just shrug. Because *yeah.*

Glacia rolls her eyes. "Wow. This isn't Undil, mister."

"Orcher said the same thing."

✳ ✳ ✳ ✳ ✳

In the morning, we meet the rest of the *Ember*'s archives team at the Embassy's gravity pod docks, just west of the city's northern sector. We're the last to arrive, thanks to me, of course. Rand is the only one who looks impatient—that is, until he sees Glacia. Then his eyes light up and he starts going on about how she'll love the gravity pods...and how he expects me to throw up at the other end.

Great. *Thanks.*

Allison seems more sober than the last time I saw her, thankfully, and Trey is fiddling with some gadget I've never seen before. Must be Dalish tech. Kile is sitting on a bench several yards away, reading a book I don't recognize. He didn't look up at our arrival, and doesn't move until Rand shouts, "*Oy, Arlington! The* real world *hasn't got all day.*" Even so, Kile takes his time closing the book, leaning forward slowly, his eyes darting back-and-forth as he speed reads to the end of the page—then snaps it shut right before Rand can knock it out of his hands.

A Dalish woman directs us to the docking area, which is farther inside the travel complex. I'm expecting to walk up a ramp and see rows of transports docked on platforms like Undil and Belvun have, but instead we go inside a chamber that has rows upon rows of massive pods...not unlike the pods we rode down the space elevator. They all go to islands around Daliona, like Baku Bala, Lastal, Marakuri, Trenchura, Kyokai, Janajon, Westin, and dozens more. Some I recognize from organizing the itineraries, others are completely foreign to me.

Obviously.

The pods are suspended between warped maglev tracks that drop into giant tubes. I stare at them in utter disbelief.

This, this...

No.

Not again.

Haven't we all thrown up enough? Do they seriously expect us—me—*Kile*—to ride *this?* I look over at him, and yup: his eyes are even wider than mine.

Rand notices, too. "Don't piss yourself, Arlington. It's just an elevator...*through the planet.*"

Glacia gawks at him. "*Through?*"

"You heard me, Haverns. Hell of a lot faster than flying, and a lot more feasible that constructing FAST tracks all over the place. Anywhere we go, it's fifty-three minutes from Point A to Point B."

Her jaw drops even more. "*Fifty-three?*"

Rand winks at her. "No shorter path than a straight line. *Basic geometry.*"

"It's not *actually* a straight line, though," Trey says, scratching behind his ear and looking at the ground. "There's a curve that accounts for the rotation—"

"Shut it, Talbot. You sound like a techie."

"But I *am* a techie."

The six of us sit in a row on the pod's upper deck and secure ourselves to the seats. We're hanging off large hinges, and Rand and Glacia rock in place as we wait for more people to board, but only three more do.

Bechi must not be a popular tourist destination.

"*Prepare for drop,*" the slurred voice says over the intercoms.

The floor retracts, leaving us suspended a few feet above the seats on the lower tier. My body tenses. I already don't like this. Being trapped. At least the space elevator had windows. Here, there are no sweeping views of the ocean or the sky or the islands, just a gray wall and whatever lies outside it. Which, I'm guessing isn't—

"*Dropping.*"

And I'm weightless.

Blood pounds in my ears. My stomach squeezes, cold chills race down my spine. I clench my fists, my knuckles pressed flat on the armrest.

We fall...fall...fall, but the pod is dead silent. I focus on breathing. On swallowing. On keeping nausea at bay. But in the corner of my eye, I notice a light: a Dalish man is watching a video on the wall. The woman with him is reading, and another man is...sleeping? How can he possibly be *sleeping?* It's like the fall doesn't faze them, while I'm up here wishing I hadn't eaten breakfast.

The seconds turn to minutes, and the minutes drag on...and on...and on. Five minutes, then ten, then fifteen. The entire time, my brain is a dizzy mess. And my body...my body...

Something is changing, though it's subtle at first. The tug of gravity is...shifting. I don't feel like I'm *sitting* anymore, but reclining slightly. When we hit the twenty-six minute mark, I feel like I'm lying on my back. Gravity is definitely not where it should be.

That's when the seats rotate. We're no longer parallel with the length of the pod, but perpendicular. The longer we fall, the more the seats rotate. And forty minutes in, we're all upside-down from how we began: the people who were sitting below us are now sitting *above* us.

The pod is slowing down. I wasn't sure at first, but now I know it is. Weight is returning to my limbs, the dragging force pulls on me as we rush up—not down. My body gets heavier...and heavier, and a weird sensation prickles my skin.

Nope, that's just nausea.

My stomach flips. My head swims. I close my eyes to regulate my breathing.

Stay in control.

It's almost over...

...right?

Yes. Another five minutes, then a shudder, and then no movement at all. The floor slides back under us and our restraints release. Kile and I don't move, afraid of what our bodies might do if we stand. Even Glacia's face is pale. Rand, Allison, and Trey, on the other hand, have no problems at all.

"It's not *that* bad," Rand says as he tries to pull Kile from the seat.

"*Says the guy...who's...done this...a dozen times.*"

"Way more than a dozen, Arlington. And this is the fastest way—"

"Emphasis on the *fastest*," Glacia mutters.

Rand shrugs matter-of-factly. "If you come up with a better way to travel four thousand miles in under an hour, I'm sure the Dalish would love to hear about it."

"Yeah, teleports."

"Teleports tend to destroy things...*violently*," Rand says. He lowers his voice. "I saw a test my last time here: the whole lab had to be evacuated."

Another few seconds go by, and then Rand's entire tone changes. He raises his voice—which only worsens my dizziness.

"Oy! Get up, you sissies. *Get. Up*. If you're gonna puke, *you're gonna puke*. So come on."

Glacia dares herself to stand first. Then me. Then Kile. My knees quiver, but other than that, the rest of my body has settled.

But not Kile's.

His face contorts, and he lurches over the disposal tube connected to his seat. Rand mutters something I can't hear and walks away.

"If you've got coats in your trunks, now's the time to get them," he says when we're all gathered again. He takes us over to where people are unloading our trunks for delivery to the hotel we're staying at. "You guys *did* bring coats, right? Our tender Undilaen skin hates the cold."

Glacia, Kile, and I all shake our heads in response. Rand points at the weather conditions displayed on a panel near the facility's exit. The only number that makes any sense to me is the temperature: -6 *F*.

Rand grabs a thick coat from his trunk and waves it in Glacia's face. "Bet you really want one of these now, don't ya?"

Glacia makes a grab for the coat, but Rand flips it out of reach and puts it on. Allison and Trey find theirs and put them on, too, leaving me, Glacia, and Kile with only our uniforms.

I have a feeling they won't be enough.

I dread every step we take toward the exit, knowing what lies on the other side. Undil's low temperatures hang around ninety degrees, and the highs get into the hundred-forties. *This*, however... Negative six...

We walk through the inner gate, and when it closes behind us, the outer one opens.

Cold air blasts in.

Air that's *beyond* cold.

Bumps swarm my skin, and my muscles contract. It's like jumping into the Hania River all over again, except this is way, *way* colder. Even my *eyes* hurt.

Glacia, Kile, and I hug our bodies, shivering like crazy, but Rand, Allison, and Trey all seem perfectly warm inside their coats. More than once, Rand glances back at us, a smirk on his face. And the harder I clench my jaw, the harder my teeth chatter. I've lost all feeling in my chin and mouth. My nose is running—and freezing in my nostrils. I wipe it on the edge of my sleeve, then stuff my hands under my armpits to keep them warm, but there's nothing I can do to protect my face from the battering wind.

No.

I do *not* like being cold.

Not one bit.

We reach the edge of the town and walk inside the first building. Coats hang on one of the walls, and boots, gloves, pullover hats, and other cold-weather clothing are scattered on shelves and tables.

Rand unseals his coat and says, "They could've put this at the other end of town and *really* made you suffer, but lucky for you, the Dalish have big hearts."

There are different kinds of coats and jackets that serve different purposes, but I'm not looking for anything fancy. I just want to be warm. I end up picking out a thick blue coat and matching gloves, then head to the front of the store. The Dalish man here doesn't look like the people in the Embassy. He's shorter and has light skin, narrow, gray eyes, and a thin nose. He scans my coat, but when I hand him my ID to pay, he arches his brow, looking like he might laugh.

"First time on Daliona, my sir? No payment here."

I step aside, and Rand walks up next to me. "*Told ya,*" he mutters in my ear.

Once Glacia, Kile, and I are bundled up, we head back outside. Now that I can actually see, I look around: the sky is grayish-blue and dusted with wispy clouds. The sun is low on the horizon, dimmer than it was it on Thorpe Island. The town lines the right side of a walkway, and a rocky cliff forms the other edge. I can hear rolling *thrums* and *swishes* as waves smash against the rocks. The ocean covers the rest of the view. I stare out, mesmerized by the view: cracked sheets of ice drift over the dark blue water, with swirls of white dust blowing across them. Snow? That *has* to be snow.

Behind the town, a field of frosty grass sweeps up a sloping hill. Without the frost, I think the grass would be brown and dark green. Patches of lavender and violet flowers sprinkle color into the landscape. And far in the distance is another, larger hill, on top of which sits a wide white dome.

My body heat circulates within the coat, protecting me from the wind as we walk to the hotel. When I look at Glacia, her face is stuffed so deep inside the hood that only her eyes and nose are showing. Windy tears form in the corners of her eyes, making them sparkle even more than usual, and the tip of her nose is reddening.

I blink away my own wind-formed tears and laugh, because she looks absolutely adorable.

Chapter
Twenty-Four

AFTER CHECKING IN at the town's lodge, we regroup in the lounge, where a long fire flickers near a circle of couches. Tall windows at the back overlook the waves that are furiously crashing against the cliffs far below. There's not much else to the lodge than that. It pales in comparison to the Embassy's hotels, that's for sure.

Everyone, including Glacia, is waiting for me to start the meeting. Rand leans forward in his chair and props one elbow on his knee.

"So let's hear it, Lance. Where are we headed?"

I display the itinerary above my holotab and bring up a map, too. "We need to catalogue both Bechi and Chesnick islands," I say, waving my hand over the map. "The Dreiden Atmospheric Observation Facility and the Chesnick marine labs are the two big ones, and there are a couple research labs in town."

"Finish by tonight, outta here by morning." Rand

slaps his knees and stands up. "How're we doing this? Teams? One group? Solo? Come on, people."

"Teams of three? Since we've got her." Allison flips the end of one braid in Glacia's direction.

"Right, so, Lance, Haverns, and Arlington." Ugh. Kile. "You three hit up the Dreiden, get some fresh air. Me, Talbot, and Vetch will get the town, and then we'll all head over to Chesnick. Sound good?"

Kile's sitting the farthest away, just close enough to be part of the circle. I haven't talked to him outside of assigning work for the archives, and he doesn't like making eye contact. Even now, he's just listening to the meeting, and whenever one of us looks over at him, his eyes fall to the side. I was hoping to be with Rand or Trey—Allison kind of freaks me out, honestly—but I guess we'll have to make do.

Bechi Island's small FAST station is south of the town and raised a few feet off the ground. Bundled against the freezing wind, Kile, Glacia, and I make our way to it. A few minutes later, we're on board the shuttle and moving southwest through the frosty fields. We glide down a hill into a shallow valley, where the track runs parallel to a stream. A cloudy layer of ice covers the water, bracing the stems of flowers and grasses against the current beneath the ice, and water dribbles out of tiny pockets that didn't freeze over evenly.

The rail curves west again and climbs the final hill. The Dreiden facility is at the top, a large two-tiered dome that stands alone on the hill. The shuttle stops inside a station built on the facility's outer ring.

In the facility's main lobby is a pale woman with a thin face and arched black eyebrows. She's sitting behind a crescent-shaped desk, swiveling in her seat and moving her hands around in the air. When she looks at us, her eyes are glowing blue, like the eyes of the Dalish men operating the space elevator.

"You are the Un-dee-laens?" she asks in a chirpy accent. "Meester Lance?"

I nod, and she makes a tapping motion in midair with her left hand.

"Director Machus shall see you shortly."

She resumes her work, so the three of us stand off to the side of the lobby. A video mural on one wall shows a flyover of the Bechi Archipelago, then fades and shows white waves smashing against black cliffs, then fades again and shows an underwater scene looking up at the ice from below the water. We stare at every image, mesmerized, until the gate at the other end of the lobby opens and a woman walks out. She's not as tall as the Dalish people in the Embassy, but she's still about a foot taller than me. She has dark brown eyes and amber hair that dangles on either side of her face, just brushing her shoulders.

"Weesh of you is Meester Lance?" she asks, eyeing up both me and Kile.

"Me," I say, though my brain is wrapped around her accent.

"Greetings." She reaches out to shake my hand. "I am Mercedes Machus. Please"—she motions at the side hall—"thees way."

Her office is located on the outer edge of the dome, with two narrow windows that face east. The sun is at the very edge, but I can't see much of the ocean because the dark green and brown hills are in the way. I can, however, see the town we came from, a tiny glint in the sun's pale light.

"You arrived here thees morning?"

"We did."

The corners of her mouth twitch upward in amusement. "And was thees your first ride on a gravity elevator?"

All three of us nod. I don't want to talk—just listen. A lot of the Dalish in the Embassy had thick, slurred accents, but they didn't pronounce many words different. Hers is so...fluid...and sharp...and *fascinating*.

"I'm *sore* it must have been an unpleasant experience. It is for many people unaccustomed to our methods of travel."

She squeezes her earlobe, which makes her pupils glow blue, and then waves her hand in the air, moving things we can't see. When she finds whatever she's looking for, she taps the corner of her desk to make a projection shimmer between us.

"President Okana spoke with me to dee-scuss the catalogue you are developing." She points at a line on the document. "He says thees RASP system analyzes our data and manufactures a web of records. Correct?"

"Yes. And an interactive map of the facility, too."

She surfs through more invisible information, transferring some of it to the hologram above her desk that we can see.

"Weesh island is manufacturing your Faustocine formula?" she asks while doing that.

"Marakuri," I answer. "We're going there tomorrow."

"Ah, so the Malamara Laboratories, one of Daliona's most highly acclaimed. I thought maybe Cavellor or

Kirandi would be tasked weeth the project." She gestures out toward the hall. "Here at the Dreiden Atmospheric Observation Facility, we monitor many of Daliona's atmospheric sciences: the magnetic field, the atmosphere, and the solar weather con-dee-tions in our local area of space."

The longer her eyes shine blue, the more Director Machus' squints and blinks, but I can't actually tell if she notices.

"I have completed the forms of consent to link Dreiden to your RASP, so, on that note..."

She hands me a stylus and points at the line for me to sign the contract. Once it's filled in, she stands and takes us farther inside the Dreiden Facility. A large cylindrical machine with data panels on its sides sits in what is clearly the facility's center of operations. An antenna rises from it and connects to the dome, and a slight whir emanates from it. All around the chamber, people with glowing blue eyes sit behind crescent-shaped desks, meticulously sliding their hands through the air like we saw Director Machus and the secretary in the lobby both do.

"Thees's where we study Daliona's magnetic field. Axial north is roughly fifty miles away, but thees machine is situated directly over magnetic north. We've nicknamed it 'Mag-Neato.'" Director Machus chuckles to herself. "Thees's probably why we don't get many visitors."

She has some of the scientists show us how the machine works. The antenna hums, a projection of Daliona floats above one of the larger panels, and a rippling, misshapen bubble—the magnetic field—materializes around the planet. It takes another minute for data to start streaming in. Patches of the bubble light up where solar radiation impacts the field. It reminds me of when we flew past Undil's sun three weeks ago, how the green and pink and red aurorae blanketed the *Ember* and the other stations.

The scientists show us how the strength of field varies over the planet, how it's in the middle of an accelerated pole reversal, and even where the field overlaps the Dalish moons. From what I understand, this is exactly how the MRRs surrounding the stations work.

"Yes, your techie Larson Remmit fee-gured out MRRs were several times more efficient than standard plasma shields," Director Machus says when I point that out. "Magnetic resonance is arguably the most versatile of the natural forces. Almost all technology relies upon it in some form or another. Why do you think I've spent the greater part of my life up here studying it?"

She shows us around the rest of the Dreiden. The facility is the heart of the archipelago, what with a central power unit, water pumps, and even a row of chambers housing large ground-based telescopes. Those aren't operational now, though, because they only scan the skies during the seven months when the sun doesn't rise over the arctic.

After the tour, we go to the Dreiden's central software array and link the facility to RASP. The data synchronizes, we secure the link, and our job here is done.

❋ ❋ ❋ ❋ ❋

We meet the others for lunch, then ride the shuttle back across Bechi Island. The sun still hasn't risen any higher, so the light is still eerily pale, but the shadows have shifted. Rand tells us it's because the sun moves sideways through the sky this far north, rather than arcing above, all thanks to the slight tilt of Daliona's axis.

The shuttle stops inside the Dreiden's small FAST station again, but this time we stay on, and soon we're speeding toward the island's western cliffs, where the track spans a wide gorge between Bechi and Chesnick Islands. Two hundred feet below, massive sheets of ice bump and grind their way through the passage.

The marine labs are built on top and down the side of Chesnick Island's eastern cliffs. Here, the director grants us access to a laboratory that monitors ocean currents and the Dalish Arctic sea life.

Ten minutes later, we're all seated in the passenger chamber of an underwater cruiser, and just like Undil's space transports, the panels on the walls let us see what's outside. Right now we're half-submerged, zooming down the Chesny Strait. Once we reach open water, the cruiser sinks below the surface. Slabs of ice float above us as we drift farther...and farther...and farther out to sea.

Then we reach the ocean shelf.

The cruiser's lights shine gray in the black waters, catching glints of bubbles and dust. Above us, the light penetrating the ice fades to black, and below, the unknown awaits. Silhouettes of submerged mountains loom in the shadows. It almost feels like we're flying through the void, where everything is the same ahead as it is behind. No ice, no bubbles, no—

Something moved.

A shadow.

A *huge* shadow.

Chills run up my spine. Prickles of fear. My eyes scan the black water, above us...to the sides... Nothing. The water is quiet. Okay, maybe I was—

Glacia shrieks and jerks back when a blood-red tentacle slaps the cruiser, sticking, sucking. It pulls off, and a...*thing*...shoots overtop the cruiser and vanishes into the depths. Then another creature rises from below. A third trails behind and loops around the cruiser, looking like it's sizing us up for an attack. Two long tentacles with wide fins at their ends propel the monster forward as its bubbled head inflates and deflates. It's fifty feet long, maybe longer. The tentacles are thicker than my neck, the head more massive than my entire body. When it flares its mouth, the thin slot becomes a cave filled with rows upon rows of hooked yellow teeth and gray flesh flexing around its throat.

"*Oookay,*" Kile whispers. He's standing a few feet back from the window. "*Didn't need to see that.*"

"Meglaquids," the marina director tells us. "Perfectly harmless...as long as we're in here and they're out there."

"Oy, Arlington." Rand knocks his shoulder into Kile's. "You could use some friends. Get out and go for a swim."

Trey and Allison both hide their smirks, but Glacia doesn't look amused. My fingers flex involuntarily, and I resist the urge to glare at Rand.

The cruiser descends farther and other creatures swim in the light. Small, grayish fish, large insect-like creatures with glowing antennae, larger fish with no eyes, and even slimy, dark green balls that spew black ink when a predator gets too close—though sometimes the ink doesn't deter the attack.

The ocean floor is dark and rocky, but flatter than it was near the islands. Streams of bubbles trickle from between crevices. A couple feet away, something kicks up a cloud of black dust, and a second later, a meglaquid gives chase to its prey.

✳　✳　✳　✳　✳

That 'night,' after having a short meeting and going for a swim in the lodge's heated pool, Glacia falls face-first onto our bed and doesn't move for a long time.

"Tired?" I ask, half-smiling.

She groans and twists sideways, gripping the edge of the bed for support. A long yawn, her eyes glistening with tired tears—and then she grabs her coat.

"Let's go for a walk."

I stare at her. "*Excuse me?*"

She just shrugs and stands in the doorway.

"But it's freezing out there," I protest.

She rolls her eyes and lifts her coat a little higher. "Well then it's a good thing we have these, *huh?*"

I stutter for another excuse. "It's...like...two o'clock in the morning."

And it's true: even though the sun is up and the sky is still pale, it's *way* after midnight. I didn't even realize it was so late until we got back from the pool.

Glacia drags me to the door, barely giving me a

chance to grab my coat on the way out. The halls of the hotel are silent, and the lobby is empty. It's creepy, knowing we're the only ones awake, and what's even *more* eerie is the fact that it's still light outside. There should be people passing us on the street, or eating dinner in one of the town's few cafés, whose windows are now dark.

We walk to the edge of the settlement and follow a dirt path that's been trampled over the years. It's the first time since hiking in the Hania Reserve that I've stepped out of a city and into nature. *Real* nature. Nature that is all but untouched by humans, left to be looked at by many and seen by few.

Even though my body aches from exhaustion, the chill air whipping against my face helps keep me alert. The path goes on...and on...and on. We walk down a slight hill and through a field of tall grasses and wildflowers. A frozen puddle sits to one side, and Glace goes out of her way to crack it open. We reach a point where the path splits in two: one branch continues straight, and the other turns toward the cliffs. Glacia pulls me to the left, and soon the roar of crashing waves reaches our ears. There's a two-hundred foot drop, but that doesn't stop Glacia from dangling her feet over the edge. I hesitate, then—keeping my eyes up—sit beside her.

A bitter breeze blows at our faces. Tears sting my eyes, my cheeks go numb, and despite wearing gloves, I have to stuff my hands under my arms. On either side of us, the cliffs line the icy ocean. There are no beaches like on Thorpe Island, so the waves smash against sharp boulders and spray upward in wild hisses.

Glacia grabs a loose rock, leans forward, and drops

it. I don't dare look down, but she watches it all the way. Then she sees me not looking and nudges my shoulder. Even though she's gentle about it, I can't stop myself from clenching the edge.

"You're fine, mister." She leans over to look at the water again. "You'd survive that fall...*probably.*"

"Don't do that."

"Do what?"

I shrug, then look away from her, up the coastline to where the town should be. I feel Glacia rest her chin on my shoulder, and for a while, we sit and stare out over the roaring waves and frozen arctic, all the way to where the dim gray sky meets the horizon. This world looks so empty—and in a way, it is. It doesn't have vast mountain ranges, canyons, deserts, or tundras that go on for thousands of miles. Daliona is the island world.

Glacia picks her head up. "Keep walking?"

I'm all too eager to get away from the cliff. My muscles don't relax until my feet hit solid ground again. The path curves inland and up a slight hill, and from here, we can see most of Bechi Island: the pale sun hangs half-hidden behind the island's tallest western hill, and there, almost invisible, the Dalish moons hang low over horizon. The yellow one is slipping out of sight.

To the left, the Dreiden sits on top of its hill, and the shuttle runs down the slope, disappears inside a valley, and reappears as a tiny line near the town.

"The island isn't that big," I say.

"Nope."

Glacia steps in front of me and stands on her toes to give me a short kiss, then presses her face down into my shoulder.

"*Mmph so wmmm,*" she mumbles.

"Um...?"

She lifts her head. "It's so warm."

I roll my eyes, and she smiles at me, her eyes gleaming with fresh wind-drawn tears. We're exhausted, we're cold, we're alone. This is how we always seem to find ourselves, first on Undil after the Induction Ceremony, again on Belvun in the Hania Reserve, and now this. It's who we are.

Two kids on an overdue adventure.

Chapter
Twenty-Five

"I'M CURIOUS," RAND says while we're waiting to board a gravity pod. "At what point did pulling an all-nighter seem like a good idea?"

"*It wasn't*—" Glacia stops to yawn. She can barely hold her eyes open. "Wasn't an all-nighter. The sun was up."

"Getting smart with me, Haverns?" Rand stares at her, then winks and says, "Maybe you'll sleep during the drop."

Ha. If only.

When the pod drops, my body wants nothing to do with sleep. Anxiety floods me again. My palms sweat, my head swims. And the longer we fall, the less I can tell which direction is which as gravity weakens around us. Halfway through the fall, I feel like I'm lying on my side rather than sitting down, and the seats rotate to correct themselves again. I feel the pod falling upward, slowing as it plummets—er, *rises* toward the end of the track. At fifty-three minutes, a gentle shudder tells us we've reached our destination.

We brought medicine this time, and I take it as soon as I'm free of my restraints. Still, it takes a while for the nausea to subside. Not sleeping, combined with free-falling for nearly an hour? Yeah. Doesn't go over well. I don't throw up, though.

The same can't be said for Kile.

Even with the medicine pouch, he vomits into the disposal tube for two full minutes.

When we make it outside, half the sky is deep orange with spots of gray clouds, and the other half is fading to black. It's only eight-thirty in the afternoon here, but I know I'll fall asleep as soon as I find a bed. Heck, the grass looks good enough to sleep on...if Rand would let me. But he keeps one hand on my shoulder, guiding me as I stagger along.

The air is warm and humid. A grove of trees stands off to the side of the path. I see a city and a mountain, and waves are splashing...*somewhere*. I can't tell where from. Probably...to my right...*I think*.

Somehow I made it onto a shuttle, and now we're getting off. Rand gives me a shake to keep me moving. Allison does the same to Glacia. My eyes itch. I'm squinting so hard, watching the back of Trey's head as we walk...walk...walk. Occasionally my gaze slides upward and I see a hovercraft, or people in cyclo suits, or the top of a glassy tower. Then we're in a lobby. Rand asks for my ID. I fumble inside my pocket and hand it to him. He hands it back. We walk into a giant room filled with plants and trees and...waterfalls. Birds are squawking. We ride an elevator, walk down a hall that smells like fruit. Rand scans my ID at the door, shoves both me and Glacia inside, and closes the door again.

✳ ✳ ✳ ✳ ✳

Even before I open my eyes, I'm being blinded by a ray of light. I turn over to avoid it, but it's so bright in here. I pick my head up and look around. I'm on a big bed with pulled-up drapes, and a large outer window is directly across from it. We didn't drop the drapes or shut the blinds last night. Too tired to think about that. Even now, I have to rack my brain to remember everything: trees, water, lights, towers, mountain, city, hotel.

Gravity elevator.

Marakuri Island.

I look over my shoulder: there's Glacia, asleep, and curled up with her face tucked into a pillow, out of the light.

I get out of bed and go to the window. The floor is padded with a soft, squishy carpet. I'm looking east through a city—except I can only see the tops of the taller towers because a dense fog is rolling off the mountain and billowing between the towers, covering the ground from view.

After admiring the view, I turn away to explore the rest of the suite. Outside the bedroom is a living area with a set of bright green couches surrounding a speckled gray table, and black chairs are arranged around a dark brown countertop in the dining area. I'm almost disappointed to see that there's no fruit covering every inch of the place like our room in the Embassy.

A huge video panel is set into the back wall, where a Dalish woman with dark bronze skin and pale brown eyes is giving a newscast on mute. A picture of Daliona's yellow moon hangs beside her head, and right next to it...wait...is that Bechi Island? Yeah, that's *definitely* the Dreiden Facility.

Curious, I step closer—and a control pad materializes in the air. The volume icon is red, so I tap it, which turns it green and unmutes the newscast. The woman's voice is lighter than I expected it to be, and her accent sounds more...*sophisticated* than some of the others I've heard here.

"*—where construction on Docho's magnetic research outpost is set to begin next month. Director Machus of the Dreiden Atmospheric Observation Facility on Bechi Island will be overseeing the project, saying the outpost will help monitor Daliona's magnetic field and further our understanding of the shifts we've experienced over the last two decades.*"

The woman pauses and the background fades from Bechi Island to an orbital view of Daliona's only continent, Kiana. Then she starts speaking again.

"*Recent reports say the populations of all species preserved on Kiana have experienced significant growth in the past three years. Kaia Sako, a spokeswoman for the Galactic Ecology Survey's Dalish Environment Preservation Committee, says thousands of land-based populations have increased by an average of twelve percent since 4317, while amphibious and marine populations are up a* staggering *twenty-five percent. This growth puts many species back within acceptable ranges for the next interstellar relocation. Discussions surround-*

ing which exoplanets chosen to harbor various species will begin next year."

I change the channel by swiping sideways over the display pad. Now I'm watching a conference being held in the Embassy. And here's news from the Westin Isles, then Gorgico, Mahan, Thocksoll, Selayche... Every archipelago seems to have its own channel.

There are other channels, too. Channels about urban life, wildlife, nature, space, ocean cruises, talk shows with leading scientists and Embassy Officials, reports from the moon base—even construction projects around the planet. I pause on a show called *Decorating Daliona*, which is currently detailing how one of Daliona's famous resorts was designed: the Pelago Hotel off the coast of Selayche Island—my team's last stop, our week of *actual* relaxation before heading back to Undil.

I sit there in awe for at least thirty minutes. Part of the hotel is submerged over a reef and has a natural aquarium. There are scenic dining areas, nightly fireworks, clubs, interplanetary mixers, live game shows, rooftop pools, seafloor hotel rooms, and so. Much. More.

It's strange. Undil doesn't have shows like this. We have newscasts from the settlements, but nothing for entertainment. Undil can't afford that luxury, and it probably won't in my lifetime. There aren't enough of us to waste time like that. We *have* to go to Secondary, we *have* to work, we *have* to raise families. Anyone who doesn't go to the Embassy spends their life back home, helping the settlement stay productive.

It's not like that here. The Dalish do what they want, when they want. And I'm sure they aren't the only ones. The people on planets like Yillos, Rygin, and Artaans probably live in comfort, too. At least Undil has Hologis. That's always a plus. I've yet to see a Hologis arena on Dal—

Woah.

I've been flipping through sporting events, and the channel I just stopped on is showing live footage from the Marak gravity run, located at the base of the Marak volcano, near Marakuri's westernmost point. A platform sticks out over the ocean, a maglev track plummets into a tube, then into the water and out of sight. Here and there, parts of the tube breach the surface, whole sections of track that twist, bend, and curve in wide arcs, long straightaways, and quick turns. According to the image in the corner of the screen, a race is taking place in a few hours.

So *this* is what Rand keeps talking about.

I mute the video feed again and walk onto the room's outdoor balcony. The sun has risen higher, and the fog has lifted. I can see plazas and all the people walking or flying below. FAST tracks slip between towers, the shuttles zooming back and forth in a blur. The wind is gusty up here, the sunlight warm. It perks me up, refreshes me despite not having showered yet. My hair is greasy, sticking up on one side and flattened on the other.

Across the way, I see a man wearing a cyclo suit standing on a balcony that's a few floors below mine. He walks to the railing, throws his legs over it—and drops off. He falls...and falls...and then swoops up and glides out of sight.

Seeing that takes my mind back to the cyclo arena. Jumping off the side of the platform and flying around the arena... *That feeling*. I'd fly off, safe, and free, and—

"Excuse me, Mr. Lance?"

I jump at the voice and look behind me: it's not Glacia, but a tall Dalish girl. No, the *projection* of a Dalish girl. She has light brown skin, perfectly straight, white teeth, and strings of yellow and blue flowers braided through her hair. Her bright orange and yellow uniform has *The Tabanca* written across the chest.

"I'm sorry to have disturbed you," she apologizes with a small giggle, "but you have brunch reservations at the Tabanca Lounge in thirty minutes. Your friend, Mr. Harmat, insisted that I notify you."

It's a good thing Rand sent her, because I don't remember making reservations. Heck, I don't even know where the Tabanca Lounge *is*.

"Thank you."

"My pleasure."

She clicks a palm-sized device in her hand and flickers out of sight.

I go back to the bedroom and poke Glacia in the ribs over and over until she squirms and opens one eye.

"*Stooooop*," she mumbles into the pillow.

"You know we have breakfast reservations in a half-hour?" I ask.

"*Hmm?*"

"Food. Half-hour."

She picks her head up. "Where are we?"

"Marakuri Island."

"Oh, yeah."

She groans, stretches, and squints—then falls back into the pillow and hides her face from the light. I shake her until she's definitely awake, and then go take a shower while she's getting ready.

The walls of the shower close around me, confining me to just a few feet of space. Jets of soapy water spin around for two minutes, cold water rinses me down, and when it's finished, a dispenser slides out of the wall and squirts some scented oil into my palm. It smells *amazing*, like some of the flowers in the Dalish Embassy. I rub it down my arms, stomach, face, and legs. My skin gleams, softer than I've ever felt before.

Downstairs, in the hotel's lobby, some of last night's groggy memories come back to me. I remember walking through the indoor plaza with the sprawling gardens. The entrance to the Tabanca Lounge is at the center, down a set of wide wooden stairs that spiral underground to a brightly lit restaurant. I immediately recognize the girl who told me about the reservations. She smiles when we walk over.

"Mr. and Mrs. Lance?" she asks, looking down at us. "Your friends are this way."

Glacia whispers something behind me, but I can't hear her over the commotion and music of the restaurant. We pass tables of people drinking colorful drinks and eating pancakes, eggs, fruit, bacon, berries, kerns, and so much more. The sounds of the sizzling pans and the smells drifting around us make my mouth water the entire way to our table.

Rand and Allison are the only ones waiting—and neither of them look like they want to be awake. Neither of them says good morning, though Allison *does* give us a short-lived smile that's interrupted by a yawn. Trey shows up a few minutes later, but none of us know where Kile is. He doesn't answer our calls, and when

Rand sends the waitress to his room like he did mine, she reports that his room is empty.

"Fine, then. We'll just order."

Five minutes later, I'm eating one of the largest breakfasts I've ever had: a stack of killari patties, honey-soaked agrans, marsellion juice, a vine of plump ganopas, and a huge bowl of sweetened oats and eggs.

I bite into one of the ganopas: the inside is yellow and crisp and cold. Down the table, Allison has already chugged her juice and is now cutting into her pancakes. Rand is chewing a tough strip of meat, Glacia is ripping her pancakes by hand, and Trey is dipping his ganopas in syrup.

"All right, so, I'm gonna make this easy for you, Lance. Listen up." Rand puts his palms together and angles them at me. "When we're done here, I'm going back to bed. I'm sure Vetch and Talbot will, too. None of us slept. Not a wink. So you do you, and then we'll catch up this afternoon." He sits back and stretches. "Or you could piss us off and tell us to get to work *now*, but I'll make your life *hell* for the next week to thank you for it. What'll it be? You're the boss."

"Not *my* boss," Glacia says nudging my knee under the table.

Rand turns to her. "Haverns, keep your mouth shut. What are you even doing here? Don't you have flying lessons with Frizzy Fallsten?"

I slap my holotab in the center of the table before Glacia can respond. I *really* don't feel like listening to them.

We run through our itinerary for Marakuri: catalogue the Malamara Labs on Kailun Island, where the

Faustocine formula is being developed. Then we'll hit up the Kolikai Oceanic Lab and the Poké Wildlife Facility.

When I'm done talking, Rand leans his head on his fist. "Props for trying to be responsible, Lance, but you still haven't given me a straight answer. Seriously, I could really use another few hours of sleep, or else I'll be half-assing my job all day."

"*He seems fine to me*," Glacia mutters so only I can hear.

"We'll start tomorrow," I say, my voice stiffer than I meant it to sound. "No later."

Rand slaps the table and pushes himself up to leave. "That's what I thought. Thanks. You avoided a disaster, Lance. And hey, how about this: I'll take you guys to the sports dome later for some fun. Sound cool?"

He looks at Glacia when he says it, not me.

* * * * *

Just like he promised, Rand calls me that afternoon and has us meet him and the others at Marakuri's FAST station. He even managed to convince Kile to join us, who looks like this is the exact *opposite* of what he wants to be doing today...which is reading, probably.

Across the bay, I see Kailun Island to the southeast, Cacha Island to the southwest, and right in the center of the bay is a submerged dome. A portion of the top sticks above the water, but the rest lies below.

"Hurry it up, people. Gotta catch the next one."

We make it on a shuttle seconds before the doors clamp shut. It accelerates out of the station, and soon we're racing through an underwater tunnel, passing by red and pink coral, colorful fish, bubbly creatures with fleshy strings sticking off them, larger creatures with flat brown-and-green shells, and—

"What are *those?*"

Glacia points at a group of giant black-and-orange...*things.* They have four rear legs, two front pincers, and a massive, shelled tail that propels alongside the shuttle. Each is larger than a person, even a *Dalish* person.

Rand slings one arm over the back of his seat, as he tends to do when he's explaining stuff to us. "Barkals. You know, the crustaceans you love stuffing into your face."

"But...those are tiny," Glacia says, confused.

"What an *astute* observation, Haverns. Really, well done." He holds his thumb and pointer finger apart. "You eat the freshly hatched barkals. The babies. *These* big boys pack a mean punch. Catching them is a bloody mess."

Rand grins at her, but Glacia rolls her eyes and looks out the window again. So he taps her shoulder with the back of his hand.

"All right, Haverns. Let's talk about these gravity runs. You might be some kind of Hologis fanatic, but the runs are a whole new beast. I'm telling you this for your own good: people have *died* on these things. I'm gonna be practicing with the Undilaen racing club a few times a week to prepare for Tahani, but there's no way in hell I'd let you take on a professional run without proper training. Stick with the recreational." He suddenly looks serious. "Nobody's dying on my watch."

Trey waves at him from across the aisle. "We've done these before," he says, gesturing at Allison, too.

"Yeah, well, you'll have to prove yourselves. I've got seniority—"

Allison coughs loudly.

"Correction: *she's* got seniority. But I'm doing all the talking, so I'm in charge."

Glacia mimics Allison's cough. "Technically, Arman is—"

"Lance is in charge of the *archives*, Haverns. Right now we're trying to have a bit of fun. I'm sure General Orcher would appreciate it if the Head Archivist and his pilot girlfriend *didn't* get themselves killed."

The shuttle curves around the dome's perimeter and enters a station, pulling in beside several other shuttles from around the archipelago that are also letting people off. The station leads into massive, crowded chamber, and the words *Kiruni Sporting Dome* are flashing above a gate at the other end. It's not just officers here. I see families and groups of teens and people our age. And when we get inside, I almost stop walking to take it all in.

The most prominent feature is a silver tube winding its way through the dome. It curves back and forth, twists in wide spirals, and gently slopes all the way to the floor. That's obviously the gravity run—a recreational one. It doesn't look too bad...*from down here*. The run I saw on the sports feed this morning looked ten-times worse.

The public cyclo arena is obvious, too. It's sanctioned off, but borders the top of the gravity run. Scattered platforms float in the air. Some are supported on tall poles, others are hovering and have ropes and obstacles dangling from them. Dozens of people are flying inside the arena, jumping off platforms or swinging from the ropes or hanging out in midair just talking, by the looks of it.

Elsewhere in the dome, there are waterslides and wave pools, maglev tracks with long, twisting cars whipping up and down along them, people shooting beams of light from their palms at targets down a range, and people riding in small, circular pods are aimlessly drifting overhead, watching everything from above. At the center of it all is a smaller dome: a food court.

"Kiruni used to be a biodome, if you can't tell." Rand points up at the sky. "A quake sunk the shelf and it slid all the way down here. Whole thing flooded and ruined the habitats and equipment and whatever else they had. So the Dalish salvaged it and now, *this*."

The six of us make our way through the crowds and ride and elevator to the top of the gravity run. The line is pretty long, so Rand takes the chance to go through the basics of racing: sway the hips, point the toes, stay focused on the next turn in the track, keep our heads down, and most importantly, *don't let go*.

He doesn't need to tell me twice.

Allison goes first. The attendant prepares a maglev sled and gives her a helmet. The sled itself has footholds at the bottom, contours for the shoulders, and two grips on either side. Allison lays flat on her back, and when the countdown reaches zero—*shooooom!* The sled shoots off into the tunnel.

We can't see what happens after she rounds the first turn, so it's another minute before the attendant gives clearance for the next person. Kile looks like he's going to be sick just from being up so high, so Rand forces him to go. After him, Trey. My heart is pounding by the time Glacia lays on her sled.

The countdown hits zero, and she's gone.

"Scared, Lance?" Rand gives my shoulder a shake—then squeezes it when he feels how tense I am. "Loosen up. *Geez.*"

I don't say anything.

The attendant puts the next sled in place and beckons me forward. I shove the helmet over my head. A display in the visor traces the best path down the track, and numbers line the edges of my immediate vision: velocity, slope, even my reaction times.

"You are new, too?" the attendant says. I nod, and he laughs. "You'll be back up in a minute. I know it."

I straddle the sled, set my feet in the footholds, and lie down. My shoulders fit the grooves, but my arms are already going weak. *What am I doing?* What if I slip? What if I roll out and break my ribs again? Why did I let Rand make me do this? Never again. No.

I fix my eyes on the countdown: *8...7...6...*

Rand's face appears upside down over me. "Remember: head up, lean into the turns. Keep it smooth, Lan—"

The sled jets forward before he can finish my name.

Air whips over the helmet. I adjust my grip as the first turn rushes toward me. Almost...almost...*now.* I throw my hips just as the sled whips to the right—but jerk to the side when I try to regain my balance, way off the golden line. I shoot down the straightaway, picking up speed as I close in on the next curve. This time I lean too late and bounce on the sled when I try to stabilize.

My helmet says I'm speeding along at thirty miles per hour, way faster than I'd like. My hands are coated in sweat and keep slipping on the grips whenever I squeeze harder. I need gloves. I *definitely* need gloves.

Dive into a spiral.

My stomach wrenches, but the track straightens out before nausea completely overcomes me. Forty miles per hour. I prepare for the next turn: wait...wait...*now*—

"*Mmphh!*"

My shoulder slams into the wall—knocks me off the sled. I hit the bottom of the tube. Skid on my back, keeping my head tucked.

No.

No.

No.

I let myself slide to a stop, then go limp and stare up, too shaken to move. My shoulders and neck ache. I'm definitely going to have bruises. The sled is nowhere to be found.

A word flashes red in the helmet: *RETRIEVING.*

"*Please remain where you are,*" a voice says in my ear, but it's not like I'm planning to go anywhere. "*No serious injuries detected.*"

A minute later, a larger sled shoots down the track from the top. It stops in front of me, and my helmet flashes: *PLEASE BOARD RETRIEVAL SLED.*

I stand up, wincing at the small aches in my hip and shoulders, and climb onto the sled. Two braces fold over me, pinning my body and arms down. Then it accelerates forward, but goes slower than when I fell.

Around the curve, down a steep drop, a long series of back-and-forth twists, and then the final straightaway.

I shoot out of the tube and glide to the very end of the track, where the sled releases me. Glacia, Allison, and Trey are lined up along the track, waiting, but a Dalish attendant takes me aside and scans my body for any injuries the automated scan may have missed. Detecting nothing, he clears me and takes the retrieval sled to a conveyor.

People are staring. And of course, *now* I notice the displays that show each run, so everyone around here saw that. Including Rand.

Dammit.

Glacia looks concerned, but when she starts talking, I can tell she's holding back a laugh. "You okay, mister?"

"Yup."

"Hey, you could've been Kile," Allison says from behind Glacia. "He got off and puked his guts out."

She jerks a thumb over her shoulder, and I see a boxy robot spraying cleanser on a splatter of vomit.

Glacia takes my hand, which I realize is sweating profusely. Great.

"Wanna try it again?"

"*No.*"

She grimaces, then lets go of my hand. "Fine. See you in a bit."

She and Allison walk away, leaving me alone with Trey. He pushes his glasses up, and turns toward the screen to watch the end of Rand's run. It isn't long before Rand himself shoots out of the tube and stops in front of us, looking bored out of his mind.

"That was disappointing. *Severely* disappointing." Without taking his helmet off, Rand rounds on me. "You.

I knew you wouldn't be cut out for this...*but damn*, man. Should've heard these two twelve year olds up there bragging about how they've never fallen. Maybe you should clear out before they get down here."

I try to ignore him. I do. But the ache in my hips makes that a lot more difficult than it should. His words echo in my head. It plays over in my head, falling, my vision rolling as I flipped off the side. Glancing around, I see people are still staring...mumbling about me, probably. My face gets hot.

Then another memory overtakes my thoughts: the car crash. Father's short yell. The stench of blood. My vision, fading. My thoughts, panicking, I thought I was going to die that day. Sometimes...

No.

Rand throws his hands on his hips and looks around. "Oy, where'd the girls get off to?"

"Went for another round," Trey answers, his eyes pausing on a Dalish girl walking by.

Rand pulls off his helmet and sets it on the conveyor. "Gotcha." He notices my distant stare. "You all right?"

"Yup."

"Wanna catch up to them?"

I shake my head and fix my eyes on the cyclo arena. Rand follows my gaze.

"You wanna flip around in the air after crashing in a gravity run? You don't wanna conquer it first? You're quitting?" Now *he* shakes his head. "Priorities, Lance. Evaluate them."

I fake a laugh.

He jabs a finger into my shoulder, pushing me off balance. "Whatever. All this means is your girl's got tougher guts than you. Nothing to be embarrassed about."

He flicks his eyebrows up then walks off toward the cyclo arena. I rub my shoulder, staring after him—but then he abruptly stops, lifts one hand, and turns back around.

"Where the hell's Arlington?"

"Puking his brains out," Trey says. He gives me one more look before following Rand.

When the current cyclo round finishes, we're sized into suits and let inside the arena. The sense of weightlessness eases the ache in my shoulders and hips. Now that I'm flying again, my mind quiets down. The visions vanish. I focus on my movements like the instructor from the Embassy told me to. I try out some breathing exercises, let my mind clear so I can feel the sensation tingle in the nodes pressed to my scalp.

After practicing for a while, the three of us land on one of the floating platforms and line up at the edge.

"How about we play a game? Make this worth my time." Rand points at the next platform, about thirty yards away. "We'll start easy. Run and jump, and whoever lands closest to the edge gets to choose what we do next."

Trey and I agree. We each take a few steps back, keeping spaced far enough apart so we won't collide, then run forward and leap off the edge. The cyclos kick in and we soar across the gap—a hundred-foot drop. I line up my target, adjust my trajectory, and try to calculate when to arc back down. Wait...wait...wait...

Now.

Rand drops past me and lands two feet from the

edge. I touch down five feet away, but Trey lands with his heels off the side.

We regroup at the center of the platform.

"Not bad. Winner's choice, Talbot."

Trey scans the cyclo arena. He glances up, then over at the ropes dangling from one of the platforms.

"Race to that, climb to the other side, then race back here."

Rand grits his teeth. "*Physical exertion?* Why do you think I left Shield? Training every day's a bitch, that's why." He looks my way and points back at Trey. "Make sure Talbot doesn't win. Play dirty for all I care. I don't like his ideas."

We line up again. Rand counts down—and then we're off. I throw my arms forward to help guide myself, and gain a slight lead as we zoom up to the ropes. Closer...closer—

—and I grab it. The rope swings one way, then the other, but I'm already climbing. I can't waste time.

Hand-over-hand.

Go. Go. Go.

I grab hold of the webbed section and clamber over it. That in itself is beyond exhausting. Rand and Trey grunt as they pull themselves along behind me.

I reach the last web, pull myself through, and drop. Falling...falling, until I ease my fall and swoop around and speed toward the platform we started on, where I land at a jog. Rand places second, and Trey comes up last.

"Now...*that*...was impressive, Lance," Rand says through heavy breaths. "Since when are you so agile?"

Since Glacia motivated me to start working out.

But I don't say that.

"So, what's next?" Rand asks me expectantly.

I scan for an obstacle—but get distracted. Most of the dome is surrounded by the bay, but the part of it sticks above the water. The sun is out there, and the clouds and mountains and islands. *The sky.* I want to fly where I can be totally free, because this dome isn't big enough to contain me. I remember the people in the Embassy who were swooping between towers, jumping off ledges, diving into the Rainbow River... That's the life I want, the life I need. And a year ago, I never would've imagined it *could* be my life, until I opened up to the world.

Rand stares up with me. "You need a license for that," he says, as if he knows what I'm thinking.

"How do I get one?"

"Train a few days a week, sign up for a license course, and it's all yours. Get on that soon, if you're serious."

"I am."

"*Can't believe I'm saying this*..." Rand puffs his cheeks. "You might have what it takes."

I can't help but grin. My heart is pounding—in a good way. That might be the first time he's ever complimented me. Usually he's busy comparing me to Glacia.

I finally come up with a challenge: if we start at the highest platform, we can drop to the next one forty yards down and several to the side. In fact, all of the platforms are spread around like that.

"How about first one to the ground wins, but you have to land on every level all the way down?"

"I'm cool with that. Talbot?"

"Gotcha."

We fly to the top of the dome and land on the highest platform, a few yards above the gravity run. I try to find Glacia and Allison in the line, but they must have already taken their second runs.

"On your count, Lance."

We look over the edge and line up our first jumps. People waiting for the gravity run watch us, curious.

"Three, two, one, *now.*"

All three of us dive headfirst off the platform and streak by the gravity run. I hear people cheering as I level out, throw my elbows backward, and slow down just enough to hit the second platform at a jog before hurling myself over its edge in another dive. Rand and I hit this one at the same time, and Trey lands as we both drop off the other side. I aim for the platform in front of me, but Rand swerves to the next one over.

Dive, swoop, land, run.

Dive, swoop, land, run.

I jar my knee on the fifth level, giving Rand a slight lead. Trey catches up and we dive off at the same time, just inches apart.

One more platform, then the ground. Rand lands...then me and Trey. Rand drops off the side, but I jump before I reach the edge and pass him midair, speeding toward the ground. Air whips through my hair and past my face, the folds of my uniform rippling.

Slow down—twist in midair—brace myself.

Hit the ground.

I skid on my back, then lie there, catching my breath and hoping I didn't break anything.

Now everything *really* aches.

A few people in the arena are staring at me. Some look unsure if they should get help, or if I'm okay. I give them a thumbs-up. Then Rand's there, pulling me to my feet.

"What'd I say about killing yourself?" He cocks his head, then turns to the people watching us. "Oy, who won?"

Everyone points at me.

"*You're all blind*," he mutters under his breath. "Seriously though, Lance. You okay? Nothing weird poking through your skin where it shouldn't be?"

I flex my knee, and it pops. It stings as I walk to test it, but I'm fine otherwise. Maybe it's the adrenaline. *This*... This is a new feeling for me.

My heart—racing.

My energy—surging.

More, more, *more*.

My brain is in overdrive. Is this how Glacia *always* feels? Is this normal? Not even Hologis makes me feel like this.

"*No fear*," I say between breaths.

Rand's face lights up. He throws his arm around me and pulls me toward Trey. "Oy! Hear that? Lance is catching on!" He gives me a rough shake. "That's what power feels like."

I disagree. I don't feel powerful, I feel *alive*. As alive as the people at the dance that first night in the Undil Embassy. As alive as the forests and rivers of Belvun. The surge. The...*excitement*. A rush of things I haven't felt in years, if ever at all.

After dinner, Glacia and I change out of our uniforms and head to the beach. The sun is setting, a dark orange circle hanging over the water. The pink-and-red sky reminds me of Belvun's sky, which was always this color, and even the clouds have taken on pinkish hues. Waves roll up the beach, the water still warm from the heat of the day. It tickles our ankles, and our feet sink in the sand as we walk toward the sunset, each new wave washing our footprints away. Some Dalish people skim across the water on hover jets, some hang from gliders, riding the air currents while white and black birds flock around them, squawking noisily.

Glacia's eyes follow the gliders. "Can we do that too?"

"You just want to do everything."

"Because there's *so much*."

"I'm supposed to be working, remember?"

She shrugs. "So?"

"And we don't really have time."

"Says who?"

"Says...um..."

"*Says nobody*. That's who." She spins around me and walks backward. "Please? I'm gonna be stuck in the Embassy for the next week, mister. It's *not fair*."

Now *I* shrug. "Tough luck."

Her expression darkens when she realizes I'm not going to lay off the act. "You better send pictures, and buy me stuff, and—*Arman, NO!*"

Glace shrieks when I shove her into the next wave. She pops up a second later, drenched head-to-toe, spluttering and scrambling to regain her footing. I make another grab at her, but she ducks and tackles me from behind, sending us both crashing face-first under the water. We wrestle a few seconds, then kick to the surface and gasp for air, laughing. Glace clambers onto my back to stay above water, and as I lumber back to shore, she kisses my cheek and ruffles the water out of my hair.

The beach becomes thinner the farther we walk, and soon the jungle is almost at the bay's edge. Trees with thick, brownish-yellow trunks and fanned leaves lean over the beach. Glace climbs onto one and carefully crawls up its length. It takes me longer, but I manage to reach her without falling. The tree bends under our weight, and the leaves sway in the wind. Across the bay, lights flicker on the other islands. The mountain tops are still crowned in the waning light, but it doesn't take long for darkness to slide up their peaks. Stars overtake the night, new constellations we have yet to learn, and to our backs, Lide, Daliona's smaller moon rises in the east.

"We should always watch the sunset together," I say. "Every planet, every city."

She looks sideways at me, and it's several seconds before she says, "Don't ever miss a sunset you have a chance to see, okay? Even if I'm not there."

We watch the sun and a sliver of Daliona's larger moon, Docho, sink below the horizon. Docho disappears first, then the sun, and soon a line of golden light is all that remains of the day.

Chapter
Twenty-Six

WE START CATALOGUING Marakuri after breakfast. Just like on Bechi Island, we split into teams of three: Rand, Allison, and Trey are in one, while Glacia and I are stuck with Kile again. The central section of the city is a research park, so many of its labs and data facilities are contained to one area.

We visit the Topographical Oceanic Current Center first, where scientists study Marakuri's local ocean currents and weather patterns. In one of the rooms, a projection array similar to the *Ember*'s StarPad displays live holographic feeds of the region's strongest currents. We add it to the catalogue, then head to the Meteorological Center, the Marine Bio Labs, the City Development Center, and a few other facilities.

We finish cataloguing Marakuri's main island on Wednesday, then move to Kailun, the larger of the two islands across the bay, where the Faustocine formula is being synthesized. Since Rand was part of the team that decided what organic samples to collect on Belvun for the formula, he hands Kile off to Allison and Trey and goes with me and Glacia to check up on the Faustocine's production.

When we step off the shuttle, I stare up at the twin mountain peaks I've only seen from a distance the last two days. Moss, trees, and shrubs cover their lower heights, and waterfalls spill from crevices into a river that flows beside the Malamara Synthesis Labs. They're disk-shaped, and sit a hundred feet up the mountain. To reach them, we have to ride a transport elevator and cross a skywalk that has a *stunning* view of the Kiruni Dome and Marakuri Island.

Two men are waiting for us in the lobby: the lab director, and Michael Rafting. Michael has already changed in the week-and-a-half since I last saw him. He's not so pale anymore, his shoulder-length black hair is slicked back and curling at the tips, and he seems more confident and happier than I've ever seen him.

"Good to see you two again." Michael shakes my hand and gives Glacia a quick hug, then offers his hand to Rand. "Michael Rafting, Ambassador."

"Rand Harmat," he says with a respectful nod. "I was a project manager on Belvun."

Michael looks impressed. "What'd you do?"

Rand runs a hand over his freshly buzzed hair. "Determined some of Belvun's extraction sites and tested the sample quality. Gotta have well-represented samples, and nothing gets by me."

"That you do. Glad you're on the team."

Michael steps aside and introduces the director of the laboratory. "This is Director Qarl Alamid."

The Dalish director is a lanky man with a pointed nose and solid cheekbones, but there are wrinkles on his long neck and bony hands. His curly, graying hair bounces on his forehead, and his light brown face is spotted with dark freckles. He doesn't *look* that old— Orcher's age, maybe—but his body seems as frail as Captain Blitner's was.

"Welcome to Malamara Laboratories. We *are* glad to be a part of Ambassador Rafting's Recovery Treatise." Director Alamid extends one hand toward me. "This is *your* team, I presume? The Live Archives of RASP?"

I don't bother correcting the name for him. "Yeah, part of it."

"I see, I see. Yes, President Okana notified me that you need access to our database."

Director Alamid pauses, frowns, and then squeezes his earlobe to make his pupils glow blue, and proceeds to wave his hands in the air until he finds what he's looking for.

"RASP was developed in Orvad and integrated with Dalish software. Good. That makes *our* job much easier." He squeezes his earlobe again, and his eyes return to normal. "I'm glad Undil has at last allowed private enterprises to borrow Dalish technology *beyond* the requests of Horizon Tower. Your space program is superb indeed, but your domestic logistics are nearly a century behind the galactic standard. But all will come in good time." He hugs his arms to his chest, sighs. "Shall we proceed?"

He takes us into the laboratory, which is mostly contained within the mountain. The halls are brightly lit so there are no shadows, and at the end of one hall, a gate slides back to reveal a large, multi-level chamber. Storage units are arranged in the center, each containing a sample from Belvun. In another chamber, Dalish chemists are recording the effects each batch of Faustocine has on the Belvish samples.

Rand looks fascinated. He's memorizing diagrams, reading data and analyses, and muttering under his breath, his grin never faltering.

"You hiring, Director? I think I've found my calling."

"We would love to take on an enthusiastic individual such as yourself. However, I'm afraid that decision is in the hands of your superiors."

Rand turns to me. "Oy, Lance, *you're* my superior."

Glacia snorts, and I crack a grin.

Director Alamid takes us down another corridor. All around us are observation windows that look into chambers where chemists are actively testing the Faustocine formula on the samples. Small trees and flowers are growing from some, bright and alive—but then there are others with black leaves and wilted stems. Analysts are poring over displays and molecular configurations as they look for solutions to test.

"The *original* formula, that is, the one we developed six years ago, was not synthesized in these laboratories," Director Alamid explains. "We delivered mobile units to Belvun, but experienced internal contamination that went undetected until *after* we manufactured the formula for application. By the time we realized the fault, the damage had been done." The director turns his eyes to the samples being tested in the lab. "The current decay on Belvun's ecosystems isn't a natural disaster. *We* catalyzed it. But by the time the negative reports came flooding in, it was too late."

"*Eco-hacking,*" Rand mutters to the side.

The director grimaces at the word. "Unfortunately, sir. But you'll find that many of Daliona's most revered scientists believe the consequences of eco-hacking can only be fixed with *more* hacking."

"But planets aren't meant to change overnight," Rand retorts. "Nature isn't so versatile. We can swallow some meds or stitch our wounds, but there's no reset button for the universe."

"I do not disagree, sir. Nature seeks balance, and on Belvun, we've tipped the scales too far, too fast. Our job was to mend an ailment, but we birthed a disease."

✻　✻　✻　✻　✻

Michael joins us for dinner that evening. Rand ends up giving him a one-sided discussion about the Faustocine formula, and is currently going off about the lack of extended research into eco-hacking, how planets are healthier in the long run when terraformed the old-fashioned way.

"*Sure, it only took a century to terraform Belvun using the experimental techniques, but look how unstable the resulting environments are today!*"

"*You can't settle a planet without measuring the untested conditions!*"

"*We could be looking at* millions *of acres destroyed by the time we get back to Belvun. The whole damn planet could burn if this fails.*"

The rest of us remain quiet, letting Rand's voice

dominate the table. Kile just stabs at his food and stuffs it in his mouth. Trey's gaze stays fixed on Rand as he absentmindedly eats crustaceans one-by-one. Allison and Glacia mutter to each other from time-to-time, and I'm left at the end of the table, staring down at the bay and Kailun Island. I can just see the Malamara Labs in the late-evening light.

"So, Glacia," Michael says when Rand finally stops talking. "Have you tried out the gravity runs?"

Glacia's eyes light up and she wipes her mouth with a napkin. "I love it. Like, woah."

"Haverns here has more guts than Lance and Arlington," Rand says, pointing his fork at her. "She went down Kiruni's run half a dozen times, but *this guy?*" He waves the fork at Kile and nearly loses his half-bitten slab of fish meat. "This guy puked after his first run. *No offense,* Arlington."

Kile ignores him. He doesn't even glance up. He just goes on chewing, his cheeks bulging.

"Lance fell off, but that happens to everyone, right? I mean, I used to break so many bones I stopped caring. Point is to reach the end." He chews another bite of fish, then says, "Cyclo suits, on the other hand? Now *there's* something Lance is good at. You should see him fly, Ambassador. Nearly broke his leg—actually no, *nearly snapped his spine*—but he beat me in a race and that's what matters." He winks at me. "Right?"

"Obviously." Michael leans forward to see me better. "Must've got a concussion, too. When I met this kid, I swear he didn't leave his room for two days once—"

"Didn't Ellin have to drag you into the dance?" Glacia blurts. Michael's expression drops. "You were trying to leave, but she made you go. Yeah. *We saw that.*"

She has a point, but she's leaving out another part of the story. Nobody here saw what happened between me and Glacia that night: she asked me to dance—*twice*—but I didn't want to, and we ended up standing by the window just looking over the Undil Embassy. Then she went off about how I needed to get over Ladia. And tried to make me smile. And practically yelled at me before I ran away to my room.

I don't miss those days at all.

"Wait a moment." Michael is suddenly grinning, and he slides his sleeves up his arms. "Glacia, wasn't it *you* who fell asleep during my treatise conference? Remember that? Man... Captain Fallsten *railed* you."

Rand bursts out laughing and claps his hands loudly. Glacia's face goes blank, and Michael holds his hand over his heart, faking an apology.

"Oh, ho-hooo, *man!*" Rand raises his glass in a solo toast. "To not being you, Haverns. To not being *you*." He tips his head back and chugs the drink. "How bad did you want to slap her across her frizzy, fire-headed face? I'm sure nothing I've been through can compare to being the object of Frizzy Fallsten's ferocious fury. I mean, *who cares* that you were conked-out during what I'm sure was a *very* stimulating conference. No offense," he says again, this time to Michael.

"None taken."

"Back to the point. Lance is getting his cyclo license next month." Rand puts a hand over his heart. "Not even *I* have my license. I like gravity runs, you like cyclos, some people like quid—"

"You don't have a cyclo license?" Trey interrupts,

genuinely surprised.

"Listen up, Talbot: gravity runs are a *real man's* sport. And besides, who actually takes their cyclos back to Undil? Not many people, because they're so damn impractical back home. You've got nowhere to charge them, first of all."

"I'm sure we could build charging ports."

Rand thumps his palm on his forehead. "Of course! Why didn't anyone else ever think to do that? Genius!" He throws his arms on the table, rattling all of our glasses. "I've got one word for you: *infrastructure*. But our delightful Chancellor Green is too concerned with shitting on the Narvidians for getting in on Gray Wall to put any real effort into developing Undil. I don't care who's building what. Progress is progress. We need a functional society, and he's impeding on aspects beneficial to the growth of Undil's infrastructure—all because of a grudge."

✳ ✳ ✳ ✳ ✳

Michael hangs back with me and Glacia when we leave, and we follow behind the others on the beachside walkway as we head back to our hotel.

"You guys leave...?"

"Friday," Glacia answers. "But I'm going back to the Embassy."

"The rest of us are going to Hossiard Island," I say.

Michael slips his hands in his pockets. "I'm staying here at least another week. Lars and Victoria are coming down Friday. I think they're bringing that other guy...the techie you hired from Orvad."

"Olivarr."

"Yeah." Michael cranes his neck to look up at the hotels surrounding the plaza. "I take it you're staying here?" Glacia and I both nod, and then he twists around and points at the third and smallest island in the bay, southwest of Marakuri. "My suite's up on Cacha Island. See that light near the peak? That's the Ambassadorial Suite."

"You're *way* up there," I say, almost jealous. Of course, I'm the one who purposefully failed my interview with Chancellor Green last year, not that I had much of a chance of becoming an ambassador anyway, after learning that Michael spent years studying to be one.

We reach the hotel and stop outside the entrance to say our goodbyes.

"Keep in touch. It's always nice to see you guys." Michael shakes my hand and hugs Glacia again. "Let me know if you *do* sign up for any of the gravity challenges," he tells her. "I'll be there to cheer you on."

✳   ✳   ✳   ✳   ✳

We finish cataloguing the archipelago before lunch on Thursday. After we eat, Rand takes me and Glacia to the sporting dome, where he coaches Glacia on the gravity run while I practice flying the cyclo. Though I love the sensation of moving freely through space, I need to stop being so reckless. One hard hit could be all it takes to knock me out—or worse.

A Dalish instructor notices me flying alone—and how uneven I am, apparently—because he comes over and shows me how to maintain better control, and even suggests some mid-flight meditation techniques. After a half-hour of those, I'm less fidgety, less prone to flailing my loose limbs. I can almost land *precisely* where I want, fly at the speed I want, even shift directions without jerking my body too hard. On top of that, I'm learning to calculate my path, rather than letting the environment catch me off guard.

When we're back on solid ground, the instructor encourages me to practice in as many different arenas as I can while on Daliona.

"You get too used to one, you cannot handle others. Everywhere is different, you must remember. Meditate. Train far and wide. Be aware of all that is around you."

I find Rand and Glacia waiting for me outside the arena. As usual, Rand is going on about how daring she is to push her limits, how precise and controlled she keeps her path, how she might be ready to take on a real run soon.

"Start training on Laka when you head back to the Embassy."

"*Definitely.*"

"It's an all-around good course for anyone serious about collecting medals."

"I'm gonna be *so* decked out."

"Not as decked out as *me*, Haverns. I'm the most decorated gravity racer from Undil."

"Yeah, well, not for long."

She's just as excited as he is. It's obvious how much they prefer the runs over the cyclo suits. Me, I need the freedom, the fluidity, the peace of mind a cyclo gives me. I live for that, because I denied myself of it for so long. But them?

They live for the rush.

"Like I said, I've had my fair share of crashes," Rand is telling her when we board the shuttle back to the main island. "Hell, the Law of Large Numbers dictates that eventually yes, you *will* crash. Nearly a thousand runs down and I've crashed dozens of times. Some weren't so bad, some put me in the hospital. It sucks, but it didn't stop me. I rode the runs until I conquered them. Point is, you gotta eliminate fear. All of it. If you're even the least bit afraid—*game over.*"

The shuttle slides out of the station and zooms into the bay. Giant barkals rise from gaps in the rocks and reefs, their shelled tails churning through the water and scaring off the other fish. Then the outgoing shuttle glides past ours, and the barkals take up chasing it instead.

Back in the station, Rand meets up with the team of Undilaen racers he trains with. Some I recognize, some I don't. They're all wearing custom gravity suits. Deitra is wearing a dark green suit with orange racing stripes and a matching helmet, Imogen is sporting a white suit with dozens of overlapping yellow rings and a light blue helmet, and Bill "the Bullet" has a blood-red suit and black helmet. He brought Rand's gravity suit with him, which is dark gray and has the Undil Embassy crest marking the chest and back.

"Because I've worked for every branch," Rand explains, patting the crest as Bill hands him the suit.

"Yeah, *not* because you're captain of the squad," Bill

points out.

They all catch a shuttle south to the Marak gravity run. Glacia and I already have other plans. We go back aboveground and follow the beachside walkway to the outskirts of the city, where the jungle begins. A map at the head of the jungle path shows us all the trails on the island: some go west to the volcano, some go north to a lagoon, and some wind through the river valley.

The jungle quickly closes around us. Shadows swallow the light, fresh odors waft in the thick, humid air. Bark is peeling off the twisted, gnarled branches, and moisture clings to the leaves, or drips on the ferns and flowers sprouting between the trees.

The trail doubles back on itself, getting steeper, and steeper, and then we enter a clearing. Flowers larger than my head bask in the bountiful sunlight that the rest of the jungle floor doesn't receive. White flowers with deep tubes streaked with orange and yellow, blue flowers with fat petals, groups of beady bulbs teetering on tall stems. Insects with bodies wider than my hand buzz in the air, moving from flower to flower. Many have wings several inches long, eyes as big as the tips of my fingers. Antennae twitch on their heads, and tubular tongues curl under their heads to drink nectar.

A rustle in the trees.

Glacia and I freeze in our tracks. A branch shudders—then a bird bursts from the lower canopy making shrill squawks. Its body and wings are black, and its tail is pure red and fans out several feet. As it flaps away, three tiny yellow birds dart out of the trees behind it, chirping excitedly.

"Arman."

Glacia squeezes my hand, hard, and makes me look forward. Farther down the path, a creature is standing completely still, staring right back at us. It has long, pointed ears, two massive black eyes, and an extremely bushy tail. Brown fur covers its entire body, stumpy legs and all, except for the mane of light tan fur around its neck.

"*What is it?*" I whisper.

"*No idea.*"

"*Didn't you see it in the book?*"

"*I saw a lot of animals in the book.*"

The creature twitches its ears as we talk, then pads forward a few steps, sniffing the air. Its eyes never leave us...until it pounces forward and traps something on the ground between its paws. We hear buzzing—then a crunch—and the buzzing stops. The animal lifts its foot and I see a giant black insect, now crushed.

"*What do we do?*"

I shrug. "*Wait for it to leave? Throw something at it?*"

"*What?! That's so mean! Look how cute it is!*"

I step forward. The furry creature perks its ears, its eyes now locked with mine. I take another step, then another, and on the third, the creature turns-tail and jumps out of sight.

"There. Problem solved."

Glacia sulks. "But I didn't get a picture..."

I just roll my eyes and grab her hand.

As we keep walking, the humid air begins to clear, and we hear a steady, muffled roar. I recognize the sound, and when we reach the next turn on the path, we're overlooking a deep river gorge. Waterfalls surge over the cliffs across from us. Their dull roar fills the ravine, and mist spews up from the lower river, which winds its way toward the Marak volcano.

Then we look all the way across the island—and see the sky. Dark clouds loom over Marakuri's distant northern beaches. A shadow blackens the ocean, and from what we can see, the waves crashing against the shore are a lot rougher than they should be.

"Okay, that looks...*bad*."

"Turn around?"

"Yeah."

Glacia practically drags me back through the jungle, trampling the dirt and dead leaves and bark as we hurry away from the storm. At one point, several black-winged bugs zip in front of our faces, causing Glacia to scream and duck out of the way. In a matter of minutes, the rich yellow glow peeking through the canopy darkens, the storm covering the whole island. Through the trees, we catch glimpses of the city and bay, but we're still hundreds of feet up.

A gust of cool air...

The chirps and buzzes go quiet...

And a new sound replaces them.

A light rush. A deep rumble. Pattering noises race toward us, and just as we reach the base of the first peak, the first drop hits me.

Rain.

Water falls around us, splashing leaves and muddying the dirt. I tense my muscles, prepared for sharp stings—and wince when the first drop hits me. But...no. Chills shoot up my spine. The sensation actually feels *good*. Even though my clothes are sticking to my body and my hair is drenched and my nose is getting stuffy, the rain is refreshing, cleansing me of sweat and invigorating me with newfound energy.

Glacia's hair doesn't fare so well. It puffs out, then gets flattened as the rain pours harder...and suddenly the pattering has grown into a full-blown roar. Thunder rumbles in the sky. Glace shouts something, but I can't make it out. She points off to the side: through the trees, the storm is raging over the bay, torrents of rain so thick it's nearly impossible to see the main city, let alone Kiruni Dome, and the other two islands are gone completely.

The trail finally levels out. We break into a jog, keeping our heads down. Our feet splash in muddy puddles. I nearly slip off a slick root, and Glacia gets smacked in the face by a low-hanging branch that's swinging in the wind.

We reach the edge of the jungle and run onto the beachside walkway. Gray waves crash up the deserted shores, and by the time we reach a building to take refuge in, we're soaked to the skin. Glacia's hair sticks to her face, and our clothes drip water all over the floor— so much so that the desk attendant has to call in a robot to dry our mess.

We're shivering, and when we finally calm down, Glacia drops her head against my chest and breaks into a fit of giggles.

Chapter Twenty-Seven

FALLING...

Falling...

Falling...

I'm adjusting to the gravity elevator. *A bit.* My stomach still flips, and blood still rushes to my head, but thanks to training with the cyclo, the nausea doesn't hit me as hard as it did the first two times I rode these. Of course, I was half asleep the second time, so I don't exactly remember *what* I felt like then. But right now, the tug of my weight is sliding from my feet to my head as we fall.

Or rise.

Or whatever direction it is we're moving.

In any case, the seats reorient us.

Glacia isn't here. She returned to the Embassy a couple hours ago to start her new week of training. She already has atmospheric and station pilot licenses, and now she's working on crew transport and supply delivery, so she'll be training in orbit most of the week.

The gravity elevator wobbles. Clamps secure the pod. As soon as the harnesses release, Kile flings his over his head—face pale—and vomits in his disposal tube. A man with dark red hair walks into the pod and helps Kile off his knees, then gives him a medicine pouch.

"You *really* gotta toughen up that gut, Arlington." To the rest of us, Rand mouths, *'never gonna happen.'*

We left Marakuri at dawn, but here it's already early afternoon, a seven-hour time difference. According to Rand, we've crossed fourteen time zones in the last week. *Fourteen.*

I'm pretty sure my body has given up figuring out a sleep schedule.

Now we're on Hossiard, an archipelago in Daliona's mid-southern latitudes. The air is chilly—not freezing like it was on Bechi Island, but still cold enough to make me shiver.

From here, we ride a shuttle across the larger part of the island to the western cliffs. I stare out the window the entire time, watching the world go by. Rugged, rocky hills sharpen the landscape, their cliffs towering over barren plains and muddy valleys. Nearer to the coast, scattered tufts of yellowed grass poke up from the dirt, then pale green grass that's several feet tall.

We leave the craggy hills behind. Now we're surrounded by cultivated life. Dozens of fluffy white animals graze in the grasses, birds half my height squabble around in ponds. I see insects shooting this way and that to avoid the smaller birds that are chasing them, nothing but blurry streaks.

The shuttle stops in a settlement, then another, and then begins the longest stretch to our destination. We cross back onto barren plains, and jagged hills rise far off to our right. When the shuttle glides down the next hillside, the island's uncharacteristic flowery fields return. Beyond those, the ocean. Waves crash along the shore, spewing yellow foam over pillars of misshapen rock lining the coast.

The shuttle stops in the heart of a settlement along the shore. Most buildings here are short and flat-roofed. Like Bechi, the Hossiard Archipelago is first-and-foremost a scientific establishment, with greenhouses, telescopic observatories, and soil research facilities—all places we need to catalogue.

We discuss our agenda, then get right to work. Rand, Kile, and I go to the greenhouses, where we meet a short man who has a bald head and sparse black stubble sprouting from his chin. His black eyebrows are huge, and his neatly trimmed mustache is even larger. He's *definitely* not Dalish, and neither are the other people working in the greenhouse. Two of the women have bright ginger hair and skin so pale it almost looks like they've never been in the sun—like, ever—and another man has wavy blond hair, bright blue eyes, and thick teeth. The women are examining a blue-stalked plant with bright yellow flowers, and the other man is retrieving soil samples from a pot.

The man who greeted us introduces himself. "Bonj, I am Rusé LeBlanche." He shakes our hands, muttering *'bonj'* each time and holding solid eye contact. "You have come to catalogue the Floral Fertility Project, *yes?*"

"Yes we did," I say, cracking a grin now. I recognize

his accent. I heard it while we were in the Embassy: he's Yillosian. His voice is thick, yet smooth, as if Standard shouldn't be—or maybe *isn't*—his first language. Now that I'm *really* paying attention, I hear the other botanists speaking a language I can't understand, just like the Narvidians always do on Undil.

"I am glad you have chosen our greenhouses, Mr. Lance," Rusé says. "Our project is a fairly new extension to the Galactic Ecology Survey, so receiving this exposure should surely help us...er...*promote* our efforts. The hope, of course, is to apply our research to infertile planets, such as Undil."

"No, see, we're not infertile," Rand says. "We're just lazy."

Rusé chuckles, taking the comment as a joke, but still shifts a confused glance up at Rand. "Ah, I see. Well, our aim is to change that, certainly. My branch researches soil fertility and subsequently determines the most suitable conditions for a variety of floral life forms chosen to undergo planetary relocation."

When he says that, I remember what I heard on Marakuri's news feeds. They were talking about this sort of stuff all week, in fact. I know, because Glacia and I would watch the news as we ate breakfast.

"I saw that," I say. "The populations grew like twenty-five percent or something."

"Indeed, sir, though land-based population growth hasn't been so dramatic as the marine. With extinction threats rising on Rygin, Belvun, and *Husteng*"—he spits out the last planet's name—"it's past time we diversify what species we have, both floral and fauna. Daliona hosts large populations, *yes*, but in that same way, we are limiting life to one mold when we should be...er...reshaping it to fit in several."

Rusé spreads his fingers and pushes their tips together, forming a ball with his hands.

"For life to thrive, it needs to...to *break free* of its shell." He tips his hands apart, as if opening the ball. "Constraining life to one planet isn't healthy, *yes?* And yet, what will happen to the birds of Daliona if we relocate them Belvun without first letting a portion of their population adapt to life here? They will go extinct—a preventable extinction, *yes?*"

Rand utters a laugh. "Yeah, until you remember that Belvun's burning up."

Rusé raises his eyebrows, which makes his mustache block his nose. "We cannot stop pushing the limits, but in the same way, we must also provide nature with an infrastructure suitable for the life forms we wish to relocate. Do this across multiple planets, and we can create species that thrive where they once could not, *yes?*"

Most of that goes over my head. I'm just here to catalogue. But Rand starts blasting Rusé with all sorts of questions:

"Which species are lined-up to relocate?"

"Which planets are the best candidates?"

"I can make this guy"—he's pointing at me—*"write up a proposal to get Undil on the radar."*

To his disappointment, and mine, too, Undil isn't next on the list, even though it's part of the end goal.

"Give it another one or two hundred years," Rusé explains, giving a throaty chuckle as he scratches the corner of one huge eyebrow. "Your planet's terraformation is not far enough along to sustain anything beyond human life."

"*Like we haven't noticed*," Rand mutters.

He shows us around the greenhouses. It turns out all of the plants here are new species, bred right where we're standing. The project monitors and alters their growth using various fertilization techniques before setting them loose in the natural world. There's a plant with a blue stalk and yellow flowers called Hiberia Coloctus, which is a derived from the Orafrid, a flower found in the Yillosian tundra. Then there's the Metosia, a vine that sprouts juicy yellow berries, and the Revens Ursus, a bulbous red and blue flower hanging precariously off a thin stem.

All of them produce edible nectars and berries that have been genetically modified for maximum nutritional and medicinal value. Rusé lets us eat some and enthusiastically emphasizes that we're among the first people in all of human history to taste them. The berries have tiny seeds that crunch between my teeth, and their sweet, watery juices quench my thirst. He even lets us eat the stems of one plant, though Kile declines. He doesn't look too thrilled about making such *important* history.

Afterward, Rusé takes us to the greenhouse database and watches Rand establish a connection to RASP.

"I am correct to assume that Belvun is the next addition to your program, *yes?*" Rusé asks as he curiously reads Olivarr's description of RASP. "Until recently, I was not aware of the...*extent* of the fallout on Belvun. Only when we brought our project to Daliona did President Okana mention it during a conference, and briefly at that. Most Yillosians are in the dark, I believe. Some of us knew about Ellaciss City, of course, but the...*severity* of the crisis surprised us." He lifts his eyes apprehensively. "News doesn't travel quickly around the galaxy, and it has been longer than a century since Yillos last did dealings with Belvun. Most of our negotiations occur through Melles, Daliona, *Husteng*, and Undil—though that is rare." He makes the same throaty chuckle as he did earlier. "And I cannot begin to say *who* does dealings with Narviid anymore."

"We do," I tell him. "Belvun, too. We have residency programs."

"Ah, I was unaware. Well, I do hope you have a chance to visit Yillos in your travels. Our tundra is home to herds of killari, and the great seasonal migration is one of the galaxy's most spectacular events to witness."

Rusé escorts us to the exit and shakes our hands on the way out, this time muttering *'rev'* to us.

* * * * *

I don't sleep that night. My body is seven hours behind Hossiard, so I'm only just getting tired when Rand sends out the wake-up call. The five of us meet for breakfast and drink unreasonable amounts of coffee and energy juice, because it turns out *none* of us slept well.

Then we start the day. We ride a shuttle across Hossiard and over a wide gorge to Bondalp, the archipelago's other main island. Unlike Hossiard, it has yet to be cultivated. No flowers bloom in the dry, grassy fields, no swathes of color decorate the barren soils.

Before long, we're zooming down a twisting slope toward an inlet, where another town sits tucked below the cliffs, and tall white domes—telescope observatories—stand on the highest hills.

We catalogue the town's facilities, and then hike a very narrow, very steep trail up the cliffs to reach the observation domes. Not only is the path barely wider than my body, but I'm not used to scaling uneven rocks, many of which are loose. By the time we reach the top, all five of us are exhausted. If it weren't for the view, I'd regret the entire—

"Are. You. Kidding. Me."

Rand points behind the domes: a gentle trail wraps around the slope, probably leading straight to the town.

That's it.

I regret the hike.

The twin telescopic domes sit on either side of the Astronomy Center, a sort of museum that looks like a StarPad exploded inside it. There are detailed maps of what some people refer to as the Bubble, the region of the galaxy humans have explored and settled. Holographic models of the other planets in Daliona's solar system float above pedestals, complete with moons, artificial satellites, and other nearby objects. Timers count down to meteor showers, eclipses, and planetary transits. But my favorite section is called the *Our Galactic Backyard*. It has holograms of wavy, colorful nebulae, churning supernovae, models of black holes and wormholes, magnetars, quasars, and more. I could spend *hours* in here. Heck, Glacia would be in love with this place. She'd never leave.

And that's why we have RASP. Not only to catalogue

these places for the Embassy, but to be able to share things like *this* with people who will never be able to visit Daliona, or Belvun, or Yillos, or the other planets. We could put this kind of stuff in Primary and Secondary, build museums with augmented tours, build stellariums for people to learn, for people to feel inspired. I get to bring all of that back to Undil.

This is part of my calling.

Once we've spent enough time in the museum—and for the record, I haven't—the observatory's director, Usef Keck, takes us into one of the domes, which houses a massive telescope. I've never looked through a real telescope before, but I've seen older versions, and these aren't so different. Forty-foot mirrors, laser-guided, multiple filters.

After we link the Astronomy Center to RASP, Director Keck invites us to come back tonight for a tour of the night sky.

Awesome.

We leave and make the easier trek back to the town. At the bottom, however, something farther along the base of the cliff catches our attention: a flock of birds waddling from the shore to the cliffs. The nearer we get, the less they actually *look* like birds. They aren't like any birds I've ever seen, at least. Their wings are stumpy, their heads perfectly round, and their bodies are gray and brown or black and white. But what sticks out most are their absurdly long yellow and red eyelashes. A lot of them are gathered at the base of the cliff, squawking noisily as they wait their turn to...*what?*

"*Seriously?*" Rand shakes his head in frustration. "I'm done. These suckers are putting us to shame."

And it's true: the birds are *hopping* up a jagged path in the cliff. The five of us watch, dumbfounded, as one leaps forward and lands on a ledge more than a foot off the ground. Then it looks up, bends over, and leaps to another rock. And another. And another. There's a line of birds...thirty feet up...now forty...and one by one, they hop over the top and wobble out of view.

"Well, this is just embarrassing."

The birds leap and climb, leap and climb. Dozens of them. Then one makes a running leap—but misjudges the distance, smacks off the cliff, and bounces to the ground, where it squawks and thrashes around before two others scramble over and use their beaks to shove the bird back on its fat feet.

"*That's what you get, you stumpy menace!*" Rand shouts at it. The rest of us can't help but laugh.

We stay on Bondalp the rest of the day and eat dinner in one of the town's restaurants: freshly caught fish, cooked-vegetables soaking in a spicy glaze, brown rice, juice that was squeezed in the Yillosian greenhouses. And when it gets dark, the sky shines with thousands of stars and the Milky Way stretches straight up over the ocean, so bright I swear it's casting a shadow. But that's how dark and isolated these islands are. Except for the dimly lit paths and a few windows, no light leaves the town, giving the observatories a perfect view of the perfect skies.

We head back up to the Astronomy Center, where Director Keck already has the telescope fixed on a patch of the sky. There's also a screen that shows us what the telescope is seeing, but looking through it just feels more...*real*. When I put my eye to the piece, I can't believe what I'm seeing: a striped, purple-and-white planet with dozens of bright dots lined-up around it.

"Vanoss," Director Keck tells us. "A gas giant."

Next we look at Merin, a rocky, yellowish planet marked with black spots, then at Galadrel, a pure blue gas planet with dim icy rings. That's all we can see in the solar system, so Director Keck rotates the telescope, adjusts the settings, and adds different filters.

Now we're looking at sprawling nebulae, pockets of dark matter, and plumes of dust and gas hanging in the void. There's so much out there that I've never knew there *could* be. So much of it is invisible to the naked eye—but there nonetheless.

Director Keck lines up the last object of the night, and soon we're looking into the depths of another galaxy, gray and blue around the edges and bright yellow and white at its center. Even before he tells us, I know what it is. It was the largest thing in the night sky back on Undil.

"Andromeda, the Milky Way's closest neighbor," Director Keck says. "A trillion stars, twice as many as are in our own. Every dot, every prick of light you see… Those are stars. The distance between each is five light-years, on average. Fantastic, no?"

No.

Fantastic doesn't even *begin* to describe seeing Andromeda up close. The stars are sprinkled around like dust in sunlight—times a million. I can't look away. What if I'm looking at entire civilizations? And what if they're looking back? It's scary to think that I could be looking at an alien, and an alien could be looking at me, and neither of us knows—and we may *never* know. Because, even in the Milky Way, we've yet to find intelligent life. Yes, we've found plants and animals, but we've never encountered another society, never come across aliens who have built cities and space stations, who are out here exploring the galaxy just like us, waiting to find another civilization, *hoping* they're not alone.

Now that I think about it, the thought sends chills up my spine: what if we're all there is? What if nobody is out there, anywhere? What would it mean to be the most intelligent life form in the universe?

Chapter
Twenty-Eight

I ENDURE ANOTHER sleepless night.

It's not just my body this time. It's my thoughts. Like how I wish Glacia was here right now. How I wish she could've seen the Astronomy Center and looked through the telescope with us. She still hasn't responded to the pictures I sent. Maybe she's training. Or sleeping. Or practicing for that gravity run. Am I worried? Yeah. Every time I picture her on that, I see her breaking a leg, or an arm, or worse. It's stupid. I know she won't. She'll be fine. She's Glacia Haverns. Nothing stops her. Nothing ever has, nothing ever will. Still, it's dangerous, and she isn't one to care that much about her own safety, I think. She pushes hard. Too hard. She said she's not reckless...but that doesn't mean she doesn't take risks. She does. She takes too many. And on a gravity run, she can't do that. If she falls, or crashes, or worse—

No.

She won't.

But I don't *know* that.

Does she say *'no fear'* before her runs, like Rand does? Or did she come up with her own motto? I don't even know. I'm not the one who trained with her every day. That was Rand. *Rand* always took her to the practice runs. *Rand* always taught her new techniques. *Rand* always bragged about how well she's doing. How she's a natural. How she's got more guts than me. How gravity runs are for the daredevils, and cyclos are for wimps.

Yeah. Sure. I'm a wimp for feeling so free when I fly around, flipping through the air, or jumping to what *would* be my death—before catching myself and soaring to safety. He doesn't know how that makes me feel. All he cares about is how fast he can go down a run. He's broken bones and bloodied himself up. Is it just a game to him? *Let's see what I can break today!* Who in their right mind *likes* that? No. *He* wasn't in a car accident. *He* didn't have to look next to him and see his dead father. *He* didn't sit there, gasping for air, scared he was going to die.

No fear. That should be *my* motto, not his. He hasn't felt *half* my pain. I lived through so much more. So much...more...

I lived.

I lived to carry Father's name.

I lived to see Mother and the twins again.

I lived, and fell in love with Glacia.

I lived, and saw the Embassy. Belvun. Daliona. The Perihelids. The Kairos supernova.

I lived, and I've been making my dreams come true. I'm doing something with my life. I didn't hide. I didn't quit. I'm trying harder, becoming better, learning more about myself and my universe. I've felt the warmth of three stars, met people from different planets, seen creatures I've only ever read about in books. And there's so much more out there for me to experience.

Because *I lived.*

✳ ✳ ✳ ✳ ✳

BOOM BOOM BOOM BOOM BOOM.

Loud, angry shouts.

I bolt awake. Stars swim in my eyes. Dizzy. So dizzy. And my holotab is buzzing like crazy.

"Lance!" Rand's irritated voice shouts from outside my door. *"We should've left twenty minutes ago! GET. UP."*

Now that I see the time, I think I got...maybe an hour of sleep.

Great.

I tear off my nightclothes, throw on my uniform, and stuff everything into my trunk. No time for a shower, which sucks. My hair's a mess and my face is greasy. But I know if I do—

"You better not be taking a—"

I slap my palm against the panel, and the door slides open. Rand is standing there, clean and shaven and angry. His holotab is in his palm, still calling mine, which hasn't stopped buzzing. He takes one look at me and scrunches his nose.

"Whooooo... You reek, Lance. Do us a favor and shower next time."

He winks and slaps the back of my shoulder before

motioning me toward the end of the hall, where Allison, Trey, and Kile are already waiting.

Catch a shuttle.

Board a pod.

And fall, fall, fall...

✳ ✳ ✳ ✳ ✳

I bolt awake.

Somebody's shaking my arm. Trey. And he's giving me a worried look.

"*Sorry,*" he whispers so only I can hear. "*Thought you blacked out.*"

I shake my head, then squeeze my eyes and yawn. It feels like we're still falling.

No, rising.

Gah. Whatever.

The pod is slowing down. That's what matters.

Minutes later, we stop. The hatch opens, Kile throws up. I stagger out behind Trey and am immediately blinded by sunlight. The roof of this gravity dock is a glass dome. Voices echo noisily in the chamber. I look at a sign to remember where we are. *Cavellor Archipelago Research Districts*, it says. Dots flash on a map, labeling some of the larger locations: the *Mizzono-Suzu Particle Collider* is to the north, the *Tavizzio Academy of Relativistic Sciences* is far to the northeast, the *Gane's Museum of Pre-Modern Technology* is a bit east of Cavellor's main island, and the *Cycloidal Gravity Wave Application Facility* is just beyond that.

From what I see, the entire archipelago is dedicated

to innovative tech and theoretical sciences...things I know will go right over my head. Olivarr Cresson would love it here, though. We'd lose him in a matter of minutes and never find him.

I'm dragging my feet, and my eyes sting, and I keep yawning, but Rand makes us get right to work. Yeah, I'm in charge, but I want to sleep...and that's not productive. So I let Rand take over for the day, and as we make our way by to the first facility, he gets me a pack of energy shots and some granola.

The Mizzono-Suzu Particle Collider turns out to be the largest collider ever built. It's submerged a mile under the seafloor, circling the entire island of Vizzona. We have to ride an underwater shuttle to the main operating facility, put on sterilized body suits, and then pass through a neutralizing chamber before we're allowed anywhere near the collider. Even then, we're still not allowed to see the machine in its entirety. I'm not complaining. This thing is nearly sixty-three miles all the way around. Walking five hundred feet is good enough for me. Still, I have no idea what I'm looking at. It's not *too* impressive, just a bunch of photonic info receptors and data panels lining the walls. But when Director Adessi takes us to the surveillance labs, she shows us real-time analyses of colliding particles. Okay. I admit: *that* is neat, like watching fireworks on a subatomic scale, because the machine is replicating some of the strongest forces in the universe.

The physicists are studying the small-scale effects of these forces in an effort to harness teleportation technology for normal matter objects, a project Director Adessi tells us was expedited by the Belvun crisis.

"We cannot afford the long resource delivery trips between planets," she explains. "If we advance beyond quantum teleportation, we could theoretically supply aid within minutes, instead of months."

But they're nowhere near figuring out normal-matter teleportation. I think back to what Rand said a couple weeks ago: so far, it's been *'violently destructive.'* Nope, I can't see how this could *possibly* be dangerous, what with smashing atoms together and creating mini black holes.

Ha.

Throughout the rest of this day and most of the next, we move down the island chain, cataloguing, cataloguing, and, of course, cataloguing some more. Most labs are dedicated to enhancing experimental technologies: cyclo suits, opticons, the Lucidity Interface, and modern hyper drives. All of those and more were conceived right here in Cavellor.

We even tour the technology museum I saw when we arrived. Some of the displays are computers with keyboards that click, cars with rubber wheels, pre-modern aerial crafts called helicopters and airplanes, wooden pencils and ink pens that people would use to write, pedal bikes, giant farming machines, and much, *much* more. Trey goes absolutely nuts, taking pictures of every exhibit and grabbing a whole bag of souvenirs, including several build-it-yourself kits.

I can't help noticing the *variety* of the technology people had back then. On Undil, we only have holotabs and work panels, one type of maglev car, one type of hovercraft, one type of stylus. It's all *condensed*. What we have works, and we don't need anything else.

After spending three days on Cavellor, we drop to the Westin Isles, a string of narrow islands rich in mineral deposits. There are salt mines in ancient cave systems that rose above the ocean as the archipelago grew, leaving the cliffs of the outermost islands stark white. The inner islands are densely forested, with river rapids surging down narrow ravines that formed as the archipelago rose from the ocean.

We get to work after eating a quick lunch. The first facility we catalogue is the headquarters of the Sedimentary and Geological Evolution Project, yet another branch of the Galactic Ecology Survey. The director shows us maps of Daliona's plate tectonics, its most active volcanic activity, how ecosystems are affected by hurricanes and eruptions, and even a time-lapse of how some of the archipelagos have changed since the first settlers arrived two thousand years ago.

Near the end of the tour, I notice Rand is missing. He's not in the main labs, won't answer our calls. It turns out he hung back with a group of geologists who are showing him what each layer of the sedimentary deposits represents, how the Westin Isles are situated on top of a convergent plate boundary and grow about four inches per century.

We visit the salt mines on the second day. The cave openings are two hundred feet above the ocean, and eight hundred below the top of the island. We have to ride an elevator to the entrances and put on ventilation masks before going inside...and I soon know why: even with the masks, the pungent smell makes me feel sick, like I'm breathing ocean water.

The caves themselves are several stories tall. Some of the ceilings have had to be back-filled and braced to prevent the land from caving in. The ground crunches under our feet and the walls are brittle to the touch, so much so that chunks of salt sprinkle down when I brush my hand across. And my eyesight... All the color seems to have been sucked away. The walls of salt absorb the light so much that we're surrounded by different shades of white and gray. And the noise that *should* fill our ears is muffled, even as scraper machines sheer off layers of salt onto the conveyors lining the caverns.

The Westin Isles don't have a cyclo arena, but there *is* a gravity run on Hashmere, one of the northernmost islands in the archipelago. Caves and tunnels have been drilled into Westin, Hashmere, and Precipice to accommodate the track.

For once, I'm actually following Kile's lead: staying back while Trey, Allison, and Rand go off and have fun. We hang out in the spectator complex, glancing up at the video feeds every so often to see if any of them have gone yet. There's another panel that lists the course records from years past—and Rand's name in fourth place, set five years ago.

I point it out to Kile. "I don't know how he does it."

He forces a laugh. "Me neither."

We get quiet. This is the first time I've been alone with Kile. I feel bad for never really talking to him, but he doesn't seem to *want* to talk, so...I guess he's fine. Even now, he's just watching the video panel. His elbows are on the table, chin propped on his thumbs with his hands blocking his mouth. I want to say something, but what? It reminds me of those first few days—*weeks*, even—of working with Captain Blitner, how we spoke only when we needed to. But then...

But then he told me stories about Father. And Belvun. And a few about Daliona. I remember when we were working in Stationary Plaza, he would look at that gray mountain, the one that stood far to the south of the Belvish Embassy, beyond the forest, even beyond the Hania Reserve. *Beautiful things should be smiled at*, he'd said. His last words. His eyes were crinkled, bright, young, and happy. His hands were folded in his lap. Did he know he was about to die? He was just...smiling at the mountain, with me sitting quietly by his side.

"Thanks for your help, Kile." Then I add, "Like, seriously."

Kile picks his head up and looks at me. "No problem. Sorry I'm not...like..."

He shrugs and looks back at the video feed.

Gah.

Awkward.

Allison makes her run first. There are two video feeds: one from her helmet, and one from the cameras placed down the track. She shoots down it, leaning this way, then that way, twisting, dipping, swinging around wide turns. The screens nearly go dark when the track curves inside the artificial caves. Silhouettes flash by, blurry shadows. The cameras shift angles as Allison zooms past them.

She bursts into the light again, enters a dense fog rolling off the cliffs, then angles down a steep dive. Her speed jumps from thirty to forty miles per hour in a matter of seconds. Her body tenses. She grips the handles tighter, stiffens her legs and stomach, forces all of her concentration into timing every turn in the track. She's *way* slower than the track average, and with no hope of making up the lost time. One more turn, and she hits the final straightaway.

That's it: two minutes and forty-nine seconds—a full fifty seconds slower than the record.

Trey's run is faster than Allison's, but he nearly tips off his sled coming out of the final dive, which spooks him so much that he slows down and doesn't even try to lean into the last turns, costing him even more time.

Then Rand sets up.

3...

2...

1...

He mouths '*no fear.*'

And his sled shoots off.

From the top, I'm in awe of his precision, how he calculates his movements. He twists only his hips—never his torso. He minimizes his movements, anticipating how the sled will react to every twitch. Rand's body doesn't turn with the sled. They flow together. He only accelerates. Allison and Trey both slid up and down the sides of the tube around the wide arcs—Rand hardly deviates from the ideal path. The momentum is his. The curves are his.

The track.

Is.

His.

When he hits the final dive, he doesn't hold back. His

speed jumps from forty-eight to sixty-two miles per hour, and he streaks across the finish line five milliseconds slower than his personal track record.

I bet he's disappointed.

✳ ✳ ✳ ✳ ✳

"It's so humid, Glace."

"Glad I'm not there, then." Glacia sticks her tongue at me. "How much longer?"

"Two days, and then we go to Noya for a week."

"Gotcha."

Glacia's still in the Embassy. She won't join us again until next Friday, when we go to Selayche Island, our final destination.

My team is on Culsaren Island now. We've been here four days, and I'm sorry, but this place *sucks*. The air outside gets so thick I feel like I'm drowning, *especially* in the early afternoon. I swear I've never sweat so much in my life. All the buildings have dehumidifier vents so we don't suffer indoors, and there are thunderstorms every single day at five-thirty—*on the dot*. Watching the storms from my hotel room is neat, but there's no way I'd get caught out there. The storm on Marakuri was nothing compared to these...*monsters*. For a full thirty minutes, the sky turns black. The wind bends the trees sideways, blowing off loose leaves and bark and dirt. Jagged bolts of lightning pierce the sky, and the thunder... The thunder rips the air. Sometimes it's so strong, the windows shake.

And then, right around six o'clock—it all ends. Blue

skies, a rainbow in the retreating clouds, and steam rising from the hot, soaked ground.

But the humidity?

That *never* goes away.

"Michael's coming out to watch me race tomorrow," Glacia says after we've been quiet for a while. A pause, and then, "I wish you could, too."

I half-laugh and look away from her hologram. She's wearing her swimsuit, reclined on one of Thorpe's beaches, and I can hear ocean crashing rolling nearby.

"Rand said he'd come out if you guys weren't so busy."

"I'm sure he would." Then I add, "Surprised he *isn't*."

"Some of his friends are, though," she says loudly over the rush of a wave cresting in front of her. "He said they might take me on the team. They're, like, scouting me."

"Cool."

"Yeah." I hear someone else's voice, and Glacia tilts my view sideways. "Kerin says hi!"

Glacia's hall mate and training partner, Kerin Richter, waves at me from another beach recliner. I force a smile and wave back.

"Hey."

Glacia snorts and turns the view back on her. "*Sooo* enthusiastic."

"Mmhmm."

"Have you been training?" I lift an eyebrow, so she says, "With the cyclo."

"Yeah. Every day. Well, not on Westin. But here I am. And I actually saw where cyclos were invented on Cavellor."

"That's cool!"

Another half-laugh. "Yeah."

I close my eyes and feel the pillow under my head. It's well after midnight. I could fall asleep. I need it. The last couple weeks have been exhausting. We just haven't stopped moving. At all. And Culsaren is wiping me out. I wish we could just go to Selayche. Anywhere but here, really. I'd even go back to Bechi at this point.

Shhhuuuhhh...whoosh.

Shhhuuuhhh...whoosh.

The rush of the waves and the wind blast out from my holotab. I don't even hear Glacia until she says,

"You awake, mister?"

I don't open my eyes. "Yup."

"Did you hear me?"

"Nope."

A pause, then, "I said I miss you."

One second...two seconds...three—

"I miss you, too."

"Two more weeks. Not even. Then we can go have some fun."

I finally open my eyes, just in time to see her smiling, but it looks just as forced as the ones I've been making the last couple minutes.

"Victoria said she's gonna meet us on Selayche," Glacia goes on saying. "Lars and Olivarr, too. They've been all over the place. And Olivarr keeps running off. It's so funny."

"Yeah."

I breathe a heavy sigh and close my eyes again, listening to the waves. I try to smile, but it falls. I miss her. I want her *here*. We're supposed to be traveling together, not separated like this. It's the longest we've ever gone without seeing each other, and it sucks. And it sucks even more when Rand talks about her. Or when *she* talks about him. Hell, he's making us have a party tomorrow to watch her race in the Laka Gravity Challenge. That's all he talked about today, actually. *'Haverns this,'* and *'Haverns that,'* and *'She'll be the captain of the racing team one day, just watch.'* His so-called team isn't even an official thing. They only race every couple years. How can they call that a *racing team?* It's not like they can practice on Undil.

Glacia sits up, and a shadow covers half her face. "I'll let you sleep, okay?"

I don't even open my eyes this time. "Okay."

"Goodnight, mister."

"Night."

I drop the holotab at my side, but it's still several seconds before the sounds of the ocean go silent.

* * * * *

"We should've gone, Lance. Let these other suckers finish cataloguing. Haverns needs us on the sidelines."

Rand elbows my arm as we ride an elevator to the hotel lounge, which has the largest video panel we could find. He ordered some food to be delivered for the evening, and when we reach the lounge, some Dalish chefs are arranging dinner platters for us.

Rand finds coverage of the Laka Gravity Challenge. The screen is divided into four sections: aerial coverage, helmet camera feeds, interior track cameras, and a chart of the Top 20 track times of the day. The aerial coverage is high above Laka Island—the island located just southwest of Thorpe. As it circles around, Daliona's space elevator comes into view, rising from the jungles of Thorpe Island and up...up...up into the atmosphere. Then the screen flicks to a view of the run from the main complex, where competitors are lined up in a queue.

The challenge has been going on for an hour already, but Glacia's time isn't for a while yet. If she completes the course without falling, she'll get a medal. If she places in the Top 20—which I highly doubt, seeing how the current Top 20 is made up of professionals—she'll be eligible to go on a planet-wide tour competing on gravity runs ranked the same difficulty as Laka until there's one winner. That person gets put in the Hall of Fame and wins vacation packages and other perks. Rand even said that the winner of the hardest challenge series gets to travel to any planet on this side of the galaxy. Undil, Belvun, and Narviid are left out.

Of course.

A panel of announcers keeps talking in the background. I can tell who Daliona's famous racers are just by how the announcers say their names.

"And we know Hollanko will be watching Bachelli today. He said Bachelli has been training six hours a day in preparation for this run. We may even see them again on Tahani in two weeks..."

"Liki Maruho has been the woman to watch ever since she shattered Gregorio Tellsar's record back on the Jukuto Run last year."

"Yerifa Coomball has had quite a nerve-racking year.

Remember he broke his collarbone in that nasty crash last April. We were all worried he might not make a comeback. But here he is, ready to redeem his name."

Even Rand knows a lot of the Dalish racers. He tells us who to root for, who to hate, who he thinks cheats, who he's met in real life. I can't tell if he's kidding or not, but *he* claims to have given out autographs. I look to Trey and Allison, but they seem just as suspicious.

"Fine," Rand says, raising his hands defensively. "Don't believe me. But I can tell you those autographs will be in the Hall of Fame one day. Daliona will never forget *Rand Harmat,* th—"

"That guy from Undil who never shuts up," Allison interrupts, smirking at him before taking another bite of her fish sandwich.

"Oy!" Rand tears into his own sandwich and chews obnoxiously, giving her an unblinking stare.

The queue of names keeps updating as people go down the run. The fastest time of the day is *2:01.32,* set by Terran Oculo. Second place was half a second slower, and the rest have ranged anywhere from point-nine to a full forty-five seconds slower.

Then Glacia's name appears on the queue, and Rand and I have two different reactions: my chest freezes, and anxiety sears through my body. I bite my lip over and over and over. A lot of people have crashed. Some slam into the walls, some tip over around a turn, or get flung off when they crest a hill. All I can think about is when I fell. How I skidded on my back. My shoulders and legs ached for days. But it could've been worse. It could've been *a lot* worse.

Next to me, Rand claps and gets ready to record Glacia's run. He keeps muttering things to himself, little pep talks like he'd give her whenever they trained.

Three more people...

Two more people...

One more person...

And Glacia sets up on the track.

She's wearing a standard Dalish racing suit, nothing special or customized like Rand's team or a number of the other racers we've watched. It's just a green, white, and blue full-body suit and a blue helmet.

The countdown flashes on the screen, and then,

3...

2...

1...

She definitely mouths, *'no fear.'*

And the gravity sled shoots into the tunnel.

A hard left-hand turn. A straightaway. A drop. Glacia's face is contorted, eyes narrowed, jaw clenched. She looks in the direction of the next turn—then flinches her legs and zooms around the curve with a slight wobble.

Her visor's video feed shows the ideal path, but she's only managed to trace that line forty percent of the time so far. She isn't going as fast as she could, either. Forty miles per hour, then fifty. By this point, other racers were going sixty or faster. There's no way she'll be in the Top 20.

Good.

Over the video feeds, the announcers comment on her technique, too. *"Glacia Haverns, a pilot from Undil. First time competing on a professional course. Not bad for a first run, of course, but clearly still a lot to learn. See how she's using her legs? Don't want to do that. Too much movement there. You want your body to remain still as it can be, of course. Keep it all in the hips. Notice how her head's a tad high, too? The drag on the air is going to slow her down more than she knows."*

Glacia dips down a short drop into an underwater spiral that gets tighter, and tighter, and tighter—then blasts onto a straightaway at fifty-nine miles per hour and swerves up an incline.

Over a hill...

...and down the other side.

That's where a lot of racers have been thrown off—but they were moving *much* faster. Glacia is already a full twenty seconds slower than first place, well out of the Top 20. It almost makes me relieved, knowing she won't be—

Allison covers her mouth. Rand sucks in a breath, cursing. Glacia's hand slipped going around the turn, causing her shoulder to roll off the sled. She swerved so far off the ideal path that she was practically sideways, the golden line out of view. Her speed drops by half. The announcers make more comments about rookie mistakes, and then she's gliding into the last straightaway...

Back into the light...

Crossing the finish line.

Her time flashes on the screen: *2:37.09.*

Rand spreads his arms over the back of the couch. "Crossing the line is what counts. The pro tracks are a lot trickier that those public ones. *A lot* trickier." He looks at me and shrugs. "Hey, now you can say you're dating a pro gravity runner."

"Ha, yeah."

She didn't get hurt. That's what matters. Nearly fall-ing spooked her, just like it spooked Trey when he nearly fell on Westin's run last week. It won't stop her, though. Even I know that. She has her medal. To her— and Rand—*that's* what matters. They live for the rush. They break barriers.

All I do is build them up.

Chapter Twenty-Nine

ONE FOOT DOWN, then the other, and I'm back on solid ground. The whir of the cyclo suit ceases... Weight returns to my body. That felt good. That felt *really* good. My best training session yet.

I just came out of a dive. Wasn't even nervous as the ground rushed up at me, because I knew. I knew *exactly* when I'd flip, *exactly* when I'd level out, *exactly* when I'd land. My timing has become precise, my accuracy has improved tenfold. And my landing was soft that I barely felt my feet touch the floor.

Rand is waiting for me outside the cyclo complex. He was training on the gravity run, one of his last sessions before he competes in the Tahani Gravity Challenge six days from now. During our stay in the Noya Archipelago, we've been training at the Gidion Sports Complex, a massive, oblong dome that covers a four square miles of Gano Island. There are three gravity runs of varying difficulty twisting through the complex, looping around each other and even going outside in some places. Rand convinced me to try out the easiest one when we arrived, but it only managed to reaffirm my anxiety.

We catch a ferry back to Noya Island, and as the boat skims over the bay, I watch the sports complex shrink against the rest of Gano Island. We cruise through the heart of the archipelago, between dozens of lush islands covered in pastures and vineyards and groves of fruit trees. They're nicknamed the Orchard Islands, and when we catalogued them, we got to keep bags of fresh fruit—and *wow*. Some had just enough crunch in the bite, some had large pits in the center, and some were so, *so* sour, but delicious all the same.

Rand leans backward on the railing. "I gotta say, you look good in a cyclo suit, Lance. *I'm serious*," he adds when I give a short laugh of disbelief. "You remind me of...well, *me* on a run. In the zone. In control."

I never told him how impressed I was with his run in the Westin Isles, so, "You're pretty good, too. At the gravity runs."

He nudges my shoulder. "Just *pretty good?*"

"That's not—okay, yeah." I can't win with him, can I? "You should stay here and become a pro."

"Nah. As much as I love that life, there are more important things. The Belvun crisis, for one. I'd rather be somewhere useful. Here? I'd have thousands of girls fawning over me, and a few guys, too, no doubt. But how's that helping anyone? Just because we're in paradise doesn't mean those people on Belvun don't exist. They have *real* problems, we don't, so it's our obligation to help them. Understand? All that matters is what we choose to do about it: ignore them and watch a whole planet die, or make an effort to help. I don't know about you, but I choose the latter." Rand looks down at me, his arms crossed. "Always choose the second option, Lance. Option two *always* does the most good."

I nod as I stare out over the water, watching the islands slide by in the distance. He's right, in a way. After Father died, I wanted to give up—but I didn't. Then I went to Belvun in search of Ladia—but came away with Glacia. When Orcher asked me to take over the archives, my first reaction was to say no—but I said yes. A year ago, I only wanted to live on Belvun, to fall in love with Ladia, and never look back. Now I'm heading up a new program and traveling around the first planet humans ever settled.

All because I chose the second option.

"Tell it to me straight, Lance: how'd you get your girl?" Rand counts off on his fingers. "You're not good with words, you've got questionable looks, and you aren't the chosen one, so what was it? She lose a bet?"

Just like that, my smile dies. I look down at the water and listen to the hum of the ferry. How am I supposed to respond to *that?* Here I thought he was making an effort not to come off as a jerk, and he says that. *Lose a bet.* Yup, that's me. Glacia's mistake. He doesn't know what she did for me—what we've done for each other. Doesn't know all those stupid times when Glacia pelted me in the face in Hologis, then turned around and tried to hang out with me when no one else would, only for me to turn her down and continue the cycle I'd trapped myself in. He doesn't know about the night she showed me the stars, or when I came back to her in the Belvish Embassy, or our hike in the Hania Reserve. He doesn't know she likes it when I call her *Glace*. Doesn't know that her favorite drink is Armici Tea—or *was*, rather. Now she likes marsellion juice. And she never puts her hair over her right shoulder, only the left. One of her eyes has a green ring around the hazel, and the other has a blue ring. When we hold hands, she walks one step behind me. When she smiles, her lips pull up higher on the left side than on the right, the cutest grin ever. When she laughs, her voice cracks.

Rand bends over the railing beside me. "Man to man, Lance." He waves a hand over the side of the ferry. "Forget all this for a minute. You wanna know why I was discharged from Shield?"

I look up—not at him, but straight ahead. He takes that as a yes, even though I meant it to come off as *'you're annoying me.'* But when he next speaks, his voice is softer than usual.

"*Professional indecency*. Me and this girl, Sasha. Met her my first night in the Embassy. I...we hung out too much for Shield's liking. It got in the way. Nearly ruined her career. Stupid of me. But I struck a deal in the hearing: if I voluntarily resigned, neither of us would get kicked and the affair would be pardoned. She could keep her job, I could find a new one. So I took up planetary sciences and worked a couple years in Horizon, then transferred to Threshold to work for Orcher when this whole thing started on Belvun. I've really gotten around, haven't I? How many people can say they worked for every branch in the Embassy, huh? Not many."

Rand presses his palms together, puffs his cheeks, and watches the last of the islands pass by before we enter Noya Bay. Then,

"I haven't talked to her in like, three...maybe four years. Shield doesn't exactly let discharged officers visit, no matter how sentimental you sound. And once you're a ranked officer, you don't leave the compound unless you're assigned to an expedition. It's a prison, Lance. A military breeding ground. All you do is train. But the day I left, my supervisor told me I wasn't cut out to be a soldier anyway, that I had more potential because I asked questions while the others stayed silent. In simulations, I made connections between things other recruits didn't even realize were pieces of the same puzzle. You *need* critical thinkers, Lance"—he taps his head with one finger—"because sometimes your brain is all you've got."

✳ ✳ ✳ ✳ ✳

Kile somehow managed to kick his puking habit. When the gravity pod locks in place and the hatch opens, all of us are surprised when he doesn't bolt for the disposal tubes. We throw glances his way for several minutes afterward, as if every little noise he makes is a sign he's about to throw up.

The gravity dock is full of commotion, and for good reason: we're finally on Selayche Island—*the* Selayche Island—home of the Pelago Hotel and some of Daliona's most popular resorts and attractions. Glacia will arrive tonight, and we'll spend the next week in paradise, our last full week on Daliona.

"Well *that* was perfect timing!"

I recognize the voice, and before I can turn around, two hands slap down on my shoulders and give me a quick shake: Officer Remmit. He greets the others, hesitating only when he goes to shake Rand's hand. They don't say much, just lock eyes. It's clear they both remember the argument they had when they first met back in November.

Olivarr and Victoria are standing behind him. Judging by the wild look Olivarr has slapped on his face, he's just as eager as I am to see Selayche for the first time.

"Thought we should catch up since we missed you back on Marakuri," Officer Remmit says. "There's no better place, really. Third time in my life I've gotten to vacation on Selayche. I love it." He jerks his thumb back at Olivarr. "Oh, you wouldn't believe how hard it is to keep track of *him*. Turn our backs for one second, and *bam!* Gone."

Olivarr gives an innocent shrug. He's only half-listening, his eyes fixed on the gate that keeps opening and shutting as people walk in and out, revealing brief glimpses of the world outside. He edges toward it, forcing the rest of us to follow. Then we're standing on a walkway lining the edge of a cliff, which overlooks a steep valley that opens toward the ocean. The sun is setting, casting gold and orange rays through the thin clouds drifting toward it. Dark green mountains line the far coast, closing in the bay and beach.

A resort sits in the center of the valley. Closest to us

are condos with large windows, pools, and patios, but the main area lies at the head of the valley. Foot bridges span narrow streams, gardens decorate hillsides, and three waterfalls flow off the top of the resort's central tower. Glowing elevators slide up and down its sides, fading from red to yellow to green to blue to purple and then red again. A marina sticks off the beach. Some boats are anchored there, and others float in the deeper waters between dozens of smaller, manmade islands that are arranged in the sprawling design of the Dalish flag.

Officer Remmit extends his arms. "This is the Mukalana Valley Resort. Don't get too excited, though. We aren't staying here."

He's speaking to me, Kile, and Olivarr. But I already knew this wasn't the Pelago Hotel, because when I watched the show on Marakuri, it looked nothing like this. It was built in the ocean, not on land, and disk-shaped tiers made up each level.

Officer Remmit and Victoria lead the way to the cliff inclines. We ride one down into the valley, then catch a shuttle and glide through the resort, passing by illuminated pools, tropical trees, crystal clear streams, and private patios. People are swimming, or relaxing in hammocks, or hosting dinner parties, or walking through the resort's quieter, more secluded areas. One Dalish couple is standing at the edge of a balcony, arms around each other as they watch the sunset.

The shuttle stops at the central tower, where some people get off and others get on, and then we speed away again. At the beach, the track curves left, toward the mountain ridge I saw from the incline. Large birds are circling over the water, and a few dive into it, then reappear with a speared fish flopping in their bills.

When the track rounds the mountain, I see it: the Pelago Hotel. It's at least twenty stories tall, that is, *above* the water. Lines of light circle every level of every disk-shaped level. But that's the last I see before the FAST track dips underwater. The world above becomes distorted, the sun too far gone to brighten the depths.

When we unload, Officer Remmit ushers us across the station and into an elevator that shoots us up several floors. We flash past lobbies, banquet halls, theatres, open-roof decks, and other areas of the Pelago, then slide to a stop and walk into a wide atrium. Ramps curve to lower levels, orbs of white light float twenty feet in the air, ambient music drifts around us. I immediately see Dalish people from all over the planet milling around: the muscular, darker-skinned Dalish from the equatorial archipelagos, like those from the Embassy, the thin-eyed, lanky Dalish from Marakuri, the lighter-skinned Dalish from the Westin Isles. But there people from other planets, too. The Undilaens are obvious, what with our yellow-tanned skin and more pointed features. Officer Remmit points out the pale-skinned Yillosians, the round-faced, shorter Ryginese, the thick-eyebrowed Hustengs, the slender Artish, the stouter Mellesians. So many foreigners, all casually vacationing on Daliona. They speak with different accents, and in some cases, different languages. I've never been surrounded by so many different people from around the galaxy.

And I absolutely love it.

I look at a map projected on one of the walls. The archipelago stretches more than a hundred miles, from the western tip of Selayche to the eastern shore of Kilache. Selayche is the largest island, dwarfing the others. There's Relico, Mulaharu, Lisha, Pavlona, and Tahani, all surrounded by dozens of smaller islands, bays, and other natural features.

Glacia arrives three hours later and meets us on one of the Pelago's north-facing decks. Rand, Allison, and Trey went off to do their own thing, but the rest of us are relaxing with some drinks. At Officer Remmit's insistence, Glacia caves and gets one, too, but I catch her diluting it with water. I nudge her leg and give her a lazy smirk when she looks up.

Music is blasting from one of the other platforms. Lights pulse and flash, we hear cheers, laughter, people singing. Our platform isn't so rowdy, but part of me itches to find where the excitement is. The new me *wants* to feel the energy. *Wants* to dance, and yell, and stay up all night and never go to sleep.

My body disagrees. We've traveled so much and had such inconsistent sleep schedules, I'm pretty sure I'm running on adrenaline right now.

So we finally decide to call it a night. Officer Remmit takes us to the lowest level of the Pelago, skipping the shuttle station and descending into a quiet hotel lobby. Several reinforced glass hallways bathed in soft white light spiral outward from it. The one we're walking down is eerily quiet, so different from the commotion above us. Only swishes of water can be heard against the tunnel. Large orbs shine farther out in the dark depths, each marking a hotel room, I think, because we pass doors that line up with them.

It seems like forever until Glacia and I reach our room. When the lights pop to life, we see velvet couches, wall panels, a kitchen, and a door at the rear that leads to the bedroom. A rug in main room is embroidered with a colorful coral reef and fish.

"Glad I'm not claustrophobic," Glacia says, whispering unnecessarily.

I've missed our nights together. I've had trouble falling asleep, but now that we're together, it's just easier. She snuggles against me, and I smile. Her arm is warm against mine. Her hair tickles my nose. I brush her cheek and kiss her forehead, and we're both asleep soon after.

Chapter Thirty

I WAKE TO a myriad of colors.

Blue. *Lots* of blue. And red and orange and pink and white and black and yellow. The reef surrounds the hotel, rugged shelves of coral spanning the sandy seafloor under the sparkling sunlight that breaks the surface of the ocean dozens of yards above. Fish poke their heads from holes in the coral and rock, and rubbery-looking purple...*things* cling to the coral, their tentacles swaying in the water.

I can't help it: instead of letting her sleep like usual, I wake up Glacia. She's groggy at first, and shields her eyes from the light. She squints—and then her mouth falls open. We stare at the reef and the fish and all the other creatures, with their fins and shells and tails and antennae.

"Remember how I wanted to stay on Belvun?" Glacia asks, her eyes following a school of silver fish as they swim overhead.

"Yeah?"

"Scratch that. I'm moving here."

A *massive* greenish creature that has four fat fins and a spikey brown shell the size of our bed swims up to the window and pauses to look inside. Glacia slides out of bed and stands face-to-face with it, giggling as she moves her hands around, trying to get the creature to follow her. Its large, black eyes don't move, and a permanent frown marks its face.

"*Get the book*," Glacia hisses, still trying to keep herself as interesting as possible so it doesn't swim away.

I search my trunk and grab *48 Light-Years*, then take Glacia's spot while she skims the encyclopedia to figure out what's staring at us.

"Spineback Sea Turtle," she recites, sliding her finger along the page for any quick information. "They eat coral and dead fish, but won't touch the living ones. They can live upward of...*two hundred and fifty years!*"

She walks up to the window and looks the turtle in the eye. "How old are you?" she asks it, as if expecting an answer. That's when the turtle finally gets bored and swims over our room, moving deeper into the blue.

We get ready for the day and go eat breakfast inside the Pelago's natural aquarium, a restaurant built around tubes that connect the ocean to the aquarium so the fish can swim right through the room as people eat. Then, eager to see as much of the Selayche Archipelago as we can, we find an information center by the Pelago's FAST station and check out all the events happening on the islands: fireworks, island tours, mountain glider rides, cave tours, coaster parks, mountain vista inclines, nighttime parties, and, of course, the Tahani Gravity

Challenge that Rand and his team will race in on Thursday.

Glacia points at something she finds on the events panel. "Look at this: *'Experience the deep ocean and come face-to-face with Daliona's favorite sea serpent, Dally.'*"

The logo for the tour is a dark green, snake-like head with slotted eyes and countless scales. It's wearing a funny red hat, probably to make the tour appealing to kids.

"What do you think?" she asks. "Next tour starts in an hour."

"Sure! Where at?"

"Relico Island."

We catch a shuttle to Numakali, the city on Selayche Island's southern coast, then transfer to a shuttle that takes us to Relico. The beach town we find ourselves in is more-or-less a public marina, with docks and shaded walkways covering nearly every inch of the inlet. A tall fence separates us from the *Relico Adventure Park*, where people are zooming along on mag-coasters and little kids are riding in pods shaped like animals. Excited screams and jingly music and sweet scents fill the air.

Our eyes stay glued to the park as we walk past it, and I know Glacia's thinking the same thing as me. *Why can't we have* this *on Undil?* It's not fair. If we had cool things to do growing up, life on Undil might not have sucked so much.

The path takes us toward the beach, and now we're walking through a crowded part of the marina. We push through the thick of the crowds as we try to find where the tour is. I have to make a conscious effort not to let my eyes wander at some of the girls we pass, especially those in their swimsuits.

It's an impossible feat.

These Dalish girls here are tall, have smooth, dark tan skin, shiny black hair, and perky faces. Others are foreigners, like the four Ryginese girls with bubbly lips, or the two Artish girls with slender legs and arms, but dull, rough-looking skin.

As if reading my mind, Glacia flexes her fingers in my hand. Her grip *definitely* tightens. But come on. Let's be honest: there are just as many shirtless guys around here who are way hotter than me. There's no way she's ignoring them.

Finally, we find an information panel and search for the *Dalish Undersea Experience Tours*. We follow the path through a shady park until we finally see a sign that has the tour's logo. We're among the last to board the submersible. There are families, couples, groups of friends, and even people who look like they have nothing better to do...*somehow.*

The guide, a thin Dalish woman with curly black hair, greets us and starts spitting out facts about the archipelago.

"*Home to fifteen-hundred fish species!*"

"*Zenith Now's Number One galactic vacation destination!*"

"*The six main islands were formed fourteen million years ago by the now-dormant Nelaniche volcano!*"

When we're seven miles out to sea, the submersible slips underwater and sinks farther, and farther, and farther. Sunlight can barely penetrate the water at this depth...and now it's totally dark. The floodlights kick on, but they're useless for now, because there's nothing to see.

Until we reach the ocean floor.

Pillars of gray and white rock stretch upward, releasing streams of gas bubbles. Arches span hundreds of yards, cliffs drop into black trenches. The underwater world is devoid of life and stranger than any place I've ever seen. The black rock contradicts the color of the islands that sit thousands of yards above us, as if the beauty has been sucked right out of this place. These are two worlds separated by a watery void. Yet I'm completely mesmerized, caught in an unblinking stare, waiting for...*anything*.

Everyone has their faces pressed to the windows, gazing at the shadows sliding over the rock. My chest gives out and a circle of fog puffs on the window, and I realize I've been holding my breath. The submersible is so quiet, even the tour guide has stopped spouting out facts.

A swirl of sand.

A long, flat fish with gray scales shoots away and dips over the side of a cliff. I stare at where it vanished, but the craft moves too far away to see. Then the floodlights pass over a pink-and-gray blob that's sitting on a crop of rock. Its white eyes stare forward, and it has no distinguishable mouth under the droopy folds of fat hanging off its face. Tiny transparent fish buzz by the window, and a second later, a long, blood-red creature with fleshy pincers and two triangular fins gives chase. They vanish into the black depths, and the water is silent once more.

The submersible moves on, and for another twenty

minutes we explore the ocean floor, all the while listening to the guide as she tells us facts about this part of the ocean, names of the different underwater structures, the types of fish we're encountering. The last part of the tour takes us up the side of a steep trench, where we begin to see light again—but only just. Up here, tendrils of dark seaweed sway in the currents, and clumps of algae and other specks float through the dim waters. Fish scurry across the sandy floor and hide in tiny boreholes.

"Is everyone ready to see Dally?" the tour guide asks, and a rumble of excitement rolls through the passengers. "We're going to call her with a sonic pulse. She's off the grid right now, so we aren't sure which direction she'll come from. Keep your eyes peeled."

Glacia squeezes my hand when a sharp *ting* resonates off the walls, and a quick shudder ripples the water around us. Now everyone is completely still, hoping to be the first to catch sight of the serpent.

A little kid squeals and jabs his finger on the window, whispering loudly to his mother. We all see it: the long shadow sliding through the water. It disappears again, so the submersible emits another *ting!*

Fish kick up sand, and the ground becomes a blurry mess—but it's impossible to miss the monster. The same kid screams and grabs his mother's leg and hides his face. Scales slide by the floodlights, green and spotted with black and brown. It moves behind the submersible, then reappears on our other side. A narrow, pale eye peers in at us as Dally swims by, her massive body flexing back-and-forth.

Dally swims through a hole in the rocks and dozens

of colorless fish burst from their hiding places and shoot off in every direction. She gives chase to one of the clusters and snaps her jaws down, trapping the fish within. That pale eye stays locked on the submersible, however, and all of ours stay fixed on the serpent. Glacia is squeezing my hand so tight now that both our palms are sweating, and I have to pull mine out before she breaks my knuckles.

"*Sorry*," she whispers, and then she hugs her arms to her chest.

Finally, the submersible emits a lower-pitched pulse. As if on cue, Dally streaks away into the semidarkness.

The ocean floor settles.

✳ ✳ ✳ ✳ ✳

"You know, I just realized I've never been on one of those undersea tours," Officer Remmit says after Glacia and I tell them about Dally. "Vicky, Olivarr. What d'you say? Up for it?"

Victoria shrugs and sips at her glass of purple juice, but Olivarr's eyes widen eagerly.

"Of course I knew *you'd* be down, Olivarr." He raises an eyebrow at Victoria. "Sure you don't want to? It'll take your mind off things."

Victoria just shrugs one shoulder and shakes her head. "I've done it before."

Officer Remmit stretches his arms, then stands and nods his head at Olivarr. "Get tickets with me?"

After they leave, it's a long time before any of us talk again. Victoria definitely isn't the same mood as she was yesterday.

"Glad you had fun," Victoria says, her voice flat. She lets out a long sigh and rubs her eyes. "Guess where *I* just got back from?"

"Where?" Glacia asks, looking slightly concerned.

"The Embassy. Orcher called me this morning, said I needed to be there for a conference of the *utmost importance.*"

She chews her lip and stares past us. After several seconds, she shakes her head, and her face gets red. Neither Glacia nor I know what to say, but, again, it's Victoria who breaks the silence, now with a shaky edge in her voice.

"Ambassador Purnell arrived from Belvun last night. He's in a *wonderful* mood."

Glacia and I stare at her, both taken aback by the news. I don't understand why he'd be here, and then it dawns on me.

"Did something happen—"

"President Garner declared a state of emergency. *Six weeks ago.* By the time Ambassador Purnell left Belvun, three more cities were evacuated, with a dozen others rising into the *'elevated risk zone.'*" Victoria takes a deep, uneven breath. "The cities were evacuated before we even left Undil to come to Daliona. There's no way *we* could have known. Not before *now.*"

She clenches one hand into a fist, her face growing redder by the second. A hard lump slides down her throat, and she knocks her fist lightly against her mouth. Her eyes stare straight ahead, unfocused, and I know what she's seeing.

The evacuation of Ellaciss.

"The ambassador said... He said when he left, the fires were still burning."

I *have* to ask. I *have* to know. "Which cities?"

Victoria flicks her eyes at me—and it's all the answer I need. "Noshton, Fleerard, Subari."

Subari.

Ladia's home.

I remember when I went to her house, the desert was creeping toward her neighborhood. The trees were dying, the bright orange grass was turning brown and flaky. The air was stale and hot, *too hot* for the Belvun I'd always heard about in Father's stories. Even the power grid was blacking out in some neighborhoods.

What happened to Ladia? Are she and her mother living in Ambassador Purnell's embassy penthouse? Will I see them when we return in two months?

I won't be able to avoid her.

Not this time.

"It's like they didn't even *try*," Victoria says, her teeth gritted, one hand held stiff over the table and the other tucked in her lap. "Like they didn't change *anything* after Ellaciss fell. No protocols. No precautions. Garner knew the risk. Saw the research. When this all...*started*. Now they've got a million refugees or more. Where will they go? The Belvish Embassy? *Undil?* And what happens when their embassy falls?" Victoria's knuckles are white. "*What. Then.*"

She stops talking and takes several deep breaths, clasping her hands behind her neck. Behind her, I see Olivarr and Officer Remmit walking back down the path toward us. When they get closer, they slow their pace. Officer Remmit knows what's happening, and he holds out his hand to stop Olivarr.

"*Vicky…*"

He crouches and touches her shoulder. She's still staring forward, and at his touch, her lips quiver, so she hides her mouth. Blinks away tears.

"Let's go for a walk. Come on." Officer Remmit gently lifts her arm. She doesn't resist, and they walk away.

Olivarr sits across from me and Glacia and nods at us. "Don't know if you heard, but, uh…" He clears his throat and smiles awkwardly. "Well, the Dalish are a day or two away from synthesizing the last of the Faustocine formula. So Belvun will be all right, and just in the nick of time, too, from what I've heard." He gives a cheerful smile, a dimple forming in his cheeks. "Oh, and I installed that upgrade we talked about, Mr. Arman. The one we discussed way back when."

"Thanks."

"Of course. That should complete my work in the fleet. The next steps will involve integrating a city-wide network into the Embassy, like what I showed you in Orvad. I don't believe I'm joining you on your expedition to Belvun, so I'll have plenty of time to work on all that while you're away. And as far as I can tell, linking the Dalish networks to RASP was a success. You just need to design the catalogue." He pinches the sides of his white-rimmed glasses, then says, "Your program's off to a good start, Mr. Arman. I'm proud to be a part of it."

"Thanks," I say again, and I mean it, even if my voice doesn't show my enthusiasm. My thoughts are still stuck on the news Victoria told us. I've seen that same look in her eyes before, and in Orcher's, too, every morning aboard the *Ember* as we flew to Belvun, when I would meet him on the Bridge. Something deeper than fear. Something that consumes them.

I'm probably not so different. After Father died, fear overtook me every time I drove through the intersection where the crash happened. And when I fell off the gravity run... All I saw were those visions that will forever haunt me, felt those feelings that threaten to ruin me. Maybe all three of us share the same fear: a fear we have to endure, because if we succumb to it, we won't be able to live with ourselves.

Rand's motto makes sense now, but not in the way he explained it. *No fear.* Saying it doesn't eliminate your fear. No, it reminds you that *you* are in control. When you say it, it gives you a moment of courage. It's the knot in your chest before you jump into cold water. The shiver that runs down your spine when you're alone in the dark. The adrenaline that rushes through your veins before a Hologis tournament.

No fear.

It's not what you say to buffer the crash. It's what you say when you reach the point of no return.

Chapter
Thirty-One

THE NEXT AFTERNOON, Olivarr and I are standing outside the Tahani Gravity Complex, waiting for Rand. When the doors open again, he struts out, a grin slapped on his face.

"It's official. Few more days and Tahani's all mine."

I look up the side of the mountain. Two hundred yards above us, the track dives from a platform, lazily switches back and forth, then dips into a long spiral before making a steep plunge into the bay. More than three-quarters of the track is underwater, though there are several sections that breach the surface. Rand points at one section in particular: the Hump, an arch that spans fifty yards and climbs twenty or so above the bay.

"People get tossed off that all the time. And more than half lose it at the Punch, right there at the end."

He points farther up the bay, where the track shoots up from the water at a forty-five degree angle and levels out at the finish line.

"Come Thursday evening, we'll be kicked-back on the beach, drinks in our hands. That's right. We'll be on top of the world."

Olivarr holds up a finger. "Ah, well, not to be technical, but we're usually *always* on top of the world, if you think about it. We can be higher and lower—"

"You know, I really hate techies, Lance," Rand interrupts. "Bunch of smartasses, the whole lot of them."

He gives Olivarr a sideways look until a grin breaks his façade, and they both start laughing.

"I suppose now would be an appropriate time extend an offer to you...a business venture I've had in mind, Mr. Rand," Olivarr says, slowing his pace to a stroll.

"I'm listening."

"Let's bring gravity runs to Undil. You and me. I've got the techies, you've got passion. We could partner up and get the ball rolling—"

"The sled sliding, you mean. *Not to be technical*," Rand adds with a wink.

"Think about it," Olivarr goes on. "People on Undil want something other than Hologis to keep them entertained, right?"

"Obviously."

"Constructing gravity runs on Undil would bring a whole new level of excitement, attract more tourists to Undil, but more importantly, we could use privatize the revenue and directly fund our terraformation. Doing so may even begin to bring us up to par with some of tech here on Daliona. Imagine, say, Orvad: tracks in the dunes, tracks in the ocean, tracks right in the middle of the city."

Rand claps Olivarr around the shoulder. "See, you Orvadian techies aren't so bad. Those Embassy techies annoy the hell out of me. Do me a favor and don't ever become one of them, Cresson."

Olivarr chuckles and pushes his glasses back up his nose, which Rand almost knocked off. "I'll certainly try not to, er, stoop to their level."

"I'm gonna come right out and say it: let's do this. Imagine a track wrapping around the Crown—"

"There could be one coming off the mesas!" Olivarr says, getting excited. "*O-o-or* even through the canyons!"

They bounce ideas off each other for several more minutes until we reach the marina and ride a ferry back to Selayche Island. It speeds several miles northwest, and soon Numakali, grows larger, the city covered in shadow as the sun falls below the western mountain ridges. Both of the Dalish moons are visible, hanging nearly side-by-side high in the east.

Nearer the shore, people in cyclos race over the water, diving into and bursting out from the bay, zooming between buoys and soaring so high into the sky that they become nothing more than tiny black dots.

And from there, they fall.

Arms spread wide.

Wind rippling their hair.

Happy screams and cheers.

The rush they must feel as they fall…fall…fall…and at the last second, swooping safely over the water, or plunging headfirst into the depths. I want to join them. I want to experience whatever *that* must feel like.

Tomorrow.

I'm testing for my cyclo license *tomorrow*. And if I

get it... *If I get it...*

I can't help but grin at the thought.

The hum of the ferry dies when the boat docks at the pier, and as we make our way through the city, Rand sends Allison a message. She and Glacia have been at the Molanis Mall for most of the evening, so that's where we go. It isn't hard to find: the mall is by far the single-largest structure in the city, spanning three blocks and rising at least ten stories. Its entrance is a rotating circular portal, half underground and half above, with colorful orbs bouncing back and forth within the ring.

Inside, I don't see any flat surfaces *anywhere*. The walls bend in waves, the floor slopes up and down, and to top it off—literally—the tall ceiling appears to ripple and gleam with sunlight for an underwater effect.

Dalish vendors shout out to customers, announcing inventions and recipes and clothing fashions that they themselves designed. Sweet aromas drift through the air from food courts and perfume shops alike, and all sorts of objects sit on disks floating behind large glass windows. Augmentation and spectrum goggles fill the shelves of one shop. In another, I see levitation boots and boards, state-of-the-art tendril gloves and opticons, and even customizable maglev sleds and cyclo suits, which you can only get if you have a license.

On the second level, there's a chamber that Rand calls a Lucidity Arcade, similar to the one in the Pelago Hotel—except much, *much* larger. Dozens of people are reclined on special seats, each grouped in sections that are linked to a different experience. The weirdest part is that everyone looks like they're sleeping, and they all have headsets strapped to their foreheads. Rand explains that they're linked to a variety of neuro-interfaces, and that everything is happening inside their heads. Some people might be playing war games, others might be exploring different regions of Daliona, like the small continent of Kiana, which is illegal to *physically* visit in order to preserve the natural habitats. Other people could be playing Hologis, racing on gravity runs, or even researching science and math.

"Lucidity feels no different than being awake," Rand explains, talking mostly to Olivarr. "You're induced into being asleep. Sometimes you won't even know because it feels just like real life. The interface slows your brain's perception of time, so you can spend hours in lucidity. Days and *weeks*, even. Say you play Hologis for an hour. In real life, you spend fifteen minutes asleep, and when it's over, you just wake up. That's the beauty of lucidity: you wake up and pick up life right where you left off."

"*Incredible*," Olivarr breathes, staring longingly into the arcade.

Rand starts walking again, and I follow him down the length of the hall. "The practical uses are infinite," he keeps saying. "Imagine if we had this on Undil. *Everyone* would be a genius. Cresson and Remmit wouldn't be so damn full—"

He looks over his shoulder and stops walking, because Olivarr isn't following us.

"*Case in point*," Rand mutters.

We find Olivarr back in the arcade, engaged in an excited discussion about lucidity networks with a Dalish techie who's a full two-and-a-half feet taller than him, and seems amused by Olivarr's boyish giddiness.

"But it's so *fascinating!*" Olivarr insists as Rand literally pulls him out of the arcade. "Can you imagine the implications if we could integrate this tech on Undil? The barriers we could break? It would revolutionize our mental capacities! Exponentially accelerate our technological progress. Years of discoveries completed in a matter of days."

Rand slings one arm around Olivarr. "And there's the flaw in your plan."

"What's that?"

"You can *learn*, but you can't *discover*. It's impossible to test theoretical knowledge in lucidity. Not without—"

Rand stops talking when Olivarr's face lights up like he just realized something important.

"Not without the Algorithm," he says slowly, his eyes staring ahead.

Rand nods. "You got it."

I look at them, confused. Olivarr chuckles and jerks his thumb at me as he says, "Mr. Arman here has no idea what the Algorithm is."

"That's because he's an archivist, Cresson. Can't expect *too* much from them."

Rand winks and pats my shoulder.

Olivarr holds his hands apart in front of him. "The Unification Algorithm is a theory—no, a *function* within maths and physics that ties together every physical force. Some physicists consider it to be the highest order of all possible knowledge. Crack the Algorithm, and we would become masters of the universe, Mr. Arman, able to travel through time, observe other dimensions, and predict, albeit with some small degree of uncertainty, every natural event that will ever occur in all of space and time."

I stare blankly at him. That went *way* over my head.

Yup, I'm an archivist for a reason.

"You don't have to worry about that stuff, Lance. Leave it to the people who think for a living." Rand turns back to Olivarr. "I, for one, hope we never discover the Algorithm."

"And why is that?"

"Well, number one, we'd never hear the end of it from you all-powerful techies." That gets a nervous laugh out of Olivarr. "But seriously, it would take away the point of life," Rand says with a heavy shrug. "All the fun is in the adventure of discovery. If we knew everything there is to know, what would be the point of waking up in the morning?"

"An admirable argument, Mr. Rand, though I'm not sure it'll convince techies everywhere to drop their research. Discovering the Algorithm *is* our ultimate goal, after all."

The gleam in Olivarr's eyes doesn't fade as we keep walking through the mall to meet Allison and Glacia. And when we find them, the first thing we notice are all the bags they're carrying.

"*Oy!*" Rand shouts from a distance, throwing his arms up. "What's all this supposed to be?" He peers inside Allison's bags. "*Clothes.* It's all clothes! Did you get a closet for these, too?"

Allison and Glacia laugh and hand over their bags to us, then start walking back the way we just came.

Outside, night has settled. Torches flicker along the piers, and the walkways glow blue under our feet. Greenish-yellow dots dance in the smooth trees lining the shore, while across the bay, fireworks shoot up from

Relico Island's marina and explode in the sky. Even from here, I can see flashes of light inside the adventure park, hear the distant screams and booming music.

The five of us eat a late dinner at one of the bayside restaurants. I get barkals, clamper shells, and a gooey meat I'm not too fond of, mostly because it feels weird going down my throat. Afterward, Rand and Allison take the shopping bags back to the Pelago, Olivarr leaves to meet Victoria and Officer Remmit, and Glacia and I decide to visit Verana Peak, the highest point of Selayche's southern mountains.

As we ride the incline pod, the city shrinks below us. The black waves of the western ocean glisten in the light of the two Dalish moons, which are nearing their peak in the sky and are slightly closer together than earlier this evening. We rise higher...and higher. There's the Pelago Hotel, and a few miles to its right, dozens of white dots shine on the water like stars for the ocean. Those must be the private resort islands I saw when we arrived yesterday.

The pod stops, and we exit with a few other passengers. Now we're standing on a wide deck that wraps around the entire peak, so we can see most of Selayche Island. The central jungle is mostly dark, except for patches of light that mark outposts and farms. Orcher said something about the kloia bean being harvested here, Daliona's signature coffee bean.

More shadowy mountain peaks poke at the sky, and the island's volcano rises to the north, the highest point of the entire archipelago. More fireworks explode dozens of miles away over one of the other islands, silent and dazzling. As we watch them, Glacia points at the horizon, at an orb of light that comes into view as the clouds shift. It's several times brighter than any of the stars, and when I look below it, I can just barely make out a thin white line.

"*The space elevator,*" Glacia whispers, her voice just loud enough to hear above the soft rush of wind.

I stare at it, totally in awe. Thorpe Island is at the bottom of that line. Here I thought the Dalish Embassy was halfway around the planet, but no. It's right there. We could probably see the glow of the city if we were any higher.

And I could be. If I pass my cyclo license tomorrow, I can fly as high as I want.

I can go anywhere.

See anything.

And be completely free.

✳ ✳ ✳ ✳ ✳

I wake up in that peaceful blue light, and for several minutes, I just lie here and watch the fish and other sea creatures swim around the bedroom. I can't imagine any way to wake up that's more beautiful than this. The sun isn't glaring down on my eyes and the only sounds are the muffled swishes and swirls of water.

A jab in my ribs. "Morning, mister."

Glacia's awake. She must've been doing the same thing as me: lying here, staring up at the fish.

She rolls onto her side, her hair falling down her back, and gives me a kiss. "Ready for today?"

"Mmhmm."

She puts her ear to my chest and listens to my heart, which is absolutely pounding, so she smiles and gives me another kiss. "*You'll*"—and another—"*do*"—and another—"*amazing.*"

Her hazel eyes reflect the watery light above us. I love staring into her eyes, so bright, so alive with everything she is. Her energy, her excitement, her passion.

I love all of it.

Glacia leaves to go have breakfast with Rand and Allison, giving me time to meditate and prepare my mind for the cyclo. *'Maintain physical awareness of your environment,'* one of the instructors I worked with kept reminding me. *'Study the environment before throwing yourself into it.'* That instructor made me stand at the edge of a platform and memorize every obstacle in the path he created for me—a straight line, but with shifting platforms and small disks and other random obstacles.

'Don't think. Just be aware.'

It took half a dozen tries, but I managed to complete the course without smacking into anything on the way down. Awareness became instinct.

So I meditate. I like meditating. My mind goes quiet. My muscles relax down my neck...into my arms...my chest...my legs. I breathe long, steady breaths. It's easy to smile, too. Smiling makes me feel good, and feeling good relaxes me even more. It's a win-win.

I catch up with Glacia and the others and grab a quick breakfast. Then we ride a ferry to Tahani Island, rather than a shuttle, because Rand insists that I need the fresh air to keep my nerves down. I look up at the gravity run as we dock in the marina. Someone shoots down the track, nothing but a blur, and within seconds they vanish below the surface of the bay.

The cyclo arena is built at the head of a shallow valley in the center of the island. There are indoor and outdoor sectors, each with its own set of challenges. The trees and cliffs of the valley have been shifted, cut, and marked for an outdoor course, while platforms, rope courses, tunnels, and vertical towers form the urban course. It's the most complex arena I've seen yet, but that's what Tahani is known for: the intensity and rigor of its extreme sports.

Rand comes up behind me and massages my shoulders like he's my personal trainer about to give a pep talk—which he does. "Just gotta show them your stuff, Lance. Fly high, swoop low. What'd that one guy say? *Stay aware.*" He gives me a light shake. "Do that, and you'll be the most decorated head archivist Undil's ever had."

"That's not saying much," Glacia chimes in.

"*OY!*" Rand sticks a finger in her face. "No one's asking for your sass, Haverns. I'm building him up, see? Quit sabotaging him!" He leans closer to me and lowers his voice. "You and me, Lance. Let's go home feeling like heroes. How about it? You ready?"

"Yup."

"No. Come on. I said, *are. You. READY?!*"

He shakes my entire body, and my face burns from embarrassment, but he isn't letting up.

"I'm ready!" I try to sound excited, but my voice cracks.

Rand hangs his head. "One of these days…"

My chest tightens as the time crawls closer to my test. I wish I could switch places with the guy going after me. That'd give me time to go to the bathroom, give myself a few extra minutes to settle down. But then a woman with squared black bangs comes into the waiting room, and I know it's time.

"*Arman Lance.*"

Heart throbbing so hard it hurts, I follow her into the next chamber, where she sizes me for a cyclo suit. Then we go into the massive arena. Pillars acting as city towers stand anywhere from fifty to three hundred feet tall, with bars and ledges sticking off their sides. Floating platforms glide through the air in different patterns and speeds, and a few are even flipping in place, while ropes dangle from others.

I'm glad sunlight is pouring through the windows. Taking this test without natural light would throw off my perception. I can't mess up. We have one week left on Daliona, and I'm determined to spend it soaring through the skies.

My suit isn't fully activated yet, so as we walk to a marked ring—my starting point—I keep moving the tingling sensation around my head. Front. Top. Side-to-side. Back. Lower.

Again.

Again.

Again.

"Are you set, Mr. Lance?"

Her voice is stern, but kind. I remember the man who gave me my driver's test in Cornell, a year before I met Ladia. He judged my every move, just looking for a reason to fail me on the first try. Not this woman. The way she smiles, one corner of her mouth curled, I know she's here to support me. Nor do her pale green eyes criticize me, expecting me to fail. And when I swing my arms to loosen them, she looks like she might laugh, which makes *me* want to laugh.

"Yeah. I'm ready."

"When is the last time you trained?"

"A few days ago, on Noya."

"Do you train fairly often?"

"Yeah, and I meditate, too."

"Excellent." She smiles that supportive smile. "You're already two steps ahead of most other foreign applicants."

She squeezes her earlobe, and like I've seen so many times before, her pupils glow blue. She waves her arms in midair, tapping icons I can't see.

"Assuming your success, do you plan to design a personal cyclo?"

The question takes me by surprise. "Um—"

"Most people do," she says quickly. "Although, being from Undil, you may want to hold off. The three Edge planets haven't yet installed charging docks, so you'd be limited in your use."

"I've heard," I say with a quick laugh.

She squeezes her earlobe again, and her pupils return to normal. "You can still decide after your test. So let's get started. I will select your course, and you will be required to complete it. If you lose control, you automatically fail and must wait two weeks before testing for another license. For reasons that should be obvious, we can only distribute licenses to users who demonstrate advanced technique."

I nod. My palms are sweating, so I wipe them on my thighs to distract myself. Breathe. Breathe and focus and be aware. Even as she tells me to stand in the middle of the starting circle, I retreat into my head and let the subtle sensations tingle my scalp.

An image shimmers in front of her, and she taps several icons to prepare the course. "There are ten checkpoints. Your goal is to reach them in sequence while following an outlined path. Do not deviate from more than ten percent of the path, or you will fail. The difficulty will increase as you progress. Most successful tests take ten to fifteen minutes to complete, but if you exceed twenty minutes, you will fail. The clock will pause when you reach a checkpoint, and resume when you leave the checkpoint. Do you have any questions before you begin?"

I hesitate to give myself an extra breath to calm down and clear my head. Then,

"I'm ready."

Her finger hovers over a green icon. "Best of—oh, close your visor. It is part of test protocol."

I hastily slap my neck, and the visor seals back into place. Then she touches the icon—and my suit activates. The gloves glow, the power disk whirs against my back, cool air seeps through the internal pressure and ventilation system. As the timer ticks down, I keep my eyes on the blue beacon that lit up when she hit the icon: my first checkpoint. And in my visor, a faint hologram outlines the path I need to follow, much like the gravity run helmets do.

3...

2...

1...

"No fear."

Go.

I jump, arms reaching forward. Weightlessness overtakes my body. I feel only the air rushing against my face as I soar toward the beacon, my mind focused on moving forward.

And...*slow down.*

I relax the sensation and plant my feet firmly on the platform. Weight returns to my limbs, I run into the beacon, and the timer materializes around me: *00:07.84.* Another beacon, preceded by a new path, shimmers to life on the other side of two rotating panels. The gap between them opens and closes...opens and closes. I need to time this perfectly.

With a running start, I fling myself into the air, thirty yards above the ground, and glide toward the gap. Open...closed...open...closed...open...closed...

Now.

I accelerate, pass through the opening, and drop onto the second platform, which immediately starts tilting under my weight. I snap my attention to the third beacon in the corner of my eye and hurl myself toward it before I slide off the platform. I free-fall—then shoot sideways.

Swoop under the wall.

Flip in midair.

Land.

Adrenaline rushes through me. I pause and reel in my thoughts to make sure I don't lose the sensation. My heart is still racing, but the anxiety is gone, replaced by excited confidence.

I can do this.

Drop off the side, fall, and shoot toward the next

beacon, which pauses on a ledge before it glides upward, pauses on a second ledge, and finally stops on top of a narrow pillar in the makeshift city. I repeat the pattern: land on the ledge, jump—land on the second ledge, jump—glide upward, stop in midair, drop on the pillar.

My eyes follow the beacon, study the path. I don't look away until I've got my timing down. Then I jump. Dodge the towers, jump off the highest platform, avoid random objects crossing my path on the way down. Land on a thin ledge, leap up to a higher one, cross a gap. Scale a wall with uneven hand and footholds. Grab a dangling rope, grapple my way to the other side, drop onto a platform that's sliding back and forth through the air, land on a narrow bar connecting two pillars.

I complete each obstacle. My confidence grows. My legs have stopped shaking when I land. My heart rate is steady, my breathing controlled. I'm relaxed, aware like never before. My eyes flick left, right, up, and down, judging the environment. I can *feel* the distance between me and the walls, know exactly how fast—or slow—I need to move to avoid obstacles or land where the beacon lands.

The arena is mine.

All. Mine.

Is this what Glacia feels in Hologis when she's sprinting around, taking people out one-by-one? A force to be feared, everywhere at once, and nowhere at all? When we played in the tournament last year, she planted spheres around the arena, led players into traps of her own devising, and knocked them all out, despite being outnumbered six-to-one.

I land on a platform halfway up the arena. The beacon flashes three times and the words *FINAL TEST* circle around me, then my current course time: *11:28*.

Not bad.

I catch my breath as the beacon lays out the final routine: drop to the next platform down, then land on one of the mock towers. Jump, land on the ledge of the tower several yards away. Jump, land, jump, land. Fly to the pillars and leap diagonally. Land on the narrow bar between the final two towers, then shoot straight up to the top of the arena, avoiding all the objects littering the open air. At the highest platform, the beacon flashes red, signaling the end.

I let it replay the routine one more time. I need to make this run count.

Deep breath. Focus.

Flex my fingers. Shake out my arms

Bounce my legs.

No fear.

I shove off the platform, slow my fall—but slam harder than I meant into the next platform. My legs feel weak as I jog to the edge, but I ignore the twinge of pain. I look straight ahead and leap for the first tower, soaring dozens of yards through the air. I bend my knees to absorb the impact and slide off the side in one motion. The thin ledge is barely wide enough for my feet to set properly. But I don't need to catch my balance before leaping to the next one over.

Then the next.

And the next.

I shove off the last tower and weave through the urban course. Once I reach the outer limits, I fix my eyes on the pillars in the opposite corner, dipping sideways at every hint of movement.

Land, set, jump.

Arc through the air.

Land, set, jump.

Falling...falling...falling.

Land.

Set.

Jump.

My legs strain under my weight when I hit the narrow bar spanning the final two pillars. I wobble in place, holding my arms out to catch my balance.

Deep breath.

Look up.

The objects above me drift at random speeds, criss-crossing, speeding up, slowing down, spinning erratically. All I can hope is that there's some sort of shut down in place if one of those is going to hit me, because getting slammed by a spinning bar won't be pretty.

...they *would* shut it down, right?

I watch for patterns—but then I realize there *is no* pattern. I need to make my own path. Just be aware.

I crouch. Whisper *'no fear.'* Spring upward. Dodge left. Curve right. Slow down. Strafe. Acceler—*flatten my body!* Barely avoid the disk. Feel. Feel. Feel. Stay aware. Look left, right, left again. Time it...time it...*now*. Strafe, stop, accelerate. There's the last opening: two platforms sliding over each other, leaving a gap for less than two seconds. Closed again. Wait...wait...drift upward, faster, faster.

Open.

Go!

Shoot straight up, stretch my arms—

And I'm through.

I flip backward and grab the top platform, pull myself over the edge, and jog to the center. The beacon flashes green and words circle around me, but I'm not reading them. My body is shaking and I'm cold. *Freezing.* I choke with every breath—no, I'm laughing and I can't stop. I drop to my knees and put my weight on my fist, breathing heavily. When I look over the edge, the obstacles have cleared the area, and the instructor is far below, standing in the ring I took off from.

I tip over the edge...and gravity does the rest. I fall. Falling...falling...just like those people who fell out of the sky last night and caught themselves at the last second. *Just like that.* I slow down, straighten my body, and land lightly on my feet.

The instructor holds out her hand. A wild grin takes over my face. It feels so good to smile, the best feeling in the whole world, and I need to make up for all the years I went without it. I remember when Glacia pushed my cheeks up at the opening dance in the Undil Embassy, forcing me to smile my first smile in years.

All because she wanted to see my glowing teeth.

"Superb, Mr. Lance."

"*Th—thank you.*" I'm so giddy, I have to clench my fists to keep my arms from shaking.

"Thirteen minutes and fifty-three seconds. Well within the acceptable time. No collisions, one particularly hard landing"—she motions at my knee, which, I now realize, is throbbing—"but nothing that disqualifies you."

"*Thank you,*" I say again, like I can't remember any

other words to say.

She starts walking toward the exit gate, but I don't move. My legs are shaking so hard, I don't trust myself to move. She laughs and gives me a gentle push forward.

"So, how about that cyclo suit?" she asks. "I can help you order a customized one, if you'd like? It will be available tomorrow afternoon."

I nod vigorously. "*Yes.*"

Ah, a third word.

✳ ✳ ✳ ✳ ✳

Rand, as always, is the first to raise his glass over the torch-lit dinner that night.

"Where do I begin? Right. When I first met Lance here, he didn't strike me as the kind of guy who'd enjoy flipping through the air or flying down a gravity run at breakneck speed—in fact, it's safe to say he still hates the latter."

The others laugh. Officer Remmit is here, along with Victoria, Olivarr, Glacia, Allison, and Trey. Even Kile showed up, but he hasn't been spending much time with us.

"I distinctly remember calling him out: *'you don't have the guts,'* or something to that effect. Details aren't important." He waves it off, then tips his glass at me. "Lance, you could've sat your ass on a bench like Arlington here and watched the rest of us have all the fun—no offense, Arlington."

As usual, Kile ignores him.

"You didn't, though. You gave it a shot, and I think

it's more than obvious you're glad you did. So I want to raise my glass a little higher"—he stretches his arm farther over the table—"because I'm proud of you. I really am. To Arman, our head archivist. A guy with no fear."

Rand winks at me as the others raise their glasses in unison, and Glacia nudges my elbow. A flickering torch reflects in her eyes. I love her smile, love the way her teeth shine and her cheeks pinch outward, how her eyes widen ever so slightly. She's always had that smile, as long as I can remember. All those times in Secondary when she wanted to brighten my day, but I blocked her out... Those memories come rushing back to me, dozens of smiles, dozens of bright eyes, dozens of pinched cheeks—and I blocked her out.

* * * * *

The sand crunches under nine pairs of feet when we all go for a walk on the beach. Rand, Allison, and Trey walk ahead of the group. Kile follows a few steps behind them. Officer Remmit's hands are stuffed in his pockets, his head raised in laughter as he walks beside Victoria, whose head is lowered in her own quiet fit of snorting. Olivarr keeps pace on her other side, running his mouth about his idea to build gravity runs on Undil...though I'm not sure Officer Remmit and Victoria are *actually* listening.

Glacia and I follow behind everyone. Fingers interlocked, we swing our arms between us and try to match our footsteps inside the ones already imprinted in the sand before the water washes them away. Then Officer

Remmit sweeps Victoria off her feet and staggers toward the ocean, her shrieks carrying through the wind until he dumps her in the water.

Glace and I stand back, stopping right where the waves lap against our feet. I wrap my arms around her from behind and set my chin on her shoulder, and we sway in place, watching boats glide over the bay and the nightly fireworks glittering above Relico Island, their distant booms muffled.

I feel a bubble swell within my chest. I'm so happy. In this moment, I wouldn't want to be anywhere else. I'm with friends I never dreamed I'd have, on a planet I never thought I'd visit. I'm in love with the girl in my arms. I've taken control of my life.

Most of all, I know Father would be proud of who I am today: the son I never was, yet the son he said I'd be.

Chapter
Thirty-Two

TODAY IS GLACIA'S birthday, and we're going on an adventure.

The sun has barely risen, but Glace and I have already been up for an hour. Right now we're sitting in a hovercraft with fifty other people, en route to Kilache Island. Though the far edge of Kilache is a hundred miles away, we can already see how different the entire island is compared to the rest of the archipelago. There's no jungle, no moss-covered mountains or misty valleys. Its beaches are brown and black, and its cliffs are crumbling into the ocean. Even the waves spray up dirty yellow foam, staining the rocks.

The hovercraft lands on a dock near the island's northeast corner, and the tour guides lead everyone to a trail that branches in two directions: one goes inland, toward a dead-looking forest that covers most of the island, and the other path heads down a hill to the blackened shores.

One of the guides gets everyone quiets and gestures to one side. "Eef you would like to see the Ferron Beaches, stand here weeth me. Or eef you would like to see the Kelihu Marshes, stand over there with Méké."

Glacia and I join the group touring the beaches and follow the guide down the trail. It gently curves back and forth—a straight descent would be too steep—and soon we're at the bottom. Black boulders and slabs of rock, some with skid trails behind them, lay inside small craters where they broke off the cliffs. Other stones litter the beach, chinking and scraping under our feet. Some of the boulders closer to the ocean are streaked with white. According to the tour guide, it's a mix of salt accumulation...and bird poop.

Lovely.

It isn't long before we come across a whole flock of birds. These aren't the chubby penguins with stumpy wings like we saw on Bondalp Island, though. These are proud, white and brown birds with bright purple feet and speckled yellow beaks. They screech and squawk as we walk through their numbers, watching us with beady blue eyes. But they don't seem frightened, or aggressive, for that matter. In fact, a few waddle beside us, heads tilted, apparently curious to see what we're doing. A few flap away, catch an air current, and soar high into the sky before diving toward the water, splashing under the surface, and reappearing with fish flailing in their fatty beak pouches.

"Purple-toed halloons," the tour guide says.

She crouches in front of one and tries to coax it toward her, but it just cocks its head until another bird bumps into it. They slap their beaks together and stomp their webbed feet on the stones and make deep-throated honking noises at each other.

"They nest een the cleeffs. The younger birds scrounge for shellfeesh een the pools, but the older ones feesh off the coast. There's a reef up ahead"—she points down the beach, where some ridges poke out of the ocean—"and that's where the *eeguanas* leeve."

Glacia grabs my arm, her eyes lit-up with excitement. Despite thinking they're so ugly, she's wanted to see the iguanas for months, ever since the first time we looked at *48 Light-Years* in my apartment on Undil.

We leave the halloons behind and continue walking up the beach. The sun has risen higher, and the black shores are bathed in a golden sheen. As we walk, the guide tells us fast facts about the different types of stones littering the shore, the cliff-dwelling turtles that have learned to access the ocean through an ancient blowhole, and the algae and other microbial life that thrive in the crevices, which some of the local lizard populations feed on. That's when we come to a part of the beach that's crowded with boulders, and among those, the giant lizards themselves—iguanas.

That's when Glacia squeals.

Everyone in our tour stares at her. I squeeze my eyes shut, but my face betrays me: the embarrassed smile, the heat rising to my ears. Even the tour guide looks mildly confused, thinking something might be wrong.

Glacia raises her hand, but doesn't wait for any acknowledgement before asking, "Can I pet one?"

The confusion in the guide's eyes turns into laughter. "Eef they let you, go right ahead. They are used to humans."

To further my embarrassment, Glacia doesn't let go of my hand as she drags me to the front of the group. Someone pats my shoulder sympathetically before I'm forced into the open for everyone's entertainment.

We reach a boulder. Sprawled on top of it is by far the ugliest creature I've ever seen: black and red skin, stubby spikes lining its spine, muscular legs with thin claws curling off the long toes, small, yellow eyes, and a smushed face. White crust clings to its head, glittering in the sunlight as the beast slowly turns its neck to look at us.

Glacia finally lets go of my hand and presses her hands to her face, suppressing another squeal. Behind us, I hear the tour guide saying how the iguanas, like many species found around the galaxy, were relocated from Earth before humanity left.

Now Glacia is bent over the five-foot-long iguana, her hands clasped tightly between her legs, and a huge, giggly smile on her face.

"*Hello!*"

The iguana blinks.

She looks up at me. "I wanna touch it."

"Then go ahead and touch it."

"Mmmm...*you touch it.*"

I scoff. "Ha. *No.*"

Glacia bites her lip and stares at the iguana, which is now licking its nose with a fat, pink tongue. It takes several more seconds, but Glacia works up the courage to scratch the iguana's stomach. It must like the feeling, because it closes its eyes and arches its neck. I look around the beach: there are *dozens* of iguanas of all colors and sizes basking in the sun, green and yellow ones, and red and orange ones, and black and green ones. The largest looks to be just over seven feet long. Each has the same smashed-in face, the same long claws and tails. Most pay us no attention, even when the rest of the tour walks into their numbers.

Glacia drops her hand away, and the iguana immediately opens its eyes and stares at her, as if wondering why she stopped.

"Touch it. It's weird."

I grimace, and then—*only* because it didn't bite her hand off—scratch the iguana's neck. Its skin is coarse. It tickles my palm, actually. I poke the spines running down the lizard's back: they're stiffer than I expected. Then again, I don't know *what* I was expecting.

We leave the iguana to sunbathe on its rock and join the rest of the group. The tour guide is pointing at an iguana that's clumsily running across the beach, its feet flopping against the ground until it dives into the water.

"They're excellent sweemmers, and leeve off a diet of algae and small plants. And as you can see"—the guide make an obvious gesture at Glacia—"they're generally passeeve toward humans. *Thees* population, at least."

She ushers us down the beach, and Glacia manages to take a selfie with another iguana before jogging to catch up.

When the tour walks around another cliff, it's as if the rocky beach has healed itself. The black stone is mostly unbroken. I spot our destination across the smooth beachfront—the path back up the hill—but as we walk toward it, an uneasy feeling comes over me. I feel...anxious. *Really* anxious. About what? I don't know.

Something feels wrong, and I'm not the only one to notice.

"Everyone feel that?" the tour guide asks. A thin smile spreads over her face. "We are walking on a slab of magnetite. Don't worry, though. Eet's just your brain reacting. We'll be clear of the effects farther up the heell."

Even though she told us why we feel so anxious, nobody can quite shake the lingering paranoia. Glacia's fingers tighten around mine. I clench my other fist. My breathing quickens, my heart rate picks up. Here and there, a shadow darts at the edge of my vision, but when I flick my eyes sideways, it disappears.

Nothing lives on this stretch of beach. No birds, no iguanas, no shellfish. The rock is slick from years of weathering, and thin lines trail across it: contours, I realize, that subtly trace the slab's magnetic field.

Before we step back on the trail, the guide points down the coast: the cliffs are splitting from the island, and massive boulders are poking up from the waves. The entire side is eroding away.

"Kilache ees the oldest island een the Selayche Archeepelago. The first to be formed, and the first to return to the ocean. Eet weell take another two to three meellion years for eet to sink completely underwater, and about thirty meellion more for Selayche."

With that final bit of information, we climb the hill, then return to where the hovercraft sits on the docking platform, a little more than two miles away. The group that toured the Kelihu Marshes is already back. Everyone has mud on their shoes and legs, and Glacia and I both scrunch our noses in disgust: they reek of dirt and rot and stale water.

Glacia leans close to my ear. *"Glad we didn't go in there."*

* * * * *

Rand chuckles when Glacia shows him the picture she took with the iguana. "Better watch it, Lance. I think this punk's trying to steal your girl." He zooms in on the iguana's stubby mouth, which is slightly open and touching Glacia's cheek. "Oh yeah, I *definitely* see some tongue action."

He tosses Glacia's holotab back to her, then folds his hands behind his head, leans back in his beach chair, and hums along with the music echoing behind us.

We're on the edge of Pavlona, the archipelago's smallest main island, facing the steep mountains of Selayche's eastern coast. Pavlona itself is flat all the way across, the entire island one huge resort with walking trails, pools, high-end restaurants, and soft white beaches like the one we're sunning ourselves on.

"Figure I'll work in one more set of runs tonight before the big day tomorrow. Anyone wanna join me?" A round of unenthusiastic mumbling answers him. "No takers? Hey, Arlington. You and me. How about it?"

Kile doesn't even acknowledge the question. He's reading an absurdly thick book called—I have to tip my head sideways to see the title—*The Winter's Winds*. It looks brand new, with a crisp cover and stark white pages.

"Whatever," Rand goes on. "You guys are putting me

on the spot, making me represent the *Ember* all by my-self. I thought we were a team?"

Allison flips over in her chair so that she's lying on her side and her thick braids pile up in the sand. She's holding a silver pipe with a hollow orb at the end that's filled with thick white smoke. She's been breathing through it the entire time we've been here. Rand forced her to take the recliner at the end of the row so he wasn't downwind of her.

"We'll be rooting for you...from a safe distance...in the air conditioning...maybe piping some kalupa..."

Rand rolls his eyes at the last part.

A wave crashes up the beach, the water receding several yards in front of our line of beach chairs. When I roll onto my stomach, I look sideways at Glacia, who's on my other side. She catches my fingers. Our hands dangle between us, fingertips lightly sweeping the sand. She grins that cute little grin I love so much, and I stare into her eyes until they fall shut.

* * * * *

Officer Remmit holds my cyclo suit out in front of him and stares at it, impressed. "That's a handsome suit, Arman. You're making me jealous." He turns it around and laughs. "I like what you did with the power pack."

I love the entire suit. Rand went to the Molanis Mall with me this afternoon and helped design it, using his personal gravity run suit as inspiration. We figured Un-dil should be one of the distinguishing features, so we requested that the cyclo's power pack be in the shape of the Undil Embassy crest, the symbolic golden triangle representing our embassy's three branches and the Crown at the center. The rest of the suit is fairly standard, with minor color changes to fit my taste. Instead of white and green like all the other Dalish cyclos I've flown, I went with a dark blue vest and helmet, and gold streaks running down the arms, legs, and chest.

Officer Remmit flips my helmet in his hands to read the inscription I got engraved on top.

"What's this? *I Lived*."

I shrug. "Just a motto. Rand has one, my Father had one—"

"I have one," Victoria says from the floor, leaning back against the couch.

Officer Remmit frowns in thought. "Come to think of it, so do I: *Thinking is*—"

"—*hard work*." Victoria smirks at him, her eyes shining. "Like we haven't heard *that* before."

Officer Remmit touches a hand to his heart. "Without us thinkers, society would be nowhere. *You're welcome*."

He stretches out on the couch that Victoria is leaning against and watches a school of striped yellow-and-orange fish swim over the underwater room.

"Where are you taking Glacia for her big birthday dinner?" Victoria asks after I put the cyclo suit back in its case.

"I'm not sure...yet."

Officer Remmit throws one hand in the air. "Have no fear, Arman. Vicky and I are experts when it comes to selecting romantic dinner destinations. *Pelago, view local map*."

A projection appears above him, a map of the Selayche Archipelago.

"I had *no idea* you could do that."

Officer Remmit laughs. "*Firsties.*" He straps on a pair of tendril gloves and zooms the map to the northern tip of Selayche Island. "Have you considered the Volocan Resort? Comes with a stunning view of the Voilukai Falls, with resort access to the Paikau swimming hole through the Monakai Cliff Passage." He scrolls the map south, to Pavlona Island. "Or do you want to experience Fiche Point? More of the party atmosphere, if you're into that scene."

"Lars, does Arman really look like a party animal to you?" Victoria twists around and grabs his hands to maneuver the map, clumsily zooming to the gray, rocky islands directly north of Pavlona. "Take her to Lisha Cove, Arman. The hotel and restaurant are carved into the cliffs, and there's a nice torch-lit walk above the cove."

Officer Remmit claps loudly. "*Yes.* Beautiful. It's settled. Go there." He clears his throat and gives Victoria a sideways glance. "I, uh, don't suppose you'd mind a *double date*, would—"

He recoils when Victoria elbows his ribs.

"Ah, *fine.* You two go have your fun. But Vicky, if they're not going to Volocan, what do you say we head down there for dinner? Be like old times. Some people say you can still hear the volcano rumble."

"That's your stomach, Lars."

He holds a hand to his stomach, which actually *did* just gurgle. "Can you blame it? Sun's almost down and I haven't eaten a thing since that late breakfast." He looks back at me. "Seriously, go to Lisha. Spend the night. Grab a room overlooking the cove."

That settles it. I leave and walk down the spiraled glass tunnel to my room, the water swishing against the window the entire way. A faint orange glow illuminates the depths as the sun sets. The reef is active with fish darting through the water as they try to catch tiny specks of food, and larger creatures—like the bulky turtles—chomp at seaweed and algae.

Glacia and Allison are waiting for me in the room. When Allison leaves, Glace puts her arms over my shoulders and stands on her toes for a kiss.

"*Sooo*, what's the plan?"

"Lisha Cove."

"Where's that?"

I start to respond, then stop, because I don't really know. "Um, like, that way." I point the direction I think is northeast. "But all *you* need to do is dress up and pack for the night."

She steps away slowly, so that our palms and fingers run together before letting go.

"*I'll be right back.*"

She disappears inside the bedroom. When she comes back out, she's wearing a sleeveless dress, one of the dresses she bought Monday. It's blue and orange, and patterned with pinkish, flower-shaped splotches and streaks of green. Her hair falls down her left shoulder, as always.

I don't try to hide my smile as Glacia crosses the room. *Beautiful things should be smiled at.* Captain Blitner's last words, the words he barely whispered as he stared at that gray mountain on Belvun.

The entire time we're riding the underwater shuttle, I'm holding Glacia's hand. When we transfer to the hovercraft that will take us to Lisha Cove, I'm holding Glacia's hand. And then we're in the air, the sunset to our backs, and I'm holding Glacia's hand.

Lisha sticks out of the ocean, which consists of two islands separated by a gorge. One island is *much* more massive than the other. There are no beaches. The steep, dark gray cliffs glow in the setting sun, and a shadow cast by Selayche's volcano forms a black wedge in the light. As we fly nearer, I notice that there aren't any buildings on top of the island, no towns, no gravity runs, nothing. The surface is too jagged and uneven to settle on, and the Dalish don't like impeding on nature. So far as I've seen, they build around it whenever possible, rather than leveling it. No wonder they chose Kiana, Daliona's small continent, to house a majority of the wildlife populations, even if it meant restricting where they themselves could live.

The hovercraft angles toward a gap and rapidly decelerates, until we're crawling along through the air. We glide through the dark gorge, which only has clusters of lanterns to mark the cliffs, but it isn't long before we see a yellow glow...and it grows brighter, and brighter. Suddenly we're in Lisha Cove—and we can't take our eyes off it. Victoria wasn't kidding: the inner face of the cliff has been hollowed out and turned into a massive cave, complete with carved tunnels illuminated by torches, wooden decks hanging over the gorge, and strings of yellow light dangling from the ceilings.

I look at Glacia, but her eyes are fixed on the cave, so I kiss her cheek and squeeze her hand gently.

The hovercraft lands in a docking chamber. Soon we're walking through a golden-lighted tunnel where the walls have been smoothed to a glossy sheen, and at the other end is a stony balcony. The cave is about a mile long, split into several terraced levels supported by decoratively designed pillars. A long pool has been dug into one slab of rock. I see people sitting on its edge, or swimming through the perfectly clear water that has a blue aura to it. Spiral staircases wrap around some of the pillars, ending in balconies or walkways that lead to other parts of the cove, each suspended fifty or more feet above the floor. At first glance, it looks like they're *dangerously* unsupported, but then I see flat disks attached to the undersides: industrial cyclo units.

Glacia and I make our way down a polished stone staircase. At the bottom, a bald Dalish man with a white cloth hanging off his forearm greets us.

"Two guests?"

I nod to answer him.

"What is the occasion?" he asks as he leads us to a table near the front of the cavern.

"Her birthday," I answer, squeezing Glacia's hand again.

"*Ahhh.*" He bows to Glacia. "A wonderful birthday to you, miss. You have dressed *beautifully*. To celebrate so far from home is a memory you will never forget." He smiles, his dark eyes glistening in the lantern light. "Can I start you off with a bottle of Sicha Wine? Each bottle is blended from the ripest harvests Daliona has to offer, then aged for exactly a Standard, to the day. You won't find a sweeter wine in the whole galaxy."

I look at Glacia, and she answers for me. "Please."

He clasps his hands behind his back and bows, then taps a disk sticking off the edge of the table. A menu appears. We look at it until he returns with two tall glasses and a clear, spherical bottle of pink wine. He aerates it into each glass, sets the first in front of Glacia, the second in front of me, then places the bottle between us and clasps his hands behind his back.

"And have you decided?"

Glacia orders Seagrass Flounder, and I order steamed barkal with boiled kern marinade. When the waiter leaves again, I reach for my wine glass. My fingers are trembling slightly—and Glacia notices. She perks one eyebrow, a small grin tugging on her mouth. I take a deep breath. But now my face is getting hot, and my mind is starting to blank on what I wanted to say.

"...*yeah*." Well, that was a great way to start a birthday speech. "You've taken me places I never thought I'd go, Glace. You've...gone through so much for me, you've been there even when I didn't want you"—I add a laugh—"even made me question my sanity at times."

Her hands are in her lap, her hair is down her shoulder, and her hazel eyes are fixed on me. I stall as long as I can, letting this image of her sink into my mind.

"You're beautiful, Glace. You're crazy. You don't let anything get in your way. You have that awesome smile...*and those eyes*. Like, wow. I just..." Another laugh escapes me. "Whatever you do, don't get those glowing blue things these people wear, because your eyes are perfect, Glace. Perfect. People look at your eyes all the time. They do, I swear. Your eyes just...*shine?* I don't know. I just like them a lot."

She cracks a smile and drops her head, then quickly

looks back up. Her cheeks are red, her smile is...quivering? And her eyes are locked on mine—but with wet tears in the corners.

She's beautiful.

"You were my second chance, and you're the best second chance I, or any guy, could've got." I raise the glass higher. "So happy birthday."

She lifts her glass and clinks it against mine. We drink together. It's chill and sweet—but not *too* sweet. It has a bit of a bite, and it's definitely better than the wine we have on Undil. I swallow half the glass before actually realizing it, and after I set it back on the table, Glacia's fingers brush the back of my outstretched hand. She stares at me...and stares at me...and stares at me some more, and then she breaks into giggles mixed with tears, and then she starts hiccupping, which makes *me* laugh. Her eyes keep darting to the side now, and she tries to smile even though she's crying, so I run my thumb over the back of her hand.

We eat dinner in silence, looking up at each other only to smile or pour more wine. Afterward, we walk along the edge of the cave, even stepping out onto one of the decks hanging over the gorge. We look straight down and listen to the water rushing far below. If I was wearing my cyclo right now, I could just...*lean over*. And fall. And fly. Because when I'm wearing the cyclo, I don't have to worry. I know my mind will stay calm, that I'll be in control. Nothing can stop me. I'll have no fear.

Flying a cyclo *is* living.

The path follows along the mouth of the cavern, lit by torches whose flames splutter in the wind but never go out. We reach the carved-out lobby of the cove's hotel and get a room with a view of the gorge, just like Officer Remmit told me to do.

It's quiet inside. And chilly. A thick, oval-shaped window forms the entire front of the room, tilted forward slightly. A hot tub takes up one corner, and a circular white bed sits in the other.

I face Glacia and hold my holotab up. "Remember your brother's wedding?"

She gives me a startled look. "*I have a brother?*"

I roll my eyes and grin, and she bites her lip and giggles to herself.

"Do you remember the song you liked?" I ask. "I think you said it reminded you of the stars."

She glances at the holotab—then back at me, her expression livening up.

"*Yes...?*"

"I got it from Jaston before we left. It's called *Stelle Adiis*. I did my research a while back and found out it means, '*The Sounds of the Stars*.' I know it's not, like, a real gift—"

"Mister."

I stop midsentence, my mouth still open. She takes the holotab and looks at it. Her mouth twitches in a smile when she sees the file, and then she taps the icon and sets the holotab on the rock shelf beside us. The music drifts out, slow at first...light and sad...beautiful and lonely. Chimes ring in the air moments before a soft, low thrum flows up from under them.

A heavy pulse.

A shattering beat.

A swing of the melody.

A rush of wind through trees.

My hands are on Glacia's waist, and hers are on my arms, and we're alone with the music, light-years from where we first danced to this same song, the song that resonates with the stars and fills the infinite void.

Chapter
Thirty-Three

RAND WALKS OUT of the prep area with the two
other Undilaen racers competing on Tahani, each of
them dressed in their gravity suits. The rest of their racing team is hanging back with the five of us to watch the
challenge from a spectator plaza.

Racers from all around the planet are checking in for
their race times and gathering in groups to watch the
ongoing competition. Looking around, I can see how
color-coordinated most of the competitors are: a lot of
the Dalish racers are dressed in the standard bright
blue, white, and green suits with blue helmets, nowhere
near as customized as Rand and his teammates. A Yillosian team has matching orange and white suits, and
three Ryginese people are wearing dark green and yellow.

Rand wasn't kidding when he said today would be
for the best of the best. The challenge began two hours
ago, and twenty-six people have gone so far. Of them,

only eleven have crossed the finish line. Eight lost their grip while rounding a turn, two got tossed off the Hump, and five flung into the walls of the Punch. Most people were fine. They just rode an automated sled to the end, like I did when I fell off on Marakuri. But three people have needed emergency evac for broken bones and cracked helmets.

Those were brutal.

"All right. We're gonna head up." Rand looks at us expectantly, flipping his helmet between his palms. "What? No *'good luck'* or anything? Okay. Glad to see you're rooting for us. See you guys on the other side."

Everyone speaks at once, our voices running together incoherently. A couple handshakes, pats on the back, thumbs-up.

Before Rand heads off, he shakes my shoulder and says, "Remember, we'll be heroes, Lance. You got your glory, now I'm coming for mine."

He holds his hand up in a wave, and then the three of them march toward the gravity complex to catch a lift. The rest of us walk to one of the spectator plazas, grab drinks, and find an empty table with a clear view of the displays.

A multi-framed projection of the races stands in the corner of the plaza. Right now, a man named Nicolay Tarles is in the middle of his run, streaking down one of the track's underwater sections. One frame shows the view from his helmet cam, and another shows the view from the cameras that line the tunnel's interior. The third screen shows his current time and speed, and the fourth frame lists the day's rankings. A woman named Margérite Vérjé, from Yillos, holds first place with a time of 1:57.051.

Nicolay finishes in three minutes, ranking 32nd, well outside the Top 20 contenders.

Three announcers commentate the runs, just like the announcers did the day of Glacia's challenge on Laka. As the queue slides along, they talk about racers they expect to do well—or not so well. Lilo Rabuka surprises all of them, sliding into fifth place when they thought she'd fall off at the Hump. Her time pushes Kulam Mako into sixth. A bunch of racers finish in around two-and-a-half to three minutes. But for every three people that make it to the end unscathed, one person wipes out at the Hump, just like Rand predicted, or even more violently at the Punch, the sharp back-and-forth curves that shoot straight into an upward arc. One man wipes out at the top of the Hump, slams into the top of the tunnel, and tumbles down the other side while his sled zooms down the track, riderless. Another racer smacks face-first into the top of the tunnel when she loses her grip late in her run. A loud *'OOOOOHHHHH'* rises from the crowds every time.

Two more racers go, and then, being the unofficial captain of the Undilaen racers, Rand steps up to the loading platform. The Dalish racing official locks his sled in place and gives him clearance to set up while the previous racer nears the end of the track.

"Here we have one of our favorite foreign runners to watch. Randeroy Harmat"—on the display, Rand rolls his eyes and mouths, *'just Rand'*—*"...hasn't competed in a gravity challenge in four years, though he has trained during his current stay. He set those yet-unbroken records on the Maligo and Hashmere courses all those years ago,*

and we're excited to see what he pulls off today."

If Rand is nervous, he doesn't show it. Behind his visor, his eyes are fixed on the opening of the tunnel. He's breathing slowly, his cheeks puffing out, then deflating.

The timer at the head of the tunnel blinks the previous racer's time, then resets. Rand's face fills one of the screens, but he's looking down the track—not up into the camera.

Ten seconds.

Rand adjusts his shoulders. Flexes his fists. Shifts his feet. His eyes don't move. Not even once.

At three seconds, he heaves a breath.

At two seconds, he blows it out.

At one, he mouths: *'No fear.'*

Zero.

The sled blasts forward. He's inside the tunnel. Dropping down the first dip.

Thirty miles per hour, cruising around the long curve that will bring him over the beach. Down...down. Streaking along at fifty miles per hour. A short drop—a straightaway out over the bay—the first steep dive.

In one screen, Rand is a blur. In the other, the tunnel whips by blindingly fast. He can see the boats and mountains and open sky as the water surges toward him—and then he plummets below the surface.

The whole view changes. Fish and eels and turtles and reefs. The track dips left to avoid a submerged cliff. Down a trench, into darkness. His visor lets him see the golden line that marks his path, but the rest is black until the track angles upward and light filters back into the tunnel. Dark, rocky walls loom on either side. Upward in a tight spiral, a dive, a straightaway, another dive.

Rand leans into the next curve and shoots toward the bay's surface, briefly skims it, drops down a short slope—and then swings up again. He's almost to the Hump. Almost... Almost...

Now.

Rand's body visibly lifts off his sled. He's yelling, filling the plaza with his strained roar as he fights to stay on the sled.

He succeeds...

...and shoots back into the bay. A straightaway on the other side gives him a short reprieve.

He curves left.

Drops beside another submerged cliff.

Rises into the light and loops around a reef.

A group of barkals chases him, but he pays no attention. White fish, yellow fish, blue, black, green, striped, dotted. This reef teems with life, almost as if it's trying to distract Rand with its beauty, just *daring* him to sneak a glance and miss the next turn.

Rand dips to the right.

Now he's shooting straight to the bottom of the trench, surrounded by darkness with only his visor and instincts to guide him. His teeth clenched, his speed rocketing from sixty miles per hour to eighty...ninety...

One hundred.

Glacia digs her nails into her palms. She's stiff, eyes glued to the display.

Terrified.

The final checkpoint: *1:46.673*. I don't know if he knows his time—maybe the visor tells him—but he's nearing the end. He's going to make the Top five. Top three, even, if he holds his speed.

On the map of the track, I see the left-right switchback that feeds into the instant upward arc. The Punch. Rand is closing in, rounding a turn, hitting a straightway. He sees it. His jaw tightens. He flexes his fingers, shifts his legs. Going one hundred-and-four miles per hour, he'll have about a quarter-second to react to each turn.

He swings to the left.

Flattens out.

Swings to the—*NO*.

Rand's fingers rip off the grips. He yells. His feet dislodge. His arms flail. He skids, bangs, flings down the track.

Glacia shrieks. Covers her mouth.

THUD.

Rand slams into the wall. His visor cracks and the helmet's video display cuts out.

The maglev sled is gone. It shot away up the track and is slowing down at the finish line. But he isn't moving. His body keels over, limp.

Glacia's already crying. Allison's mouth is hanging open, her eyes red. Kile is looking the other way. Trey dropped his drink, and it shattered on the ground. I didn't even hear it break, because *everyone*—the people in the plaza, the crowd on the beach, the people passing by on the street, *everyone*—utters the same drawn-out '*OOOOOHHHHH.*'

And then silence falls.

No more *ooohhh*s.

No more muttering.

A siren wails in the distance: the rescue team. It fades when they dive underwater. Rand's teammates, the ones who were sitting with us, are already gone, running out of the plaza to the gravity complex.

Glacia sounds like she's choking now. Allison's face is growing redder, tears finally falling. And my chest feels hollow. I'm shivering, rubbing my fingers in my fists, legs shaking. Eyes watering. He just—I just saw him—did he just—?

I can't bring myself to think the word.

He can't be.

Not Rand.

He hasn't moved, and the emergency crew hasn't reached him yet. One of his arms is bent the wrong way. One of his feet is twisted the wrong direction. Blood is soaking through his racing suit, dripping from his nose and mouth.

Nobody can tell if he's breathing.

Part 3
The Aurora

Chapter
Thirty-Four

I STARE AT the darkness above.

I'm alone the hotel room. The lights are off. The swirls of water seem dull, blending into my thoughts like the hum of the *Ember*'s engines would. The fish have retreated for the night, and the blue waters have darkened to black.

Glacia hasn't come back. She stayed at the hospital, but I couldn't put myself through that. To *see* him. I've seen too much, *felt* too much. My thoughts have broken me again, the memories I swore I'd hide from. But they're leaking through my head, every thought of Rand dragging in one more thought of Father.

My body shudders—violently.

Rand's arms flail, his body flips off the sled. Glacia screams. Glacia, crying. Rand, skidding down the track, smacking into the wall. Going limp...

...and then I see Father. His head is slumped, blood is pumping from his temple where the shard of glass ripped him open. My eyes couldn't find his. The stench overwhelmed me. My world was spinning, my vision was darkening. I couldn't speak. Couldn't scream. My fingers fumbled for the lock on his belt, but I was weak. The voices...the voices. The sting that split my stomach.

I can't—couldn't—breathe.

I thought I was going to die.

And now I'm reliving it.

Somehow I managed to keep myself from slipping too far. When they released me from the hospital, I wanted so bad to just...to just...

My vision is blurry from tears that won't fall. I rub my eyes. Squeeze them shut and cross my arms over my face. I hear nothing, see nothing, want nothing.

I should have taken Father to Emerson's ice cream plaza. He would have told me a story, and I would have sat and listened to him. I could have told him how Erinn and Flavia were growing up so fast. But I didn't do any of that, and he's dead because I didn't.

Father was the man the galaxy respected. The man who built a legacy. I was just his son, just a boy obsessed with a girl. This one, *stupid* girl I turned my back on in the end. The Embassy doesn't need someone like *that*. The Embassy doesn't need *me*.

The Embassy needs my father.

❋   ❋   ❋   ❋   ❋

I've been lying here for two hours, the silence weighing down on me. Because the door is shut, I don't hear when Glacia comes back, not until light floods the bedroom.

But Glacia shuts it quickly when she sees I'm in the dark. She must think I'm asleep. I don't hear her walk over, though.

Why won't she come over?

Please come over here, Glace.

Please.

The sounds are muffled. I wasn't sure at first, but now I know she's crying. Whimpering, sucking breaths through her nose to stay quiet. A soft *thump* as she leans on the door, then slides down it. She must be sitting on the floor. And I'm not there for her. I haven't moved. I can't make myself turn over, let her know I'm awake.

A heavy breath…

I hear her stand…

Light floods the room—then darkness.

＊　＊　＊　＊　＊

When I wake, the water has a light blue tint, with gray shadows drifting through the sunbeams. By the time I roll over to wake Glacia up, the reef…

Wait.

Glacia isn't here.

I press my face to the pillow, then force myself out of bed. I find her in the main room, still wearing the clothes she was wearing yesterday, her shoes knocked to the side. Her knees are bent, and she's shivering, her arms hugging her sides because she doesn't have a blanket. She looks so miserable. How long was she awake last night? I should have told her I was awake, that I know she came into the room and heard her crying against the wall.

Crying for Rand.

I sit in the empty space, in the crook of her knees, and reach one hand out to touch her arm—her elbow. I need to do something. Like go back to the bedroom and get her the blanket. But before I can stand up, her eye opens. She's watching me. A tear wells up and slips over the bridge of her nose, landing on the couch.

"*He's in a coma,*" she tells me, her voice cracking in a whisper.

First I laugh, a gargled choke that doesn't leave my throat. Then I nod. "He's not—"

"*No.*"

I take a deep breath and look away from her.

"Okay."

She doesn't move. I don't move. Every time I look down, her eyes flick away. I don't know what that means. I know what I *don't* want it to mean, but that's the only thing it *can* mean. Like I'm losing her. Looking into each other's eyes usually makes both of us smile. Except now she isn't letting me look at her.

I pull my hand back, clench it tight. I need *something* to hold onto, because that...that *twisted* thought is making me sick. The thought that she—*they*—could have ever... Except I know *she* wouldn't. Not Glacia. She wouldn't do that to me. Would she? Rand always had his eyes all over her. '*Haverns, Haverns, Haverns.*' The way he would say her name, the way she would grin, her eyes wide and ready for a new day of training with him. When's the last time she looked at *me* like that? I race through my thoughts, looking at her face in every memory, but she's never looking at me. Not in any of them. She's staring at a gravity run, or at Daliona, or at the cove, or the iguanas, or the ocean. Never *me*. Not until her birthday. When I gave that stupid speech and she started crying. Why would she start *crying?* Was it because there I was, spilling my love for her, and she wasn't telling me something? And she didn't talk to me as we ate, even though usually we can't shut up. Is that it? *Why would she do that?* When I gave her the song, *she* started dancing with me. She looked so happy, like there was nowhere else she'd rather be, like we meant everything to each other and nobody, *nobody* could take that away from us.

I'm shaking. My arms, my legs... Even my head is twitching, my eyes shifting at her now, but I can't tell if she's looking back. Tears build up in my eyes. I wish I wasn't here. Anywhere but here.

Get. Me. Out.

So I stand up and go to the bedroom, grab my uniform, and go take a shower. I don't look at her as I cross the main room again, even though she's facing the bedroom. I don't want to see her looking away.

※　※　※　※　※

I take as long a shower as I can. Cold, then hot, then cold again, in cycles. That relaxes the muscles. When I finish, I rub on the scented oil I've been wearing every day, but this time I use a lot. It's so strong that even *I* think I overdid it. But I want it to cloud my head. I don't want to think. I don't want to worry. I'm on Daliona, for crying out loud. *Why do I feel so awful?*

Glacia isn't laying on the couch when I come back out. Even her trunk is gone from the bedroom.

I go eat breakfast in the Pelago's natural aquarium. Music chimes around me, people from all across the galaxy gorge themselves, or stare at the fish and eels and turtles swimming through the tubes crossing the room. I'm sitting alone at first, but it isn't long before someone else sits across from me: Kile.

We look at each other. He smiles, I nod back.

"I saw Trey and Allison over there," he says, pointing in some direction. "But I figured…"

He trails off and shrugs, maybe because I'm not looking at him anymore. I leave him to silence, keeping my hands folded over my chin. But he doesn't leave when he's done eating. He keeps flicking his eyes at me, or down at my half-eaten food.

"Finish your book?" I ask, breaking my silence.

He shakes his head. "Nah. I'm going to save it for the expedition home. Plenty of time then. It's like two thousand pages."

"*Geez.*"

"Yeah." He taps a finger on the table. "Do you read?"

Now *I* shake my head. "Not unless I'm like *really* bored."

"Ah."

Silence again. But Kile doesn't leave. Not until I do.

✳ ✳ ✳ ✳ ✳

There's no gravity elevator between Selayche and Thorpe because they're too close along the curve of the planet, so we have to take a hovercraft. The trip is thirty minutes longer than a gravity elevator would take—and these islands are relatively *close* to each other. I can't imagine how long flying halfway around Daliona would take.

As we fly, I close my eyes. And when I close my eyes, I see Rand's final words form silently on his lips.

No fear.

I see the sled shoot into the tunnel.

No fear.

He had complete control.

No fear.

What did he feel before he slammed into the wall? Was there enough time for him to feel fear? *Would* he have?

I remember what I told myself, that saying *'no fear'* only gives you the courage to push yourself off the edge. After that, whatever happens, happens.

There's no turning back.

✳ ✳ ✳ ✳ ✳

The Thorpe Archipelago grows from a bump on the horizon, to a lush, mountainous set of islands. The space elevator is in our sight the entire time, rising from the depths of Thorpe Island's jungles and vanishing into the atmosphere. On the other side of the mountain range, the Embassy shines on the eastern shores. We circle over Laka Island, fly beside the massive elevator, and descend toward the short-range passenger docks. I see the complex where—almost a month ago—we first rode a gravity pod to Bechi Island. Bechi, where the sea turned to ice and the sun never set. Director Machus told us the shadow months were closing in around the Dalish Arctic, that the top of the world would plunge into darkness.

A short walk through the docks.

Now we're riding a FAST track, gliding through the Dalish Embassy's twisting towers, over its vast, colorful plazas, across the winding Rainbow River. People in cyclos zoom between buildings, drop into plazas, dive into the river and come up dripping. I watch them, letting my eyes flick from one to the next. I wish I could jump out and join them. Just...*jump.*

The shuttle stops in Thorpe Plaza Station. Back on the ground, we meet Orcher and President Okana in the courtyard at the base of Thorpe Tower, along with a mix of other top Dalish and Undilaen Officials.

Orcher gives us—me, Kile, Trey, and Allison—a sad smile. Even President Okana's large, bronze face softens, a sign of his own condolences.

"*Arman.*"

Orcher waves two fingers for me to follow him. We walk down one of the paths shaded by those fat brown and yellow trees, and he waits until we're a good distance from the others before speaking.

"The *Drake*'s and the *Blazar*'s teams are already back. Lon Kelvin and Elliot Writway reported to me"— of course *Lon* did. He's always doing Baxter's job—"and I gave them small assignments to complete." His eyes fall to the ground, and he hesitates before saying, "I was in contact with the hospital. Mr. Harmat will be fine. He's in stable condition. Bruised up, broken right arm, severe concussion...but he's hydrated and nourished, and his vitals are showing fine. All he needs to do is wake up." Orcher frowns and tips his head. "Of course, that begged the question: what to do with him until then? After...well, after discussing this with our own medical officers, we've decided it's best he remain here, on Daliona, until such a time when he is fit to rejoin us."

I nod harder than I mean to. "How long is that?"

Orcher scratches his chin. "Nobody can be sure. Really, it depends on *when* he comes out of the coma. A few months at the earliest, if he were to wake soon. If, however, he were to remain in this state for an extended period..." A sad look comes over his eyes. "You must understand, Arman. For someone in his condition, spaceflight is just...*not safe*. The gravity acclimation, the time adjustment, the mental duress. If he were to wake up on Undil, and not know *how* he got there... Well, we want this to go as smoothly as possible for him. He'll need to undergo extensive psychological examination before he makes anymore interstellar trips."

Orcher looks back at the group of Undilaen and Dalish officers. My small team is standing a few yards to the side. Kile's standing with his head bowed, his heel rhythmically scuffing the path. Allison and Trey are both staring into the city.

"The Dalish doctors explained a recovery technique they've put some other patients through," Orcher says, his voice stronger than it was a moment ago. "Again, I discussed it with our own medics, and we decided to proceed with the idea. The hospital has linked Rand's mind to the Lucidity Interface."

A cold shiver prickles my neck. "What will that do?"

"You can imagine Mr. Harmat isn't the first person to sustain severe injuries from those gravity runs. It's a dangerous sport, Arman, and with the risk comes the cost. Tahani is particularly notorious for death and mental and physical damages. The doctors said that hooking him into the interface will...*in effect*...give him a normal life until he wakes up."

I shake my head. I think I know what he means, but that just seems...*wrong*.

"It's nothing experimental," Orcher explains. "This method has been tested in the past. They've already generated a world for him to exist in. He'll be told what happened. What he does with that information is up to him. In the meantime, his subconscious will stay occupied. His mind won't deteriorate."

My heart begins to race, my thoughts swirling around as I try to make sense of what Orcher is telling me. I'm confused. I'm *so* confused. No, I *understand* what he's saying, I just don't *like* it.

"But the whole thing is a lie?"

Orcher hesitates, his mouth slightly open as he searches for a better explanation. "I wouldn't say so. It's an interface generated from his strongest memories, like an induced lucid dream to keep his mind active."

I think about the lucidity arcade on Selayche Island. Fifteen minutes in real life was an hour in the interface. Rand could literally spend months...*years* in this dream, only to have it all ripped away when he wakes up.

Orcher clears his throat again. "This is for the best, Arman. He'll come around soon."

His quick smile isn't convincing.

That evening, I host a short conference with President Okana in Thorpe Tower's foreign council chamber. I'm sitting with my team leaders behind four podiums, and our respective teams are off to the side, out of the way. We're waiting for President Okana to begin, whose eyes are glowing blue as he moves his giant hands around in the air, collecting invisible data documents related to RASP. At last, he slides his hand all the way to one side, and a data array appears in the center of the chamber.

After we discuss the initial summary of our completed work, I recite all the facilities my team linked to RASP, first listing those we got on Bechi Island, then Marakuri, then Hossiard, and so on. Baxter delivers his information next, then Sam and Elliot. As each of us speaks, the locations glow on a projection of Daliona floating beside the data we reported so President Okana can cross-check them.

"Excellent," he says when Elliot finishes the final section. "I spoke with your man, Olivarr Cresson. He told me now that our facilities are linked, this program will provide automatic updates to the catalogue."

"That's only when a fleet equipped with RASP visits Daliona," I correct.

"Of course, of course." President Okana claps his hands together, a booming thud. "Your man also mentioned plans to eventually link all nine planets to this catalogue?"

"That's the goal."

"An admirable mission, Mr. Lance. You've been thorough in your work."

"Thank you."

"I will, of course, be eager to see where this program goes. A comprehensive galactic catalogue has only been attempted once, and not on this scale. An encyclopedia called *48 Light-Years*. Have you heard of it?"

I grin. "I actually own a copy."

"Do you?" He laughs, bobbing his head. "Then I suppose you know how very different your program is. *48* covers ecosystems and species associated with the planets, where your program details our technology and planetary science divisions. A daunting task, no doubt." President Okana opens a new document and reads the abstract. "This database will be mutually accessible, correct? *Any* Embassy can access your program?"

"As long as RASP's mainframe is installed in their archives sector or interstellar fleets," I explain.

"I see. Daliona will, of course, request the installation. Tell your man, Olivarr, that we will send envoys to Undil later this year to offer a number of services in exchange."

An idea pops into my head: Rand and Olivarr kept talking about bringing gravity runs to Orvad. Now, though...after *that* happened...I'm not sure if Olivarr still wants to. But I tell President Okana anyway.

His strikingly white teeth appear in his large grin. "Did he, now? A private Orvadian run? Interesting... I will get in touch."

Chapter Thirty-Five

CONFERENCES.

From morning to night.

For two days, *that's my life.*

My teams and I have to sit in on meetings ranging from proposed exoplanet expeditions to maintenance projects on gravity elevators. Orcher wants us to get a feel for how formal conferences are run on a planet as advanced as Daliona. And now we're in the last one, the conference I've been dreading ever since I heard we had to attend it: discussing the state of Belvun.

Ambassador Purnell is sitting in the center of the conference chamber. Ladia's father. He looks annoyed, sick of waiting around for President Okana and his advisors to open the meeting. And to make things even more awkward, Ambassador Purnell keeps looking at me—*glaring*, actually. I'm the guy who ditched his daughter for another girl. Me, the son of the galaxy's most influential ambassador.

Victoria was right: he looks *pissed*. I might not be a techie genius, but I know why he's angry. I was his leverage. I was power. My name can get anything done. Ambassador Purnell *needed* me. But now he only has Michael Rafting, some no-name Latecomer who doesn't even particularly *like* Ambassador Purnell, judging from what Michael told us about their time spent together.

I'm front and center on the panel. I get to deliver questions, not answer them. Orcher is beside me, and my team leaders are on either side of us. President Okana and his advisors are up one tier behind us to oversee the conference, and Orcher's fleet lieutenants are seated at the remaining panels.

"This session is meant for archival purposes and shall be recorded as such," Orcher tells everyone in attendance, just like he's done at all the other conferences. "It will be documented in Undil's Live Archives Program as supplementary data for our catalogue of Belvun. So, Ambassador. If you would."

Ambassador Purnell clears his throat. "I stated this in our conference earlier this week...*obviously*...but it bears worth repeating, apparently: my Embassy no longer has the means to quell Belvun's deterioration. After your crew's departure last summer, analyses showed accelerated decay in regions where organic samples were removed. Our precautionary efforts, however, did *nothing* to prevent the inevitable.

"Fires broke out in the midst of a lightning storm above Fleerard Forest on the Seventeenth of October, Standard Four-Three-One-Nine...*obviously*," he mutters under his breath again. "Fleerard City was evacuated after the first report of these firestorms. On October the

Nineteenth, flames had engulfed the central district. A violent super cell that spawned half a dozen tornadoes struck Noshton on October Thirtieth. Subari's western forests, *my home*, went up in flames three days later, following three years of severe drought, in a way reminiscent of the fall of Ellaciss. Eighty-percent of the neighborhoods were lost.

"Evacuees from all three districts have been sent to our embassy. Cleanup efforts, gauging from the report I received before leaving Belvun, are futile. Our emergency services simply do not have the capacity to handle all these regions while threat levels across the entire planet are rising. We asked for volunteers to assist and received a turnout of less than one-percent of all evacuees. Morale is low, and understandably so. These storms have increased in frequency as conditions further deteriorate. Super cells and tornadoes are appearing in unprecedented numbers. Where it still rains, the water is heavily acidic and destroying our soils and crops. A report estimates that upwards of sixty-percent of Belvun has undergone severe droughts over the last four years, and temperatures across the planet have risen every year since Standard Four-Three-One-Four. Our ice caps have melted and rivers have flooded watersheds, driving even more people to seek refuge in the Embassy and other yet-unaffected districts." Ambassador Purnell slaps his hand on the podium. "Conditions, as you can imagine, are deplorable. We simply *do not have the resources* to manage this crisis."

He changes screens, looks at the report he's summarizing, and continues speaking.

"President Theodore Garner sent me and other envoys to Undil and Narviid in January of this year, pleading Chancellor Green and Chancellor Kraatz for aid and refuge until the Faustocine is delivered and Belvun is once again safe to inhabit. Before I left Undil to come here, Chancellor Green *graciously* sent a fleet to supply my people with what little resources Undil could spare. I know not of what actions Narviid has taken to assist us, as they are already doing so much to equip our Embassy fleets with the latest technologies they developed after their partial acquisition of Gray Wall Industries in the Joint Space Tech Treaty...which, you should know, Chancellor Green continues to firmly oppose despite Narviid's offering of compensation for mining rights in the Perihelid asteroid field."

Ambassador Purnell stops talking to catch his breath. His eyes flick up in my direction again, but then fix on Orcher.

"David, upon your return to Undil, I *strongly* advise you call a mandatory conference with your chancellor and persuade him to reach *some* agreement with the Narvidians. If Belvun is lost, Undil is the candidate to take Belvish refugees. But without fiscal aid, Undil cannot possibly maintain two planets' populations. You know that as well as I. The Narvidians are willing to negotiate. They *want* to help both our societies, but your *callous* chancellor doesn't see that. We need *someone* to strike a deal, or the crisis on Belvun will be irreparable, and our political ties destroyed."

That's when Ambassador Purnell stares at me and doesn't look away. I know exactly what he's thinking. But he doesn't understand: I can't be that mediator.

Father would know what to do. Father would start

working on a way to persuade Chancellor Green as soon as this conference ends. Not me, though. I'm an archivist. My job is to catalogue and report, not tell the leaders of entire planets what to do.

Orcher shifts in his seat, tapping one of his fingers. "I will have Ambassador Rafting propose a deal, Jem."

"Are there any questions from the panel?" President Okana says from behind me.

My heart races. Pounding. Pounding. Pounding. Because yes, I do. In all the time he's been away from Belvun...has the situation worsened? Would word have been sent to Undil?

I force myself to speak. "Do you know if there've been more fires and evacuations?"

Ambassador Purnell bites his cheek. Even from here, I can see his face reddening. "Head. Archivist. Lance. I have told you all that I know. It has been *seven weeks* since I was last in contact with Belvun. Ten more cities could have burned to the ground and I *will not know* until I return. Does it change the situation? Do more people need to watch their homes burn, do more people need to *die* before you show an ounce of sympathy?" He slams his fist on the podium so hard it cracks the screen. "*My people are suffering!* And you're doing...*what?* Tell me, have you enjoyed your little vacation, Mr. Lance? Did you get a nice tan? *Hmm?* What is your work doing to help—"

"*AMBASSADOR.*"

The chamber goes silent in the wake of President Okana's booming voice. Ambassador Purnell is glaring past me now, and I can almost feel the President glaring back.

"You will *respect* all members of the panel, or I will request your removal and we will settle these matters without your presence."

Ambassador Purnell's mouth drops into a rigid frown. After a moment of deliberation, he switches the central display to images and videos of Belvun, and moves on with the presentation. Most of the councilors present have already seen the footage, but to me and my teams, they're brand new. Some images are from the outskirts of the cities, others are orbital images showing the spread of the firestorms. Up close, whole trees burst into fire even before the flames reach them. Rivers and lakes are swamped with thick ash fluttering down from the noxious columns of yellow and gray smoke, suffocating the forests and fields and cities with layers of ash.

Before: a sprawling red forest.

After: miles of black, smoldering stumps and splintered tree trunks.

One video shows lines of people boarding hovercrafts out of Fleerard, hovercrafts flying under the shadows of the smoke trails. More orbital images show smoke rolling for miles, billowing through entire mountain ranges, sinking through valleys, blackening Belvun's orange hue.

Ambassador Purnell's voice stays flat when he describes what we're seeing. "The air is becoming poisoned. Cleanup crews reported uncovering dead wildlife in the ashes. Extinction threatens dozens of species, so relocation is a secondary necessity we must act on after my people are safe." His eyes flick up at President Okana. "If you haven't screwed it up this time, the Faustocine is Belvun's last hope of recovery. If not, we will let the fires run their course and start from scratch in a few decades. Hundreds-of-years of progress, ruined, Dillon. And that is why I'm going to call for Belvun's finest environmentalists compile *extensive* reports on the *illegitimacy* of Daliona's *renowned* eco-hacking and present them to the Galactic Embassy Council. With any success, eco-hacking as a terraformation process will be forbidden, and extreme measures will be taken to enforce that doctrine, much like the continued prohibition against artificial intelligence, which, unsurprisingly, was another of Daliona's greatest innovative failures."

President Okana lets out a large grunt. "When is the last time you read a history book, Purnell?"

Ambassador Purnell shuts down the display. "I'm finished." He looks at Orcher. "I'll be on Belvun awaiting your fleet's arrival, David. I've wasted enough time *here.*"

And he marches from the conference chamber without another word.

President Okana lets out another grunt. "*Hundreds of years...* The man wouldn't know progress if it beat his scrawny arse red. Lazy. That's the Belvish for you. *Damn the people*, it's the planet we need to preserve. Kiana's populations will be ready for full-relocations in the coming years, and Belvun's the ideal candidate, *if* we recover it. We need life to thrive. Nobody said a damn thing about what species."

Chapter Thirty-Six

THE SHUTTLE SPEEDS through the city on its way out toward the pastures and mountains of Thorpe. A thin fog trails through the towers, the dawn's yellow light dispersed within it.

A man in a cyclo flies past our shuttle in the opposite direction. He's the first one I've seen this morning, probably going for a quiet morning flight before the airspace gets crowded. It must be beautiful, to wake up and fly... But I never got the chance to go solo. Never got to fly in the open air, free to *be*. Free to feel the chill wind, to dive into the Rainbow River and come up soaked and refreshed and ready for another daring plunge. All the hopes I built up these last few weeks...gone.

I wish the ride to the space elevator was longer.

The shuttle races across the vineyards and pastures before dipping into the side of the mountain. We slide through the cave where those leeches dangle from the ceiling, and then we're racing toward a light.

Exit.

Walk up a ramp.

Board the space elevator.

The slurred Dalish voice prepares us for the lift...but I hardly react when the pod shoots up its tube and bursts above the jungle canopy.

Rising...rising...rising...but there's too much going on in my head to feel anxious, or sick, or whatever it is I should be feeling. I don't want to leave. I know what's going to happen when I get to the *Ember*: I'll be isolated, trapped with my thoughts. When I'm trapped, I think too much. And right now there are too many things I don't want to think—but they're the only ones filling my head. How I left Glacia alone that night. How she wouldn't look at me. How she cried for Rand. Rand, crashing. Rand, limbs twisted. Rand, slumped on the track, not moving. His crash—*my* crash. *My* world, spinning. *My* head, pounding. Smelling blood. Seeing Father slumped in his seat, blood bubbling from his head, his eyes never meeting mine. No more stories, only regrets and fading memories. And now...*now*...

Thorpe Island shrinks to a green speck in the bright blue ocean. The whole planet is slipping away. The mountains, the jungle, the Embassy. Islands I've yet to explore, people I've yet to meet, sights I've yet to see.

I close my eyes.

I'm crying.

I don't. Want. To leave.

I'm aware of the light, brightening. Of the pod, accelerating. Feel the pressure of rising...rising...rising, like I'm so used to doing these days. I'm always rising...*and*

■ ■ ■

falling.

When I sense the sunlight dim, I open my eyes and see Daliona's teal-blue oceans, the curves of its horizons, the swirls of clouds that stretch hundreds of miles.

Above the planet, thousands of stars glitter in the darkness. Dalish space fleets surround us, hanging silently in orbit...and then the pod climbs higher and they shrink to nothing.

Rise into the spaceport.

Lock into place.

Unfasten our restraints.

The hatch opens and Dalish Officials guide us to the top of the ramps and to the docks, where our transports are waiting to take us back to the *Ember*, the *Drake*, the *Blazar*, and the *Doppler*. The stations to which our lives will be contained for the next two weeks. I board one and fasten myself to the seat. Someone sits beside me—but it's no one I know.

As more people board, I listen for Glacia's voice and silently hope that she'll take the other empty seat beside me...but no, a woman takes it. I should have waited, should have stayed in the docking room until Glacia walked in. Would she have cared? Would she have looked at me? Would she have *wanted* me to wait for her? What *does* she want?

Engines whir, thrusters flare, wall panels flicker to life. My transport lifts off...slips through the silvery light into the nothingness. The spaceport's artificial gravity vanishes and weightlessness overtakes my body. But it's stranger than usual... I'm used to the cyclo's weightless effect, where my motion felt concentrated around the suit. Now I feel loose, like any piece of my body could just drift away. I'm not in control. I *need* the cyclo.

Shivers race up my spine when the woman's hair brushes my arm. If she was Glacia, I wouldn't care. I *wish* I could feel Glacia's hair now, bouncing around her head in massive, wild waves. I *wish* I could see her giggly smile. She loves this part of spaceflight...even if she normally throws up when it's over.

I need to take my mind off her. We'll talk again soon. I know we will. This is just a phase. She's upset and I don't know how to help her. Once she's better, we'll be fine.

Stop thinking.

Look at Daliona.

The planet looms to our right. It's so far away, and every horizon is visible. Docho and Lide, those yellow and white crescents, hang a bit off to the side. I don't want to leave. Not *ever*. I don't want to go to the *Ember*. Or to Undil. Or Belvun.

And you know what?

Screw them. Screw their problems. Screw Ambassador Purnell. President Okana was right: the Belvish haven't done anything to try and stop the desert from spreading. They live in their big houses in the forests with their trimmed lawns and their big cities, then complain and expect everyone to fix their problems when a tree catches on fire. I *hope* they have to evacuate. They'll get a taste of the shitty lives we Undilaens have to deal with every single day. No more grass. No more trees. No more shaded porches and neat little gardens. No more pink skies or cold rivers. Because guess what? Undil is hot. Undil is dusty. There's nothing to see, nothing to do but wish you were born somewhere else. Because no one wants to live there—not one single person—and anyone who says otherwise is lying.

✳   ✳   ✳   ✳   ✳

"I'm afraid I haven't had much practice preparing your coffee as of late," Orcher jokingly admits when he comes out of his private office with two steaming cups of Bersivo Blend. "But we have a long trip ahead, more than enough time to perfect it again."

He goes to hand me mine, then pulls back.

"Remember, mind your grip."

I'm well aware of that. Every little move I make comes twice as hard as I intend. My muscles ache to feel the tug of Daliona's heavy gravity, but we've gone back to living under Undil's. The first time walking down the hall yesterday, I nearly banged my head on the ceiling from taking too strong a step. And I have to be careful not to stab my throat with the fork at meals, or roll off the bed when I turn over. I slept for exactly two hours last night. That's how much energy my body has stored. If I want to keep the muscle I built up, I'll need to spend *a lot* of time in the fitness center *and* stick to my Dalish eating habits...yet that still might not be enough.

I take the cup from Orcher, forcing my fingers to grip it as gently as possible. The coffee is darker than I'd like, of course, but screw it. I don't care.

Orcher takes his usual spot across from me, overlooking the Bridge as we speed farther into the darkness. Daliona is far behind, indistinguishable among the stars, and Undil is light-years ahead. The

Bridge is quieter than I remember, too. Usually officers are gathered around workstations, or running system checks, or discussing expedition reports. But right now most everyone keeps to themselves, too exhausted to interact like normal. Even Captain Fallsten isn't her usual self. She's absent from Glacia's shoulder, analyzing every little move...

Glacia.

I can't take my eyes off her.

Her back is to me, her head tipped forward and her hands on the flight controls. It's the first time I've seen her since...two days ago? I think? Her hair is braided down her back, rather than being loose and pulled over her shoulder. It looks too...*professional?*...too formal for her. I don't like it. She's supposed to—

"Lars told me you got a cyclo," Orcher says, taking my attention off Glacia.

I nod and reach for my coffee.

Nope, still too hot.

"I was never into those." Orcher sets his mug down but doesn't let go of it. "Your father and I, we were always men of politics. But Lars and Lieutenant Hofhen still have that...that *spirit* to them. Those two are always on the move." Orcher glances down at Victoria, who is sitting at her work panel two levels below, reading through station data. "Several years back, before she became my lieutenant, in fact, she and Lars were always going on ski treks, glacier hikes, river cruises... I believe they rented a cabin in one of the forest ranges, if my mind serves correctly. They were a little older then than you are now, still eager to travel. I'm not saying they aren't eager *now*, but..."

He sighs heavily, then takes an especially long drink from his coffee, as if trying to hold off his next words as long as possible.

"None of us fared well after Ellaciss, Arman. We all lost the spark of adventure. Even your father. Nobody joins the Embassy hoping to risk their lives. We all want to explore... We all want to see everything, *do* everything. In a perfect life, we'd all be pioneers, artists, scientists, and inventors. What other purpose to the universe is there but to create and discover?"

Orcher pauses again and stares ahead, at the stars that dot the void. I watch them with him, and I can *see* how far away they are, almost as if I can sense the distance. And I truly appreciate how far we've come. Not just me, but *us*.

Humanity.

"Then you see a side of things you wish you never had," Orcher goes on saying. "Sometimes you wish you'd chosen differently. You finally realize you aren't here because you're privileged. You're here because you dedicated yourself to a cause. That's why your father spent thirty years of his life writing treatises, Arman. That's the purpose of the Embassy Program: to pave the path for future generations to follow."

He looks at me for a second, then extends his hand over the desk for me to shake.

"You've done a fine job with your new program. I appreciate the work you've put in. Really, Arman. Thank you. Your father would say the same."

"Thanks," I say. It's all I can manage right now.

He folds his hands on the desk. "All that's left to *this* expedition is organizing the catalogue and compiling reports. When we get to Undil, we'll switch gears, take a short break, and then set our sights on Belvun. Let's finish this. How about it? *And Arman.*" He looks down at Captain Fallsten. "Just make your reports thorough. I don't want to set Miranda off."

"Got it."

I grab my coffee to take with me—but stand a bit too fast and end up throwing myself off-balance, spilling coffee down my arm and on Orcher's desk.

So much for easing up my movements.

When I get to the archives chamber, Lon—that is, a *projection* of Lon—is talking to Allison and Trey about the *Drake*'s morning reports. He's doing Baxter's job, as usual.

Kile is hunched over his own work panel, typing up a morning report regarding the status of the Life Support systems.

"Oy, Arman. I'm thinking of filling in for Rand until you find someone else. I don't mind doing a double-shift."

"We're fine."

"Seriously, my team doesn't need—"

A pair of disembodied hands suddenly shoves into Lon's chest, and he falls backward on the floor with a loud grunt, his hologram passing right through Trey.

"*Oy!*"

He slides a finger along the visor to bring the *Drake*'s archives chamber into clear view on his end. Of course, everybody but Lon on the *Drake* is invisible to us, so we have no clue what they're doing.

"Bax, *I swear...*"

Lon gets back on his feet and rubs his elbows where

they slammed backward into the floor. He reaches out and pulls an invisible chair to the empty work panel.

"Just finish the stupid reports," I say, rubbing the back of my neck with both hands as I try to ignore everything that just happened.

Kile deactivates his screen and sits with his arms crossed. "Hey, Arman. Life Support's done."

Sure enough, his report appears in an icon on the side of my work panel.

"Thanks."

"Should I work on the catalogue?" He sounds more eager than I've ever heard him before.

"Go for it."

Lon ducks sideways, laughing, then swings his own punch—

"*Do your damn reports!*"

I didn't mean to shout. It just happened. And now they're all staring at me. Heat rises into my face. I can't even *look* at Lon. He apologizes, and his projection disappears.

"*Dang,*" Trey says. "Didn't think I'd see that."

I return to my own screen. "Yeah, well, if everybody worked like Kile, we'd be done in an hour."

A murmured '*thanks*' reaches me.

✳ ✳ ✳ ✳ ✳

As we walk back from dinner, Olivarr points at every projector we pass. "My teams linked them all to the ACIs, Mr. Arman. Operations are normal and the systems are set! I'm pleased to say the entire fleet is yours to roam. Now, we had to modify some of the processing units, of course, but it all came together. My teams never fail, Mr. Arman. Perhaps you could, er, put a word in to the Chancellor for me. Just a thought!"

He gives a half-hearted laugh, but I know he's not kidding.

"I will if I get a chance," I say.

"Ah, thank you! I certainly appreciate it." He pinches his glasses and grins up at me. "I hope it isn't long before we get around to integrating the Undil Embassy. RASP's systems are *very* useful. I'll speak with my advisors, see if we can't organize a proposal of our own if you don't have the time. The more Dalish tech we incorporate, the better off we'll be, right? Believe me, Mr. Arman, RASP will revolutionize Undil, bring us up to par with other planets in the galaxy. It will bridge gaps we've yet to cross. Suppose you need to visit Orvad, or Holistead, or, *for some odd reason*, Petrarch. Imagine it: no more long flights, no more unnecessary meetings to schedule. Just slip on a visor and you're there! You'd never have to travel again..."

He trails off as we get on an elevator, and his face quickly loses its excitement.

"On second thought, I'm not so sure I'd like that. Yes, it'd minimize travel time and maximize efficiency, but all the fun lies in the adventure. Hmm. What a *classic* conundrum. I guess it comes down to what kind of life you'd like to live!"

Olivarr gets off on Floor 12. Finally, some quiet. I need it. I like talking to him, but there comes a point when he just never shuts up.

Up in my room, I lie in bed and stare at the ceiling. I

should go to the fitness center. Glacia and I would always go after dinner. Just because we haven't talked in a couple days doesn't mean I shouldn't. I need to keep up a routine, if only for the trips between planets. Glacia would go. She's probably there right now. She's always keeping herself in shape, especially now, with how lean and strong she got on Daliona. I can't resort to sitting in bed all day. My body feels so good right now. Imagine having this strength on Undil. We'd be the strongest, fittest people on the entire planet.

I wasn't wrong about Glacia.

She's on the upper body machines in the back corner. I don't throw her anything more than a quick glance, and she's not looking when I do. Did she even see me walk in? Maybe. I don't know.

I find an open treadmill, and run. One mile...two miles...three miles... I keep going and going and don't even break a sweat until mile five. Then again, it's not on a tough setting. Just a flat run with Undilaen resistance. If I want to keep up my strength, I should double the settings and go from there.

I don't change it right now, though. I'm too far in. I'll puke if I try to finish with harder settings. So I push myself farther. Seven miles. Eight. Nine. When the display blinks *10*, I push myself harder, run a little faster. Make this the fastest mile. Finish strong.

She's leaving.

She hasn't looked back, not yet—but then she does, right as she's walking out the door. I don't even know if we made eye contact. Her head turned, her eyes pointed somewhere this direction, like she was looking for me. Maybe she didn't look directly at me on purpose. Maybe she knew where I was, but didn't want to look at me, just wanted to show me that she knew I was here. That's probably it. She would've said something if she wanted to talk. This is *Glacia*.

But...if she wasn't upset, she'd have said hi. Right? So she's angry. Now she's avoiding me. *Why?* Why won't she just talk to me? It sucks not talking to her. But it's not like I can just message her, or go knock on her door and pretend everything's okay. No. She'll come to me. I know she will. Right? This is Glacia.

Stop running.

Drink water.

Go to the machines.

My legs are shaking from running so much, but I have to work my arms and torso. Round after round after round. Lift. Lift. Lift. It's hardly a struggle, even at the heaviest resistance settings. I remember the first expedition to Belvun, how I out-of-shape I was. Back then I was only pulling ten, *maybe* fifteen reps, if I was lucky. Now I'm pulling an easy sixty.

Leave.

Shower.

Go to bed.

I lie there, trying—and failing—to sleep. I knew this would happen. Sleep. I need sleep. My heart pounds harder the more anxious I become. The darkness should've helped, or even the *Ember*'s constant dull hum...the hum that lulled me to sleep every night when I was alone. Now it fills my head alongside all my thoughts.

The thoughts. *The* thoughts.

The ones that won't go away.

Rand, crashing.

My car, slammed sideways.

Rand, skidding down the tube.

My world, spinning.

Rand, slumped over, blood staining his gravity suit.

Father's head, limp on his neck, blood sliding down his cheek and neck.

Rand's helmet, cracked.

My ribs, broken. My lung, punctured.

I can't keep the memory away. The air stunk of blood. My eyes stung. One was bleeding and I couldn't cry, couldn't scream, couldn't *breathe*. The air was leaving me. I was going to die. I was—until I woke up in Cornell's hospital, on that bed with that tube in my arm, the tube pumping the liquid that was holding the pain at bay, the pain from the ribs that punctured my lung, the reason I couldn't breathe—

I'm crying. No. Hyperventilating. Panic overtakes my mind. I twist onto my side and tuck my knees and stare across the room. I can't breathe. I can't. Breathe. Arms—shaking. Hands—squeezed into fists. Glacia's not here. She won't whisper to me. Won't hold my hands. Won't look into my eyes.

I'm alone.

Like I was on the trip to Belvun.

And I hated every minute of that trip, right until the day...until the day we became *real* friends. That morning when she got off her shift and we met in her room and she fell asleep next to me. I would give anything to go back to that morning...to feel how I did...to feel what I felt for her on Daliona.

Not this.

Anything but this.

Please.

I press the pillow to my face. Breathe hard through my nose. Dry my tears. I roll onto my back. Suck in a long breath. Let it out slowly. Stare up into the darkness that is the ceiling. Not the sky. Not the void. I'm trapped in a box that's inside a bigger box, and it's closing in. I want to be free. I need to be free.

I close my eyes, but nothing changes. Darkness *never* changes. My head is just as dark as the room, except now, little blue and red sparks burst behind my eyelids when I press my palms into my eyes. Sparkly, spinning red lines...blue circles and squares. They zoom in and out, warp and bend. Then come the thoughts, because I can't help but think these stupid, freaking thoughts.

Rand flips off the sled. His body skids down the track, hits the wall—

—my body jolts.

I felt the crash again. It keeps. Coming. Back. My world spins. Glass shatters. Heat erupts in my stomach. My rib snaps. A sharp lump pokes from my skin. But I don't—didn't—*can't*—care, because Father is dead. *His* blood. *His* head. *His* eyes.

It should have been me.

Don't. Think. That.

...it should have been me.

■ ■ ■

Chapter Thirty-Seven

I PUT ONE hand on the back of Trey's seat. "You got this?"

"Olivarr ran me through the software a few times." He cracks his knuckles and looks up at me. "I'll make it look good."

"Cool. Can't wait."

I leave Trey to his own. He's reformatting RASP's catalogue software to generate a 3D visualization of the locations we linked. I'm not sure how it'll look just yet. Even Olivarr seemed a bit wary when Trey suggested the upgrade, not wanting anyone to mess with his brainchild, but in the end he agreed that he'd like to see RASP become as interactive as possible. He thinks there might even be a way to link RASP directly to the ACI, to make Trey's update fully immersive, instead of being solely hand-operated.

For now, there's still not much I can do but wait. We're only a couple days into the trip back to Undil, and

I've stuck to my usual routine: meet Orcher, analyze the station data RASP collected overnight, write the morning reports, collect the reports from across the fleet, and send them to Orcher and Captain Fallsten.

All-in-all, life on the *Ember* isn't much different than it was during the expedition to Belvun. Sleep sucks. Work is long. The food could be better. I'm exhausted, and running off adrenaline most of the time. Each day is a few minutes longer than the previous...which doesn't mean much anymore. The difference will be noticeable when we fly to Belvun and add six hours to our day, but out here, in the void, adding an hour means nothing. There's no sun, no moons—nothing to count by but the clocks that tell us how much longer we have before we reach Undil. When I leave the archives chamber, the countdown reads: *319:27:46.* A full three hundred and nineteen hours until we reach Undil.

Ugh.

Back in my room, I toss my holotab on my bed, then lie next to it and hold my arms over my eyes to block out the light. It's not lunchtime, but I'm starving. And I'm exhausted. And I'm just miserable in general. I wish the *Ember* was bigger. I could fly the cyclo and at least feel a little better about being stuck here for another ten days. The halls are too cramped and the ceilings are too low. The only two places with enough room to fly a cyclo are the Bridge and Observatory, and I'm not sure Orcher—or Captain Fallsten, for that matter—would appreciate me flying around the Bridge. And the Observatory? Just...no. What about outside the *Ember*?

Ha. No way.

So I'm stuck.

I sit up and squint in the light. No. I can't do this again. A year ago I would have locked myself away after work, then lie around waiting for the days to end. That's not who I am now. Not anymore. Now I'm...well, I'm Arman Lance, the *Ember*'s Head Archivist. I'm an Interstellar Traveler. A Licensed Cycloist.

Ha, it's just like Rand said: I'm the most decorated head archivist Undil has ever had. Not that that means—

Bzzzzz.

A message on my holotab.

My heart rate spikes.

What if it's from Glacia? Do I read it? Do I ignore it? Do I pretend I'm asleep? Wait—why is she messaging me? Isn't she on a shift? Is she on lunch? Why would *she* be messaging *me?* She could just come to my room. It's not like she doesn't know where I live. She only slept here like fifty times. Why, why, *why?*

Look at it.

My palm is sweating and my hand is shaking. Stupid. What's wrong with me? It's just Glacia. She doesn't hate me—probably. *Hopefully.* I don't know what's wrong. Why is this happening to *us?* Why can't I talk to her? Her birthday was the last time she ever smiled at me. The last time I ever kissed her. The last time I *actually* talked to her. Then...Rand crashed. And I lost her. And I don't know—

The message isn't from Glacia.

I'm still shaking even as I read the message. It's from Orcher. And...*yep.* Captain Fallsten decided today's morning reports weren't thorough enough, and he wants us to double-check the engines' dark matter propulsion outputs from now on, because apparently Captain Fallsten thinks reporting *No Fluctuations Detected* isn't detailed enough for the *Engine Energy Fluctuations* question slot on the report. She wants numbers. She wants charts. She wants to know the rate of dark matter decay from hour-to-hour.

'...I've spoken with her multiple times,' Orcher's message says, 'but she isn't letting up. So from here on out, include those in your reports. Tell the other teams.'

Screw Fallsten. Seriously. She thinks she can tell us how to do our jobs?

I pass the message on to the other team leaders—except Baxter. Instead, I tell Lon, because I know *he'll* get things done. He practically does Baxter's job.

Now what?

Now...I'm still holding my holotab. And it's open to the messages. I could send her one. Just a quick one. Just...to see what's up. If she wants to talk.

I type: *'Hey, can we talk?'*

No, that's too direct.

'What can I do to fix us?'

Gah, too desperate.

'I'm sorry, can we be us again?'

The most insincere apology ever. Besides, I don't even know what's wrong anymore.

'Are we okay?'

Ha, obviously not.

I don't know what to say. What do you say in a situation like this? Why can't we just be normal? How am I supposed to talk to her if I don't even know what happened? I kind of do—but not really. I mean I *tried* to be there for her the morning after Rand crashed, when she slept on the couch. I sat with her. When I took a shower, *she* left. *She* disappeared, not me. So why am *I* the bad guy? Why do *I* have to feel like this? Why do I feel like I can't talk to her anymore, like I need to avoid her, like just making eye contact with her is going to make me cry? I'd give anything to go back to that night, when we danced to *Stelle Adiis* in Lisha Cove. Go back to when we ran through the storm on Marakuri, when we kissed over the Rainbow River. Daliona was supposed to make us stronger than ever—not ruin us. Now I'm alone, with no one to talk to, no one to smile at, no one to hold at night and whisper to in the dark.

Where did she go?

Where?

✳ ✳ ✳ ✳ ✳

It scares me, how the ache in my heart shrinks as the days pass. I miss her...but it doesn't hurt now. Not as much as it did the first few days. It's so easy to avoid her. Her shift is longer than mine, so I eat lunch with Allison, Trey, and Kile. She works out after dinner, so I start going *before* dinner. She doesn't come knocking on my door, so I don't visit hers.

I still see her in the mornings, even though she doesn't see me. I still glance down when I'm drinking coffee with Orcher. But I don't get excited. Instead, I wonder what she's thinking. Does she know I'm watching her? Has Captain Fallsten yelled at her for anything recently? Has she told Kerin, or Allison, or *anyone* about how we haven't been talking? Sometimes Allison waits to eat lunch with Glacia, leaving me, Trey, and Kile by ourselves, but she hasn't said a word to me otherwise, not even given me a weird look.

Trey has been too busy recoding RASP's visual catalogue to think about anything else, but Kile? He might have noticed how my mood has changed. I can't be sure. Whenever Trey goes off about the project, Kile gives me quick sideways looks, as if he knows my mind is elsewhere. He never says anything, he just...gives me space, I guess.

When I can't sleep, when my mind starts flashing through the thoughts I can't suppress, I go to the Observatory. Lying under the dome, gazing out at the stars... It helps. It really does. Most nights, I stay until one or two in the morning. Sometimes I fall asleep and wake up in time for breakfast. And when I'm there, I listen to *Stelle Adiis*, just like I did when I was alone on the *Ember*, hanging in orbit above Undil before departing for Daliona. The music keeps me calm when those memories overwhelm my mind. When I hear the chimes, my chest throbs and my face tightens, tears threatening to well up in my eyes. When I hear the wind, chills tingle my spine.

The shudders, the pulses, the swinging beats, the thrums and distant echoes. The music carries the harmonies of the universe...

It carries the sounds of the stars.

Chapter
Thirty-Eight

MARCH 12
INTERSTELLAR TRANSIT
STANDARD YEAR 4320

IT'S BEEN TWO weeks since we left Daliona.

Right now I'm in the *Ember*'s conference chamber, about to discuss RASP's catalogue, Trey's modifications included, and the broader goals we have in mind for the Live Archives Program. Orcher, Victoria, Michael, and a number of other officers from the *Ember* are sitting at one end of the conference room, and the members of my teams are sitting at the other. Everyone from the *Drake*, *Doppler*, and *Blazar* is using the Augmented Conference Interface, so whenever one of them speaks, the voice sounds disconnected from the projection. It's annoying, but it's all we've got.

Orcher looks at me once everyone is set. "Shall we

begin?"

I'm glad I have experience giving these kinds of presentations, or else I'd be a wreck right now.

"So, aside from the Embassy, my team"—I gesture at Allison, Trey, and Kile—"catalogued a total of seven archipelagos. Bechi, Marakuri, Hossiard, Cavellor, Westin, Culsaren, and Noya. Here—"

I load RASP on the room's panel and display our work. A large orb materializes in the center of the room—Daliona. I see Orcher and Michael nodding, impressed. But this isn't even the main part of it. Once Trey applied his modified software to the locations each team linked...*wow*. The catalogue, in my opinion, looks beautiful. Now we get to show it off.

"*RASP*," I say, keeping my voice clear, strong, and confident, "*locate Daliona, Bechi Archipelago.*"

The projection of Daliona rotates in place—then zooms in on Bechi. Icons pop up across the two islands: the Dreiden Atmospheric Observation Facility, the marine labs on Chesnick Island, the FAST track stations, the gravity elevator dock, and a few buildings within Bechi's small town.

When I touch the icon above the Dreiden Facility, the archipelago fades and images of the facility's lobby form.

"It's a fully interactive catalogue," I say. "You can move through the halls and rooms and read data feeds from certain panels and equipment." I demonstrate by sliding my hands apart and passing through a gate into the Dreiden's main research laboratory. Different machines highlight or fade as I spin the image in place to look around the room. "If you select the highlighted regions, you can view data associated with that specific program. When we're in transmitting range, the feed will update as a live stream. When we *aren't* in range, RASP shows the last-recorded data."

"What constitutes *range?*" a man who works under Officer Remmit asks.

"For Daliona, we've set the live stream to activate when planet-to-fleet feedback time falls below point-six-five light-seconds," Trey explains for me. "That's just above one hundred and twenty thousand miles, the farthest orbital distance from Daliona that space fleets are legally allowed to maintain."

The man makes note of Trey's calculation. "Thank you."

Olivarr leans over his panel to look past Michael at Orcher. "Isn't this impressive? Not even I thought to program RASP this way. To think that I've been using *lists* and *pictures* all these years. Careful! I might have to hire Mr. Trey at CSI."

He gets a few laughs in response, including a wide grin from Orcher. But Officer Remmit rolls his eyes and says, "If Trey is as genius as you say, he should be working for *me*—"

"I *was* working for you, Lars," Trey says, holding his hands behind his head. "Then you referred me for *this* job."

"Yes, well." Officer Remmit pretends to brush something off his panel. *"That's beside the point."*

I back out of the Dreiden, so that the projection shows the entire archipelago again. Then I say, "RASP: locate Daliona, Marakuri Archipelago."

As before, the planet spins and zooms in on the

group of islands, with pulsing icons floating over every facility we linked. The Malamara Labs on Kailun Island, the Halima Oceanography Facility, and the Kiruni Sporting Dome, among a number of others. You can tour each and gather readings from every accessible database. The names of all the directors, of scientists associated with specific experiments and labs.

I show one more example—the Cavellor Archipelago—then hand the presentation over to Sam Scott, who details the nine islands the *Doppler*'s team catalogued, and then Baxter gets up to discuss the *Drake*'s portion of the catalogue. Lon might as well have done the entire presentation, because Baxter needs help explaining the purpose of various research and tech facilities, and then he just stands off to the side and let's Lon finish for him. He even holds his hands behind his back as if he's supervising.

Yeah. Sure.

I've made up my mind: I'm promoting Lon and getting rid of Baxter. For being one of the oldest members in my program, he's done nothing but put the work on Lon. So much for being responsible.

Elliot stands last, gives a shorter presentation for the *Blazar*'s team, and then I stand up again.

"We'll upload this into Threshold and update it after each expedition," I say. "Are there any questions?"

One woman asks about how we plan to utilize this catalogue in the Live Archives Program, and I tell her we can watch how other planets operate, mimic the techniques and technologies that work best, and avoid those that seem to fail.

"Terraformation takes a long time," I say, thinking

about something Rand said once. "If we want to develop faster, we'll want Undil to be an attractive destination so that other planets are interested in aiding our development."

"So that's why I proposed we construct gravity runs in our cities," Olivarr chimes in, raising his hand. "Mr. Rand and I talked about this, General Orcher."

"Oh, shut it, Olivarr," Officer Remmit says before General Orcher can respond. "Please, for *all* our sakes. What, you want to turn all of us *craaaaazy* Undilaens into the galaxy's finest athletes? *Ha!*"

They share a quick wink.

"We can discuss that at a later time," Orcher says, stopping Olivarr before he can open his mouth again. "Are we finished?"

Nobody has any other questions, so he dismisses the conference.

⁕ ⁕ ⁕ ⁕ ⁕

The next evening, we drop out of FTL and hurtle into Undil's solar system. Within a few hours, the brown dot grows larger...and larger, and soon we're close enough that I can see the yellowish shimmer of the atmosphere.

When the fleet reaches orbit and glides to the vacant harbor bay, I notice a Belvish station attached to harbor bay designated for foreign fleets. It can't be the station Ambassador Purnell is traveling on—he's flying straight back to Belvun. This might be for some of the first Belvish refugees, living way up here, staring down at a planet that isn't theirs.

I board a transport with Trey, Kile, Allison...

And Glacia.

When we first meet in the docks, her eyes fall to the side. That's it. That's all I see because I don't even dare to stare. Now my palms are sweaty. Now my body is shivering. Now my mind is racing. If nobody noticed something was wrong before, they'll definitely notice now. We aren't talking. We aren't even looking at each other. Why do we have to be stuck in the same transport? Avoiding each other was so easy—now this.

Yup, Allison just frowned at me and cocked her head. So Glacia *didn't* say anything.

Strap into the restraints.

Wait for the countdown.

The thrusters flare, the transport shudders. Drifting down the dock...and through that silvery light. Gravity vanishes. And like Daliona two weeks ago, Undil looms below us, golden brown and reddish in the waning sunlight. The transport dips through the Undilaen space fleets and drops down...down...down...

From the upper atmosphere, the surface is barren. Then shadows of mesas and ridges and gorges take shape, and a triangle of light shines in the distant darkness: the Undil Embassy. There's the Crown, the gold and white pinnacle rising from the city's center, taller than the other towers. Threshold and Horizon stand in the eastern and southern corners, and Shield stands at the western, closest to the docking platforms.

The transports circle the city and gradually land one-by-one. The restraints release, the exit hatch hisses. A stale wind blows down the hall, and once outside, we reluctantly breathe Undil's dusty air. My lungs already hate this. It's not fresh, or salty. Even the recycled air on the *Ember* is cooler than Undil's coldest nights, nor does it sting your eyes or dry your skin. After being on Daliona for so long… After using those moisturizers and oils in the showers…

I just want to go back.

As we head to the maglev station, noises reach us. Cars gliding down the streets, horns honking, empty gusts of wind. Rows of yellow-lighted windows dot the towers. But they're so dull. I miss the rush of waves and the squawks of seabirds, the rustles of the jungle and the music and fireworks. The patter of the rain—even those torrential storms on Culsaren Island. The accents of the people from all across our bubble of the galaxy.

Undil has none of that, and I need it.

The monotonous voice in the maglev station announces the arrivals and departures of the trains. One slides out of the tunnel, stops, and opens its doors. After a moment's hesitation, we step inside and get seats all the way at the end, because three transports' worth of crewmembers are boarding with us.

The train stops at the Interchange, where several of us transfer to a train that's headed to Ceremony Station. A few officers from Horizon Tower are riding this train, too. One of them frowns and whispers something to his colleague, who just shrugs.

"You in Orcher's crew?" the first man asks.

"Yep," somebody I don't recognize answers.

"Got that Faustocine?" Several people—including me—nod in response. "Good. Belvun needs all the help it can get." He steadies himself as the train accelerates. "Don't know if you heard, but an entire natural reserve went up in flames about a month ago. That's the fourth fire since November. Whole planet is out of control."

For the remainder of the ride, people mutter about Belvun, how things aren't like they used to be.

"*This all could've been prevented if the Dalish had just done their damn research.*"

"*The Dalish? It's the Belvish Embassy's fault! Planet's been deteriorating for years, but they didn't get all panicky until Ellaciss fell.*"

"*Sad, though. So, so sad. Think about all those homes, lost.*"

"*It's the animals that've gotta worry. Where're they supposed to go?*"

"*I'm not getting caught in those evacs. I'll pick up work in the Embassy if I have to.*"

The walk to the apartment complex doesn't feel as far as it used to, probably because we're so used to walking around Daliona, where most of the cities were larger than the Undil Embassy—*especially* the Dalish Embassy. It was even bigger than Belvun's.

The woman in the lobby smiles at us like she always does, as if nothing has changed. And for her, nothing has. She hasn't experienced life outside Undil. She's never hiked through real forests, swam in real oceans, heard real birds, or gazed at real moons. She doesn't know what it's like to come back here after seeing all that. I felt utterly *alive*, and so many people on Undil will never experience that feeling. Most of them will walk around, wishing they could get off this ball of dirt until the day they die.

"Get some sleep," Allison says when she steps off the elevator on Floor 5. She gives both Glacia and I a concerned look before the door shuts again.

Then we're alone.

I feel sick.

So sick.

Every nerve in my body is on fire. My head is swimming with hundreds, thousands, *millions* of things to say to Glacia. I stare down at the floor. Clench my fists inside my pockets. What. Do. I. *Say.*

Floor 6...

Floor 7...

Floor 8.

The door opens, but I don't get off. I scuff one foot forward. The door closes again, and I look back at Glacia to say—

She's crying.

My mouth gapes, but no words come out. The elevator rises, beeps at every floor. It stops at 12.

The door opens.

"Move."

She pushes past me and disappears down the hall, leaving me alone. And I don't know what to do.

She said it softer than a whisper. But I heard her tears, her anger. A few days ago, I thought I'd never hear her voice again, and now that I did, I wish I hadn't. The last time I heard *that* voice was when she threw me to the ground in Hologis last year. And now I ruined us. Me. The guy who came back for her after he'd run off in search of another girl.

Why.

Why am I like this.

Why do I do this to myself.

Why haven't I given up.

I slap the icon for Floor 8 and slump against the wall. I need sleep. I know my mind isn't going to let me, though. Definitely not tonight. But I'd do anything to forget my life right now. I need the Lucidity Interface. Just put me down and never wake me up, because I can't control my life.

Rand knew what he was doing. He'd know what to do in this situation. He had to do it before, kind of. With that girl from Shield Tower. He chose to leave her so that she didn't get discharged, and now she's a ranking officer.

What am I supposed to do? I can't just leave. There's nothing *for* me to leave. Nowhere to run. Nowhere to—

Wait.

I can go home.

Tomorrow. Not for long...maybe a day. Glacia doesn't have to know. It'll give me time to clear my mind. My sisters will make sure of that. Yeah. That's what I'll do.

I'm going home.

Chapter Thirty-Nine

I LEAVE BEFORE DAWN.

I managed to sleep. Not long, but at least I did. My trunk is already packed, so I grab it and leave the apartment complex. The sky is still dark, the Embassy still lit by streetlights. And the roads are quiet. No one is walking on the sidewalks. In the maglev station, I'm the only passenger.

When I reach the docks, I check the flight schedule: the first hovercraft to Cornell leaves in thirty minutes. That gives me time to eat.

I almost forget to pay. On Daliona, everything was free. Here...not so much. *And it's eighteen shims for breakfast?!* When did that happen? Geez. You can get a buffet at the Shady Barchan for twelve, why is this so much more—wait. *Now* I remember: Undil shipped food and resources to Belvun.

Great.

I finally board the hovercraft and take off, bound for

Cornell. The Embassy disappears in the haze as we zoom eastward, racing away from the crest of dawn. The ground is pockmarked with craters, crags, ridges, and mesas, and the reddish landscape is lightening to tan. Now I can see the hovercraft's shadow racing thousands of feet below.

I stare around the empty passenger lounge. The first time I flew to the Embassy, it was the five of us: Michael, Ellin, John, Glacia, and me. John stuck his hands on the window and stared outside, totally in awe of what he was seeing. Ellin would put her hand on his arm whenever he started getting excited—*too* excited. And Michael would just stare at nothing.

Some of us have changed. John...not so much.

To kill time, I look at all the pictures I took on Daliona, because Erinn and Flavia will want to hear another story. There's the space elevator, a white line shooting into the sky at night. The electric arc dancers, the fireworks. The cliffs of Bechi Island that drop into the frozen sea, the Dreiden Atmospheric Observation Facility, and the meglaquids that live in the Dalish Arctic. The Marakuri jungles, the salt and mineral mines of the Westin Isles, the penguins and telescopes of Hossiard, the marine iguanas of Kilache.

Daliona is so full of *life*...

...but Undil is ridden with death.

✳ ✳ ✳ ✳ ✳

Cornell slips over the horizon an hour and a half later. The pilots adjust the course to avoid a dust storm blowing a few miles south of the city, and before long, we're descending. A slight shudder, the pilots give the all clear to exit.

I leave the lounge and head inside the dock. Now I'm back in the waiting room where I first met Ellin, John, and Michael. *Formally*, met, that is. I saw all of them during the Placement Report.

And then my plan comes to a halt. It's so early in the morning, I'm not sure if Mother will be awake to get me. The sun is just peaking over the horizon... How early do she and the twins wake up these days?

I call her. And listen to the buzzing on the other end. And wait.

"A—Arman?"

My voice takes a second to work after hearing Mother's. I'm choking up.

"Hey, um—"

"Where are you? In orbit? The Embassy?"

"No." Take a deep breath. "Can you come get me? I'm at our docks."

"Are you okay? You sound—" In the background, I hear a loud clatter and two sets of giggles, followed by Mother saying, *'Girls, girls, be careful.'* The twins must be eating breakfast. *"We'll be there soon."*

"Okay."

I cut the connection and find a bench to sit on. Thump my head back on the wall. Close my eyes. Focus on breathing. Footsteps pass by, a woman's voice announces a hovercraft's departure. The whir of an elevator door...several sets of footsteps...harsh accents.

Narvidian accents.

I strain my ears to listen. I'm still trying to pick up

new words, despite forgetting a lot of the ones I used to know.

"*Embiisill aeli vakians ami,*" one of them says.

I recognize the voice, and open my eyes: it's Ambassador Jarvis Gantz, the man who waved goodbye right before Father died. His back is to me, and he's talking to a group of other Narvidians.

"*Chancellor Green atiill vakii amar ill Gray Wall tratiis, shims, naas edall Belvun.*" He hangs his head, shakes it side-to-side, then looks up and salutes the men around him. "*Maak, maak.*"

A chorus of *'maak'* answers him, and the Narvidians salute Ambassador Gantz before he turns and walks up the ramp to the hovercraft I just flew in on.

Most of that went over my head, even though Narvidians tend to speak slower than Standard speakers. I picked up *embiisill*, *tratiis*, *shims*, and *maak*, but that's it. From what I could tell, he's going to speak with Chancellor Green about...making a treaty with Gray Wall and paying Belvun?

That doesn't sound right.

I spend the rest of the wait trying to work out what I heard, but the words are slipping from my mind. Now I only remember the easy ones.

Then the elevator to the waiting room opens, and two little girls scream with excitement.

"*I miss you I miss you I miss you I miss you!*"

I don't have time to stand before Erinn throws herself onto my lap and does her best to hug me. Flavia stays back, a shy smile filling her chubby face, cheeks blushing. She waits for me to get up before wrapping her arms around my waist. Even with Erinn in my arms,

I hardly feel her weight. Thanks to Daliona, they're as light as pillows—and suddenly I'm conscious of my every movement. I could crush them if I squeeze too hard.

When I put Erinn down, Mother steps forward and gives me a hug. "I didn't think they'd let you come home," she says. "I heard about Belvun…"

"We leave again in two days. I wanted to see you, though."

Mother sizes me up. "You've…changed."

She squeezes my bicep, which is tighter and thicker than it's ever been in my life. And with her hand next to my arm, I can see how much darker my skin is compared to hers.

"Is it really *that* different there?"

I shrug. "We got acclimated to it on the trip out, but it was heavy at first. *Really* heavy." I laugh. "Sleeping was like a workout."

Erinn grabs my arm and dangles off it. I barely feel her hanging there. She starts kicking her feet and giggling, but Mother stops her.

"Let's do that at home."

"*Ooooookaaaaaay.*"

Hearing that wipes the smile off my face. *Home.* I'm home…but I feel like I've lost it. The only reason I came here is because of *them*, Mother and the twins. I'd take them across the galaxy if I could, get them off this rock and show them what life is like out there. Cornell isn't a home. Undil isn't a home. Not yet. Home should be the place you're happiest—but I hate it here.

I ruffle Erinn's wavy blonde hair as we ride the elevator to the dock's main floor. The twins have grown from the last time I saw them. Their heads come above my waist now.

Mother and I don't talk on the drive to our—my—*their* house. The twins keep giggling and whispering in the backseat. Sometimes one of them taps my shoulder to make me turn around, and then point at each other when I narrow my eyes suspiciously.

We stop at the intersection that lets us turn onto the Main Throughway. *The* intersection. It was more than eleven months ago. Sitting here, watching cars stream in from the neighborhoods as people drive to work... I picture it over and over: *that* car crashes. And *that* car crashes. And *that* car crashes. In my mind, they all get smashed from the side. In my mind, they all spin into our lane. In my mind, glass litters the street.

I'm pressing myself to the seat, every muscle tense. I don't even let myself breathe until we make the turn and drive west.

"How long will you be gone?" Mother asks when we walk inside the house.

"I'm not sure. Probably until the Faustocine formula starts working." I flick my eyes at the twins, then lower my voice. "This was Father's idea. It'll work."

Erinn's eyes flick to mine when she hears me mention Father. Flavia, on the other hand, goes on sucking the juice out of her slice of pricklefruit without so much as a quick glance up.

"Hey." I lean toward Erinn and Flavia. "I have a surprise. Wanna see it?"

Just as I expected, their eyes get huge.

"Yeah yeah yeah yeah!"

They follow me into the front room, where I grab the cyclo suit from the bottom of my trunk. All three of them stare at it, wondering what *it* is. Part of me wants to fly…but the other part remembers that, fully charged, it's only good for forty hours of flight. And Undil doesn't have charging ports. But still…

"It's called a cyclo suit."

"What's it *do?*" Erinn asks, poking the power pack.

"It lets me fly. When I wear this—"

"*I wanna see!*"

"*Yeah!*"

I look at Mother, who smiles and shrugs. I shouldn't, though. I *know* I shouldn't. But it's so tempting. I haven't flown in so long… I miss being up high, feeling the air rush by my ears. It would be my first time in the open sky, no dome or arena to hold me back. The world is mine.

All. Mine.

"*Please please please!*"

The twins tug on my shirt, push the cyclo into my chest, grab my arms and try forcing them into the suit.

I'm doing it.

We walk out to the driveway, where I pull on both halves of the suit and secure the helmet. Clamp down the latches, fit my hands and feet into the gloves and boots. And when I activate the power pack, the cyclo pressurizes to account for Undil's atmosphere.

"Ready?"

Erinn and Flavia nod, and I catch Mother smiling, anxious to see what the suit does. I take a deep breath, let the sensation swim around my head—

And lift into the air.

A few inches.

A few feet.

I finally beat Undil.

This planet held me down for twenty miserable years, and now I'm laughing at it. I rise straight up, until the western neighborhoods are just lines on the ground. The northern neighborhoods, where Glacia lives, sprawl out in the distance. There's Gray Wall Industries on the other side of Cornell. Everywhere else, the yellowish, rocky desert stretches to every horizon, the horizons that closed me in until the day I left for Belvun. Now I don't need a transport, or a hovercraft. Now I can escape just by willing it.

Then I stop thinking.

I go up...up...up...

Stop briefly in midair...

And fall...fall...fall...

I spread my arms and legs, let my body lay flat. The air whistles in my ears. The ground rushes toward me. Windy tears sting my eyes. I'm falling farther than I've ever fallen before. Thousands of feet. The horizon flattens. Depth returns to Cornell, spaces appear between the buildings, cars are gliding down the Main Throughway, people are walking down the street. I can see Mother and the twins, their faces pointed to the sky.

Straighten out my body.

Feel the sensation.

Slow the fall.

And land.

Erinn is screaming with excitement and clapping her hands. Flavia's mouth is gaping, as if she can't believe what she just saw. Mother looks terrified—but somehow happy at the same time, like she can see how happy I am. How *free* I am.

"That was the most coolest thing I ever seen!" Erinn hugs one of my legs, wraps her arms and legs around it. *"I want to fly!"*

I bend at the waist and tickle her until she lets go. "I can't take you up that high."

Her mouth falls into a droopy frown. "Why not?"

"Because it's too high up for you, silly."

"But I'll hold on *really really* tight."

Mother steps forward. "You can do it when you're older, sweetie. You can get your own one day and fly with Arman. Would you like that?"

Erinn nods vigorously.

Then I have an idea, and hold my arms sideways. "Grab my arms and don't let go."

The twins each latch onto one arm, their now-sweaty fingers fumbling for a secure grip. Mother frowns a bit, but I smile to reassure her and let the sensation tingle the nodes. My feet lift a few inches off the ground, and Erinn and Flavia giggle and kick their feet. I rotate in a circle, sway forward and backward, even rise a little higher—two...three feet off the ground—but then catch Mother shaking her head.

The moment I touch back down, the twins let go and collapse in a fit of giggles and start squealing about how much fun that was, that they were *flying*. Of course, it technically *wasn't* flying, but there's no way to explain that to them.

After they settle down, we head back inside and spend the rest of the afternoon together. I show them all the pictures of Daliona, and even Mother can't hold back a breath of awe at the planet's blue aura, at the green mountains and grayish-brown cliffs, the tall white waterfalls, the colorful fish and birds and flowers and odd-looking trees. Her eyes glisten, tears welling up at the corners, which I catch her wiping away.

All of them laugh at Glacia's selfie with the iguana and the story of the penguins jumping onto the rocks. They listen with bated breath when I tell them about the bottom of the oceans, of Dally the sea serpent and the meglaquids of the Dalish Arctic. It's just like when Father would come home and sit on my bed and tell me his adventures. I'd look through his portfolios and ask if I could go with him on the next expedition. He'd smile and put his hand on my shoulder and tell me I'd join the Embassy one day. It was supposed to be us, Father and son, traveling the galaxy and making it a better place.

❉ ❉ ❉ ❉ ❉

Mother cooks an early dinner—roasted potatoes, sautéed vegetables, and killari steak—and when we're finished, we put everything in the washer and get ready to go back to the docks, because my flight back to the Embassy leaves in a half-hour. I pack away the cyclo and the twins 'help' take my trunk outside.

An uncomfortable, heavy silence fills the car. Erinn and Flavia don't squirm and giggle and whisper like they did on the ride to our house. They sit perfectly still, staring out the windows at the desert, at the hazy dust storm south of Cornell, at the cloudless blue sky.

Mother parks the car. Erinn and Flavia stand side-by-side and wait for me to get my trunk, then walk next to me when we go inside the dock. Erinn holds my one empty hand the entire time.

Back in the waiting room, I crouch and ruffle Erinn's hair as cheerfully as I can. "I won't be gone long."

"You were gone a long time last time though."

"That wasn't very long," I say. "Do you want me to bring you back something special?"

"Can I have a bird?" Erinn asks in a gloomy voice, her eyes falling to the side.

I laugh and press my cheek into the top of her head. "I don't think I can bring a bird back."

"Why not?"

"We're not allowed to have pets on Undil."

"*Why not?*"

"Um... Because..."

I rack my brain. There's a regulation against pets simply because Undil isn't at the level of sustainability for life beyond humans. We're still struggling to keep ourselves from burning up, so pets would just add pressure.

"Because it's too hot," I finally say, and Erinn accepts that as an answer.

"*Now boarding Flight 826,*" a woman's voice says over the intercoms.

Erinn starts crying. She sniffles into my neck and tells me she loves me and misses me and wishes I didn't have to go, and I promise her I'll bring back gifts, tell her that when she's older, we can fly the cyclos together, and maybe one day Undil won't be so hot and she can have any bird she likes. It's not so far from the truth. Regulations evolve. Maybe the Embassy will construct a real park where people can have pets, just like on Belvun and Daliona. With Olivarr still talking about building gravity runs in Orvad, I'm sure anything is possible.

I let go of her, then hug Flavia and Mother. We spent one day together. No, *less than* one day. Maybe I shouldn't have even come. Maybe I shouldn't have let them know I was back, let them believe we flew straight from Daliona to Belvun. I would have spared them the pain of saying goodbye.

Erinn is still crying, but that doesn't stop her from giving me a wave as I walk away. One of Flavia's hands is clenched on Mother's shirt, while the other hangs at her side, her face expressionless. Mother wipes her own tears away—

And then I remember.

I remember the last time Father left. The *final* time he left. It was two days after my eighteenth birthday, another birthday he'd missed. He had just gotten back from Artaans after securing the Watershed Irrigation Treaty. He'd been home for only a day, and we were in the middle of dinner when his holotab buzzed. Mother was too busy feeding the twins their baby food to see his face drop. But I saw the look he made. I was *always* watching him. His gaze fell to the table, then to me. Right then, I knew something was wrong, and he knew that I knew.

Father had motioned at the front door. I didn't question him, just followed him outside. We stood on the driveway. He wasn't talking. *Why wasn't he talking?* I wanted to know—*needed* to know what had upset him.

He broke the silence.

"I have to go on another expedition."

I stared at him—and he couldn't handle it. In the

light, I saw a tear glistening on his cheek, saw his chest heaving in and out as he tried to steady his breathing, trying to stay calm for *me.*

I tried to do the same for him. I needed him to know I was okay, even though I wasn't. Needed him to know I understood, even though I couldn't. Not back then.

"Where are you going?"

He had laughed then, but there was a whimper in his voice, too. He turned back to me. His eyes were hidden in shadows.

"Belvun."

My heart leapt when he said that. Thoughts of Ladia flooded my head. He was going back! And I could go. I *had* to go. I'd do anything, *anything*, even if I had to pay my way. I'd saved up thousands of shims while working for Gray Wall—that *had* to be enough.

"Can I come?" I had asked, crossing my fingers in the darkness.

"No. You need to finish Secondary."

My fingers tightened into a fist. "But Ladia came here. We could—"

"*That was a treat.*" His voice was suddenly stern. "We can't keep sending kids out there just to see friends."

I clenched my jaw and didn't say anything. His eyes flicked at me, then back to the sky.

"I'm sorry," he said, his voice quieter. "It's...too short of notice to get you permission. I would try if there was more time." He gripped my shoulder and gave me a shake. "*I would*, Arman."

My mouth went dry. My excitement was gone. My hopes were crushed.

"When do you leave?" I had asked.

He hesitated. I remember seeing his chest stop moving, like he was holding his breath.

"General Orcher will be here in the morning to escort me."

My face got tight then. I started to shake. It wasn't fair. How could the Embassy send him back out after he'd been home for only a day? Why did it have to be *him?* Didn't they know he'd just met his baby daughters for the first time? That he had a wife and a son who lived without him for months at a time? Why couldn't they choose someone else?

"There's been a *mistake.*"

I didn't know it back then, but he was talking about Daliona's mobile laboratories, how they had contaminated the samples in the original Faustocine formula, which was supposed to reverse the short-term effects of the eco-hacking that was supposed to alter some of Belvun's ecosystems 'for the better.' If Daliona had gotten the formula right the first time, all of this could have been prevented. Belvun would be safe. But here we are five years later. Forests are burning, a drought is sweeping the planet, and cities are being evacuated.

"They need me to keep order while things get sorted out," Father had told me after not speaking for a long time. He had been fighting back tears. "Belvun is...is threatening to boycott negotiations with Daliona."

"*It's not fair.*" My voice was shaking, tears were welling up in my eyes.

"You know I'm the only one anyone trusts to handle this."

"I don't...that's...*no.*" I couldn't splutter out more

than a few words. "*It's not fair.*"

"I know," he had said. His voice was softer, trying to reassure me. "I know."

That's how I lived for most of my life. I understood the duties of being an ambassador, but I also had to live with the consequences.

More than three years have passed since that night, and I'm leaving my mother and sisters the same way Father left me. I joined the Embassy, and now I have to keep abandoning my family for weeks, months, sometimes maybe *years* at a time. But that's the sacrifice. That's my duty to the Embassy, my duty to Belvun, my duty to humanity. Father never wanted to leave us behind, but he had to because he was working for the greater good.

And he made a difference.

I remember Father's motto, the motto engraved on his plaque in my living quarters: *'I work so you may have a future.'* When we were on Belvun, Captain Blitner told me something else Father once said: *'We are not a part of the future, so it's our job to make sure there is one.'*

It hurts to leave my family behind. It does. But I'm doing it because Father did it, and so have countless others. We are *all* responsible. We *all* play a part. We *all* have a purpose.

And I'm finally accepting mine.

Chapter Forty

EARLY THE NEXT morning, I head to Threshold Tower to write up Daliona's expedition report. My new-found sense of purpose hits me hard with guilt. I should have written this yesterday, *before* visiting Cornell.

The old Records Room has since been converted into the new Live Archives Chamber. It's several times larger than the room on the *Ember*, with twenty panels lining the curved walls, one for each member of my team. Data orbs used to hang off the walls, but they're gone now, stored away. A currently non-operational ACI has been built into the wall opposite the room's entrance, and at the very center is the area designated for viewing diagrams and other projections, such as RASP's catalogue of Daliona.

The urge to open the catalogue overcomes me. I just love the way it looks. Trey did an awesome job. I grab a pair of tendril gloves, and when I walk to the center of the chamber, a square display with a list of options materializes a foot or so in front of my chest.

Well, that's new...*for Undil.*

"RASP," I say out loud. "LAP Planetary Catalogue."

Just like it's supposed to, the display fades and a collection of nine rotating orbs appears in its place, each labeled with the planet's name and scaled to their relative sizes. Yillos is the largest, and is mostly white except for its equatorial mountain ranges and tundra regions. Melles is the smallest, pale green with swathes of white washed in. Only Daliona is highlighted, though, because it's the only planet we've catalogued.

That lifts my mood a bit, the thought that I'll have a complete catalogue one day. I'll be the one to link all the planets. I'm the one who started this program, and I'll be the one to see it through. Nine planets. Nine *settled* planets. Another selection would have let me see every exoplanet and moon we've discovered, but there are tens-of-thousands of those and would take forever to get through.

"Oy. Morning, there."

I look up at the voice: Lon and Chloe are walking toward me, both of them transfixed on the giant hologram of Daliona.

"Wrong planet, Arman. Shouldn't we be prepping for Belvun?" Lon flashes a grin, and then they walk around the room to check out all the new equipment. "Horizon should be jealous. We've got state-of-the-art *everything*, by the looks of it."

More people from the teams arrive over the next several minutes. Sam, Carrie and Heather Vale, Baxter—whom I still have yet to fire—Kile, Langston, Tomme, Jaclyn, Hazel, Noah, and the rest of the archives team...

■ ■ ■

Minus Rand.

We settle into our projects. After I complete the expedition report, I walk around. It makes me feel somewhat responsible. This is the first time all of us have been in one room, working as a team. A *true* team, and I'm in charge of them. Tomme is collecting data about the Embassy's maglev trains. Lon's starting his morning report, and Sam and Elliot go around assisting their individual teams.

"*Scuse me*, Mr. Lance," a gruff voice says, accompanied by a knock on the door.

Gort Buntem, the Secretary of Threshold Tower, is standing in the doorway with Olivarr Cresson. Gort's a full foot-and-a-half taller than Olivarr, and rougher-looking, too, compared with Olivarr's smooth, chubby skin. I'm sure this is how we looked next to some of the Dalish.

Olivarr beams a smile at me and steps farther into the chamber. "All's well, Mr. Arman, I hope? Systems running properly? No glitches in the catalogue? Are the holograms too fuzzy? Or is that my eyes? I can call someone up right now and smooth out the pixilation, if you need. Maybe it's just the lighting..."

"It looks fine," I say. "And I tested out the full catalogue earlier. I can't wait to add the other planets."

Olivarr adjusts his glasses. "I'm excited for that day as well, Mr. Arman. On another note, have you analyzed the network flow of the Embassy yet? I've always been curious to see how data is transferred around this city. Orvad's network is a double-spiral, if you remember me showing you."

"Nope, not yet."

He taps his chin thoughtfully, and his eyes slide over the room. Then he seems to bring himself back to the moment and motions me toward him.

"Can I have a word?"

We leave the chamber and walk a bit farther down the hall, to a window that overlooks Julian Street.

"I'm returning to Orvad," he says, his voice uncharacteristically quiet, almost solemn. "I have unfinished business at CSI I've clearly been neglecting, but now it's catching up with me." He takes my hand in his and shakes it vigorously. "You gave me an adventure, Mr. Arman. Never, *never* did I ever think I'd travel as far as I did these past several months. You know how many times I visited the Embassy before meeting you? Exactly zero. *Zero!* My projects always get to my head and keep me pinned down, and sadly, I don't expect I'll be traveling anywhere for another long while. If, however, you're ever inclined to visit Orvad, don't be a stranger. We always love to show off our projects! And if your program could benefit, I'd be delighted to continue our partnership."

"I'll definitely let you know."

"I'd also enjoy staying informed on your developments with RASP. It's about time the Embassy employs outside tech. For a while there, a lot of us thought Orvadian innovations wouldn't ever see the light of day! There are those of us in Orvad who've been fighting to have a voice in the galaxy, Mr. Arman, and you've given us that. *Thank you.*"

Olivarr takes my hand and shakes it again. Then he starts backtracking toward the archives chamber.

"And I *am* going to push for a gravity run in Orvad.

Something to honor Mr. Rand, carry out my end of our deal. I think he'll like that when he returns, don't you?"

I grin at the thought. "He definitely would. Out on the dunes, like you guys said." Then I remember, "Did President Okana talk to you?"

"He did! Thank you for dropping my idea on him. He's sending envoys in the next few weeks to gather a layout. The only obstacle is Orvad's zoning committee, of course, but I see no reason for them to deny my request. I run the city's information network, after all! They wouldn't want to get on my bad side."

He winks at me, and then we go back inside the archives chamber. I return to my panel as he enthusiastically bids everyone good-bye, repeating over and over again how much he appreciates being selected to contribute to our program. And then he's gone, escorted away by Gort.

When they're out of earshot, Baxter shakes his head and says, "Somebody should tell that guy to cut back on the coffee."

Some people laugh, but I roll my eyes simply because it was Baxter who said it.

Besides, Olivarr doesn't drink coffee.

✳ ✳ ✳ ✳ ✳

The elevator opens. Glacia is standing in the corner, arms crossed, frowning, and wearing her hair in that not-Glacia braid. I look at her, she looks at me—we both look away.

We're going to the Shady Barchan. Not alone,

though. John called us so we could have another recruit reunion, and repeatedly hinted at a big secret he has to tell. So that's where we're going.

Glacia steps off the elevator as soon as it opens and walks ahead of me all the way outside, forcing me to jog to catch up when she crosses the street—right before the signal changes. Then she beelines for Ceremony Station without checking if I'm still following.

When we board, I sit two seats in front of her. The hatches seal, and the train glides forward.

That's when she takes a sharp breath, and says, "Ready to talk? Or what?"

My chest tightens. It takes me a few seconds to work up the nerve to look at her. Words buzz inside my head, but I know none of them will fix what happened.

So I stall.

Glacia's face gets red. Her lip starts quivering. She blinks a few times, then looks out the window even though there's nothing to see.

"*I don't know why I'm like this.*" I'm looking at her reflection when I say it. Her reflected eyes meet mine, then drop away. "I don't *want* to be like this."

"Then just"—Glacia sniffles, quickly rubs one eye—"*talk to me.*"

The train rounds a curve. We're almost to the Crown, halfway to Arena Station.

Glacia finds my eyes in the window again. "Where were you yesterday?"

Take a deep breath—let it out. "I went home."

I shouldn't have said that. Her eyes drop again. The color leaves her face, the corners of her mouth twitch, and her tear streaks visibly reflect in the window.

She wipes her cheek. "Did you have fun?"

"Yeah."

No response.

The train stops in Crown Station. The hatches open, a few people get off, and a few others board. Two of them sit a few seats behind us. Then the train takes off again.

Glacia heaves a long sigh, then twists around and sits with her back to the wall. I do the same so that we're basically sitting side-by-side, even though an empty seat separates us.

"I should have gone with you. Seen Jas and Sophie. My parents."

"Yeah..." Then I remember something. "I showed my sisters that picture of you and the iguana. They thought it was hilarious."

Glacia gives me a sideways glance. "That was funny."

"Yeah."

We both get quiet again. Every few seconds, we share a quick glance, but that's it. That wasn't so bad. I'm still burning with questions, but we talked. And it wasn't bad. Not really.

Glide into Arena Station.

Make our way to the surface.

Walk to the Shady Barchan.

The moment John catches sight of us, he jumps up from his seat and suffocates us in a too-tight hug.

"You guys have no idea how *boring* it is around here without you," he says as he sits between Michael and Ellin again. "Mind-dumbingly boring."

Mind-numbingly, I think to myself when Ellin doesn't correct him. She's watching us, her hand covering her mouth.

"Now that we're all here, it's time for my big secret!"

John drums the edge of the table, shaking our water glasses so hard that Ellin has to hold hers in place.

"The Embassy selected my maps to use as the latest standard models! *My* maps! I've been doing *a lot* of traveling *alllll* over Undil." He throws his elbows on the table and counts off on his fingers. "The Embassy, Cornell, Orvad, Holistead, Petrarch, Monal, Sessoor... *Oh!*" He facepalms himself. "I even finished mapping the Perihelid asteroid field from...*that-one-guy's* data."

"Officer Remmit?" I suggest. I remember helping Officer Remmit collect data from the field during the expedition to Belvun, so that people like Horizon's cartographers could generate maps for future expeditions.

"Yes, *that* guy. Larson Remmit. Sometimes I call him Larry, but only when I'm by myself. Do you think he'll care? Does anyone else—"

Ellin grabs his arm to keep him from almost knocking his own glass over, her eyes boring into his. "Just call him Officer Remmit, okay?"

"*Okay...*" John's flare of excitement falters, and Ellin lets his wrist go. Then, "I'm just...*so excited.* He's using my map. *My* map!"

"And so did the other expeditions."

John's attention suddenly snaps past me and Glacia, and he stands up in his seat to see over the balcony. I turn around, and there's Officer Remmit himself, walking into the Shady Barchan with Victoria. As soon as they reach the top of the stairs, John jumps out of his seat, and—

"Nice to meet you in person at last, Officer Remmit!"

He throws his hand outward. "I'm John!"

"Jonathan, congratulations! I have to say: your maps are *superb*. The techies in Horizon told me you had a knack for neuro-optic holography, but I admit, I didn't believe it until I saw your work." Officer Remmit motions for them all to sit down, then props his elbows on the table. "You've got quite a brain, to be able to include so much detail."

"That's what they all tell me, *Larry*."

Ellin's face twitches, but she keeps her eyes fixed on the menu.

"Just call me *Lars*," Officer Remmit says, laughing politely. "Only Vicky is allowed to call me Larry." Victoria scoffs, to which he says, "Well, she should start. I think it could catch on."

"*Ha-ha*."

"Vicky here's no fun," Officer Remmit says behind his hand to John. "She also tells the *lamest* jokes."

John bites his lip to keep from laughing. Officer Remmit winces, and I assume Victoria just kicked him under the table.

A little while later, sizzling platters of chopped steak, sautéed vegetables, and fried rice are sitting in front of us, and we're all scooping good-sized portions onto our plates. Glacia nudges my hand away when I reach for a third helping of potatoes—then snatches the scoop and takes the rest of them for herself.

I raise an eyebrow. "I just want some potatoes."

She shrugs, stuffs her face…

And that's the end of that.

Officer Remmit chuckles. "Eat up, kids. This is the last quality dinner you'll have for a month." He gestures at John. "Are you coming with us this time, Mr. Mistin?"

"No, no. I'm afraid not, Larry—*I mean Lars.*" John snickers to himself, then settles down and speaks in as formal a voice as he can muster. "You see, I've only just finished the easy part of my job. After I submitted my maps of Undil and the Perihelids, the Narvidians offered to pay me good money to make maps for them. I had to clear my mental exam before the agreement was finalized, obliviously, but I did it!"

I can't help but cringe when he says that. But again, Ellin doesn't correct him.

Obviously, John. Obviously.

"I've been granted a residency contract," he keeps saying. "The first Undilaen in *years* to be granted a residency contract on Narviid! I'll stay there a few months, maybe even a few years, honing in on all the tricks of the trade. Imagine that. Me, a resident mapmaker!"

"You're making a name for yourself, there's no doubt," Officer Remmit compliments. "Have you ever heard of Mitchell Corder?"

"Sadly, Lars, I can't say I have."

"He was one of the most famous cartographers in the galaxy once. Man was an artist. Captured the essence of every planet he ever visited. He could draw mountains and rivers and entire forests in such beautiful detail. His maps moved, too. A field of grass would sway in the wind, suns would forever fall and rise over the same horizon, and streams flowed like real water."

"He...sounds...amazing."

"He was! And he worked in an era before we settled Narviid, Belvun, and Undil. It's been a *very* long time since we've had a mapmaker who matched the likes of him."

"Are you saying...?" John's eyes widen, his mouth falling open slightly. "*Nooooo.*"

Officer Remmit tips his head. "The techies believe you could match his work, maybe even surpass it, because you have—"

"My NEO Visor!"

"Right on, Mr. Mistin. You're the first cartographer to use neuro-optic holography, so you're the pioneer of your field. You could be the next Mitchell Corder."

I jump in my seat when Ellin's fork clatters on the plate and bounces to the ground. She picks it up, apologizing several times. Then she bumps her head under the table when she goes to sit up again, spilling her and John's glasses of water. Her face gets red, and she avoids looking at any of us except to let Glacia help clean the spill.

John's eyes stay fixed on her. "*She hasn't been sleeping very well,*" he whispers. "*Our—*"

He stops abruptly when Ellin gives him a dark look. But I know what he means. Ellin once told me about their mother. Her condition must be worsening.

Victoria glances at Ellin, then reaches across and touches her hand. "If there's *anything* we can—"

She pulls back and drops her hands to her lap. Her mouth is twitching, and she's shaking all over.

"The Narvidians are helping cover the expenses in return for my work," John says, speaking slower than usual. "That's why I got the residency."

Officer Remmit folds his hands and clears his throat. "Any chance you'll be joining us on the trip to Belvun, Ellin? The *Ember* needs you, you know. You were one of the brightest new techies we've got. Sad that you couldn't come to Daliona with us. I told Olivarr all about you, and he said he'd consider hiring you in Orvad if you ever wanted a transfer."

"Oh! You'd love Orvad, sis," John adds. "It's right by the ocean. Remember how I showed you? You'd *love* the ocean. You should've seen the marinade."

Ellin's lips twitch, and she chokes up a laugh. "The *marina*, John."

He springs to his feet and wraps his arms around her shoulders, pressing his cheek into hers and letting his smile go completely unrestrained.

"You're my favorite dictionary, sis." He lowers his voice again and whispers loudly in her ear. "We'll be okay. By the time I get back from Narviid, she'll be better. You'll see."

※　※　※　※　※

The morning of our departure, we have to attend a conference on what to expect in terms of logistics when we arrive on Belvun. The first hour is dedicated to delivering assignments to specialized teams, as decided by Horizon's planetary sciences and Shield's civilian management sectors. Then we go over evac procedures in case the locations go critical while the teams are distributing the Faustocine, and teams are instructed to stick to specific schedules, thus minimizing the strain on Belvun's resources. On top of all that, Horizon and Shield have elected to send additional scientists and military personnel on the expedition, meaning we'll take one of Shield's cruisers along with us—the Saros—so we'll have five stations in our fleet instead of four.

During the second half of the conference, officials discuss the conditions we are projected to encounter and the last known numbers of evacuees, and *their* situations.

Ambassador Catria Blayson of Belvun returns to the podium to finish her presentation. The Belvish station I saw above Undil two days ago belongs to her.

"All-in-all, a little more than a million people have been displaced," she reports. "One hundred and sixty-five are dead, and two thousand are missing, presumed dead."

She flashes pictures of Noshton, Subari, Fleerard, and Boronulli—the last city to evacuate before she traveled here. Charred forests, collapsed bridges, smoke billowing down city streets... People running to evac transports, carrying children or breathing through their shirts. Only the scattered Belvish emergency crews have masks and suits.

"These are the most recent images, taken minutes before we broke out of Belvun's orbit. They reached us about an hour before we entered FTL. It was, as you can imagine, fortunate that we received them at all."

"Yes, as if we needed more evidence of Belvun's *disastrous* situation." Ambassador Ravad, the man who was responsible for the Joint Space Tech Treaty with Narviid, grunts with annoyance. His thick gray eyebrows come together when he frowns. "The planet is *lost*. This discussion is over."

Ambassador Blayson shakes her head. "Belvun has managed to contain at least *some* of the outbreaks."

"Ha!" Ravad barks. "Tell me: *how are you going to feed the damn population?* How long have you got, Ambassador? Six months? *Three?* Do you even know? How do you plan to keep people alive beyond that? What resources are there to spare? Even if Artaans chooses to fulfill the premature resource supplication, it'll be half a standard or longer before Belvun sees one scrap of it."

A buzz rises in the council chamber. He raises a valid point. From Undil, a flight to Artaans takes almost two months. It's three from Belvun. The time it takes to send word to Artaans, prepare food stocks, and deliver them to Belvun is, *at best*, six months.

"Ambassador Propp is already en route to Artaans with the necessary payment and instructions," Chancellor Green responds.

Ravad tilts his head back and mouths something we can't hear. "I said it then, and I'll say it now: *you're wiping us clean, Raymond.* What's an emergency resupply going to cost, may I ask? Or have you not noticed our own food costs rising?" He spreads his arms and looks around the room for an answer to his question. "Does no one have the figures? What, we're plunging into debt but we don't even know how much?"

Several people scramble to check the data. As they do, the pictures of desolate cities and smoldering forests and fields still flicker in the center of the room.

Chancellor Green hesitates, shifting in his seat. "It's a temporary setback."

"*Temporary*..." Ravad mutters. "You're dealing on the galactic scale now, Chancellor. You're asking Artaans to provide a surplus they may not be able to fill. There are massive widespread ramifications you're too blind to even consider! *Maybe* there would be no fallouts if Undil had a working agriculture, but you have neglected to allocate funding for our continued terraformation. We're already *decades* behind standard terraformation procedures. You've invested too heavily in our technology sectors and abandoned one of the fundamental requirements to wean Undil off its dependence on other societies."

Chancellor Green has no response, but it wouldn't matter if he did. The whole chamber erupts in arguments and counterarguments. Many people side with Ravad, others stand firm with the Chancellor. Two men end up in a furious shouting match and are escorted out of the conference. All the while, Ambassador Blayson stands in the center of the room, watching all these Undilaens argue over the future of *her* planet. And I'm sure if Ambassador Purnell was here, he'd be spitting in Ravad's face for suggesting we give up on Belvun.

"They are *pissed*," Trey mutters next to me.

"Just a bit."

Across the chamber, I see a group of Narvidians clustered in the lowest rows of seats. One of them is Ambassador Gantz. It feels strange, having seen him just yesterday in Cornell, and now *here*. When our eyes meet, he lifts his hand up in a quick wave. I pretend not to notice. Last year, his wave was the last thing I saw before the crash killed Father.

Somebody found the financial figures, because now the center of the room is filled with past budget reports and future projections related to assisting Belvun.

Ambassador Ravad is standing now, and he's facing Chancellor Green. "These last five years have nearly *bankrupted* Undil, Chancellor. If it wasn't for the Joint Space Tech Treaty with Narviid—"

"A treaty I *did not approve.*"

"—then we *would* be bankrupt." Ambassador Ravad gestures at the man who found the budget report. "Please deduct the profits Undil received as a result of that treaty."

A line of the report from almost six years ago disappears, and the number at the bottom of the display drops into deep negative figures. Ambassador Ravad turns to Chancellor Green and holds his hand up at the display to prove his point.

"If our work on Belvun fails, who can say how long it will take us to recover? Years? Decades? So I must ask: why should Undil forfeit its stability to save Belvun from Daliona's negligence? We've sent enough aid. Narviid has repaired what it can...and yet the Dalish have done nothing, blind to Belvun's cries for help. If they won't put in substantial effort, neither should we. Undil cannot hold up to the pressure, Raymond, and as your ambassador—*as a citizen of Undil*—I advise you surrender this cause. You're fighting a force of nature. *Let it run its course.*"

Ravad's speech is met with applause from the Narvidians and several dozen Undilaens. He's not Undil's most popular ambassador. Even Father used to say that Ravad has done more political harm than good. But I mean...he has a point.

Belvun's Ambassador Blayson is holding her hands behind her back, her head bowed. I'm not sure what she thinks of Ravad's speech. He's in favor of an immediate evacuation, which the Belvish only want as a last resort, but he's also not blaming them for Belvun's deterioration like I've heard so many other people do. He's laying the responsibility on Daliona. I'm not sure if any Dalish leaders have visited Belvun since the first attempt at a Faustocine formula, and that was six years ago. Even *I* can't let that go unnoticed. But still…

All eyes are on Chancellor Green now. The entire audience is waiting with bated breath. He's in the middle of conferring with his councilors. Their hushed voices echo within the chamber, leaving it eerily quiet when they finish.

It takes the Chancellor several seconds to begin talking. He still looks like he's arguing with himself. "You're saying evacuate Belvun…*now*."

Ambassador Ravad rolls his eyes. "Yes, I am. And the Narvidians are willing to provide us with the necessary resources to accommodate the Belvish refugees."

Chancellor Green rubs his chin. His eyes are narrowed, and his leg is shaking under his panel. He's mulling something over, his lips forming silent words as he talks to himself.

"*There's a price*," he says at last. He turns toward the Narvidians, addressing Ambassador Gantz. "And what *is* that price?"

The Narvidian ambassador stands and holds one arm across his chest. His harsh, choppy accent echoes across the silent chamber.

"I spoke with representatives at Gray Wall yesterday. We reached a preliminary agreement contingent on your council's approval." He pauses, but even *I* already know what he's about to ask for. "As per the Joint Space Tech Treaty, Narviid is willing to compensate Undil for partial mining rights in the Perihelids."

"*No.*"

Ambassador Gantz pinches the bridge of his nose, his forehead creasing. After a moment, he holds his hand out and says, "Raymond, listen: the profits you obtain would provide Undil with the means to support both the Belvish and Undilaen populations off the Artish resources—perhaps for a decade or more."

"You assume Artaans' resource production will suddenly multiply to meet our needs, and that is not—"

"*And whose fault is that?!*" Ravad interrupts, throwing his arms out. "Had you gotten Undil back on its scheduled terraformation, this crisis would not be an issue!" Murmurs buzz around the chamber, but Ravad speaks over them, saying, "Narviid has a claim in the Perihelids. Why are you refusing to recognize it?"

Chancellor Green's fists are pressed onto the desk. Both Ambassador Ravad and Gantz are on their feet, facing him, but when it's clear the Chancellor isn't going to reply, Ravad purses his lips in frustration.

"I suggest a recess," he mutters. "We should reconvene when we've *properly* thought this through. Do you agree, Jarvis?"

Ambassador Gantz nods. "I extend the motion."

All eyes go back to Chancellor Green, and he eventually nods.

The conference is dismissed, but nobody has stood to leave. Ambassador Blayson shoots Ravad a glare, then marches out of the chamber, and by the time people start filing out, more arguments have swelled in the crowds.

Chapter
Forty-One

NOBODY WANTS TO go back into the void.

Yet we all want to leave Undil.

Flying to the *Ember* is the fun part. How could it *not* be? But once we're there...once it hits us that we'll be trapped for another month...the enthusiasm fades.

I spend the first hour in the archives chamber with Allison, Trey, and Kile to scan the primary systems. And after we compile a pre-expedition report, I go up to the Bridge and sit with Orcher to watch the departure, listening to the painful exchange as Officer Remmit and Captain Fallsten force themselves to act friendly.

"Coordinates set, Remmit. Preparing—"

"Hold it, Cap. Still warming up the engines."

A pause, then, *"Primary engines are reading stable and functioning at max capacity. Check again, Lars."*

"Negative, Cap. I haven't—"

"Larson, let her do her job," Orcher interrupts.

This time, it's Officer Remmit who takes a long time

answering. *"Confirmed, General. All systems go."*

"Do your damn job, Lars," Fallsten hisses. *"Nobody wants to f—"*

"Miranda, confirm launch sequence," Orcher says, his eyes sagging from exhaustion.

Down in Station Control, Captain Fallsten has each station pilot relay their statuses. Once they confirm, she says, *"Prepared to initiate launch sequence on your command, David."*

"Initiate."

The *Ember* unlocks from the harbor bay and backs out, with the *Doppler*, *Drake,* and *Blazar* following in turn. The *Saros*, the cruiser housing the additional Shield and Horizon crews, will intercept our fleet before we reach FTL.

Undil slides out of view below us. The sun is almost fully behind the planet, and a fiery red and yellow arc burns on the horizon, shrinking...shrinking...gone. All that remains is the glittering backdrop of the void and the glowing core of the Milky Way. When we flew to Daliona, the bulging arm stretched upward, but now it's running parallel to our path, pointing the way to Belvun.

Pointing at the dying planet.

✳ ✳ ✳ ✳ ✳

"He just *jumped*. Like, we're talking from thirty thousand feet. Took him all of like five minutes to touch down."

The projection of Chloe looks at the projection of Lon. They joined me for a late breakfast before we all head off to work. Kile happened to be here when we walked in, so we sat with him.

Lon cuts into his patty and holds the slice in front of his mouth. "Nope, seven minutes. Two in free-fall, five with the wings."

Chloe tells us about the caving trip she went on back on Daliona, how it was so dark underground she couldn't even see her hand when it was right in front of her face. How there wasn't a set path, they just had to scale a cave wall to reach the bottommost regions.

"That's where it got weird. Those worms live down there—like, the leeches or whatever. Same thing."

"Worms and leeches serve two *entirely* separate roles in the ecosystem," Lon corrects. "So no, *not* the same thing at all."

Chloe ignores him. "And there were these beetles. Like, *huge* beetles, bigger than my hand! They were everywhere. On the walls, on the floor, on the ceiling. It was disgusting. I'm *so* glad they couldn't fly."

She pulls her arms tight to her body and shudders.

"We saw a sea serpent," I say.

"*Dally.*"

The three of us look at Kile, who's been sitting off to the side, trying to read another book. He somehow finished that huge one on the trip back from Daliona.

"I went on the tour while you were getting your cyclo license," he tells me, then goes back to reading.

Lon puts down his fork when he finishes his third serving of patties. "You guys hit up any arctic islands?"

"Bechi," I answer. "Freezing up there."

"You're telling me. We had to catalogue Falsaboro, down there by the south pole. Dropped to negative fifty-five degrees. Even my *bones* hurt."

Geez. And here I thought six degrees was bad.

I'm the last to finish eating, and then the four of us put our trays in the cleaning units. Lon and Chloe say goodbye to me and Kile, then to each other, and then they both vanish into thin air.

Kile and I go up one floor to the archives chamber. Trey and Allison arrive shortly after we do, and the four of us analyze the data RASP collected overnight. Only Trey finds anything: a temporary power fluctuation in the fitness center when a man went for a late-night cardio session.

Ah, the thrilling life of an archivist.

✳ ✳ ✳ ✳ ✳

"So."

"So."

I'm inside my room, and Glacia's outside it. She still has that not-Glacia braid down the center of her back, but I'm not about to tell her I don't like it. This is pretty much the first time in three weeks that we've willingly seen each other, not counting the night we met up with John.

"Can...I...come in?"

I stand aside, and Glacia sits on the edge of my bed.

"Who first?" I ask after the door shuts.

She shrugs and takes a deep breath. "I have a lot to say. I don't know about you."

"I'm the one who should be sorry."

Her eyes drop to the side. "No, it's both of us." She

pats the bed. "Come here."

I hesitate—then sit next to her, keeping a few inches between us. I don't like having that space there. It's not...*natural* for us. But I'm also dead scared of getting too close too soon, pretending everything's okay when it's not.

"I'm not...mad," Glacia says after several long seconds. "I mean, *I am*. But I don't want to be. And I know we aren't going to fix this tonight—"

"Me, too."

"—but I hate being like this. I do, Arman." She waves gestures between us. "This? This isn't *us*. I don't even know if you're angry, and not talking doesn't help. Well—it did, a bit. Kind of. After, like, being mad at you for a while, I settled down enough to think about what happened. Because I miss you. *A lot*. And I want to know what I did to push you away like that. Obviously I did *something*, Arman. And I think before I can start moving past this, I need to know *what* I did."

I'm fidgeting with my hands in lap, tapping my fingers, folding my hands and unfolding them. Biting my lip. Breathing as quietly as possible, even though anxiety is flaring inside my chest and my heart is pounding, pounding, *pounding*.

"Like..." This is so hard to say. My voice keeps catching. "Like, when Rand crashed. That freaked me out, I think. Because it reminded me of...*my crash*."

"On the gravity run?"

I shake my head. "The car. With Father."

Out of the corner of my eye, I can see her nodding, her head tilted a bit my direction.

"That's all I could think about. *For days*. I still do

* * *

491

sometimes, but not as much. And I didn't have anyone to talk about it. I didn't have *you*. Because I thought... It's, like..." *Deeeeep breath.* "When you came back from the hospital that night, I was awake. I heard you crying. And I didn't help you. And I should have."

I'm starting to choke up. My voice is shaking harder. Even my eyes are starting to burn.

"When I saw you on the couch, I felt *awful*, Glace. I shouldn't have left you alone. And then you wouldn't look at me, and I knew you were thinking the same thing. But I thought..."

My voice trails off. I can't say the next thing I want to. She'll hate me for thinking it. I shouldn't have even *thought* about her and Rand. She wouldn't do that to me. This is Glacia. She wouldn't.

She *wouldn't*.

"I thought you were in love with *him*."

Glacia doesn't say anything. It's stupid. So. Stupid. I shouldn't have said that. Now she knows I was jealous. That I was scared. That I couldn't stop imagining *them*.

"Arman...you know I love you, right?"

A tear slips down the side of my nose. "*I know.*"

"Rand was a friend. He's cool...but...he's...*intense*. And he's got nothing over you. You came back for me, and you actually care, and you make sure that we do fun things together." She tucks her hands under her arms. "I mean...we went so long without anything, like, *bad* happening to us. This was *bound* to happen. It sucks that it did, but if we're going to fall apart over this..." She shrugs and shakes her head. "That's not *us*. We're better than *this*. I know we are."

"I do, too."

Glacia takes another deep breath. "I don't want to go back to how we were. Not yet. I do *want to*, though. But I'm still, like..." She holds up her hands. "Trust me. I need a little more time. But I want to know that we're going to be all right. That you're not going to shut down again, especially not before we reach Belvun. I don't want to get there and screw something up because we're mad at each other."

"Mmhmm." I squeeze the edge of my bed. "Hey, Glace?"

"Yeah?"

"Can we...*do things* again? Work out and eat and such?"

The corner of her mouth twitches. "Yeah."

She grabs the edge of the bed, too, her hand *so* close, and rocks side-to-side, her shoulder barely nudging mine. I look at her, and she looks at me, and I tear up again, because it's been so long since I've looked into her eyes, so long since I've felt okay about us.

We're not falling apart.

But then the moment ends. She stands up and wipes each of her eyes. "I'm gonna go to bed, okay? But let's make tomorrow different. No more fighting. Or being angry. Or whatever we are. Promise?"

"I promise."

She backs away...slowly...and stops with her back to the door. "So...goodnight?"

I haven't moved. I'm just watching her, thinking about her, relieved, and happy, and calm. And my mind isn't racing. And I think—

"Mister."

She's waiting for me. *Duh*. Of course. And I'm just sitting here like an idiot.

Of course.

I walk over, and we hug for the first time in a long time. I almost forgot how much I missed holding her. Feeling her heartbeat...smelling her hair...not wanting to let her go, ever.

* * *

Chapter Forty-Two

TODAY WAS THIRTY hours and twenty-four minutes long, two-and-a-half hours longer than a day on Undil. We're living under Belvun's gravity, which is slightly lighter than Undil's and close to half of Daliona's. My muscles vibrate with pent-up energy. It's affecting the entire crew—those who traveled to Daliona, at least. We're always restless, always hungry, always tapping a finger or shifting our feet. I find myself awake long into the night, every night, and usually end up going to the Observatory, like now.

It's nearly twelve-thirty in the morning, the beginning of the thirteenth day. The *Ember*'s dull hum fills the empty halls and ramps, then fades when I reach the Observatory.

I lie on a lounger and look out at our fleet: the *Doppler* flies to the left of the *Ember*, and the *Blazar* to the right. The dark belly of the *Drake* hangs overhead, slightly to the left, outlined by the blinking red lights. The bulkier figure of the *Saros* hangs slightly to the right. Twelve days, and I still haven't gotten used to seeing Shield's cruiser in our formation, though, admittedly, it *does* balance the symmetry.

Millions of dots are sprinkled all around us. From one edge of the Observatory to the other, the stars glitter in the blackness. The Milky Way stretches through them, giving some depth to the endless expanse and reminding us that we're a very small part of a universe that could be infinite. Belvun is out there. And behind us, Undil. All of humanity is scattered inside our little bubble of the galaxy. Daliona, Narviid, Yillos, Melles, Artaans, Husteng, and Rygin. They're all out there, and here *we* are, in the middle of the void. It doesn't even look like we're moving. Not from a distance. But close up...like when Glacia showed me the Barrier three months ago...I saw that shimmer in space, that ripple in the void.

My holotab buzzes, just like I expected it to. Even before I read the message, I'm looking around the dim darkness, looking for her.

'Mind if I join you?' Glacia's message says.

I tap, *'Please do,'* then strain my ears and eyes, listening for the buzz and searching for the light.

...bzzzzz.

Right there, to my left, two loungers away. I slip off my couch and make my way to her hiding spot. Getting closer, and closer…almost there…

Bzzzzz.

My holotab buzzes in my hand.

"That was subtle." Glacia climbs over the back of the lounger and falls onto it, stretching out to take up as much room as possible. "I'm tired, go find your own."

She bites her lip and perks her eyebrows, not letting up the act. This is how it's been the last few nights. If we can't sleep, we come to the Observatory, just like we used to. Otherwise we'd stay in our own rooms, alone.

Lately, both of us have *'had trouble'* falling asleep.

Tonight I end up sitting on the floor with my back against the lounger she's lying on. We don't talk, but I tip my head back so that it's barely touching her side…and it doesn't take long for her to start playing with my hair, just like I'd hoped.

✳ ✳ ✳ ✳ ✳

I wake up with my head slumped against Glacia's arm. My legs are numb and my knees ache, so I stretch—then tense up in pain when the needle feeling swarms my legs. Okay, don't move…don't move…*gahhhhh* that hurts that hurts that hurts.

Nothing signals the beginning of the new day except the change in time. The Observatory is still dim, the void is still black, and the red lights outlining the *Drake* and *Saros* are still blinking above us. We left Daliona more than a month ago, and in the time since, we've gotten less than three days of actual sunlight—*not even*—and all of it came from Undil's sun, the one sun I hate. Now, however, I'd gladly take it over this constant, sunless infinity.

Our stomachs are sour, so Glacia and I go to the food court and stack our trays high with beef patties and fruit and kerns, and neither of us speaks until we've finished off the last crumbs. Glacia sucks down her juice, then slouches, yawns, and puts her forehead on the table. A moment later she picks herself up, lifts her arm, and pinches the underside.

"Look at this. I'm getting all flabby."

My skin feels even looser than hers. "Me, too."

We couldn't keep our exercise habits up. Working out using resistances that mimicked Daliona's gravitational-equivalent just wasn't sustainable when the gravity we're living under is nearly *half* Daliona's. And not only have our muscles begun their inevitable deterioration back to normal, but our tans have long since faded. My arms are the same color as my palms, maybe even paler. Meh. I liked my skin being dark. I felt so *confident*. I was a different person, a better person. Now I'm just...me.

We head to the Bridge ten minutes behind schedule. Glacia gives me an exhausted sideways hug before she goes down to Station Control for her shift, and I trudge up the ramps to Orcher's platform. He's already got my Bersivo Blend stirred to a medium tan, while his coffee is straight black, as usual. But his eyes are red, and dark circles hang under them. He sips at his coffee, grimacing when it burns his tongue.

"I can't say my mind has ever gotten used to bouncing so quickly from one calendar to the next. When we aren't given a chance to catch up, as is quite common these days, well… Time's a funny thing, Arman, and our perception of it even more bizarre."

He tests his coffee one more time, then sets it aside and folds his hands in his lap. His eyes stare out over the Bridge, sometimes following a data orb as it drifts from one level to the next, other times just looking straight ahead at the stars. At one point I see Glacia's head drooping, and less than two seconds later, Captain Fallsten springs out of her seat and marches over, demanding a good excuse for her slacking—not that Glacia has much to do today except monitor trajectory readings against the interstellar currents.

Orcher doesn't seem to have noticed the exchange below, because he's chuckling. Wait, has he been talking the entire time? Without looking at me, he says, "Yesterday, I forgot we even stopped at Undil. I asked Lars if he'd seen Olivarr lately, and…well, as you know, Olivarr stayed behind." He runs a hand over his mouth and chuckles again. "Funny…how memories can slip around like that."

He's tapping one finger on the desk now, never ceasing. *Taptaptaptaptap*. He furrows his forehead. Narrows his eyes. Frowns.

I sip my coffee to distract myself. These days, I count every cup of coffee, one for each day. Counting seems to help the expedition pass quicker. *Thirteen cups*. That means seventeen more until we reach Belvun: five until we reach the Perihelids, two while we're in them, and ten to end the trip.

I'm going to savor the final cup. Belvun might not be beautiful anymore. It's covered in blackened forests and fields of fire. The gray lines won't be mountain ranges, but plumes of smoke and poisoned clouds. That morning's coffee could be my last Bersivo for a long, *long* time.

I'm not surprised to find Lon walking toward me when I step off the elevator on Floor 11. I told the team leaders of every station to meet me in the *Ember*'s archives chamber every morning for daily updates, and I'm almost fifteen minutes late. Lon flickers whenever he switches between projectors, and he randomly side-steps to move out of someone's way on the *Drake*, even though the *Ember*'s hall is clear. I still haven't gotten used to that. You can be walking right next to someone, and then they're suddenly ten feet behind you because they had to avoid something.

"Oy, we were all wondering where you are, man," he says. His voice is coming from my left, totally separated from his body. "Morning reports are done. Yours is the last one we need."

"Thanks."

In the archives chamber, Trey and Allison are leaning back in their seats, talking, and Kile is sitting off to the side, scrolling through station data. He glances up when I walk in, twitches a smile, then looks away again. He has another book beside him, his holotab stuffed between the pages.

"You can leave if you want," I offer.

He shrugs, seems to give it some thought, then grabs the book and walks out.

"What does he *do* all day?" Lon asks. I didn't even realize he was still behind me until he spoke.

"Reads," I say. Lon gives me a disbelieving look. "Seriously. He brought every book he owns."

"No one reads *that* much."

"Kile does," Trey says off to the side.

Lon gives me a look. "Weird."

"How's containment holding up?" I ask to change the subject.

"Stable. Climate control hasn't budged since I adjusted it last week"—he holds up a finger to keep me from speaking too soon—"but I *did* have to pressurize the chamber because of an overnight C-1. Minor, *minor* leak, nothing not normal."

That's no surprise. All four stations have had C-1 breaches during the expedition. And on the way back from Daliona, the *Ember* had two in a week. A team goes out in pressurized suits to repair the damage, and that's that.

"Hit me up if you want to meet for dinner or something."

"Will do."

Lon vanishes. I turn back to my panel, access the reports, and read through them—like I do every morning. Then I analyze my portion of RASP's data, compile my report and send all of them to Orcher, Officer Remmit, and Captain Fallsten.

Like I do.

Every.

Single.

Morning.

Chapter
Forty-Three

"THIRTY SECONDS TO DROP."

The countdown in the Bridge ticks...ticks...ticks.

"Twenty seconds to drop."

The station pilots prepare for the dropout, setting the thrusters and trajectories to their proper levels.

"Ten seconds to drop."

Silence overtakes the Bridge. Every passing second is equal to millions of miles.

3...

2...

1.

"Dropping."

The main thrusters power down. A gentle tug forward, my coffee rocks lightly in its cup, and then the drag equalizes. Slower...slower...and then a black line forms in front of us, cutting through the galaxy's twinkling backdrop:

The Perihelid asteroid field.

* * *

The star at the center of the solar system shines pure white. It's so tiny from this distance, barely larger than any of the other stars. Its rays streak through the dust, tracing unbent shadows behind the asteroids.

"Activate floodlights," Captain Fallsten orders.

Bright beams shoot out around the *Ember*. At the same time, the floodlights of the *Drake* activate, then the *Saros*, the *Doppler*, and the *Blazar*.

Closer…closer…closer…

And then we're inside the field.

The MRRs deflect asteroids from hundreds of yards away, keeping the rocky behemoths clear of our fleet, diverting them up, down, and around us, until the boulders are no longer within the magnetic influence. They arc safely over the stations into new trajectories, which RASP and Officer Remmit are tracking so we have an idea of where they'll be for future expeditions. I remember Officer Remmit telling us how it's all about the math. *Every interaction in the universe has an equation,* he had said. *The tricky part is calculating them, but I leave that up to people who are good with numbers. I've already got enough thinking to do.*

To Officer Remmit—to every member of his team logging the forces acting on the fleet and nearby asteroids—everything is an equation. Thousands, *millions* of equations, one for every sizeable chunk of rock. Some could get flung from the field, and others could fall toward the sun, or wander to the outer limits of the solar system—and beyond.

It's calculated chaos.

"Forty hours, people."

Captain Fallsten drops down from her elevated seat

and walks up the ramps to Orcher's platform. I stand to let her have my seat before she makes it up here, but she doesn't even acknowledge the gesture.

I say goodbye to Orcher and head down the ramps, passing Victoria on her platform. She's in the middle of conferencing with Lieutenant Marlick of the *Blazar*, but still smiles as I walk by.

The *Ember*'s halls have no windows. Without windows, you can't see the asteroids and the dust and the stars. That's why I like the Bridge, why I like the Observatory. There's so much going on outside these halls, and I'm restless to return to it.

Write the morning reports.

Collect the morning reports.

Deliver the morning reports.

Even though I know what's on the other side of this expedition—even though I know we might have to evacuate Belvun, and that people have died, and that cities and forests are burning—I don't *feel* like there's any danger on Belvun. I don't *feel* like people have been driven from their homes. So what *will* I feel when I see that world, a world so altered from my last visit? Will I be scared? Will I have to save someone's life? Or will I be stuck on the sidelines, kept out of the danger?

Do I *want* to play a part?

I don't know.

✳ ✳ ✳ ✳ ✳

When Glacia and I go to the Observatory that night, we don't even try to sleep. Not at first. There's too much to see, so much more than a blanket of stars. We watch those disfigured shadows moving just beyond the range of the floodlights, listen to the *clack, clack-clack, clack, clack* as specks of rock clatter against the Observatory, the smaller chips and chunks that go unaffected by the MRRs.

"*It almost sounds like rain*," Glacia whispers.

She yawns, then nestles into my shoulder. I rest my cheek on her head and smile, hearing her words over and over again in my mind. It's true. It *does* sound like the rain. Like the time we got caught running down the jungle path on Marakuri, or when I would sit by the window on Culsaren and watch those torrential downpours storm the archipelago.

So we close our eyes and pretend the clattering chips are really raindrops. My holotab buzzes, threatening to distract me. But I'm used to meditating, used to blocking out the world. My mind is at ease. I don't have to think about what lies at the other end of this expedition.

I can pretend it was all a dream.

Belvun is still beautiful. The fires never burned, the clouds are white and the rivers are cold. The gray mountains loom above the rest of the world, washed in the light of pinkish sunsets and crimson dawns. The Dell Washers will still be pecking the grasses for twigs to build their nests. Captain Blitner will be sitting in Meekman's Café eating a pastry, and Barimus will be laughing while he prepares a customer's order. Ellaciss City will be noisy and crowded, surrounded by a lush forest where Belvish families go for long walks. Victoria's memories won't haunt her. Father never went to

Belvun. He never had to write the Recovery Treatise...

...it all could have been a dream.

Flash.

I open my eyes.

There was a light. It brightened my eyelids. But now...now I see only the floodlights and shadows and the darkness beyond.

Glacia's asleep. Her light blue nightclothes rise...and fall. Her eyelids flutter. Her face is relaxed, her hand is in mine. Her elbow is digging into my arm, so I adjust my shoulder.

Flash.

Out of nowhere—a ribbon of green. It whizzed high above us, forming on the other side of the *Blazar* and vanishing beyond the *Doppler*. The Observatory glowed in the soft light...and darkened when it faded. Then another hazy green ribbon races through the fleet, and another one, farther down near the Bridge. Two at once, merging and crossing and flowing in a thick stream.

Three bursts. Four. Swelling so bright that even a few asteroids pass through the aurora until it dissipates. The ribbons keep materializing, sweeping beneath the *Drake* and *Saros*, whipping around the *Blazar*, or rippling along the hulls of the *Ember* and *Doppler*. They trace the contours of the MRRs, some of them gathering in tight circles before dissolving into darkness.

I remember this: when we left for Daliona and flew by Undil's sun, we entered a flare of solar radiation. An aurora enveloped the fleet, and vanished when we left the sun behind.

These ribbons blaze and twist and bend, flooding the gaps between the stations. Now I think of the Rainbow

River in the Dalish Embassy, how the canal wove through the city, coloring the night.

I can't let her go without seeing it.

"*Glace.*"

I nudge her side, give her a small shake. But I think it's the buzz of my holotab in my pocket that startles her awake. Bleary-eyed, she lifts her chin to look at me.

"*What was—?*"

"Look up."

And she does.

I don't need to point it out. The aurora illuminates everything: the Observatory, the *Ember*'s hull, the dust and asteroids. While she takes it in, I watch her eyes, because they reflect the brilliant green.

Glacia sits up, entranced by the lightshow. Her eyes flick left and right, catching every burst of color like when we watched fireworks on Daliona. But there are no thunderous booms, no crackling, no sizzling.

Pure silence.

"It's been going for a few minutes," I say. "I think it's from the sun."

"From a flare."

"Yeah. Like when we left for Daliona."

She scoots to the other end of the lounger so we're facing each other, and hugs her knees to her chest. The bottoms of her nightclothes pull up over her ankles.

"It's so beautiful."

"*Yeah.*" Then I grin, suppressing a short laugh.

My holotab buzzes a third time—then starts beeping and doesn't stop. I'm used to it buzzing at night, usually just notifications from RASP, but beeping?

It's *never* done that before.

So I check it.

And freeze.

RASP sent me a notification nearly ten minutes ago:

Intense Radiation Field Interaction.
Magnetic Resonance Repulsors Strengthening.

And another notification, two minutes ago:

Radiation Field Critically Intense.
Magnetic Resonance Repulsors Weakening.

And now, with the beeping:

Radiation Levels Critical.
Station Personnel Notified.
Activating Alarms.

"BURR, BURR, BURR."
"BURR, BURR, BURR."

A ring of light flashes in time with the alarm. And it's not just the *Ember*: through the aurora's green fog, I see emergency lights flashing on the bridges and observatories and windows of the other stations.

"Arman. What's—"

"The shields."

"BURR, BURR, BURR."

Glacia stares at me, her jaw tightening. And she's shivering, her face going pale. She lets go of her knees and sits up, one foot on the floor.

"All pilots report to the Bridge," an automated voice says over the intercoms, shutting out the alarms. It repeats over and over. *"All pilots report to the Bridge."*

"Glace." She's frozen to the spot. "Glace, we *have* to."

I take her, and she resists when I try pulling her up.

But I manage to. We're both shaking. She's breathing loudly—I'm trying to stay calm. Retreat inside my head.

Stay. Calm.

I coax her to hustle down the ramp to Floor 15, then turn the corner—and we nearly slam into dozens of people, mostly pilots, who are jogging to the Bridge.

"BURR, BURR, BURR."

Everyone gathers in Station Control, where Captain Fallsten is waving her hands and ordering three new pilots to take control of the *Ember*.

"Hold course! Find an open patch!" She rounds on the other pilots. "Molters! Safeguard Formation! *KEEP— US—CLEAR.* Jespon, impact status?"

"*None confirmed*," a pilot to her right answers, reading from a panel linked to RASP.

"Two patrols over the Bridge and engines," Fallsten orders, speaking to two head pilots. "Hold intervention until the MRRs fail."

The pilots rally their squadrons, and more than two dozen people run back out the gate.

"*Saros has activated turrets*," Jespon reports.

"Open a line with *Saros*!"

We all look up. Through the aurora's green haze, we see the *Drake* and the *Saros* hanging directly above us. Even from here, I can see the *Saros'* external defense turrets blasting lasers into the darkness, some zipping dangerously close to the *Drake* and *Blazar*, others shattering asteroids into smaller chunks with explosive force.

"*Contact made.*"

"This is Captain Fallsten of the *Ember*. DO—NOT— ENGAGE—TURRETS. Molter Safeguard Formation *ONLY* until I give further directives."

"*Confirmed*," the captain of the *Saros* acknowledges. "*Dispatching units.*"

That's when Captain Fallsten spots me and Glacia standing at the back of the crowd. "*Out!*" She shoves her way past people, pointing at me. "*GET OUT!* Haverns, you're with Kroner's squadron. *Kroner!*" The pilot named Kroner stands at attention. "Rogue Formation. Authorized for primary engagement at your discretion."

"Aye, Captain." He turns and shouts, "*On me!*"

But Glacia stares at Fallsten, frozen on the spot.

"*NOW, HAVERNS!*"

She shoves Glacia forward, toward me, and pilots run around us. I grab Glacia's wrist. We're both shaking. Both stumbling. Both—

"*Arman I can't.*"

I tighten my grip. We're falling behind the pilots.

"You have to—you *have* to."

"*Please no. Please Arman...please!*" Her voice is shrill, caught in a stutter. "*No... No... No...*"

"Remmit's on RASP!" a man shouts at me as he jogs by. It takes me a second to realize it was Orcher, but he runs through the gate before I have time to shout back.

"Glace—"

She's crying, resisting me. The other pilots are waiting for the elevators, and they're looking at her. Looking at me. And I realize we've stopped walking.

"*Arm—Arman.*" Desperate.

Kroner marches over to us. "Haverns—let's go. Off."

Glacia's eyes find mine, pleading. "*Not out there. Not out—*"

"Glace." My hand is turning purple, she's squeezing

my wrist *that* hard. "We'll be fine. We'll be fine. I promise."

She's clinging to my arm with both hands. My other arm is around her back, holding her to me. I need to let go. She needs to let go. Neither of us can.

But then Kroner wrestles Glacia's hands off my arm, cursing at us as he does. "You really think any of us want to go out in that shit? *Do you?* Think again, Haverns." He looks at me. "I've got her. Go to your damn post."

He drags Glacia away. Her voice is reduced to whimpers. She and Kroner get on the elevator, more pilots join them...

And the door slides shut.

The moment it does, I choke. My lip is quivering. And my eyes sting. And I'm shaking. So. Much. The door is shut. I can't follow. I didn't even *try* to stop him from taking her. I didn't know what else to do. But resisting him wouldn't have ended well. I have a feeling he would have thrown me to the ground. Or broken my arm. Or punched my face.

I half-jog, half-stumble to the ramps. Turn, turn, turn down four levels, jog into the hall of Floor 11. But I stop. Lean on the wall. Rub my eyes, take a deep breath.

"Dammit." I rub my eyes on my shoulders. "Dammit. *Dammit.*"

Calm down.

Glacia.

We'll fix this.

Glacia.

It'll be over in a few minutes.

Glacia.

Stand up.

Straighten myself out.

Go.

I hear their voices even before I'm inside. Officer Remmit, Kile, Allison, and Trey. Kile's monitoring external video feeds, projecting them on the empty wall opposite the panels, and communicating with someone on the Bridge so they can see the same feeds. Allison is analyzing the MRR readings, Officer Remmit is scanning the maps of the Perihelids, relaying coordinates of nearby empty patches in the field to the station pilots, and Trey is using the augmented interface, transmitting information to one of the other stations.

"What can—"

"Arman!" Officer Remmit spins around. "The *Drake* needs to strengthen its MRRs around the engines and containment units. We can't have the Faustocine contaminated. Not again."

I grab an ACI visor, strap it on, and select the *Drake*. Then I'm there, in the *Drake*'s archives chamber, with the blue outline of the *Ember*'s overlapping it.

"...the hell is—? Oy!" Lon jumps back in surprise.

"Protect the engines and the containment units," I tell him.

Lon turns and shouts at Anna, who's speaking with the *Drake*'s head tech officer, Nick Garlan. They immediately open the operations panel and surge power into sections of the *Drake*'s MRR field.

Officer Garlan turns to me. "Our shields are holding up. Minimal depletion. My guess is the bulk of the *Saros* is shielding us from the rads. What's your status?"

"We've deployed squadrons—" I hear muffled

shouts. Lon and the others are staring at me, waiting for the status. "*Keep them powered up.*"

I rip off the visor just as Allison says, "Radiation is *flooding* the Observatory."

Officer Remmit jumps next to Allison, takes one look at her readings, and curses. "Lock it out. Seal *everything* and internalize the local MRRs." He switches comms links. "*Remmit to Wilder—depressurize the Observatory. We're internalizing.*"

Allison taps an icon to lock down the gates to the Observatory, then gets to work modifying the MRR grid. The field contours aren't covering the dome anymore, but have withdrawn to hold max coverage starting at Floor 15. At the same time, readings from Trey's panel start spiking. Every system in the Observatory is shorting out. The StarPad. The vents. The gates. On one of Kile's internal video feeds, I see sparks bursting, entire panels catching fire, pieces of metal *dripping* from the intensity of the radiation.

The bulk of the aurora is within a few yards of touching the hull of the *Ember*. Sometimes a ribbon grazes the surface—and sparks fly.

"Protect the Bridge, the engines, the docks," Officer Remmit orders. "Keep control of the—"

Thud.

A long, hollow echo reverberates in the walls. Metal groans. The floor shudders. Officer Remmit's knees nearly collapse from under him, so he throws himself in the chair beside Allison and opens communications with the Bridge as Kile scans the video feeds and finds one in particular: dust, chunks of rock, a dent in the side of the *Ember*. The asteroid that hit us broke apart and the boulders ricocheted into the black.

"Confirmed impact," Officer Remmit announces to the Bridge. "Floor 7, Northwest."

"*Confirmed*," Orcher's voice says above the shouts in the background of his comms. "Internalize the shielding, Lars. Systems are prior—"

His voice cuts short.

"Orcher?" Nothing. Officer Remmit smacks the comms panel. "*Orcher?*"

"Internal comms are out," Allison says when she checks. "Nothing's open."

Officer Remmit scrambles to internalize the MRRs, protecting as much of the hardwiring as he can to preserve the power systems. But that means losing the outer shields. And that means—

THUD.

My feet leave the floor. I slam backward into the wall. Kile flips over the back of his chair and almost gets tossed out the open door. Allison, Trey, and Officer Remmit are secure in their seats, but they still have to fight the heavy drag. I'm pinned to the wall, limbs splayed outward. The *Ember* is spinning, and spinning, and spinning...

I slip down an inch. The spinning weakens...I fall to the ground, gagging, choking. My back stings. My head pounds where it banged the wall. But the station pilots still have control. That's all I need to know.

Until I remember Glacia is outside.

In the field.

I can't stop the tears. She's out *there*, and I'm *here*, standing here against a wall.

If we lose power.

If we lose the engines.

If we lose the Bridge.

Dots of light race across the video feeds. Molters. The pilots who were sent out to protect the *Ember*, protect the fleet. Lasers burst from the Molters and explode against asteroids that are otherwise invisible in the darkness. The floodlights swivel, revealing more, and more, *and even more* asteroids headed for the fleet, undeterred. No shields to deflect them. Nothing but the Molters to protect us.

Thud...

Thud...

THUD.

The floor doesn't stop shaking. The lights flicker, the panels and projections get blurry, then clear again. Kile's still conscious, slumped beside the door and moaning incoherently. The metallic groans echo, the force of each impact knocks me off-balance. The pilots fight to keep the *Ember* steady, using the external feeds to anticipate every collision as best they can. But standing in the open is too risky. I need something to hold onto. Something to control—

The cyclo.

I have to do it. I'm useless here. Kile's in no shape to stop me. Nobody's watching.

Set my feet—push off the wall.

Jump through the door, into the hall.

Up. I need to go *up*.

Breathe...*focus*.

Not the elevators. I can't risk it. One flicker of power—I'm done. So I run to the ramps. Run up, turn the bend, run up.

Floor 12.

Run...run. Pump my arms. Push off the wall. Pump my arms. Push off the wall. Breathing steady. Keeping my mind clear.

Floor 13.

Floor 14.

My room is to the right, near the end of the corridor. I fumble in my pocket for my ID. Slap it on the scanner. Squeeze through the—

Thud.

The impact throws me forward and up, and I tuck my head to keep from smacking headlong into the ceiling—then fall face-first into the bed and fall off the side, ramming my knees on the floor.

My stomach, twisting. My brain, spinning.

Close my eyes and just *breathe.*

In...out.

Come on. Stay in control.

I grab the edge of the bed and pull myself up. My trunk is upside-down against the far wall, but it's still closed.

Unseal it.

Dig to the bottom.

Grab the cyclo.

I throw open the case and haphazardly pull the suit onto my feet, my arms, my head. It pressurizes around my body, and I retract the helmet visor.

Activate.

The whir of the disk...I become weightless, feet dangling off the ground. *You are not flying,* the first instructor I ever had on Daliona told me. *You are moving through space.*

I drop to the floor and jog back to the ramps—where I stop. Up, or down?

The Bridge, or my team?

A succession of bangs. Shouts echo, but from where, I can't tell. My muscles twitch when the floor shudders. The lights flicker. Darkness...light.

I choose *up*.

The Bridge gate is open, and officers are running out. They shove past me, shouting to one another. Most ignore me. One or two give me a look, a flicker of wonder when they see what I'm wearing.

Run through the gate.

Data orbs are bouncing off the walls and ricocheting in every direction. The rear of the *Drake* looms above us, perpendicular to the *Ember*. Its engines are still glowing, despite the weak aurora engulfing it.

Thud.

The *Drake* swings out of view. An explosion flashes in the dust, a Molter colliding with the *Ember*. Debris clatters on the windows. Another Molter swerves up to avoid slamming into the Bridge—and explodes on an asteroid headed our way, cracking it apart. More Molters swarm outside, unleashing lasers at asteroids, dissolving them into smaller chunks. Rockets whizz past and pound into the largest asteroids—at least, the ones the pilots can see.

I jump into the air, twist around, find Orcher. And when I land beside him—

"*Here*," he says into his holotab, probably to Officer Remmit. "He's here."

There's the *Blazar* now, slanted away from us. Its engines flare, burning bright blue amid the green aurora. And just as the *Ember*'s pilots manage to stabilize us, a fireball erupts from the *Blazar*'s left engine—snuffs out—blows to shreds.

"*BELLY UP!!*" Captain Fallsten screams from Station Control. "*TIP US OVER!!*"

One pilot slides her hand down her panel, and the other two ignite the micro-repulsion thrusters. Orcher clings to his desk as the *Ember* tips...tips...doing a barrel roll in free space—but not quickly enough.

CLACK, CLACK-CLACK, CLACK.

CHINK, CH-CHINK.

THUD. THUD. THUD.

Debris smacks the *Ember*'s windows. Torn metal. Broken rock. Thin splinters crack through the glass. Outside, a Molter slashed by a shard of metal swerves out of control over the Bridge...flies back...back...

And smashes through the Observatory.

A section of the dome collapses. Glass glitters in the dust. Support beams flail, snapping off and hitting asteroids and the *Ember* alike, gouging the top of the station. Sparks flash, flames flicker and snuff out. Chairs and loungers and tables that have been getting tossed around finally break free among the debris.

Thud.

A cloud of dust kicks up over the Bridge. Zero visibility. Brown and gray. When it clears, two Molters zoom across the floodlights, lasers firing, crumbling an asteroid to smaller bits, then vanish inside another dust cloud. Two more swoop down from above—and are both engulfed in a ball of green and pink.

Another aurora.

Molter shields can't withstand that much radiation.

It cripples their systems. Their engines go dark, their lasers stop firing, they swerve out of sight—

Th-thud.

Two explosions.

The platform shudders, but the station pilots maintain control. Hold steady. Captain Fallsten has given up shouting and resorted to helping them maneuver the *Ember.*

Orcher's holotab starts beeping. It's Lieutenant Rivets, of the *Drake.*

"Go for Orcher."

"*We still have shields,*" Lieutenant Rivets says. "*Weak, but functioning.*"

"How far out are you?"

"*Two miles. We sent evac your way. So did the* Saros. *One way or the other, somebody should be there any minute. Negative visual on the* Doppler. *No contact. No floodlights. The* Blazar*'s looking like it's about to go down, too.*"

"*Blazar*'s engines are gone," Orcher informs Rivets. "Divert evac to them. We've still got support."

"*Copy.*"

Orcher searches the darkness. The *Drake* is still flying on course, a hazy spot of light in the thickening dust. Several bright dots are moving toward us from it, just like Lieutenant Rivets said.

THUD.

Orcher slams into the railing—grunts in pain. I jumped, but my legs clipped the railing. Pain sears in my ankles, and it's all I can do to not scream. I'm jerking, writhing, twisting out of control. Tears sting my eyes, my legs...throbbing...

I need. To. Focus.

THUD.

The Bridge goes dark, and the outer floodlights, too. The dust, the debris, the asteroids—*everything* vanishes. All that remains is the pale gray light pouring through the windows. Black shadows slide over the walls, the platforms, the people scrambling below.

"EVERYONE OUT! EVAC! EVAC!"

Captain Fallsten's order spreads fast. Other officers start shouting with her. The station pilots abandon their posts. Then the power comes back on, except everything is flickering, shorting out: the panels, the lights, the projectors. And when I look at people's faces, I see smears of blood, bruised eyes, broken arms and noses and...and...

My stomach lurches. I try to hold back, but end up choking, and vomit spills from my mouth, some into my cyclo suit, the rest onto the platform below me.

I spit and gag—fall straight to the floor and collapse to my knees, smelling the sour stench of my own splattered puke that I'm kneeling in. My ankles *burn*. I can't feel them, and I can't work up the will to see if they're moving.

Thud.

My knees and fists drag sideways, but the impact doesn't knock me over. I hardly felt the shudder.

Stand. Up.

But I can't. I can't put *any* weight on my feet. At all. I can't walk. *I can't walk.* I can only fly.

I rise off the floor, high enough to see what I need to. People are jogging down the ramps, evacuating the platforms. Orcher's on his way down, and Victoria is running up to help him. Before I fly to the gate, I look for Captain Fallsten, but she's still in Station Control—with no plans to leave. She straps on a pressure suit, seals the helmet, and secures herself to a seat.

She has sole control of the *Ember*.

I fly outside the gate and hover off to the side, avoiding the people stampeding through before they slam into me. Orcher and Victoria are almost to the lowest level. Orcher's limping, Victoria's holding his arm.

Flash.

I glance up: a Molter is engulfed in a pink aurora. It goes dark—careens sideways—smashes the Bridge.

All I hear is the explosion. Then a screeching whistle. My ears pop. I slap my neck to activate the cyclo's visor, muffling the screech and fully pressurizing the suit.

Air drags around me, threatening to pull me into the Bridge. A hand grabs the side of the opening. I grab it and yank. A man tumbles through, rolls behind the wall. I hear screaming, but I don't know—

I feel something behind me: the panel that will close the gate.

Wait.

Wait.

But no one else comes.

And I know there are—*were*—more people inside. But I don't check. I don't know who got out. There were still so many people in there. Twenty...maybe thirty.

Orcher.

Victoria.

"*CLOSE IT!*" The man's voice sounds so far away.

I panic.

People are still in there!

Do it!

They aren't out!

The man's mouth is moving, but I can't hear him. His head lolls to one side. He's still looking at me, his face turning red, and darkening.

I slap the panel.

The gate seals. Silence fills the hall, but as the seconds pass, the sounds return. Shouts, footsteps, echoes.

The docks.

We have to get to the docks.

The man drags his hand across the wall, pushes off, and tries to stand—but collapses. He pulls his knees up, holds his head back, his eyes watering, his face bright red.

I sink to the floor, legs stretched out and my back pressed against the wall. A noise escapes my raw throat as a new spike of pain slices my feet.

Thud.

The hall shakes. The air shakes.

Thud.

Each collision sounding like it could be the last.

Thud.

"Go. Go, dammit. *Go.*"

The man is on his feet. He grabs me and forces me up. I float beside him as he stumbles down the hall, holding my arm, gasping for air. I'm using the cyclo's recycled supply.

Th-dud...dud...dud...

The reverberations follow us into the ramps. Down...down...down the ramp, turn left, faster now, turn left. Turn, and turn, and turn. The docks are on Floor 3, we're passing Floor 9.

Halfway there.

Where's Officer Remmit? Allison? Trey? Kile? Are they still in the archives chamber? Do they know we're evacuating? Are they okay? Alive? Orcher can't be. Victoria can't be. I don't know if Captain Fallsten survived, that is, if she wasn't hit by the Molter. But—no. The *Ember* isn't spinning out of control. She *has* to be alive. The rest of them... They could be anywhere. *Anywhere*. Are they waiting for us? Hoping we're coming to the docks? How long will they wait? When will the last transport leave?

Th-dud...dud...dud...

Down, turn. Down—

The man slips and falls, dragging me with him. Water sloshes around us, flooding the ramp. Water from the pools in the fitness center.

I help him up. His arms and legs and back are soaked now. He clenches his teeth, groans, and keeps walking. We *have* to keep moving, except now we're slower, because the water is gushing down the ramps.

We reach Floor 3 and hear shouts before stepping out of the ramps. Officers line the hall, collecting the stragglers. Smoke hangs on the ceiling, dimming the flickering lights, threatening to choke out anyone who isn't wearing a mask.

"Evac's here! Go, go!"

Down the hall, through the gate to the docks. Smoke rolls across the ceiling from the transports that were thrown in the collisions. Near the front, the last people load transports, all of them headed to the *Drake*. The crafts leave in quick succession, slipping through the silvery light...and into the thick of the Perihelids.

I board a transport, open the cyclo's helmet, and breathe the cold, clean ventilation, not the sickly smell of my vomit dribbles. And as I look around, I see that only two dozen other people boarded with us, all donning pressurized space suits from the transport's rear compartment.

I sit down, strap in. The pain in my feet is starting to numb. But they ache. I know I can't walk, and at this point, I don't know if I'll ever *need* to walk again. The thought crosses my mind:

I am going to die.

The thrusters flare. The transport lifts up, sways in place. Accelerates toward the silvery light. Gravity vanishes, and a deadly darkness swallows us.

I swallow, hard. I try not to think, try to look away from the video panels. But it's impossible. The shadows, the flashes, the dust and smoke. The radiation has passed the fleet. None of the stations are being swarmed by hazy green auroras, so the darkness is gray and colorless. Disfigured asteroids move closer...closer, and then farther...farther. The *Ember* shrinks behind us, the dock's silvery glow fading. When I look to the Bridge—the glass crater that *used* to be the Bridge—I see a single dot of light.

Captain Fallsten is in control.

But she's piloting an abandoned station. The Observatory is a gaping hole. Panels have been sheared off the hull, and the Bridge itself is irreparable. As the *Ember* rotates in place, I see one engine has been torn off, clinging to the others by a few cables and getting knocked around as asteroids drift by.

A Molter zooms past our transport and blasts lasers

across our path, crumbling an asteroid before it smashed headlong into us.

Thump, thump, thumpthumpthumpthump.

Chunks of rock batter the hull, but we keep flying, keep powering our way to the *Drake*. Following the squadron, protected by only a—

Flash.

A green ball engulfs the Molter escorting us. The craft careens into the darkness.

The *Drake* is still more than a mile out. Behind us, there's no sign of the *Ember*. Rays of dim sunlight etch gray shadows amid the dust and debris. The squadron flies through it all, a dozen or more transports all bound for the *Drake*. There have to be more out there. The *Blazar* and *Doppler* evacuated, too. They *had* to. But everywhere I look, there's no sign of the other stations. Only the *Drake*, the hazy beacon ahead of us that's growing brighter with every passing sec—

An asteroid rams into transport that's three ahead of ours. We watch it fall...fall...fall into the shadows.

Gone.

A green aurora blazes around another transport. The craft loses power, goes dark, swerves out of the squadron.

Gone.

The remaining transports dip side-to-side, dodging, swerving, thrusters flaring, pushing for the *Drake*. What few Molter escorts we still have can't protect all of us—or themselves. One arcs upward, lasers blasting apart a boulder twice its size, then an asteroid clips its rear thrusters, and the Molter spins...spins...spins...

Our transport dives.

In the floodlights, I see a massive dust cloud...and a station surges through. The *Doppler*. Its windows are dark, pieces of its Observatory flail, a gouge is torn where the docks used to be. And then it returns to the swells of dust, black among the shadows.

We're closing in on the *Drake*. It's still pushing forward through the asteroids, but we're gaining on it. A thousand yards...nine hundred...eight... So close, we watch a transport slide into the docks, safe. Five...four—

Flash.

Green light swarms us.

The thrusters die.

The panels go dark.

People shout. Hoarse screams. Some unfasten their restraints, bang on the walls, pound the cockpit door. But it won't open. I seal my helmet and activate the cyclo's lights, just as other people turn on their pressure suit lights. All around me, faces half-hidden in shadow. Hands holding hands, or gripping the restraints, or clinging to the walls.

Drifting...

Drifting...

Drif—

BANG.

Jerked sideways—spinning. Dizzying dots flicker in front of my eyes. I focus...but I can't focus.

BANG.

A whistle pierces the air: a section of the wall rips outward. My body lurches toward it, but I'm still secure in my seat, dragging...dragging...and then it stops.

No more yelling, even though I can see mouths moving. No more bangs, only dull reverberations. Distant echoes. And when I unlatch my restraint, when I push myself out of the seat...

Silence.

My breathing fills my helmet. My heartbeat thuds in my ears. The gentle hiss of the cyclo's pressure unit is amplified, and even the whir of the disk on my back sounds like a dull engine.

I turn around and see people gathered around the torn wall. We're moving *with* the field. Some asteroids pass by faster than others, but most seem to hang in place. A rock the size of my head passes in front of our helmet lights. Dust drifts into the chamber, fogging our vision, and debris clatters against my visor louder than my own breathing.

Spinning...there's the *Drake*, a distant beacon, drifting farther...farther...farther into the dust.

The haze thickens.

Shadows reclaims us.

The wall thumps my arm, pushes me with it. Blood splatters my helmet—bubbles and freezes—and then I see the body impaled on the ripped wall. The face is contorted, the suit shredded. Someone pushes the body outside.

Pricks of light flicker in the dust. Lasers. Pilots fighting a lost cause. They'll be near the *Ember*, or one of the stations, at least. Do they know we're here? Do they know the *Drake* is gone, the *Doppler* destroyed? What happened to the *Saros*? The *Blazar*? Is the *Ember* safe?

Glacia.

My heart rate spikes. Every muscle in my body tenses. She was out here. She might *still* be out here. But I can't call her. My holotab is on the *Ember*. What if she's calling me? What if she's looking for me? What if she went back to the *Ember*, thinking I stayed behind?

I'm sweating. Trembling. Holding back from crying. I feel so sick, but I can't open my helmet. I can't wipe away the tears that threaten to form. I have to keep control. It's all I can do. Breathe. Focus. Come on. Calm. Down.

I can't.

I can.

Death.

Life.

We're trapped, staring into the pale gray light for any sign of rescue. But there's no one coming. I know that. Everyone knows that.

I have to do it.

An asteroid that's at least ten times larger than the transport drifts past, and several smaller ones follow in its wake, a cluster of rocks and small boulders. The walls shudder.

I'm not going to die.

I steer myself to the hole. The others look at me, confused, angry, scared. Some of them must realize what I'm about to do—jump outside—but they think it's a suicide mission. It is, though, because even though I have the cyclo...

My heart catches in my throat.

I'm going to die.

I push through—and then I'm outside, in the void, and I don't look back. I know the transport is drifting away. That everyone inside is drifting with it. That they'll die, because there's nowhere they can go. Even *my* plan is futile.

● ● ●

I'm not going to die.

I rotate until I'm facing the direction I saw the laser lights. But I don't move. I wait. I watch. Shadows stretch within the dim darkness. Dust clouds my visor light, rocks bump into me, an asteroid passes a few feet away. The only sounds are my breathing. The *th-th-thump, th-th-thump* of my heart. The whir of the cyclo. My head feels tight, and hot, and my arms and legs feel weak, and cold.

I'm not. Going. To die.

I take a deep breath, flex my fingers, feel the sensation tingle in the nodes touching my head. Study the darkness, memorize where I think the *Ember* should be, focus on getting to that point. It's my only hope. My only chance to live.

I count down from three.

Two.

One.

No fear.

End Book 2

ACKNOWLEDGMENTS

Thank you, thank you, *thank you* to my beta readers: Alex, Adi, Victoria, Sydney, Karina, and Shannon. Without you, *Resonance* wouldn't be what it is. I appreciate all the hard work you guys put into helping me revise! (And your onslaught of UPPERCASE WORDS IN ALL THE APPROPRIATE PLACES).

Next I want to thank my friends, both at school and home. You've shown so much positive support that has helped keep me going. Thank you for all the great times!

To everyone on Tumblr who's been following this journey and showing support. Thank you for your fan mail, your words of encouragement, your hilarious comments, your slew of '*congratulations!!!*' when I finished the final draft, and, of course, for helping spread word about *Embassy* and *Resonance*. You guys have helped expand my readership from one city to the entire world!

Lastly, to the readers. I hope I've inspired you to look up at the stars and wonder if you, your children, or your grandchildren will walk on another world. One day, Earth will be a dot in someone else's sky, the sun a part of someone's constellation. Think about that.

The universe is waiting.

Sincerely,

S. Alex Martin

CPSIA information can be obtained
at www.ICGtesting.com
Printed in the USA
FSOW01n1257271115
13951FS